THE TOWER

Asura Press books by Paul B. Spence

Darkness Rising
    The Sorcerer
    The High Priestess
    The Tower
    The Judgement (Forthcoming)
    The Hanged Man (Forthcoming)

The Awakening
    The Remnant
    The Fallen
    The Madness Engine
    The Sleeping and the Dead
    The Dark Plaza

The Endless Realms
    Project Brimstone
    Riders on the Storm

The Hand of Providence
    I Won't Cry for Yesterday
    The Instruments of Faith
    Wheel in the Sky

THE TOWER

BOOK THREE OF DARKNESS RISING

Paul B. Spence

Asura Press

THE TOWER

An Asura Press Book

PRINTING HISTORY
First Paperback Edition 2025

ISBN: 978-1-929928-55-2

www.paulbspence.com
author@paulbspence.com

For Grace, as always.

CHAPTER ONE

Drake used the Instrumentality to apport Xia and himself to their favorite restaurant in Albuquerque. Since the enemy already knew of Xia, it didn't make much sense to try to hide any longer. Drake worried about assassins finding Brygida but hoped her anonymity would conceal her. Not many people knew of his relation to her. Not many knew of his relation to Xia, either.

"You've been gone a long while, Father," Xia said once they were seated. "What has been happening? Where have you been?"

"I've been to the ends of the Earths," said Drake. "I've spent time in both the Ruined Courts and the Golden Kingdom recently. It's had an effect on the elapsed time for me."

"The Golden Kingdom? You weren't seeing that princess of yours again, were you?"

Drake laughed. "Funny that you should mention her. I did see Monika again while I was there, but not for a romantic encounter. It turns out that we had a daughter together, a few decades ago."

"Really? I have another living sister? When are we to meet?"

"Whenever you like. Her name is Brygida, and she's in this Realm, in Cincinnati, right now."

"Tough decision: have enchiladas or meet my sister? Both of these things appeal to me equally. If you didn't know you had a daughter with Monika, why were you in the Golden Kingdom?"

"It's somewhat complicated. I met Brygida in another Realm, while helping a friend. Brygida knew who I am, and our relationship, which she informed me of. My friend whom I'd been helping also had business in the Golden Kingdom. Some of the Northerners were trying to start a war with the South and trying to kill him. An attempt was staged to make it look as if I was behind the attack."

"That's interesting. Do you think it's linked to the assassin who tried to kill me?"

"I hadn't thought so, but now that you mention it, I cannot dismiss the possibility. The North doesn't have shapeshifters, but they could have found and recruited ones from the Realms as easily as the South could. Would you like to eat first or go now to Cincinnati?"

"Eat, I think. I'd like some time to prepare mentally before meeting Brygida. Also, I don't get down here for food as much as I should. I take my classes at the University of New Mexico, here in Albuquerque, but that leaves little time for other things."

"Do you ride the train?" Drake asked.

"I apport, as we did just now."

Drake sighed. He should have thought to warn her about apporting. "That's probably how the enemy found you."

"Do you think it likely another attempt will be made?"

"I wish I knew the answer to that question. Were many people killed?"

"Three locally-hired security guards were slain. Their families have been compensated. It caused a bit of a stir, as the

Institute works as a think tank for the military in this country. The prevailing public theory is that some foreign power wanted to steal secrets."

"So the problem has been contained."

The server arrived then, and Drake ordered beers and double enchiladas for Xia and himself.

"I wouldn't say that it has been contained," said Xia. "The Families were quite troubled by what occurred."

"I can imagine. However, I was referring to local authorities."

"Yes, that seems under control."

Drake didn't trust the Families and knew that the feeling was mutual. He didn't trust them because he didn't completely understand them. They had a vast trading empire yet never sought any kind of political control in the Realms they invested in. They didn't trust him because they'd had too many encounters with people from the South. Not to mention what had happened to Xia's mother.

The food and beer arrived, and they ate with gusto. Xia was the only one of Drake's children in recent memory whom he'd been able to have an active hand in raising. She was very dear to him.

After her mother was killed, he'd taken Xia to House Drake in the Courts. They'd spent the first few decades of her life together there and at his fortress in Nandegurth. After Xia was initiated into the Omphalos, she'd joined the House military and rose up through the ranks to become a captain of the House forces. Drake was proud of her.

"How are things back home?" Xia asked.

"The Ruined Courts are much as they ever are," said Drake. "Intrigues and shifting alliances. The Emperor remains steadfast. House Cyryth has become more active. They manipulated Imperial orders to kill a unit of my men, and then had imposters attempt to kill my friend Jon, who is of the

Golden Kingdom. So I insulted their duke and killed a flunky of theirs in Court. I had Imperial sanction on the kill, so they couldn't call me out."

"That must have put Emrys in a difficult position."

"The Emperor has chosen his side. It was never truly in doubt."

"Are you expecting war with Cyryth?" Xia asked. Her eyes sparked green as she spoke.

"Do not sound so eager," said Drake. "A war between the Houses would result in billions of deaths. The Ruined Courts can't afford something that would weaken us to that extent. The Golden Kingdom came closer to winning last time than anyone wants to admit."

"You think they'd attempt to invade again?"

"Don't you?"

Xia sighed and shook her head. "I admit that I don't know much about our Northern cousins. I had thought that, while they may have come close to taking the palace and central plaza, the Courts are far too large for them to conquer."

"If you hold the central plaza, you hold all of the Courts," said Drake. He shook his head. "Well, it will give you something to discuss with your sister."

"I suppose she would have considerable knowledge of the Golden Kingdom. She was raised there?"

"Yes, but try remember that her mother, Monika, was against the war, and go easy on her."

Xia laughed. "I shan't interrogate her, Father. Are you close to her?"

"I have become so in the last few weeks."

"What is she like?" Xia asked.

"You wish for my assessment instead of just meeting her?"

"Yes, actually. You often have insights others miss."

Drake nodded. "She is smaller than you, built more like her mother. She has Cynosure. She's not a sorcerer but can walk the Realms and conjure. I have seen her fight only a little; she was strong, capable, and unafraid. She was trained by Prince Dominic, so she is undoubtedly highly skilled with a blade."

"It would be interesting to cross swords in practice with her. Tell me more."

"What she lacks in stature, she makes up for in intellect. Brygida has a brilliant mind and is a skilled telepath. She studied physics and genetics, and has advanced degrees in both. I believe she intends to teach at the local university in Cincinnati."

"Great, maybe she'll help me with my math homework," said Xia.

Drake laughed. "She'd probably be happy to. She's friendly and giving in nature."

"Does she know about me?"

"She does."

"Good. That could have been awkward."

The server brought the check, and Drake settled up.

"Will you come meet Brygida tonight?" he asked.

Xia sighed. "I'd like to, but I need to get back to the Institute. There will be an inquiry about today. Some people are not going to be happy that we showed up in force to a public place."

"Well, I imagine they would've been even less happy if I hadn't been who I said I was. Please be careful, Xia. You know of my brother through the House records, but he is not to be trifled with. He is more dangerous than you could possibly know. I would like to know more of this tower you saw in the mind of the assassin."

"I wish I had more information for you. The assassin didn't live long, so I wasn't able to get much from his mind. You needn't worry, I'll be vigilant." Xia pulled a notepad out her pocket and scrawled a note. "This is my cell phone number. Please give it to Brygida, tell her to call anytime. When you come to visit next, maybe you can bring her along."

"I think that would be good. I'm sure she'll want to meet you, soon."

They walked out of the restaurant together, and Xia gave Drake a hug under the huge central tree in the plaza.

"You should be careful, too," she said. "You take too many risks, and we can't afford to lose you."

"I will do my best not to die, as always."

Xia's form shimmered with rainbows and was gone.

Drake breathed in the crisp, dry air and then apported away to Cincinnati.

⊙

Brygida was at that time driving her rented Jeep across the bridge.

Geoffrey was in the passenger's seat; Jason was in back, behind Geoffrey. They'd all gotten fresh clothes and taken showers. Brygida privately thought it was a considerable improvement. Her senses were not as keen as her father's, but they were more sensitive than most people's.

"Where are we going?" she asked.

"LaRosa's Pizza in Cold Springs," Geoffrey replied, "if you don't mind."

"We just passed a sign for one of those," said Jason.

"The Covington place isn't as good. Doesn't have the same atmosphere."

Jason sighed and looked back out the window at traffic.

Brygida knew Jason was upset about the state his house had been in. She would have been, too. The place had been a disaster. She was confident they could get it fixed up, though. She knew Geoffrey would help. She would help, too.

Traffic was light, at least compared to Tokyo. She took the

Cold Springs exit and followed Geoffrey's directions. The pizza place looked like a little hole-in-the-wall restaurant, but Geoffrey seemed to think it had the best pizza in the region.

She'd looked up Japanese restaurants in the phone book at the hotel room. There was a Japanese steakhouse on the other side of Cincinnati. She'd have to take them there and introduce them to proper food. She would eat just about anything, but she was craving fresh sushi.

The inside of the pizzeria was totally at odds to the appearance from the outside. The dining room was dimly lit, with candles on the tables. Low music was playing, and the restaurant smelled wonderfully of rich spices.

Brygida asked for a booth away from everyone else, and the hostess seated them in the back of the restaurant. It was quieter back here. A server took their drink and appetizer orders promptly and then left.

"I like this place," Brygida said.

"Wait till you try the food," said Geoffrey.

"If it tastes as good as it smells, then I'm sure to love it."

The server returned with hot garlic breadsticks and dipping sauce. Jason ordered a steak hoagie. Geoffrey ordered a large thin-crust pizza with six meats. Brygida just ordered a small double pepperoni pizza and a salad. If she was still hungry afterward, she'd steal a slice of Geoffrey's.

It took them a while to work through all that food. Jason snagged a piece of pizza from Geoffrey, too. All of the food was really good. Brygida settled up with the server after replying that she didn't have room for dessert. She could imagine *anyone* having room for dessert after those generous portions.

"Brygida, are you really going to stay around here for a while?" asked Geoffrey.

She nodded. "It will probably take me a couple years to work out all the bugs in Gerhardt's engines and coldsleep technology. It's one thing to understand the principles and another to actually build the things."

"I still can't believe it," Geoffrey said. "I mean, sure, Drake and Jon have spaceships, but the Earth is about to, as well! *This* Earth – you know what I mean."

"I do, and yes, it is cool. I'm excited to be a part of making that happen."

"What do you think they'll find out there?" Jason asked.

"I don't know," Brygida said. "I'm not sure which universe cluster this Realm is a part of. There could be lots of aliens, or none at all."

"I hope there are lots," Geoffrey said. "I'd like to meet an alien."

"You know I'm not human, right?" Brygida pointed out, laughing.

"It's easy to forget," said Jason.

"Thanks, I think."

"I didn't mean it as an insult. You just seem like a normal woman to me."

"Well, you may be the first person to ever call me *normal*," said Brygida. She waved away his protest. "I know what you mean, though."

Geoffrey yawned hugely just then. "Sorry."

"Don't worry about it. I'm tired, too," said Brygida. "Why don't we go back to the hotel? I'll get you guys a room, and then we can go over and look at the house in the morning."

"I feel weird about leaving it," Jason said.

"It's uninhabitable right now. You can't stay there tonight."

"Yeah, come on, man. If you stay there, I have to," said Geoffrey. "I really don't want to, either."

"Okay. You win." Jason laughed.

Brygida stood up. The restaurant was empty except two servers cleaning tables. She waved to them as they left. No reason not to be nice to the people who brought her food. She's be wanting to visit again, for sure.

The trip back to the hotel was uneventful.

Brygida started making a list of things she needed to buy. She'd probably just rent a house instead of buying one. She might see about leasing a Jeep like the one she was driving. She really liked the handling and the space inside.

She said goodnight to the guys and crashed on her bed.

She could really build a life in a place like this.

She could be happy.

CHAPTER TWO

Drake arrived outside Jason's house much where he had a year before.

Of course, it had only been six weeks for him. The air was still hot, and humid enough to dampen his hair, even at night. The smell of freshly cut grass and spicy-smelling weeds greeted him as he walked to the front door. The cleaners had left a little note there stating that the paint would still be wet inside.

Drake entered the house.

He hadn't gone into Jason's home the time before; there had been no reason. He had been tracking Geoffrey and the intruder who turned out to be Jon. He hadn't cared about the men who had died in the house, or the ones taken away by the government. He'd had bigger problems to worry about.

The house smelled of disinfectants and fresh latex paint. Someone had sprayed an air freshener throughout the rooms, as well. It didn't quite cover up the smell of rot from the spilled blood. That was a hard smell to remove once it seeped into wood.

Prince Drake, I'm sorry to disturb you, his ship, Hephaestus, said through his datalink. *The remote sensor you left on Kai picked up your name being spoken. Given the context, I thought it warranted your attention.*

Send it to my helmet, Drake said, unfolding his helm over his head. Hephaestus wouldn't have bothered him if it wasn't important.

Drake recognized Lolani's voice speaking. "Drake, I don't know if can hear me. Fuck, I feel stupid talking to the sky. Drake, Jon is gone. His ship is still here, but he isn't. Orbital control logged an unauthorized landing this morning. I think we need your help."

It has to be the Alliance, Drake thought. *Some people just don't learn. Hephaestus, meet me at Kai.*

Heading there now.

Drake found paper and pencil in an upstairs desk drawer and wrote a hasty note. He didn't have time to hunt his friends down and let them know what was going on. If the Alliance had taken Jon, then the Ancient Enemy was almost certainly involved.

That meant Jon didn't have much time.

Drake left the note in the kitchen, weighed down with a dagger.

He brought up the Instrumentality and focused on Hephaestus' bridge. With proper application of energy, he was able to apport through hyperspace and all the universes between. It wasn't something he would normally do, but he was in a hurry. The time rate was slightly slower in Jon's Realm, which worked to Drake's favor.

"We are over Kai now," said Hephaestus. "I've spoken to orbital control."

"Thank you. I'll go down and try to discover what has happened. You may want to dust off your weapons."

"Full weapons systems are always available at your request," Hephaestus replied haughtily. "Planetary or space-borne threats?"

"Watch for ships," said Drake. "I'll be back as soon as I can."

Drake apported down to the landing pad. The *Chwyldro* and the *Ahi'iwa* were still here, but the pad held no other ships. There *were* fresh scorch marks that could be indicative of a rapid vertical takeoff. Jon and Lolani tended to taxi down the runway to pick up speed and save fuel.

"Drake!" Lolani called to him.

She was standing outside the bar they'd eaten at frequently. A tall woman was with her, someone Drake somewhat recognized from the night he'd first met Lolani. From the fresh, healing scars on her face, she'd been fighting recently. She was almost as tall as Drake. He thought she'd be a good match for Jon.

"Thank the gods, Drake," said Lolani. "I can't believe that actually worked."

Drake retracted his helmet. "What's happened?"

"We think Jon was taken by the Alliance," the other woman said. She had a rich voice with a hint of an accent he didn't recognize.

"Did anyone see Jon taken?" Drake asked. "Where was he when it happened?"

"He was with me," the woman said. "We're lovers." He liked the challenge in her eyes. She'd been rejected because of her height and build many times, he guessed. Well, there were fools everywhere. She was lovely.

"Take me to where he was," said Drake. "And tell me what you know, starting with your name. I don't know you."

"I'm Aradhana Daevika," she said. "Jon and I had just made love and fell asleep. I woke up the next morning, and he was gone. I had a bad headache and stiff muscles, and there was a tang to the air. I think we might have been gassed."

"Why would you think that?" It seemed an odd conclusion to jump to first. Most people would have assumed their lover had left. If the two of them had been drinking before their lovemaking, a headache wouldn't have been odd, for humans.

"I used to be Alliance, Special Operations. We used a non-toxic nerve gas for extractions."

"Jon knew your history?"

"We had spoken of it," she said cautiously. "I won't apologize for having been poor and serving in the military. I was through with that life, building a new one here. Jon was okay with that."

Drake nodded. "I wasn't judging you. We all do what we must to survive. I have to ask you, though: did you have a part in what has happened?"

"I did not."

"I trust her," Lolani added. "I wouldn't have introduced them if I didn't."

"You're friends?"

"Yes. I've known Aradhana for years. She wouldn't have been a part of this."

"Very well. I hope you understand, and forgive me for asking. I am Daeren Drake, as I'm sure you know. I have come to consider Jon and Lolani as friends – family, even. I hope that you will be, as well."

"It's an honor, sir."

"Just call me Drake. Is this your flat?" She'd led him across the town and up some stairs to a worn front door.

"Yes. We were in the bedroom."

"Jon was taken this morning?"

Aradhana nodded.

Drake entered the apartment and went toward the bedroom. It was a small and modest place, simply furnished. There were a few knickknacks on shelves, including an Alliance service medal. Aradhana hadn't tried to hide who she'd been; that was a good sign. In the bedroom, Drake could smell something metallic in the air. It had left a faint, almost imperceptible residue on the surfaces. He nodded and apported them all to the roof.

"Fucking hell, Drake, a little warning next time," Lolani exclaimed.

Drake ignored her and checked the ventilation stacks. "Here," he said, pointing. "Someone drilled into the system. They probably inserted a hose to direct the gas down into your bedroom."

"That's standard operating procedure for an Alliance team," Aradhana said with a growl. "The bastards couldn't just leave us alone."

"I know it is little enough consolation," Drake said, "but they were after Jon. We're going to get him back. I promise you that."

"Well, we know how," said Lolani. "We suspect who. We need to know where."

"For that, we're going to need help," said Drake. "I need to go back to my ship."

"I'd like to go with you," Lolani said. Aradhana nodded to her. "We both would, if you don't mind."

"I think it would be fitting for you to be there when we rescue Jon. I have to warn you, though, I shall not be merciful to the Alliance. They have been warned. They chose to ignore that warning."

"The Alliance isn't going to listen to anything less than you smashing a fleet," said Aradhana. "As usual, the common soldiers are going to pay for the idiocy of the politicians."

"I assure you that those in power will pay, as well."

"Let's do this," Lolani said.

Drake nodded and apported them to the bridge.

"Hephaestus, I'm sure you remember Lolani. This is Aradhana."

"What's up, bruh?" said Lolani.

"It is a pleasure to meet you, Aradhana. Lolani, welcome back aboard."

"Who?" Aradhana looked confused.

"Hephaestus is the machine intelligence who wears this ship as a body," said Drake.

"Right, okay, sure."

"Hephaestus, Jon was abducted this morning," said Drake. "The extraction team took off in an orbital shuttle. They probably boarded a larger space vessel. Can you track it?"

"You want me to track a vessel that was in orbit over five hours ago?" Hephaestus asked. "I'm sorry, but stellar winds will have destroyed any traces of the engine exhaust."

"Damnit!" Lolani muttered.

"There are other options," said Hephaestus. "The simplest would be to jump to an Alliance held system and find a ship to interrogate."

"I doubt the crew of any random ship would know what happened to Jon," said Aradhana. "That sort of sensitive information would have been compartmentalized."

"I didn't say anything about the crew," Hephaestus said.

"Do it," said Drake.

Hephaestus immediately moved out of orbit.

"I don't understand," Aradhana said.

"Hephaestus is going to find a ship, disable it, and hack into the Alliance defense network," Drake said.

"Those systems are heavily encrypted with shifting meta-phasic code-keys," said Aradhana. "They're impossible to crack."

"Nothing is impossible."

"I've analyzed Alliance systems before," said Hephaestus. "They weren't terrible, for primitive security. It actually took me seconds to break the codes."

"Hephaestus' core is an ancient quantum computer two meters across," Drake said. "Trust me when I say he won't have any trouble."

Aradhana just nodded.

Sections on the bridge deck retracted, and two acceleration couches flowed up into position.

"We're getting ready to jump," said Drake. "We'll probably be going straight into battle." He gestured to the acceleration couches. "You'll be safe in those."

Drake settled into his couch and brought up his secondary tactical displays. Hephaestus jumped as he was doing that. The screens showed hyperspace swirling past.

It was a short jump. As they came out of hyperspace, the screens filled with the view of a planetary system with three main sequence stars. All three were orange, although one was much larger than the orbiting pair.

"36 Ophiuchi," said Hephaestus. "There's an Alliance vessel near the gas giant. Jumping now."

"There's only a single gate in this system," Lolani said. "Other side of the suns from here."

There was a slight blur as Hephaestus jumped across the system.

Drake enlarged the view of the Alliance ship on the main display.

"That's a destroyer," said Aradhana. "Crew complement of two hundred, armed with missiles and beams both."

"Alliance vessel," Drake called over the com, "this Prince Daeren Drake aboard Hephaestus. The Alliance has broken the terms of our accord. Stand to and prepare to be boarded."

"Unknown vessel, this is Captain Ubadah of the *Eadwyn*. You're in Alliance space illegally. It is you who will surrender or be destroyed."

"They're coming about and arming weapons," said Hephaestus.

"Captain Ubadah, don't be a fool," Drake said.

"They've fired missiles."

"Can you disable the ship and ensure the computer systems are intact?" asked Drake.

"I doubt it," Hephaestus replied. "That ship looks fragile."

"Then I'll do it myself. Stand by to infiltrate their systems. Do you have a scan of the layout?"

"Transferring it to your helmet now."

"Drake, what are you going to do?" asked Lolani.

"I'm going over there. You'll be safe here. Nothing will get through Hephaestus' screens."

Drake stood and closed his helm over his head. He drew his sword and pistol. He didn't want to apport over there, but the Alliance weren't giving him much choice. Drake struggle to keep his rage in check. The Alliance had defied him and taken Jon, but the crew on that ship didn't need to die.

"There are two hundred personnel over there," said Aradhana.

"Then pray to your gods that they surrender before I have to kill all of them."

CHAPTER THREE

Geoffrey helped Jason position the new couch in the living room and then collapsed onto it.

The living room looked close enough to the way it had before they left. The television, though, was bigger, widescreen, and flat, which was cool. He was waiting until he had some money to buy a new PlayStation; he missed it, but he could live without it. He was going to have a lot to do anyway, with school and work.

Brygida had taken them that morning to buy furniture on the corporate credit card. She said it was the least Gerhardt owed them, under the circumstances. Geoffrey would have liked to have gone crazy and bought everything, but he'd didn't want the card to be taken away.

"That's the last thing, right?" he asked.

Jason sat down heavily next to him. "Yeah. I mean, you'll have to set up your new bed, but this is the last of the big stuff. I still need to replace the floorboards in the hall and foyer."

Geoffrey nodded. They'd tracked down the foul smell to the floorboards just outside the living room. Geoffrey could still remember the shocking spray of blood when Jason slit the throat of the man in the hall – the man who had been about to kill Geoffrey.

It had been almost two months ago for him, but it was still fresh in his mind.

"What are you doing for Gerhardt, anyway?" asked Jason.

Geoffrey shook his head. "I don't know, actually. I start Monday as a paid intern. I don't even know what I'm being paid. I could use the money and the experience, though."

"When does school start back?"

"Two weeks. Gerhardt said I could work weekends and evenings after classes begin."

"You're going to be busy. Sticking with history?"

"For now. I'm going to take some other classes and see if anything piques my interest. You never know. Maybe I won't have to be a history teacher, after all."

"Do you know what Brygida's going to be teaching?"

"No. She's had an interview at the university this afternoon. I think she wants to teach physics. She was headed to the interview right after she took me to the bank. Did you get your truck running?"

"Yeah, just needed a jump. I was able to use the battery charger once the power was back on."

"So we can go to the grocery store?"

"Yeah. I went to the bank earlier. They gave me a temporary card."

"Brygida said she was going to try to get our wallets back and stuff," said Geoffrey.

"I wish her luck."

"It's never going to be the same, is it?"

Jason sighed. "You mean after having traveled through different universes? No, I don't think it'll ever be the same. How could it? At least we survived. It'll take a while to get back to where we were, but things will be calmer, I think."

"Do you really want that? I thought I did, but now I'm not

so sure."

"Brygida is still around. Drake will be back after he takes care of whatever he had to go do. I'm sure you'll still have some adventures."

Geoffrey chuckled. "I'll probably be so busy with work and school that I don't even miss it."

"That's usually how it works."

A car horn honked outside.

Geoffrey glanced out the window, and Brygida waved to him.

"It's Brygida. Looks like she needs something. Hold on."

Geoffrey walked out front.

Brygida had several boxes and bags unloaded from the Jeep. "Grab the food and drinks," she said.

Geoffrey opened the side door and grabbed the large fast food bags and a cardboard carrier with drinks. Brygida had the boxes balanced on her shoulder and was carrying the other three large bags. Geoffrey kept forgetting that she was lot stronger than she looked. He'd left the door open, so he went in, put down the food, and then came back to grab two of the boxes from Brygida.

"Thanks," she said. "Hey, Jason."

"What's all this?" Jason asked.

"I figured you guys wouldn't have made it to the store yet, so I brought lunch."

"I meant the other stuff."

Brygida pulled paper plates out of one of the bags. "Just some housewarming stuff."

"Thanks," Geoffrey said. "You bought White Castles?"

"Is it not a good place?" she asked.

"You just went there because it was a castle, didn't you?" said Jason.

Brygida grinned. "Smelled good, too."

"Yeah, it's good."

"I bought a twenty sack of the cheeseburgers, and three each of the fries, onion chips, chicken rings, and those cheese stick things."

"That ought to be enough for Geoffrey," said Jason. "What are we going to eat?"

"Hey!" Geoffrey had been sorting the sacks out into three piles. "Just for that, Brygida and I are going to eat the extra burgers."

"Oh, no, I'll starve," Jason said. "Thank you, Brygida. It was very thoughtful. How did your interview go?"

"It went okay."

"You didn't get the job?" Geoffrey asked.

"Oh, no. They hired me," said Brygida. "I'll be an adjunct instructor teaching basic intro-level courses the first year. It's only part time, but my pay from Gerhardt should make up for it."

"That's still good news, right?"

"I hope so. It's just that I only have two weeks to develop a syllabus for the freshman-level physics course I'm teaching. At least it will give me some time to catch up on reading the literature here. I don't know for certain that the laws of physics are the same here as where I went to school."

"Are they different in different universes?" asked Geoffrey.

"Sometimes," she said. "This Realm is real close to where I was, so things are almost certainly the same. However, even a slight difference in one of the constants can add up to big changes."

Brygida picked the pickles off her sandwiches and ate daintily.

Geoffrey wolfed down his share of burgers. He loved sliders when they were fresh but couldn't afford to buy them often. When he did, he normally bought a bag of ten and split them with Jason.

"You got chicken rings, too! We used to call these chocobo

rings," said Geoffrey. "It's from a game."

"Yeah, *Final Fantasy*," Brygida said. "That's kind of sick, dude. Chocobos are cute."

"Great," said Jason, "another gamer."

"Speaking of which," Brygida said. She opened one of the larger boxes. "I think this box is for you." She handed it to Geoffrey.

"You bought me a PlayStation? And games?"

"You'd mentioned that yours had been stolen."

"Thank you! Oh, man, you must have bought fifty games."

"I didn't know what you like, so I bought one of each. There's an extra controller and headphones in there, too."

Jason groaned. "Now he'll never do anything around the house."

"Nonsense. He'll be good. Won't you?"

"Absolutely," said Geoffrey.

"Don't think I left you out, either," Brygida said to Jason. She handed him a smaller bag. "I think these are yours."

"My silver flatware?" He looked stunned. "How did you find it?"

"I checked all the pawn shops in town. Found them in Covington. Everything is there except the spoon you found and a missing fork. Apparently some kid came in and bought the fork to make a ring. Sorry."

"Wow, thank you. I mean it. You have no idea how much this means to me."

"I'm not done with you yet." She shoved the other box over to him. "A coffee maker, creamer, sugar, and fresh-ground coffee."

Jason pulled a small bag out of the box and took a deep sniff of the contents. "That's good. Now I just need a mug."

Brygida grinned and handed him a mug wrapped in paper.

He unwrapped it and lost his smile.

"What?" asked Geoffrey.

Jason showed him the mug.

It was printed with the words *Instant Human – Just Add Coffee*. Geoffrey thought it was funny as hell. Jason was grouchy in the morning if he didn't get his coffee.

"Very funny," Jason said.

"I thought you'd like it."

"I do." Jason laughed and shook his head. "I think I'll go use it now." He picked up the box and went into the kitchen.

"That was a good one," Geoffrey said. "And seriously, thank you. I was thinking earlier I'd have to save up and buy a new console."

"Well, I got a sign-on bonus from the university," said Brygida.

"You didn't drop it onto that plastic?"

"It didn't seem right to buy gifts with someone else's money."

"Thank you." Geoffrey stood up and hugged her. "Do you play?"

"I saw some of those games at the store. They were a lot cooler than what I used to play."

"Some of these are two-player," said Geoffrey. "Racing and fighting games. I can set it up."

Brygida laughed. "I can see that you're eager to play. You go and set up. I'm going to check on Jason."

Geoffrey was really excited. He'd never had the money to buy more than a few games. Now there were dozens that he'd never had a chance to try. He couldn't wait.

⊙

Jon shivered in the darkness of his cell.

It wasn't particularly cold, but he was more frightened than he'd ever been in his life. He was strapped into a chair that didn't let him move. Even his head was strapped down.

He couldn't even kill himself, and he'd considered it. Anything to avoid the horror of becoming something like the enemy. He wouldn't let the Ancient Enemy use him.

Jon had tried to call up the Cynosure, but here in the darkness, he couldn't concentrate enough to hold it in his mind. He suspected he was drugged. He seemed to be in a fugue state most of the time. He had no idea how long it had been since he was abducted; it could have been hours or years.

Obviously, they'd thought of preventing him from dying, as well. Hoses went into his body to feed him and keep him hydrated and force air into him. There were no meals to break up the day. He couldn't starve himself to death.

He'd been a fool.

He'd let himself think he was safe on Kai.

Drake was right: he wasn't really safe.

Jon wondered how they'd found him. He hoped with every fiber of his being that Aradhana hadn't betrayed him. He couldn't dismiss the possibility, though. He remembered the soldier checking her pulse. Why would the Alliance soldiers have cared if she was okay? If she was an enemy, then Lolani was in danger, too.

This was the fear talking, he knew. He trusted Aradhana. Even more, he trusted Lolani, who wouldn't have set him up with someone she didn't completely trust. Lolani was a good judge of character, in her own way.

Lolani would find some way of saving him. She'd get in touch with Drake. Maybe it would be months, but Drake would check on him. Then Drake would make all of these people sorry they'd captured Jon.

He had to hold that in his mind.

Drake would come.

Sometimes, the visions washed over him in waves. The sensory deprivation didn't allow him to block anything out.

Had the enemy known that? Was that why he was locked into this machine? He wasn't even sure that his current situation wasn't just a particularly strong vision. Was he still in bed with Aradhana, and all that had happened here was yet to come?

Either way, fire and blood were in his future, he knew.

Suddenly the visions turned into one stronger than ever. He was lost in a sea of possible futures, falling into the depths. So many horrible possibilities lay ahead of them, and in all of them, Drake died screaming as he was torn apart by monsters. Jon couldn't accept that future, but it wouldn't leave him alone. No matter what choices he made, Drake always died, alone.

He had to tell Drake. He had to live, and remember, and tell Drake about the visions.

Drake couldn't go into the Eye.

If he did, he'd die.

CHAPTER FOUR

Drake apported directly to the bridge of the Alliance destroyer.

The acceleration couches – more like chairs – were too upright to be truly practical and stood arranged in an arc around the command chair in the center of the bridge. Other stations were placed around the circular bridge. A large view screen dominated the front of the bridge.

A red alert klaxon started screaming out its warning.

Two guards near the door to a lift drew their sidearms as he appeared. Drake shot them through their heads with his needle pistol. One of the guards fired his pistol as he died, and a beam of energy sliced across the bridge, killing an officer at one of the side stations.

"I am calling on you to surrender," said Drake.

The captain slammed his fist down on the intercom. "Security to the bridge!"

"That will only result in more death," said Drake.

A nearby crewman snatched a pistol from a rack, and Drake removed the man's hand with a flick of his sword. Maegril cut through flesh and bone with equal ease. He didn't allow the blade to dissolve the man. Another flick destroyed the racked pistols.

The ensign fell to his knees screaming as blood pulsed from the wound. Another crewman leapt to try to staunch the blood. Drake approved of the compassion, and of the intelligence to know when they were beaten.

The captain had taken advantage of Drake's momentary distraction to leap to the attack. Drake turned his head just as the man punched him in the face. The captain screamed and stumbled back. He'd loudly broken several bones in his hand against Drake's helmet. Drake slapped the side of the captain's head with the flat of Maegril, to shut him up. The captain collapsed unconscious just as the security team burst in from the lift.

They all fired on Drake at once. The particle beams cut his coat to ribbons but didn't affect him through his armor. Well, it annoyed him. Drake shot each member of the security team in the head without looking as he walked to the command chair.

Drake punched the button for the intercom. "This is Prince Drake. You may have heard of me. I have taken control of the bridge. Most of the personnel here are still alive at the moment, including your captain. Stand down, or I will have to kill all of you, and I don't want to do that."

He pointed his blade at the woman sitting behind the most complicated displays. "Are you communications?"

"Y-yes," she stammered.

No one else on the bridge dared move.

"Open all channels, no encryption. I want direct Alliance network access."

"Don't do it!" someone across the bridge yelled.

Drake fired a round into the panel in front the speaker. It exploded, and the person cried out in fear and pain. Some of the shrapnel had cut them.

"I didn't have to shoot the panel instead of you," said Drake. "Another word, and I won't miss next time. I am fully capable of killing every single person on this ship and taking what I want over your steaming corpses. I'm being courteous and allowing you to live. Do not disrespect me again."

"We surrender!" the captain said, getting up from the deck with a groan. "Don't kill anyone else."

"Announce it," Drake ordered.

The captain complied and sat heavily in his chair. He didn't look like a man used to defeat. No one in the Alliance was, really. They'd never faced anyone capable of fighting back, until now.

"Now, the network," said Drake.

"Do it," the captain ordered.

"I've opened the channels," the woman called out.

Hephaestus? Drake thought through his link.

I'm in the network. Hephaestus replied. *Jon is being held aboard the Alliance flagship* Endeavor. *The bulk of the Alliance fleet has massed at Proxima Centauri. They intend to trap us there.*

I'm not worried, are you?

Certainly not.

Once I'm clear of this ship, disable and silence it.

You don't want to destroy it?

I told them I'd let them live if they complied. I will not be forsworn.

Understood.

Drake apported back to Hephaestus' bridge. Beams flicked out and sheared off the Alliance ship's communication arrays. Other beams punched holes through the primary engines. The ship was dead in space. They'd be able to use secondary thrusters to limp to the nearest planet, but they certainly weren't a threat anymore.

⊙

Jason carefully rinsed out the new coffee pot and started it brewing.

He was deeply moved by Brygida's gift. She'd really gone out of her way to find his old silver flatware. He heard her tell Geoffrey she'd bought the gifts with her sign-on bonus from the university. Geoffrey might be too young to know it, but that really did make it more special.

Jason next washed each of the pieces of silverware. He'd had them made so he didn't have to wear gloves all the time when he ate. Wearing gloves to handle flatware was a possible point of vulnerably. If anyone had seen him, they might have figured out his secret.

That had been in the early eighteen hundreds. The United States had only recently been birthed into the world with a scream and a bang. What a shock that had been. He'd never expected the people of this world to develop real democracy.

He'd known then that other nations would follow suit.

A form of democracy had existed in ancient Greece, he knew, but it didn't really count. That had only been for rich men. He'd been saddened that classism, racism, and sexism prevented the forefathers of this country from making everyone eligible to vote, but it had still been a glorious start. He'd watched with interest, over the years, as first men of color and then women were allowed to vote.

Slowly, this world was reaching for something good.

Jason still hoped that one day he'd make it home, to his real home, but it had been so long that he despaired of that ever happening. This world wasn't so bad, though. Hell, Brygida was running around all over the place without anything covering her ears, and no one cared.

Granted, Brygida's ears weren't as pronounced as his.

She'd obviously never been persecuted for having pointed ears.

That wasn't entirely fair. Brygida had suffered while she was in school. She'd been ostracized and harassed, but no one had tried to cut her ears off or burn her. So there was that.

Brygida came in and began drying the flatware.

"Was I thinking too loud?" Jason asked.

"Not at all," said Brygida.

Somehow Jason didn't think she was telling the truth. He knew she heard thoughts that were directed at her, and he'd been incautious. He hoped she understood that he didn't mean anything by it.

Brygida shook her head. "I just thought you'd like some help washing this stuff. Geoffrey's busy setting up his game console. He didn't need me getting in the way."

"I can't believe you bought him that thing. All those games and stuff must have cost you a fortune. Geoffrey doesn't even realize."

"What else am I going to use the money on?"

"You could buy yourself something."

"I don't really need that much. I've never needed a lot to get by. I leased my Jeep. I like that. Over the weekend, I'm going to look at houses to rent. I don't wear jewelry or fancy clothes. I'd rather buy things for people I like."

"You're renting a house?"

"I know, I don't really need a full house."

"I'm sorry I don't have another bedroom," Jason said. "I'd offer it to you if I did."

"Thank you. I do appreciate that. I'm going to try to find somewhere close. If you don't mind."

"Why would I mind?"

"I don't want to be a bother."

Jason sighed. "Brygida, I'm glad you're here. I don't have many friends, you know. It's a relief having one around who knows… about, you know."

"Not comfortable talking here?" she asked. "Even in your own house?"

"I keep thinking the government must have bugged the place."

Brygida leaned back against the counter. "They could have," she said. "Or Gerhardt may have. I wouldn't put it past him. I'll look into it."

"Thanks."

"You really don't mind me being around?"

"If I had another mug, I'd even share my coffee with you."

She raised her eyebrows at that. "Really? Wow. I guess you do like me."

Jason laughed. "Well, I can't be grumpy all the time."

"No, you can't," she said. "You can't hide forever, either." She glanced pointedly out of the kitchen, toward where they could hear Geoffrey muttering as he connected things.

"Maybe once we're sure the place isn't bugged."

"Well, I guess *maybe* will have to do. You going to come in and see him try it out?"

"Yeah. Let me get my coffee, and I'll be in."

She patted him on the shoulder and left.

If she ever suggested that she'd be interested, he'd definitely ask that woman out.

Jason poured his coffee. He decided to have the first one pure and black. The coffee she'd bought was expensive and smelled amazing.

He sipped it.

It tasted every bit as good as it smelled.

It was funny. He hadn't like coffee at first. He'd started drinking it because everyone else drank it, and he didn't want to stand out. He'd preferred tea, once upon a time. Americans didn't have as strong a stigma against drinking tea as they once did, but somehow it still wasn't what normal people drank.

The coffee places on every city corner were an indication of that.

CHAPTER FIVE

Drake told Lolani and Aradhana what he and Hephaestus had learned.

"That's a lot of ships," said Lolani. "Maybe a hundred or more. They really want to make sure you don't get to Jon, don't they?"

"I believe the Alliance didn't care for my ultimatum," Drake said. "Jon is mostly just the bait."

"But you're going in there anyway?" asked Aradhana.

"Indeed. You'll be safe here on Hephaestus. In case of critical damage, the acceleration couches hold stasis field generators. Those are impervious to any weapon from this universe. Hephaestus would fall back to Kai and recover."

"What about you?"

"After the initial phase of the space battle, I'll be retrieving Jon from the *Endeavor*. I doubt the Alliance has anything that can touch Hephaestus, though. He was built at the height of my people's technological prowess, over a million years ago. I dare say he has a few weapons the Alliance has never seen or nor even thought of."

Drake settled into his acceleration couch. "Are you ready?"

Lolani and Aradhana nodded.

Hephaestus jumped through hyperspace.

They arrived close to the third planet, where the seat of Alliance government was located.

"Where are all the enemy ships?" Drake asked. Only twelves ships were visible in orbit.

"They are cloaking visible wavelengths," said Hephaestus. "Mass readings show an additional eighty-eight vessels currently moving to englobe this position. The *Endeavor* is hailing."

Drake stood before the main screen. "Put them though."

A tall, dark-haired, arrogant-looking man appeared on the screen. He was seated in a command chair, much like what Drake had seen aboard the other Alliance ship. "I am Commodore Donovan. You must be the Precursor everyone has been talking about."

"You have something of mine," said Drake, "taken from a world I warned the Alliance to stay away from."

"Right to the point. I like that," Donovan said. "I could pretend that I don't know what you're talking about. I could offer you terms of surrender, or tell you to leave our space, but we both know that my orders are to destroy your ship. You're too much of a threat."

"I appreciate your candidness. To be honest I was considering offering you terms of surrender, as well, but have decided against it. Destroying your hundred ships will be more of a statement, I think."

Donovan's face twitched slightly as Drake mentioned the cloaked ships.

"However, my friend who is your captive prefers to avoid bloodshed," Drake continued, "so I will give you one last chance to hand him over and save your ships and crews."

"That isn't going to happen."

"I don't suppose we have much more to say to one another, then." Drake cut the transmission and returned to his seat.

"They are locking weapons," said Hephaestus.

"Lock hyperspatial missiles on those ships. Avoid the *Endeavor.*"

"They've fired two missiles from each ship: antimatter warheads, fifty-megaton yield. Hyperspace shielding is holding."

"Return fire," Drake ordered.

Hephaestus generated a flickering field around the hull that opened into hyperspace. Matter and energy encountering the field were deflected into hyperspace and destroyed. The ship shook with explosions as the field breached the magnetic containment on the incoming missiles and they detonated.

Ports opened along the hull, and ninety-nine hyperspatial missiles launched, dropping briefly into hyperspace to bypass Hephaestus' own shields and skipping into the mass of the enemy ships before returning to normal space.

The missiles carried one-hundred-megaton warheads, but most of the weapons' energy was from their speed. They reentered normal space inside the enemy vessels at ninety-nine percent of the speed of light. The missiles' matter was converted into energy upon impact with interior bulkheads. The results were catastrophic, the energy release in excess of one hundred gigatons each. Just one of those missiles could crack apart a small moon.

To Drake, it appeared as if hell had been unleashed around them. Ninety-nine little stars exploded and the plasma washed over Hephaestus' hull with deep bass rumbles. The *Endeavor* was caught in the wake of the explosions and tossed around like so much flotsam.

"Gravitic cannon," Drake ordered.

The pulses from Hephaestus' cannon struck the *Endeavor*'s prow and washed through the ship. The cannon didn't do much direct damage; they just produced a powerful gravity wave. As the wave passed through the *Endeavor,* its interior bulkheads temporarily produced gravitation fields five times higher than Earth's. The crew would be thrown forward and then back into the bulkheads, over and over again. Any who survived wouldn't be in great shape for mounting a resistance.

"That should've softened them up," said Drake. He started his apport, only to stagger and cry out in pain.

The enemy ship had an interdiction field in place.

"What happened?" asked Lolani.

"They have some technology that they shouldn't," Drake said. "It prevents apportation."

"What are you going to do?"

"Board the ship the hard way," he replied. "Hephaestus, interdict the entire star system. I don't want anyone in or out. Shut down all the gates throughout the Alliance, too. Where does the enemy's field begin?"

"It extends ten kilometers from their hull."

"Okay, I'll be back with Jon soon."

"The planet has launched thousands of missiles at us," said Hephaestus. "They will arrive in ten minutes. They appear to be aimed at both ships. While we can weather that firestorm, I doubt the *Endeavor* can. I suggest you change into heavier armor."

Drake sighed. Hephaestus was right, of course. His current armor couldn't take a hit from one of those missiles, but his combat armor had a stasis field generator that protect him from just about anything.

He apported to his quarters and changed into the heavier armor, and picked up his star fusion rifle while he was at it. He didn't think he'd need it, but with one of the Ancient Enemy on that ship, he should be prepared.

"Eight minutes," said Hephaestus as Drake apported back to the bridge.

"Have you located Jon's cell?"

"Highlighted on your display."

Drake apported halfway to the enemy ship.

Glowing shells of gases were still expanding from the explosions. The enemy ship was inside the magnetic field of the planet. The cities below would have been hit with powerful electromagnetic pulses from the orbital detonations, resulting in thousands if not millions of civilian casualties.

It couldn't be helped, Drake thought. *They chose their battleground.*

Line-of-sight apportation still worked inside an interdiction field. Drake apported to the hull of the enemy vessel. The *Endeavor* had taken a beating from the destruction of the other ships and was now listing and venting atmosphere.

Drake slung his rifle when he reached an exterior airlock. The door control was inoperable, but it had a manual override. He forced the door open and cycled the airlock.

"Seven minutes," Hephaestus informed him.

"I'm working on it," Drake growled.

The interior of the *Endeavor* had been hit harder than he'd realized. Alliance ships really were quite fragile. The overhead lighting was intermittent. Electrical arcs sputtered from blown panels. Debry clogged the corridors. Screaming, broken crew lay contorted against the rear bulkheads.

Drake hoped Jon was all right. He hadn't considered how the gravitic cannon was going to interact with this ship's artificial gravity. He considered it odd that he felt badly about the wounded on the ship and the planet below, when he'd just killed thousands on the other ships.

Well, he hadn't intended for anyone to actually suffer.

"Six minutes," said Hephaestus.

Drake ran through the ship. He ignored the few people who fired at him. They would be dead from their own missiles soon. He couldn't afford to be slowed down.

He was worried about the Ancient Enemy. Unlike the Endeavor's crew, it wouldn't have been disabled by the gravitic weapon. It could be waiting for him. Almost certainly was.

Drake pulsed his rifle for a nanosecond to melt a sealed hatchway. The thermal backwash ignited the atmosphere and incinerated the crew in the corridor behind him. He tried not to flinch at the screams. Normally it wouldn't have bothered him, but he wasn't feeling as excited by the battle as he normally did. It had been too one-sided.

This wasn't battle; it was slaughter.

"Five minutes."

Drake entered the detention area. Jon's cell door was standing open. Drake approached it cautiously, slinging his rifle and drawing Maegril. Jon was within, strapped into a chair, with tubes running into and out of him. It hurt Drake to see his friend in this condition.

Commodore Donovan and a woman he didn't recognize stood next to Jon. Donovan was bloody from a head wound. The woman appeared unscathed and was holding a sphere, which Drake recognized as an ancient portable interdiction device. Donovan had a pistol to Jon's head.

"Don't come any closer," Donovan said.

"You're aware the planet below has launched against your ship?" said Drake.

"Yes. We'll all be dead in a few minutes," said Donovan, "and you with us."

Drake used the Instrumentality to fuse the internals of the commodore's pistol. Then he unfolded his helmet. "Let's talk about this."

"There is nothing to talk about." Donovan spun around and tried to fire at Drake, but he couldn't even pull the trigger.

Drake slapped the pistol out of Donovan's hand and knocked him down. "Get out of my way."

He froze as the woman dropped the interdiction device to the deck and then knelt.

"Master," she said.

Drake slipped the point of his sword under her chin and raised her head. Blood dripped from her chin. "What are you talking about?"

"I didn't realize it was you, master. I was just trying to follow your orders."

"Three minutes, Drake," said Hephaestus. "You need to hurry."

He'd missed one of the warnings. He was running out of time, but he needed to know what the woman was talking about. He didn't know her, but she was definitely the enemy. What was her game?

"Preta! What are you doing?" screamed Donovan.

She flicked her wrist, and dark fire washed over the man. He screamed and writhed on the deck as his body rotted away. Drake thought about killing him but didn't have time for the distraction.

"Tell me who you think I am," Drake demanded.

"You test me, master. You are Agarwaeth, the redeemer, the most powerful of us. You who came back from death. The prophet, the master, the returned god, th—" Drake cut her off by plunging Maegril through her head. Her last thoughts surprise and an image of someone who looked very much like Drake, wreathed in dark fire.

This one, you can eat, Drake thought to his sword.

"Two minutes."

Drake sheathed Maegril and started pulling the tubes out of Jon. He didn't have time to be gentle or careful. Jon groaned as Drake threw him over his shoulder.

"One minute"

"Drop the interdiction!" Drake ordered.

Drake apported back to Hephaestus' bridge just as the first missiles struck the *Endeavor*.

CHAPTER SIX

Jon groaned and struggled to focus his racing thoughts.

He knew he'd been rescued, but he could still feel the hallucinogens coursing through his body. He hurt, and was naked and cold. Drake was carrying him. Well, he assumed it was Drake – who else could carry him so easily? The corridors looked familiar, but then, most starship interiors did.

"Drake?" he managed.

"You're safe, Jon. I'm taking you to Medical."

"Drake, you need to know…" Jon couldn't quite remember what he wanted to tell Drake. It was all fading now. The visions were gone. The memory was almost gone, as well. It had been important. Drake needed to know. Jon had to tell him.

"All I need to know is that you're going to be all right, friend."

"No!" He knew he had to tell Drake. He just couldn't articulate what it was.

"Jon! Jon, it's me. You're safe!"

Lolani? He thought. *Why is she here?*

"Hold on, Jon."

That sounded like Aradhana. It couldn't be, though. Jon's

confusion deepened.

"Drake! Don't go into the eye!" That was it. That was what he needed to say.

Drake leaned down over him. Jon was vaguely aware that he was in some sort of pod. "What are you talking about, Jon?"

"He's waiting for you in there," Jon said. "You'll die! You *always* die!"

"He's hallucinating," said Lolani.

"I don't think so," Drake replied. To Jon, he said, "You've seen me go into the Eye? For a battle?"

Jon wept and nodded. He'd been unable to bring up the memories before. Now he couldn't make them stop. The horrors he'd seen – he couldn't make it stop. He couldn't save Drake, no matter what happened. No matter how many variations he ran.

"Do you see me fail?" Drake asked.

"What?" Drake's question jolted Jon out of his memories.

"When I go into the Eye, *do you see me fail?*"

"I see you die."

"That doesn't mean I fail."

"Drake, you can't go in there! You don't know what awaits you!"

"Shush, Jon. Rest and heal."

"No! Wait—!"

Drake closed the lid of the pod over him. Jon felt sudden claustrophobia. He was trapped in the metal box and couldn't move. Then he felt a strange sensation in his head, and all of the pain went away.

Is this what dying feels like? he thought as darkness took him.

⊙

Drake checked the systems and made sure the medical pod

was taking care of Jon. Not that he had any doubts, with Hephaestus watching over everything. Drake double-checked anyway, mostly to give himself time to get his emotions under control. Jon's words had struck him deeply.

"What was he talking about?" asked Lolani. "What eye?"

Drake sighed. "There is a place, beyond space and time as you know it, called the Eye. There is something within the Eye, a place of darkness. I've been into it before. I may have to return there to fight someone I had very much hoped was dead. I'd rather not speak more of it at this time."

"Why was Jon saying for you not to go there?" Aradhana asked. "How does he know even about it?"

"Jon has seen the Eye, from afar. He also has… precognitive visions sometimes."

"Visions that come true?"

Drake nodded. "I suspect he was drugged and in sensory deprivation aboard the *Endeavor*. That would have made the visions worse. Well, more intense, at least. You may like to know that Dr. Preta is dead, Lolani. I killed her aboard the *Endeavor*."

"Okay. Good. She was the one that messed up the jump pilot program. The one responsible for all the deaths. Why was she on the *Endeavor*?"

"To use Jon to start a new Alliance jump pilot program, and no doubt to watch Jon suffer."

"Then good riddance to the bitch. Brygida will want to know. Can we please leave now?" Lolani asked. "I don't like being here, bruh."

"I'm afraid not," Drake replied. "I've destroyed most of the Alliance fleet, but the Alliance is still a threat to those I care about. The Alliance must understand why it is a bad idea to hurt my friends."

"You've destroyed their fleet. What else are you going to do?" asked Aradhana.

"Teach them that it could have been worse."

Drake apported back to his quarters and changed into his normal armor. His coat had finished repairing itself, and he pulled that on over the armor. He liked the look. He racked his rifle; he wouldn't be needing it.

"Hephaestus, open up the communications channels to the Alliance worlds, as you did the last time we were here."

"Do you wish me to allow ship traffic, as well?"

"Allow ships in transit, but ban all others."

Drake called up the Instrumentality and apported to the surface of the planet. He arrived in the center of the government plaza, and as before, troops poured out of the building in front of him. Drake incinerated the troops and their weapons this time with the Instrumentality. They had been warned before.

He was no longer in the mood to be forgiving, not after seeing the state Jon had been in. Jon's body was broken. His mind had almost broken, too, but he would recover.

Drake walked through the barred doors into the congressional hall. Two snipers took aim, and he boiled them in their own juices. Drake once again activated their public address system.

Hephaestus, are the channels open? Drake thought.

Open and broadcasting.

You recorded the space battle?

If you wish to call it that.

Play it back over the address system, if you don't mind.

Drake watched impassively as the enemy vessels uncloaked, fired on Hephaestus, and then exploded seemingly for no reason. People around the chamber cried out as they viewed the recording; some of these people had family in the Alliance fleet. A few minutes later, missiles arced up from the surface of the planet and destroyed their own flagship.

"My name is Prince Daeren Drake, as some of you will no doubt remember. What you just witnessed was an unprovoked attack against my ship by the Alliance fleet. I destroyed ninety-nine of those ships. Your own Alliance destroyed the last one. I hadn't destroyed the flagship because an Alliance team had illegally infiltrated Kai and abducted a pilot who is a friend of mine. I was aboard that ship rescuing my friend when the missiles stuck."

Drake let everyone think about that for a moment.

"President Satō, your government was warned what would happen if you continued your aggression. Currently all Alliance jumpgates have been shut down. They will remain that way until I am satisfied."

"What do you want?" Satō called out to him.

"What I wanted before," said Drake. "For the Alliance to recognize the independence of the worlds that wish to be free. For the Alliance to stop attacking civilians and firing on ships unprovoked. Your fleet has been destroyed. Your defense networks indicate you have less than twenty ships remaining at the moment. I am willing to allow you to keep them, assuming that my terms are met and there are no further acts of aggression."

"Of course we agree to your terms. We need those jumpgates to feed our people!"

"There is one last thing that I desire," Drake said. "I want the heads of those who were responsible for these actions." Drake then named the senators and commanders who'd plotted the abduction of Jon and the trap for him.

"You can't expect for us to take your word that those people were involved," Satō said.

"It doesn't matter what you think," said Drake. "The request wasn't meant for you. The people of the Alliance have heard my demands. They are the ones suffering from your inaction. How long do you think it will be before they take matters into their own hands? To those listening, broadcast publicly the piles of heads, and the jumpgates will be restored."

"It's barbaric!" Satō cried out.

"So was the abduction and torture of my friend. Farewell, Alliance. Pray that you never see me again. I shall not be as generous and forgiving if there is a next time."

CHAPTER SEVEN

Drake had been gone for two weeks, and Geoffrey was starting to worry.

Brygida didn't seem concerned, but she was busy with getting ready to teach.

Not that Geoffrey wasn't busy, himself. He'd started working for Gerhardt Industries as a gofer in an engineering lab and being very well compensated. He'd finally gotten a cell phone. Which would have been much cooler if he had anyone to call.

His university advisor had grudgingly accepted Geoffrey's explanation that he'd been working for Gerhardt on a classified project for the last year and hadn't been able to let anyone know. The full scholarship from Gerhardt certainly helped reinforce that idea.

Geoffrey's selection of classes was somewhat limited, since he signed up just before they started. He ended up mostly filling in general studies courses. He signed up for Brygida's Intro to Physics course; he needed a science class and knew he liked the instructor.

His first day of classes didn't go well.

He raced around all day, trying to find the classrooms. He'd forgotten the layout of the huge, sprawling campus. He'd missed orientation, because since he was a junior, he hadn't thought he needed to attend. The bookstore had only half the books he needed.

He barely made it to Brygida's class in time and had to sit in front. He hated sitting in the front of a classroom. To make matters worse, it seemed that everyone else had managed to buy a textbook. The room was auditorium-style, with built-in tables for each row and separate chairs, Geoffrey sighed and took out a notebook and a pencil. At least he had that.

Brygida came into class precisely at three PM.

She surveyed the class and made no indication she recognized Geoffrey. He hadn't really expected her to; she had to maintain her profession reserve. She was dressed in a dark red suit. Her red hair was sticking up in every direction, as usual. She wasn't wearing any makeup at all, which was normal. Under the florescent lights, her eyes were very bright green.

"I am Dr. Bry-gi-da Ha-ku-bi," she said slowly enunciating each syllable in her name as she wrote it on the board. "You may call me *doctor*, *Dr. Hakubi*, or *professor*. I would not advise calling me anything else where I can hear you, and I warn you that I can hear very well. Young man in the seventh row, third seat from the right: Yes, I can hear you. Yes, I am a woman. Now, shut up or get out."

She glared at them all.

"You will open your textbooks to the introduction. If you do not have a textbook find someone to share with. You will need to get your own book before next class, as there will be a reading assignment. A quiz… is… *probable*."

The woman sitting to Geoffrey's right slid her book over so he could read it, too. "Hi. I'm Elena Mitchel. you can share mine."

"Thank you very much. I'm Geoffrey Meeks. The bookstore

was all sold out. I only just got back from traveling two weeks ago."

"No worries. We can trade numbers. You can borrow my book if you need to. It's always a good idea to have a study partner."

Geoffrey gave her a curious glance. She was pretty, but he didn't think she was hitting on him. He certainly appreciated her letting him read from her book.

"Students at the left end of rows: You will find a stack of syllabi. You will take one and pass the rest down the row until all have a syllabus. Read it. Understand it." Brygida turned and began writing on the blackboard again. "We have much to cover this semester: mechanics, fluids, heat, waves and sound, electricity and electromagnetism, optics, atomic physics, and nuclear physics! You will *not* be able to just read and take tests. You must be able to discuss and problem-solve. This course is intended to be your introduction into science!" She waved her hands over her head as she concluded.

Geoffrey smiled at Brygida's enthusiasm.

"Now, read the introduction. Then we will discuss."

Geoffrey took a syllabus and handed the extras to Elena.

The syllabus had everything Brygida had just mentioned, plus many bullet-pointed subheadings, with page numbers. She must have read the entire textbook before writing the syllabus. It also had Brygida's contact information, along with her office location. He'd wondered where she was working from, but he hadn't had a chance to ask her.

Brygida sat on the edge of her desk, swinging her legs as she watched everyone reading the textbook's introduction. Geoffrey thought she looked ridiculously young, like a kid playing dress-up. He respected her, though; he knew Brygida was probably the smartest person he'd ever met, and that included Drake.

Elena read at about the same speed as he did, so it worked

out well. He really appreciated her letting him share. She smelled nice, too. Her hair smelled of rosemary and mint.

"Okay, enough of you have finished that we can have a discussion. Who is brave enough to ask the first question? When called upon, say your name, so I can begin to learn them."

Elena raised her hand.

"Yes?" Brygida pointed at Elena.

"My name is Elena Mitchel, Dr. Hakubi. The textbooks spends a lot of time on the history of physics, but your syllabus doesn't mention it."

"Well, at least one student may pass," said Brygida. "I'm am glad that you also read the syllabus. We will not be spending much time learning the history of physics, because I don't care about it. Who cares who discovered what or when? I want you all to learn the basics of what physics is, and to have an understanding of science itself. Who can tell me the single most important physics discovery of this very year?"

Geoffrey looked around the room, only Elena had her hand up.

Brygida pointed to her.

"Did you want me to repeat my name again, professor?"

"No Elena, tell me what you think was important for this year's discoveries."

"The Higgs boson at CERN."

"Very good. Can you tell me why it is important? Anyone?"

Elena looked sheepish and kept her hand down. Geoffrey didn't even know what a boson was, much less CERN. He thought maybe the latter was a particle accelerator, but he wasn't sure enough to say anything.

Brygida sighed. "The Higgs boson, so-called god particle by the media, is proof of the existence of the Higgs field. By the way, it was actually called *that goddamned particle* by the physicists who worked on the project, because it was so hard to discover. The media censored that, hence the inaccurate nomenclature. Yes, hand raised in second row?"

"Name's Mike Smith, professor. What's a Higgs field?"

"I am glad you asked," said Brygida. "I hope you all have seen *Star Wars* – if not, *get out*. I'm not joking." She waited, glaring at them. No one dared move. "The Higgs field is like the Force. It's an energy field that binds the universe together. This is an energy field in spacetime that applies energy to massless particles, slowing them with mass. The Higgs boson is that mass. It decays very rapidly, but the particles keep picking up new bosons. They do this because all particles are lazy!"

About half the class laughed.

"You think I'm joking. Particles try to reach the lowest energy state possible, the ground state. Much like freshmen. Is this universe at its lowest possible state?"

No one answered. Geoffrey thought Brygida should be careful with the *this universe* stuff.

"No, it is not!" She pounded the table. "The energy balance of this universe is very delicate. Do you know what happens if something changes this? Say, two supermassive black holes collide energetically and pull too much energy from spacetime?" She jumped up on the desk, waving her hands over her head. "*Boom!* A shockwave would race out and reorder all mass in the universe to a lower ground state. For the record, this would be bad for living things." She glanced over at the clock on the wall. "We have five minutes. Let's call it a little early. Read the first three chapters before next class. You are dismissed!"

"Wow," Elena said quietly. "She is really awesome."

"She's certainly enthusiastic," said Geoffrey. He'd sort of followed along with what Brygida talked about, but he had a lot of catching up to do.

Elena wrote her number on the back of his syllabus. "If you want to study, shoot me a text. I was talking to Jen Miller before class – the girl next to me – and we're getting together to study tomorrow at the library, if you want to join us."

"I will. Thanks." He watched her leave. Jen was a lot taller than Elena. She whispered something to Elena, and they looked back at him. Geoffrey smiled. From the look, he thought that Jen might like him. He hoped so. She was very pretty. It would be nice to return to normal life and date again. Maybe something a little less intense than with Kalea.

He was startled when he turned back and Brygida was standing right in front of his desk. He was raised up, so she looked even shorter than she was. She had her hands behind her back and was tapping her foot.

"What'd I do?" he asked.

"I didn't know that you were signing up for my class. I was surprised to see you."

"Did I do something wrong?"

"You know you won't get any special treatment."

"I didn't expect any."

Brygida suddenly grinned. "Cool. If you'd like, you can borrow a copy of the textbook. They gave me two." She'd had the book behind her back.

"I tried to buy one, but they were sold out at the bookstore."

"So I heard."

Geoffrey grinned back. "Thank you. I'd appreciate borrowing one until I can buy one."

"Try online."

"I will."

"I see you're already joining a study group. This is good."

"Elena is putting together the group. Yeah, I think it will help a lot. I've never been really good at science."

"You'll get better at it," said Brygida. "You just need the confidence. I'm guessing your previous schooling didn't make a good case for the importance of science."

"Elementary through high school? No. We dissected frogs and worms and things."

"That's disgusting. No wonder so many people dislike science. You didn't study physics or chemistry or anything?"

"Just the basics," Geoffrey replied cautiously. He wasn't up to being grilled on what he may or may not have learned in school before.

Brygida just nodded. "Well, I'm glad you're taking my class. It was nice to see at least one friendly face."

"You're nervous?" Geoffrey asked. "You didn't seem nervous."

"Thank you for saying so." Brygida took a deep breath. "Well, first day down."

"Yep, I'm off to catch a bus."

"I could give you a lift. I'm just the next street over."

"That would be great!'

"Of course, people might think you're trying to sleep with me for a better grade," Brygida said with a mischievous grin.

"I'll take my chances."

CHAPTER EIGHT

It took Jon a few minutes to figure out where he was.

His first thought was that Aradhana had gotten up early. Then he realized he was in his old cabin aboard Hephaestus. Then recent events came crashing back into his head, and he had to lay there for a few minutes trying to sort it all out.

Clothes were laid out over a chair. They looked as if they'd fit him, so he got up and dressed. His body felt odd to him, heavier. He used the toilet and washed his hands and face. The face in the mirror was his, but not as gaunt.

He decided the unusual feeling in his middle was hunger. It had been a very long time since he'd felt that. He'd always had enough, growing up, but he'd often simply forgotten to eat. After he joined the jump pilot program, his vagus nerve had been damaged, and he only ate when others did or when he became dizzy and lightheaded.

Drake was sitting in the galley drinking tea. "I sent Lolani and Aradhana back down to Kai when it looked as if you were going to sleep the whole week."

"How long did I sleep?" Jon asked. "What happened?"

"You remember that the Alliance abducted you?"

"Not likely to forget that anytime soon."

"They didn't actually have you for very long."

"Long enough."

"I'm sure it felt longer," said Drake. "You were in rough shape, drugged, when I found you. You slept for two days after getting out of the medpod."

"I remember." Jon decided on tea, since he remembered Hephaestus' galley was worse than his own. "What happened?"

"The Alliance hoped to lure me into a trap by taking you. They set up an ambush with most of their fleet, one hundred warships, most of which were cloaked."

"Shit." Jon sat down and sipped his tea. "Is Hephaestus okay?"

"I was unharmed, Jon," Hephaestus replied. "Thank you for asking."

"The only ones harmed were the Alliance crews," said Drake.

"You disabled their ships?"

"I destroyed them. I didn't have time for subtly. Also, they'd been warned. If it makes you feel any better, I did give them the option to hand you over without bloodshed."

"A little, yes, thanks."

"They fired first. We responded. Afterward, I boarded the flagship. Many had been wounded. I would have allowed them to live, but the Alliance fired on the ship and destroyed it."

"Did Preta get away?"

"No. I killed her myself, after she killed Donovan."

"That helps. I take it you threw down the gauntlet with the Alliance?"

"I already had. This was me carrying though with my threats."

"You didn't cut off the Alliance worlds, did you? Innocent people need that food and commerce."

"The destruction of eighty-four percent of their fleet was a strong statement," Drake said. "Hephaestus shut down the gates temporarily. He was also able to infiltrate Alliance systems and discover who planned and orchestrated your capture and the trap for me. The people of the Alliance seemed quite willing to deliver the heads of those responsible in return for the use of the gates."

"Ouch. Are all the gates working again?"

"All are restored, yes."

"Look, Drake, about what I said when you brought me…"

"You remember?"

"I do. I've been having precognitive visions of doom and gloom for a long time now. Ever since we met, your future was all fire and blood. There on that Alliance ship, I was able to run possibilities – it distracted me from the pain and fear. If you go into the Eye chasing your brother, you'll die."

"I know," Drake said and then took a sip of tea. "I've lived a long life Jon. I'm not afraid of dying. I'm afraid of failing."

"What about *falling*?" Jon asked. "I saw you being horrifically tortured."

Drake sighed. "I'm not my brother. You saw torture and madness in my future if I went to the Golden Kingdom, too. It didn't happen."

"You knew about that?"

"I've had some form of precognition all of my life, Jon. I understand how overwhelming it can be. You start worrying about the repercussions of your actions, to the point where you're afraid to take action. I've heard it said that a man often meets his fate on the road to avoid it. I think that's probably true." Drake stood and washed his cup.

"But we're talking about you dying, Drake."

"You can't see if I succeed. Neither can I. Someone has to go into the Eye. Maybe not today, but soon. I have an army that is trained to fight the things in there. If you've ever met someone more qualified than I am, please let me know. I'd gladly let them do it."

"Would you?"

"You think I court death?"

"Sometimes, yes. I think you take foolish risks. Like when you almost died back on Earth to a punk with a monomolecular rifle."

"If my brother finds a key, he can open the Stasis Tombs," said Drake. "You don't understand what that means. You thought the thing on Earth and Dr. Preta were horrible monsters. They were children. There are things in the Eye millions of times worse. There are things in there that *I don't think I can beat*. Things I don't think *anyone* could anymore. We don't have the technology that our ancestors did. If I don't stop my brother, he'll unleash those things upon the universes. I cannot allow concern for my personal safety to stop me from doing what is right."

"Would you feel the same way if it wasn't your brother? How much of this is personal?"

"Of course it's personal, Jon! My parents were torn apart in front of me when I was a child. My brother was tortured and turned into one of those *things*, somehow." Drake sat down heavily. "I lead an army in there every ten years or so. I have for the last twenty thousand years. I have literally led millions of people to their deaths in there. It's time for that cycle to end. There has to be a way to destroy the Tombs, and the answer almost certainly lies within the Tombs themselves."

"What if you're wrong?"

"Then I die, the Emperor picks some other dumb bastard to take over, and the cycle repeats."

"I meant about being able to stop your brother."

"That, I can do," said Drake. "Maegril can destroy anything, even another of the relic swords."

"Couldn't they use someone else to carry your sword?"

"Someone of my bloodline? Not a lot to choose from.

Brygida would die first. So would Xia. All my other children are dead."

"Xia is that other daughter you mentioned? What about other descendants?" Jon asked. "There must be a lot of people with some of your blood."

"Direct son or daughter of the wielder. Even grandchildren are too far removed. They'd die if they touched it."

"Then how could I have used Joseph's sword?"

"Your genetic code is similar enough to read as a child of his. If you were a clone of him, you might read as a brother, and it wouldn't work."

"Couldn't you just nuke the place or something?"

"You have no idea of the scale we're talking about. The inside of the Eye is a flat plain almost infinite in size. The black hole that it resides within is three hundred thousand lightyears across."

"I've seen it," Jon said. "I guess I just didn't think about the implications."

"Even if a nuclear weapon would work in there, I'm not sure how you'd get it to the Tombs. I don't think it would work anyway. There must be another solution."

"I can't talk you out of it, can I?"

"I do appreciate your concern, but it is unwarranted at the moment. I'm not ready to mount an offensive. It will be years before I do. Many unexpected things can happen on that timescale."

"Promise me you won't go in there without at least talking to me first."

Drake nodded.

"Okay, that'll do." Jon's stomach rumbled. "Hephaestus, did you do something to me?"

"I fixed the medical problems you had," Hephaestus replied, "including the damage to your vagus nerve. I was unable to fix any of your psychological problems."

"Is that a joke?"

"Of questionable humor," said Drake. "Are you hungry?"

"Yes, actually."

"Then how about we pop down to the surface and have dinner with Lolani and Aradhana, before I head back to check on Brygida?"

"That sounds great."

Jon was a little frustrated that he was unable to make Drake really understand. His visions had been more than a possibility of failure. If Drake was being tortured, then he'd failed. There wasn't a way around that.

He sighed and pushed it out of his mind. Drake knew what he was doing. Jon desperately wanted to see Aradhana again, to reassure himself that she was okay. The memory of that soldier checking her pulse bothered him.

"Ready, Jon?"

"Yeah, beyond ready."

CHAPTER NINE

Geoffrey did a double take when Elena and Jen came into the room at the library to study.

Jen was wearing a close-fitted dress of dark green velvet with lots of buttons, an outfit that wouldn't have elicited comment on the streets of the Golden Kingdom. She was tall and lithe, and the outfit really showed off her curves, which he hadn't noticed before. He thought the dark green went well with her brown skin.

"Oh, the dress, yeah. I know it's weird," said Jen.

"I don't think it's weird. It looks good on you," Geoffrey said. "Are you in a play or something?"

She laughed. "Thanks. I'm in the SCA, and we had a college group meeting that just ended. I haven't had time to change."

"The Student Conservation Association?" Geoffrey asked. It was the only *SCA* he knew of. He couldn't figure out why she'd need an outfit like that, unless they were doing a play to raise money.

"No, the other one."

"The living history one," Elena added. "She's always trying to get me to join."

"You probably think I'm a freak," said Jen.

Geoffrey shrugged. "First of all, there's nothing wrong with being a freak. Second, I did always want to learn how to sword fight."

Elena groaned. "OK, you two, talk SCA later. This is study time."

"I've read the first three chapters," said Geoffrey. "Not sure if I understood everything.

"I thought you didn't have a book."

"Brygida – I mean Dr. Hakubi – let me borrow one of her copies after class."

Jen cocked an eyebrow at him. "*Brygida*, hmm? Just what did you have to do for that?"

"What? No, she just offered to loan it to me. She'd heard me say I couldn't buy one."

"Oh, I'm sure she offered. I'm just wondering what you did to earn it."

"I…" Geoffrey didn't know what to say. Should he tell them he knew Brygida through his internship? Would Brygida be upset when she found out what they were thinking? Maybe he shouldn't have taken the class, if it was going to cause problems for Brygida.

"Jen's ribbing you," said Elena. "She likes you."

"What? Oh, okay. I'm Geoffrey, by the way."

"See, I told you he was articulate," said Elena.

Geoffrey shook his head. "You two *must* have known each other before this class."

"He's bright, too," Jen said. "I think I'll keep him. Maybe he has a brother *you* can hit on."

"I have a housemate."

Both women laughed.

"Jen and I went to high school together," said Elena. "We were the school's cool geeks. Physics, chemistry, math through calculus one. Why would Dr. Hakubi loan *you* a book?"

"I knew Dr. Hakubi before taking her class," Geoffrey said. "We worked together."

"Do you secretly have a Ph.D. and are slumming it?" asked Jen.

Geoffrey smiled. "No, I work as an intern for Gerhardt Industries, Aerospace Division. I have for the last year. Dr. Hakubi is a consultant for them."

"Seriously?" Elena asked.

Geoffrey dug his work badge out of his backpack and showed them.

Jen gave him a cool, appraising glance. "Okay, pretty and smart. I can dig it. How'd you manage to score a gig like that?"

Geoffrey blushed. He wasn't used to someone calling him pretty. He realized they were waiting for him answer how he'd gotten the internship. How could he answer that? He certainly couldn't tell them the truth. "My, uh, uncle Drake knows Gerhardt. He's a mercenary or something."

"Yeah, that was totally believable," said Jen. "I think I would have believed you were sleeping with Dr. Hakubi before that."

"Drake did some work for him. Something secret. Ask Dr. Hakubi, if you don't believe me."

"You mean *Brygida*?" Jen asked.

Elena glanced at Jen and giggled. Geoffrey realized they were teasing him again and sighed gustily. He shook his head and grinned while they laughed a bit.

Jen reached over and gripped his arm. "Okay, we'll stop messing with you."

"Why stop now?" Geoffrey asked.

"So, if you know *Brygida*, then you know what she's working on for Gerhardt," said Elena.

"She's working on fusion containment and the sustained thrust problem for the main engines of the *Roald Amundsen*," Geoffrey replied. He knew that one, at least.

"He sounds legit, Jen," said Elena. "Now pump him for

information that we can sell to the highest bidder on the dark web."

"I'm not going to do that with you watching, perv."

"We're here to study, right?" said Geoffrey. He was a little unnerved by the turn of the conversation. Not to mention that the thought of being pumped by Jen was borderline intoxicating.

"He does have a point," said Elena.

"Speaking of points, what is up with her ears?" Jen said.

"What?" Geoffrey had almost forgotten Brygida's ears were pointed.

"Surgery or natural?" Elena asked.

"Her ears are natural," Geoffrey said cautiously.

Elena and Jen both sighed.

"Must be nice," said Elena. "So you really do know her?"

"Yeah, she's really nice. And funny. She's also the smartest person I've ever met," Geoffrey said. "She's a bit shy, though, and self-conscious."

"How old is she?" asked Jen. "We're thinking she has to be older than she looks, at least thirty, to have two different Ph.Ds."

"I think she said she's in her forties," Geoffrey replied cautiously.

"Get out of town!" Elena exclaimed.

"She's Japanese?" said Jen.

"Uh, maybe?" How in the hell was he supposed to answer that? She wasn't even human, at least not entirely. Was her mother human? "Maybe half? I know she went to school in Tokyo."

"Well, I suppose we really should actually study," said Elena. "First chapter is *Kinematics*, Second Chapter is *Newton's Laws*, and then the third is on momentum and energy. That's a hell of a lot to cover. Do you really think we'll have a quiz?"

"Yeah," Geoffrey said. "I do."

"Then we'd better dig into this," said Jen.

"I outlined the chapter and made notes on what I thought was important," Geoffrey said helpfully. "I didn't take any of that stuff in high school. I may need some help understanding as we dive deeper into this book."

"What did you focus on in high school?" Jen asked. "Art?"

"Baseball."

"Ew! You're dating a jock," Elena said with a laugh.

"We're not dating yet," Jen said hurriedly. "Nothing binding has been said."

"Naw, you guys are totally dating," said Elena. "You just don't know it yet." She kicked Geoffrey under the table. "Ask her out."

Geoffrey was amused by their antics. They were obviously close friends. "Want to go out with me?"

"Not if you're going to take me to a baseball game," said Jen.

"How about the art museum?" Geoffrey suggested. "Then lunch, this Saturday?"

"Run, Jen! He knows your secret weakness!" said Elena, laughing.

Jen ignored her. "Ten AM, Eden Park, but you have to come to an SCA thing with me Sunday morning."

"Now you're in trouble," Elena said.

Geoffrey shrugged. "Sounds fair."

"Okay, now that the hormones levels have ebbed, can we get back to kinematics?" Elena asked.

They all laughed and dug out their books and notebooks. He liked these two. Even if nothing happened between him and Jen, he hoped they could all be friends, at least. If they ended up going to the art museum again later, he should see if Brygida wanted to go along. Not only would she like the museum, she'd probably like Jen and Elena, too.

☉

Jason spent most of his time working on his house and yard.

The people Gerhardt hired had done an adequate job, but they hadn't exactly gone above and beyond. There was still broken glass to pick up, and trash in odd places, behind bushes and in the trees. He'd replaced the broken casing on the front door and replaced the locks. He'd also managed to replace the damaged flooring and match the wood stain.

Brygida had gotten his wallet and keys back from Gerhardt.

Life was almost going too well.

Jason fought down his reflexive paranoia.

For the first time since he'd come to this Earth, he actually had a few friends. Drake and Brygida were powerful friends to have. He was confident that Drake would bail him out if anyone actually found out about him. It wasn't as if Jason was a threat to National Security or something. He'd been on the planet for more than a thousand years without causing trouble.

Jason sighed and finished gluing the rocking chair together. He'd started it before he, Geoffrey, and Jon had been dragged off on that wild adventure. He still had trouble believing some of the things he'd witnessed. There was a lot more out there in the universes than he'd ever imagined.

He heard Geoffrey arrive home and wondered what he'd been up. Geoffrey had put his class schedule up on the fridge, so Jason knew he had only one class in the morning on Tuesdays. He washed up and went back into the house.

Geoffrey was making a sandwich in the kitchen. He had a big smile on his face. Jason had seen that look before.

"What's her name?" he asked. He grabbed a beer from the fridge.

"What?" Geoffrey said. He looked surprised.

"Oh, come on. How long have I known you?"

Geoffrey laughed. "Her name is Jen Miller. We're going to the art museum on Saturday."

"Damn. Fast work. Let me guess: tall Nordic blonde?"

"She's tall," Geoffrey said. "Everything else about that was wrong."

"So are you going to keep me in the dark?"

"Since when do you care about my love life?"

Jason grabbed a bag of pretzels and took his beer into the living room. He didn't really care about that, but he cared about Geoffrey, and he knew Geoffrey wanted to talk about it.

"She's almost six-foot," said Geoffrey, coming in and sitting on the couch. "Brown hair, brown eyes, brown skin."

"Sounds pretty."

"Well, she's also really smart," Geoffrey said. "Smart and tall tend to attract me."

"I thought it was boobs."

"Yeah… She doesn't have much in that department."

Jason shook his head. "I still can't believe you don't find Brygida attractive."

Geoffrey shrugged. "You date her, then."

"She's not interested in dating, or I might've asked."

"Jen has a friend, you know."

"College girls are too young for me," Jason said. He smiled a bit at the irony. Technically, Brygida was a few thousand years too young, too. He would have made an exception for her, though. She had an amazing mind and a great personality.

"Actually, I met Elena first," said Geoffrey. "We sat next to each other in physics class. She's really smart, too."

"Yeah?" Jason said. He finished his beer.

"She's short," Geoffrey gestured to around his chest. "About the same height as Brygida. Brown hair, grey eyes, pretty. She's single. Think about it."

She did sound attractive, Jason had to admit. He *would* have considered dating Brygida if she'd shown any interest, despite her relation to Drake, because he liked her and she already knew the truth about him. He couldn't date anyone who didn't know; it wouldn't be fair to them. Of course, it might make a good cover. He'd dated in the past to pretend to be normal.

"I'll think about meeting her," Jason said finally.

CHAPTER TEN

Brygida surprised herself by how much she enjoyed teaching the two intro physics courses.

A few of her students dropped out after the first day, but that always happened. Her morning class wasn't as much fun. There didn't seem to be any really bright students in that class. They all kept their heads down and just did the work. They didn't engage with her. They were boring. At least no one caused any trouble.

Her afternoon class was another matter. She had four or five bright students, including Geoffrey. She'd liked the young man, but she hadn't expected him to take to physics. He'd aced his first exam, though, along with the two young women who sat next to him. The three of them answered questions in class. They studied together, and it showed.

Her work with Gerhardt was a little more frustrating.

The scientists who'd been working on the engines flew in from Los Alamos. They'd been irritated at having to fly to Cincinnati, and even more irritated at Brygida for telling them that their design was flawed. She hadn't seen any way to sugarcoat that, though. The sooner they got their heads out of their asses, the sooner the engines would start working.

She'd given Gerhardt a design for the coldsleep chambers, but she hadn't heard back from him yet. It was different from what they'd been trying, but then, they hadn't been successful at all with that project, either. The engines had worked better.

Brygida hadn't made any new friends.

The scientists who worked for Gerhardt resented her. They would use her ideas, but they didn't like it. Her colleagues at the university were all very busy teaching classes. They also didn't seem interested in making friends with a part-time professor who might be gone the next year. At least they weren't hostile.

She missed hanging out with Jason and Geoffrey. They'd become good friends while traveling with her father. She even missed Jon. He'd started to loosen up around her by the end. She missed Lolani and Erin, too. Hell, she was just lonely.

Her new house was nice, but it was empty.

She didn't have the energy or the interest to decorate it. A service took care of the yard. She'd started buying books, but they could only hold her interest for so long – a book was a very one-sided conversation. She thought that maybe she should buy a television and catch up on science fiction movies and shows. She'd seen on the internet that science fiction had entered into something of a renaissance in the late nineties on this Earth. There were even *Star Trek* shows and movies she hadn't seen.

Yes, there was a store not far from her. She could get what she needed, maybe some snacks as well, and indulge in some relaxing behavior for a change. It would have been more fun to have someone to share the shows with, but she was sure she'd be absorbed enough by the fiction to not think about being lonely.

The mega grocery and department store was packed with people, as always. Brygida bought a large flat-screen television, a Blu-ray player – the clerk said it was better than a DVD – and a cart full of shows and movies. She figured that would keep her busy for a while. She spied a box of microwave popcorn in the checkout lane and bought that, too.

Two burly store employees insisted on helping Brygida out to her car. They said it was store policy, although she'd seen people loading their own large items into cars as she came in. She figured it was because she was small. She watched with amusement as they struggled to put the television into her Jeep. She could have lifted the television with one hand.

"I'll get the rest, thanks," she told them. She could load the videos and popcorn without help.

She caught some motion by the cart return and approached cautiously.

A small, tortoise-shell kitten had gotten its head stuck in a fry box. She caught it and helped it remove the box. There wasn't any food in the box; it had been licking the salty grease. The kitten couldn't have been more than two months old. Its brown, tan, and black marbled fur was matted, and it had fleas. It was very skinny and obviously very hungry.

"What are you doing out here all alone?" she asked as she petted it.

It didn't struggle; it just looked at her with a quizzical expression that made her giggle. She set it down, and it head-butted her hand. Then it sat down and started to groom.

It was adorable.

Brygida sighed and walked back to her Jeep.

The kitten followed her.

"What? I don't have any food," she said.

It peeped piteously at her.

"Oh, fuck me," she muttered.

She scooped up the kitten. It started purring. She opened the passenger door and put it on the floorboard. It sat down and started grooming again. She'd have to do something about the fleas.

"Don't go anywhere."

She lowered the window just a little, and shut and locked the door.

She went back into the store and bought a little pet carrier, catnip, kitten food, flea shampoo, a litter box, and litter. Upon extra reflection, she also bought a cat tree, toys, and a laser pointer. The little scamp would need exercise.

She'd never had a pet, but she always wanted a cat.

The kitten was sitting on the passenger seat when she went back out. At least the seat was leather. She put together the carrier and then coaxed the kitten inside. It didn't give her any real trouble. That surprised her. She'd heard horror stories about getting cats into a carrier.

The kitten meowed a bit as she drove home.

She hoped she wasn't taking it away from its mother. She didn't think so, though. It was too lean to have a momma kitty helping it out. She hadn't seen any other kittens, but with a major highway nearby, they might simply have not made it.

Brygida carried her bags into her house first. Then she carried in the television. It really wasn't that heavy, just a bit awkward. She took the kitten into the bathroom and shut the door before letting it out of the carrier. It needed a bath before she'd let it loose in the house.

She drew some warm water in the sink and placed the kitten in it. The poor little thing wasn't happy about that, but it would be happier once the fleas had drowned in the soapy water. She gave the kitten a good wash and a rinse. There were quite a few dead fleas in the water that went down the drain.

She dried the little beast and noticed as she did that it was a girl.

When Brygida placed her on the floor of the bathroom, the kitten followed her into the kitchen.

"I think I shall name you Tadeo," Brygida said. "It is a boy's name, but like me, your gender isn't real obvious. I'm a girl, too, for your information. The name means *loyal*, because you follow me around."

Tadeo meowed at her, she had a burry meow. Brygida didn't know whether that was normal or not. It suited the little beast though.

"Right, food." Brygida gave her bowl of kitten chow and a bowl of water. She pounced on the food and started eating, purring and growling a little as she did. Brygida petted her tiny head.

She spent the rest of the evening setting up the litterbox and the cat tree. The television stayed in its box. She didn't care. Tadeo was a little sweetheart. After the kitten had eaten, she went straight to the litterbox and used it like a good kitty. Then she ran around the house, checking things out.

Tadeo had climbed into the bed with Brygida and curled up on her stomach as she read.

Brygida fell asleep to the feel of her tiny purr.

☉

It was an unusually clear evening on Kai when Drake waved from the beach and apported away. Jon was almost sorry to see him leave. Almost

Reports were coming in from all over the Alliance of worlds breaking free. It was a cause for celebration. The people on Kai were certainly getting into the spirit. People were partying in the streets.

Jon wished so many innocent soldiers hadn't died for it, though. He didn't care that much about the politicians Drake had casually ordered to be murdered. The people on those hundred ships – those, he felt bad about.

He felt as if they'd died because of him.

Jon didn't blame Drake, though.

Drake was just being Drake. He killed people who attacked him, even if they weren't really a threat to him. The Alliance fleet obviously hadn't been a threat to Hephaestus, but they had been a threat to the worlds that yearned for freedom.

Maybe Jon just needed to accept that.

"You look like a man wrestling with things that should be left alone," Aradhana said as she walked up to him. "Drake left?"

"Yeah. He's gone again. He's leaving Hephaestus in orbit for a while, just to be certain the Alliance doesn't try anything," Jon said, then sighed.

"You think you're responsible for all the people who died."

"Yes."

"I know how you feel. I killed when I worked for the Alliance, Jon. I did what I was told, and I didn't ask questions. The people on those ships were like me."

"That doesn't make me feel better."

"It should, though. I made a choice and left the Alliance. The personnel on those ships could have done the same. Drake gave them multiple chances."

"How could they have left? Mutinied?"

"You'd be surprised at how often it used to happen," said Aradhana. "The people on those ships choose to fire on a *Precursor* ship, Jon. Most of the ships were stealthed. They fired everything they had. Antimatter warheads are banned from use in Alliance space because of the hazards. Do you know what warheads those weapons had?"

"Antimatter?"

Aradhana nodded.

Jon sighed. "So that justifies killing all of them?"

"Maybe I'm not the right person to ask. Maybe that's something you should have spoken to Drake about, if it's really bothering you."

"Little late now."

Jon knew he should have said something, and yet what difference would it have made? Drake wasn't going to change how he acted. Maybe it was wrong for Jon to want him to change. Jon would probably be dead a few times over if not for Drake.

"Well." Aradhana shrugged. "I can't begin to understand someone like Drake, but I'm glad you have a friend like him. Otherwise I wouldn't have you back."

"Aradhana, something else has been bothering me."

She'd been about to put her arms around him, but she froze. "What?"

"When I was taken, one of the soldiers checked your pulse. I got the impression he wanted to make sure you were okay. That seemed strange to me. I want to know why he'd do that."

Aradhana smiled sadly. "That's because you were never really a soldier." She waved away his protest. "I know you served in the military on Rhyddid. You were a transport pilot, though, not a soldier. I was awake and unable to move when they took you. I assume you were, too."

"Yes."

"I left the Alliance," Aradhana said. "I termed out and left with a good service record. The mission brief that extraction team received would have had details about me. They would have needed that information in case I was able to fight."

"That doesn't really answer my question."

"I knew him, of course. I knew all of them. They sent my old team for the extraction. The Alliance likes to do shit like that as loyalty tests. Is it so hard to believe that the soldiers who took you were actual people?"

"It's a lot easier not to."

Aradhana nodded. "They all died, Jon. They would have still been aboard the *Endeavor* after the extraction. I'm sad that they're dead, but they had a choice, too. They could have gotten out, the same as me. They stayed in. So they died. That happens to soldiers a lot, you know."

Jon pulled her into an embrace. "I'm sorry."

She hugged him hard enough to pop his back, and then backed off with a laugh. She took his hand and pulled him toward the beach. "Come on!"

"I don't have swim trucks on," Jon said.

"You won't need them."

CHAPTER ELEVEN

Drake felt a certain urgency as he walked the worlds.

The Earth he was walking toward held four people dear to him. That alone was enough to make him nervous. That Realm would make a good target for the enemy, should they discover its importance to him.

Contrary to what Jon may have thought, killing the tens of thousands of people on those Alliance ships hadn't been easy for him. Drake killed often, because it was usually the fastest way to achieve a goal. He didn't like to kill. He just wasn't going to let a life get in the way of something he felt he had to do.

That was another thing that had set him apart from his brother, Galuchin. Drake enjoyed the skill of combat, the strategy and the tactics. His brother had actually liked to kill. Drake had overlooked that about Galuchin, because it seemed to be a necessary part of what he was doing. They were both young: very close in age, unusual for his people. They had fought together for thousands of years.

Drake missed his brother.

It had been a very long time since he lost Galuchin. The pain of finding him fallen had almost broken Drake. Geoffrey's poor mother *had* been broken; Drake had almost given her the mercy of the blade. He was glad he hadn't. Geoffrey had grown into a fine young man.

He sighed and pushed away his dark thoughts before they led him into dark Realms.

That was a very real problem for those who walked the Realms. A person had to hold an idea of where they wanted to go in their mind. If they let psychological pain creep into their mind, it could lead them into places where that pain would manifest as something *physical*.

It had taken Drake a few thousand years of continuous warfare to figure that one out.

The sun was setting across an arc of the Ohio River as Drake arrived in the desired Realm. The roads were clogged with cars and trucks, belching out fumes and honking. Drake walked across the pedestrian bridge into Cincinnati.

The park with the strange statues cast distorted shadows in the last rays of the setting sun. Drake wasn't sure why he found this place so unsettling. At least it didn't take him long to walk to the Gerhardt building.

The security guards tensed when he entered the lobby. He would have thought they'd recognize him by this point. Or maybe they did. There was only one receptionist at the desk this time.

"I'd like to speak to Dr. Brygida Hakubi," said Drake.

"Dr. Hakubi has left for the day, sir."

"Could you tell me where she lives?"

The receptionist glanced at the security guards. "I'm sorry, I can't disclose that information."

"Of course," Drake said. "Thank you for your time."

He turned away and left the building before the guards decided to try something stupid. Geoffrey would know where Brygida lived. She might even be staying with Geoffrey and Jason.

Drake turned down an alley and then apported to the street where Jason's house stood. Drake liked the neighborhood, with its many trees along the road. Drake had always felt it was important to not shut oneself away from nature.

The house and lawn looked better than they had the last time Drake was here. He knocked on the door and waited. College Hill was between the sunset and him, and the last rays enlivened the treetops with a blaze of red.

"Drake!" Jason said as he answered the door.

"Hello, Jason. sorry I had to run off so quickly the last time I was here."

"Don't worry about it," said Jason sid. "Come on in. Geoffrey should be home from school soon."

"Ah, so some time has passed here. I had wondered how much."

"About two weeks." Jason led him into the living room. "Can I get you a beer or something?"

"A beer would be good," Drake said. "Thank you."

Once Jason had left the room, Drake stepped out of his armor and used the Instrumentality to clothe himself – it would have been rude to damage Jason's furniture with the weight of his armor. Drake was shrugging on his coat when Jason came back into the room.

Jason handed him a dark beer and gestured to the couch. "Have a seat."

"Thanks." Drake sat and looked around the room. "I see Geoffrey didn't waste any time getting a new game console."

"Actually, Brygida bought that for him. She found my missing silverware, too. Well, most of it."

"Is Brygida living here, as well?"

"No, she's renting a house a street or so over," Jason said, gesturing east. "I think Geoffrey has her phone number."

"How have *you* been?" asked Drake.

Jason shrugged. "The house and yard kept me busy for a

while. I've started woodworking again."

Drake knew Jason wanted to ask him where he'd been, but Drake didn't want to have to repeat the story, and he wanted to talk to them all about Jon. He also wished to speak to Brygida privately. She'd want to know about her sister.

Geoffrey came home before the silence grew too awkward. He did a double take when he saw the armor and then looked around for Drake. He sat his backpack of books against the wall.

"Hey, Drake. How's Jon?"

"He's okay. I want to talk to all of you, to let you know about things. Jason says you may have Brygida's phone number."

"You want me to call her?"

"Yes, please."

Geoffrey dug a small, flat device out of his backpack and entered a number. "Hey, Brygida. Sorry to bother you. No, I didn't forget anything at school. Drake came back. Yes, he's here, sitting on the couch and drinking beer. Right, I'll tell him." Geoffrey disconnected and put the phone in his pocket. "She was driving home, says she'll be here in just a couple of minutes."

"Sounds good," said Drake.

Geoffrey left the room to get a beer.

"Geoffrey is seeing someone new," Jason said.

"Hey!" Geoffrey came back with his beer and punched Jason lightly on the arm.

"That was fast work," said Drake.

"She's in my physics class," Geoffrey said. "I'm not sure I'd saying we're *seeing* each other. We study together and have our first date tomorrow."

"Nervous?" Drake asked.

"Not really."

Drake heard Brygida pull up outside. A minute later, she

knocked on the door. Geoffrey let her in. Drake stood up so she could give him a hug.

"You look good," he said. Her hair had grown out a little, and she was wearing a business suit.

"Thank you."

Drake sat back down while Geoffrey fetched a beer for Brygida. Once she'd sat next to him on the couch, he told Geoffrey, Jason, and Brygida about what had happened to Jon.

"Jon's okay, though?" Jason asked.

"He's fine," said Drake. "Lolani and his girlfriend, Aradhana, are keeping him safe. I doubt the Alliance is going to be a problem again. Also, Brygida, I thought you'd like to know that Preta was killed."

Brygida nodded. "That does make me feel a little better. You were right about her? She was Ancient Enemy?"

"She was Fallen," said Drake. "I'm not sure if she was Ancient or not. I'm inclined to say not. She did not recognize me as myself."

He could see that Brygida had more questions, but she nodded when she met his eyes. She'd ask him about it later. Some things were too close to home to discuss in front of others.

"I don't think I realized that those things might not all be ancient monsters," said Jason.

"They aren't common," Drake said. "Many of the younger ones seem to be no more than mindless animals."

"Hungry ghosts," Brygida said quietly.

Drake nodded.

⊙

Brygida finished her beer and sat the bottle on the coffee table. She was glad Jon was okay after his ordeal. She was even happier that Preta had been killed. The woman had caused too much suffering. Maybe now Jon and Lolani would forgive her.

"Sorry, guys. I've had a long day. I need to get home," she said. "Maybe we can get together tomorrow or something."

"Off to feed your cat?" asked Drake.

"You got a cat?" Geoffrey said. "My *landlord* won't let me get one."

"You won't clean up after yourself, much less a cat," said Jason.

"How did you know I have a cat?" Brygida asked curiously.

Drake gestured to her ankles.

Brygida turned her leg. She could see a few tiny, multicolored cat hairs on the cuff of her pants. Sometimes her father's perception frightened her. She didn't think she'd have noticed that on someone else.

"Little ankle-twining beast," she muttered.

"Perhaps you'd introduce me to your cat?" Drake asked.

He obviously wanted to talk to her alone. Brygida sighed. She really did just want to go home and set up her new television. She'd been looking forward to not being around people at all over the weekend. Not that Drake was really a burden on hospitality.

"Sure."

"You'll be around, Drake?" asked Jason.

"For a few days, at least. I won't leave without a word this time."

Jason walked them out while Geoffrey picked up the beer bottles. "You're leaving your armor here?"

"If you don't mind," said Drake. "It tends to draw unwanted attention around the city."

"You're wearing a sword," Jason remarked.

Drake glanced at his hip as if he'd forgotten. "So I am." He removed it and tossed it into that pocket space he used.

Brygida would have liked to know how he did that. Maybe

it was only something that one could do with Instrumentality. She still wanted to learn how to use that.

"See you guys later," Brygida said with a wave.

Drake kept pace with her as she walked out to her Jeep.

"How are you adapting to life here?" he asked.

"Well, I think," said Brygida. "It can all be a little overwhelming."

Drake nodded. "I can barely remember what it was like when I left home. I left a wife and a young daughter. I thought I was walking to meet my doom."

"Sounds like you do that a lot," said Brygida. "Walk to your doom, I mean. You were married before?"

"I've been married many times," Drake said. "I've loved many times more men and women over my long life."

"Do our lives seem fleeting to you?"

"No!" Drake denied vehemently. "No, not at all. Each moment of my life passes much as any other's. I've known people with long lives who passed their time in a fugue. It never made sense to me. As long as I continue to breathe, I shall take in everything life can give me, one moment at a time."

Brygida unlocked the Jeep, and they climbed in. "I found a house nearby."

"Jason indicated as much."

They didn't speak anymore until they reached her house.

She saw Tadeo sitting in the window, waiting for her. It hadn't taken the kitten long to learn her schedule. Tadeo was an intelligent little monster.

The kitten was nowhere to be seen when they entered the house, but Brygida could hear her peeping from the kitchen. Brygida had left dry food and water out for her, but she'd given her a can of wet kitten food when she got home from work the day before. Tadeo remembered.

"She's in the kitchen," Brygida said.

"So I hear."

Drake knelt down, and the kitten ran right over to him. She did a little kitten war dance at him and then flipped over and began kneading the air at him. He gently rubbed her belly with a single finger, and she purred loudly.

"She's very cute," Drake said.

"I named her Tadeo."

"A good name for her."

Tadeo jumped when Brygida said her name and scampered over to her. Brygida picked her up and kissed her head, then set her back on the tile floor and got a can of food from the cabinet.

The kitten pounced on the little bowl of food. Brygida checked the other bowls. Tadeo had eaten about half of the dry kibble and drank some of the water. Brygida refilled both of the bowls and watched affectionately as the kitten devoured the wet food.

"I've always liked cats," said Drake.

"They probably remind you of yourself," Brygida said.

Drake laughed and shook his head.

"Can I get you anything?"

"I'm good," Drake said. "I do want to talk to you, if you don't mind. I know you're tired."

"I'll be fine. This little bundle of fur is rejuvenating."

"A stray?" Drake asked.

Brygida nodded.

"Those are the best kind."

Brygida hung her suit jacket over the chair and gestured back toward the living room. "More comfortable chairs in there."

CHAPTER TWELVE

After Drake and Brygida left, Jason went back inside and starting thinking about dinner.

He'd been looking forward to having a meal with everyone. He'd been feeling a little lonely recently. It was funny; he'd *literally* spent decades at a time without talking to anyone. Now, after being around people constantly for a few weeks, he longed for continued company.

He understood that Drake wanted to talk to his daughter alone, though.

"Was that strange?" said Geoffrey, coming out of the kitchen.

"Was what strange?" Jason asked. Drake was always strange.

"Those two leaving together like that."

"I don't think so."

"So you don't think...?"

"What?" Jason had no idea what Geoffrey was hinting at.

He knew Geoffrey had been present when Drake introduced Brygida as his daughter. Sometimes Geoffrey acted as if he didn't know. It was weird. Jason thought he should just point it out to him, but if Drake had blurred Geoffrey's memory, he'd probably a good reason to do so. In either case, it wasn't his problem to fix.

"Nothing, I guess. Anyway, what are you doing tonight?"

"Just eating dinner and catching up on some reading, I hope," Jason said. "Why?"

"I kind of thought we'd spend some time together. I didn't expect Drake to leave again."

Jason sighed. "I think Drake has some science thing he needs help with. Don't worry. He said he'd be around for a few days and wouldn't leave without saying goodbye. Drake gets pretty focused when he has a problem to solve – you know that."

"Yeah, I know."

"You're nervous about tomorrow, aren't you?"

Geoffrey sat down heavily. "I just don't want to blow it. I like Jen."

"Then don't blow it," said Jason.

"You make it sound easy. Why am I asking *you*, of all people, for dating advice?"

"What's that supposed to mean?"

"Well, I've never known you to date."

"I've dated, Geoffrey. I'm older than I look. No, I haven't dated *recently*. So what? Not everything in life has to be about sex. You know what your problem is, Geoffrey?"

"Enlighten me," Geoffrey replied sourly.

"You're hungry."

"What?"

"You get surly when you haven't eaten. Why don't we go out and get some food? Something real, like a steak or something?"

"That sounds great!"

Jason didn't normally like going out to eat, since he had to be careful with the cutlery, but Geoffrey needed a distraction. Hell, so did he. He'd been cooped up in the house for too long.

Time to get out.

⊙

Brygida sat down on the couch.

Tadeo climbed up and curled in her lap, purring. Brygida was very happy she'd rescued the little creature. It felt good to be loved.

"What did you want to talk about?" she asked.

"Well, first I wanted to give you this," said Drake. He handed her a small sheet of paper.

"A phone number?" She didn't recognize the area code.

"You sister Xia gave me that to give to you. She'd like to meet you, at least talk to you."

"I'd like that. Was there something else?"

"Just before I met with her, someone tried to kill her. I am worried that someone may make an attempt against you."

Brygida rubbed Tadeo's ears. "Why would anyone come after me?"

"I'm not even sure why they went after Xia," Drake said. "It's just a feeling. I'm worried about you."

"I thank you for your concern, but I'm fine, really. I can take care of myself."

"I never thought you couldn't. Brygida, I'm sorry that I had to rush off without saying anything. I know we haven't known each other very long, but you are dear to me. I love you."

Brygida blinked back tears. "I love you, too, Father. Please forgive me. I'm not angry. I'm just tired. It's been a long week. I had planned to retreat in private and recharge."

"And I am causing you stress," Drake said. He stood up. "I should go."

"No, please. I have a guest bedroom. It is a little plain, but…"

"I'm sure it will be perfect. Thank you." Drake looked around and then gestured toward the television, still in its box. "I could set that up for you."

"That would be great."

For a few minutes, Brygida watched him trying to figure out how to open the box, and she then giggled. "You've never put together this kind of electronics, have you?"

"Well, no," Drake admitted. "I mostly deal with things that just sort of *work*."

Brygida kissed Tadeo on her tiny head and placed her on the couch. Then she stood quickly before the kitten could get back in her lap. "Pull the white tabs out on the bottom, all the way around, and then lift the box off."

"Ah."

They spent the next few minutes unpacking parts and stripping plastic wrappers off things. The kitten had fun pouncing the long plastic box straps. It didn't take long to set up the television and disk player. Brygida put the batteries in the remote and sat back down on the couch.

"Maybe we should order food," she suggested.

"Would it be rude to order pizza when Geoffrey isn't here?" asked Drake.

Brygida laughed. "Nope. He's had pizza at least twice since we've been back. Maybe more, if he and Jason ordered it alone."

"If you'll order it, I'll buy," Drake said.

"What do you like on your pizza?" Brygida asked.

"Meat and cheese and sauce. I'll eat anything, though."

Brygida called the closest pizza place and ordered two large pizzas with all the meats, two salads, and breadsticks. If her father didn't want the other salad, she'd put it the fridge and have it for lunch tomorrow. She didn't know if she'd have leftover pizza – she'd seen him eat – but if there was any, it would make a good dinner the next day.

"I have beer, soda, and bottles of water in the fridge."

Drake stood up. "What would you like?"

"Beer, thank you." She wasn't used to having someone get things for her. "In the bottle is fine," she called.

She heard Drake rattle around in the kitchen. He came back in with two opened beers, plates, cutlery, and napkins. Brygida relaxed a little in his company. Her father was quiet; he seemed to know she needed a little time to process her day.

He answered the door when the delivery person knocked. Tadeo bristled and hissed at the door. Brygida thought that was very cute: the kitten was protecting her.

A minute later, Drake placed the food on the coffee table.

"It smells good," he said.

"I hope you like it."

He placed a salad in front of her, with a fork, and then split the breadsticks between them. He seemed to enjoy the pizza. She certainly did. It was a bit of a guilty pleasure. She'd not had pizza all that often before coming back to this world. At one time, she might even have turned her nose up at it.

They didn't have pizza in the Golden Kingdom. Their loss.

"When did you see my sister?" Brygida asked.

"Two weeks ago," said Drake, "right before I ran off to help Jon."

"I'd better call her, then. I don't want her to think I don't want to talk."

"I don't think she'd think that. You can relax tonight. Call her tomorrow. Maybe we can both go see her."

Brygida sat her phone back down with relief. "That would be good. I think I'd be a bit nervous, meeting her alone."

"No reason to be nervous. I think you two will get along well. She's only a little older than you, but newer to the central Realms. She's from the Ruined Courts."

"Is she a shapeshifter?"

"Yes." Drake gestured at the television. "Would you like to watch something together?"

"Sure." Brygida looked through the stack of DVDs and choose the first of the new Marvel movies. She'd been a fan of the comics but hadn't seen any of the new movies. The old ones from the seventies and eighties had been, well, *terrible*. She hoped these were better.

She collected the dishes and leftovers. Her father offered to help, but she declined the assistance. Some things she liked to do herself. Leftovers went into baggies in the fridge, and none for the kitten, no matter how much she begged, garlic is bad for cats. Brygida quickly washed the dishes and then popped a couple bags of popcorn. The kitten could have some of that.

"Would you like another beer?" she called.

"Yes, thank you."

Brygida smiled. The evening hadn't turned out the way she'd planned, but it had gone well nonetheless. She picked up the beers and popcorn and went back into the living room, dodging the kitten, who tried to trip her.

CHAPTER THIRTEEN

Geoffrey hadn't been too nervous until now, but he was getting there.

He hadn't bought many new clothes since he got back. It hadn't seemed like a priority. Now, he was getting ready to go on a date, and he'd already worn all the clothes he owned around her.

"Geoffrey if you don't hurry up, you're going to miss the bus," Jason called to him.

"Shit."

He'd already decided on faded jeans and a tee shirt. He grabbed a long-sleeved shirt and wore it open with the sleeves rolled up. He didn't think he'd worn that to class before.

"Geoffrey!"

He ran down the stairs, double-checking that he had his keys, wallet, and pocketknife.

"You're wearing that?" Jason asked.

Geoffrey froze. "What's wrong with it?"

"I thought you'd dress up."

"I don't have any nicer clothes!"

"Your clothes are okay." Jason said. He looked at Geoffrey's head and shook his.

"What's wrong? Is my hair doing that thing?"

"No, you your hair is fine." He shook his head again.

"What?"

"It's that exposed part above your collar that worries me," said Jason.

"The what…? Oh, fuck you, man," Geoffrey said when he realized Jason was harassing him.

"Not me or anyone else, with that face."

"If I miss my bus, it's your fault!"

Geoffrey ran out the door.

He didn't miss his bus, but it was a close thing. Geoffrey rode the bus downtown and then transferred to the Mount Adams route. He walked up the long hill to the art museum, trying not to think about how much he was sweating in the summer heat and humidity.

Jen stood in the shade near the entrance, dressed in a casual fashion not much different from what Geoffrey was wearing. She smiled and waved when she saw him.

"Hey, Jen," Geoffrey said as he walked up.

"I'm glad you didn't dress all fancy," she said. "You're so serious all the time, I thought you might show up in a tie!"

He'd considered it.

"We're college students," said Geoffrey. "We can be serious after we graduate."

"You ride the bus?"

"I don't have a car. I caught the transfer from College Hill."

"That's cool. I rode in from Clifton. Riding the bus is the better, greener choice."

"You ride the bus because it's better for the environment?"

"That and because I can't afford a car."

"Mostly the last for me," Geoffrey said. "I mean, I care about the environment, but it isn't really a *choice*, you know?"

"I do." Jen bowed slightly and gestured toward the door.

"Shall we?"

Geoffrey grinned and opened the door for her.

It was cold in the museum. He was glad he'd worn the extra layer. He couldn't remember if there was a charge to get in, but turned out to be free to the public; only the special exhibit cost extra. Jen wasn't particularly interested in that, so they wandered the halls looking at all the amazing artwork.

The lower level held many historical artworks. Geoffrey liked the Egyptian and Greek stuff the most, although the early modern work from the US was interesting to. Most of the paintings were upstairs, and they spent a few hours walking the galleries and looking at people who'd been dead for hundreds of years.

"So, why did you sign up for physics?" Jen asked.

"Well, talking to Dr. Hakubi over the summer started me thinking that my history degree wasn't really worth much. I could do a lot more than just teach high school somewhere. I'm not from a rich family – first in my immediate family to go to college."

"Brothers and sisters?"

"Only child. You?"

"The same." She sat down on one of the benches. They were alone in the gallery. "What about your parents?"

"Just my mother," Geoffrey said. "Never knew my father. You?"

"Parents still together. Doing well. My mom's white."

"So is mine," said Geoffrey.

Jen laughed. "You're funny, you know?"

"Me?"

"Most guys are kind of dicks to women in STEM fields. Not to mention women of color."

Geoffrey shrugged. "That never made any sense to me, people are people. I mean, no one is forcing a guy to date a college woman. I don't get why it would be a problem anyway.

We're all human, all the same people. What difference does it make if our reproductive organs are inside or out? Or some people have more melanin?"

"*Stargate* reference – nice," Jen said, nodding. "Maybe you really are a geek. Elena thought you were, but I wasn't sure. I thought you might be a poser, just trying to pick up hot geek women."

Geoffrey hadn't been trying to quote anything, but he'd take it. He wasn't sure how he felt about being called a geek. He knew the term wasn't an insult in most places, but it had been a *hard* insult where he was from. Of course, most people where he was from never read a book, either.

"I can't help how I look," said Geoffrey. "I'm white and blond. I know I look like a jock. I played baseball in high school because I was expected to play a sport, and baseball was the one I hated the least. I read, and I play video games. I watch science movies and shows."

"Easy, tiger, we're good. I'll accept you for now, but I reserve the right to quiz you on video games later to establish your full cred."

"How do I know *you're* actually a geek?" he asked.

"Oh, ho! He turns it around. Well done, grasshopper."

"I grew up watching reruns of *Kung Fu*, *MASH*, and *Star Trek*," Geoffrey said. "And the *Incredible Hulk*, which was a lot like *Kung Fu*, now that I think of it."

"*Space 1999*?"

"I liked the shapeshifter in season two."

"Everyone liked Maya."

"I liked how she could turn into a tiger."

"Hmm. Sure it wasn't her skimpy outfits?"

"Now you sound like my housemate," Geoffrey said. "Besides, most of the women on *Star Trek* wore less."

"True."

"Would you like to have lunch with me?" he asked.

"Dutch?" she asked.

"I willing to buy, but that's your choice."

"Good answer." Jen took his hand and stood up. "We should go someplace other than the café here. The prices are crazy."

"I've never eaten here, but I'll take your word for it."

They walked down the hill together. The day had turned hot, but it wasn't too bad in the shade of the trees.

"Where do you want to go?"

Geoffrey shrugged.

"What's you budget?"

"I'm working as a paid intern and have a full scholarship. I'm pretty flush."

"Maybe I *should* let you buy me lunch, Richie Rich."

"Ouch."

"Okay, I'll let up before you cry. How about we head across the river?"

Geoffrey laughed. "Okay. Lots of good food over there."

"I'm from Kentucky, by the way," said Jen. "I went to school in Florence."

"I'm from Mount Sterling."

"Okay, a point in your favor."

They caught a bus across the river and a transfer to the TANK bus headed for Florence.

"Your parents still live in Florence?" Geoffrey asked.

"Well, actually they live in Oakbrook. I just went to school in Florence. Okay, you have to pick a place to eat."

Geoffrey tried to remember what was in Florence. "Applebee's or Steak and Shake?"

"Hmm. Sensible, middle-range restaurants with decent food. I know I should say Applebee's, but I'm going to go with Steak and Shake. I like the atmosphere better."

"Better shakes, too," Geoffrey added.

"Well, that goes without saying, doesn't it?"

They hopped off the bus at Turfway Park and walked to the restaurant. Geoffrey was glad he'd spent so much time walking with Drake. It had built up his stamina. Playing baseball hadn't really been vigorous, and he'd been out of high school for a few years now.

Geoffrey got two double cheeseburgers, fries, and a banana shake. Jen raised an eyebrow at his order, but she ordered a cheeseburger, onion rings, and a bowl of chili, along with a strawberry shake. They picked a table away from the other customers.

"This is a test, you know," said Jen.

"What is?" Geoffrey asked. She'd let him buy – not that it was expensive.

"Some men won't kiss a woman who's eaten onions." She slowly and deliberately bit into an onion ring.

"Some men are fools," said Geoffrey.

"You realize, of course, that I may withhold a kiss anyway."

"I would never presume."

"Hmm. You are curiously charming and likable. Almost too much so. Why hasn't some other woman snatched you up and hidden you away from the rest of us?"

Geoffrey smiled. "I was dating someone, when I was on… Hawaii." He'd almost said *Kai*. "Last summer."

"Hawaii?" Jen asked dubiously. "Did you get that fishhook there?"

"I did. And the tan, for that matter. It was part of my internship."

"Shit, sign me up for some of that. I've never been outside the Tristate." She meant Ohio, Kentucky and Indiana. "Was it serious?"

Geoffrey nodded.

"Well, I guess you're not a virgin, then."

"Nope. You?"

"I should have seen that coming."

Geoffrey tried not to laugh. She threw an onion ring at him. He caught it and ate it.

"Now we both had onions."

"Clever," Jen said. "On the other hand, maybe I won't kiss a man who's eaten onions."

"Nah."

"Why do you say that?"

"Because you're not a fool, either."

"Well, at least you're perceptive. Maybe I should see if you want to go on another date, before another woman steals you."

"You already asked me out on a second date: your historical thing tomorrow. You may be stuck with me now."

"We'll see. Most people run away when they see what a strange hobby I have."

"Taken a lot of men to these things?"

"Touché." She watched him over her milkshake as she finished. "Okay, smarty, you still have a jock cup?"

The sudden non-sequitur threw him off. "I think so. Why?"

"Wear it tomorrow, and I'll kick your ass with a sword."

"Okay."

"Okay? Just *okay*? No macho reflex?"

"You know how to sword fight. I don't. So if we fight with swords, you'll almost certainly win. I'm okay with that."

"You really are a catch, aren't you?"

"I'm smart and good looking," said Geoffrey. "So are you. No matter what happens, let's agree to be friends, at the least? Okay?"

He held out his hand, and she shook it solemnly before starting to giggle.

"At the least, huh?" she asked.

He held onto her hand and looked into her eyes. "Yes, at the *very* least."

She blushed. "Okay, time to head back home."

Geoffrey cleaned up the table and followed her out. He

bought some gum out of the machine on the way out and gave her half. She laughed at him but chewed the gum all the way back.

They caught the bus back to Covington and transferred to Cincinnati. They kept the conversation lighter on the way back, mostly talking about their favorite books; their lists had a lot of overlap.

They parted ways at the Metro station. Geoffrey was headed back home to College Hill. Jen was staying in the student dorms in Clifton. She responded passionately to his kiss and sighed deeply as he stepped back.

"Damn. Okay. I will see you in the morning. Eden Park, by the old reservoir wall, ten o'clock."

"I will be there. With protection."

She blushed again.

"I meant my cup."

"I know!" she squeaked. "You go now. Get!"

Geoffrey smiled and got onto his bus, which was leaving a few minutes before hers. He waved from the seat. She blew him a kiss.

He leaned back in the seat as the bus pulled away.

The day had gone better than he'd had any right to expect.

It had been a little over a month for him since he'd left Kalea on Kai. He couldn't and wouldn't forget about her. He'd loved her. The pain of separation had been with him the entire time since, but he felt as if it was starting to ease now.

Jen was the kind of woman he could love and settle down with. She was smart and funny. She was also damn sexy. Her body had felt good, pressed against his as they kissed. He couldn't wait to see her again.

Jason was going to be jealous. Maybe he should see about setting him and Elena up on a date. They might make a good couple. Then they could go on double dates, and Geoffrey might not have to ride the bus everywhere.

CHAPTER FOURTEEN

Brygida stepped into the back yard late in the afternoon and gathered her courage to call her sister. The air was warm and humid, but the trees in the yard provided good shade. That was part of why she'd rented this particular house.

Maybe I should have just let Father introduce us, she thought.

She dialed the number.

A woman answered on the second ring. She had an unfamiliar accent. "This is Lucy."

"Hello. I was trying to reach Xia Jaiying."

The woman said something in a language she didn't recognize – Brygida thought it might be one of the Chinese languages. Her voice was slightly higher than Brygida's.

"I'm sorry, I don't know what you said."

"Who is this?" the woman asked.

"My name is Brygida."

"Oh! Brygida! My sister! It's been a couple of weeks since I gave Father my number. I didn't think you were going to call."

"He had something urgent to do in another Realm and just now got back here."

"Yeah, that sounds like him."

Brygida wasn't sure what to say. She'd always wanted to have a sister, but this woman on the other end of the phone was just a voice. She didn't know who she was. She didn't even know if the woman wanted to meet her.

"I don't want to bother you. I just wanted to call and say hello."

"You're not bothering me, Brygida. Hold on a moment."

Brygida felt something uncomfortable between her shoulder blades. It felt as if she was being watched, like the feeling she might sometimes feel when walking alone at night and hearing a nearby footstep that wasn't hers. Then there was a rainbow distortion in the air and a *whoosh* as a woman appeared.

"That should make things easier," the woman said. "Hi, I'm Xia."

Xia was taller than Brygida had expected, at least fifteen centimeters taller than Brygida herself. Her long hair was coppery red, like Brygida's, but streaked with jet black. The irises of her eyes looked like fractured fragments of stained glass.

"Brygida," she managed. She hadn't expected her sister to apport here. She turned off her phone and put it into her pants pocket. She hadn't known what to say on the phone, much less in person.

Suddenly she was engulfed in a tight hug. "Oh!"

Xia held onto Brygida's arms as she stepped back and looked her over. "Dad said I had a little sister, but I didn't realize he meant it literally."

"I also said we should be careful when apporting," Drake said from the kitchen door.

"I've apported through the Cincinnati airport before. I went there first. This was just a little side jump. No one will notice."

"I noticed," said Drake.

"You were right inside. You probably heard I was coming anyway."

"Well, I'm glad you're here. We should have dinner later,

the three of us." Drake turned and walked back inside.

"He's worries too much," said Xia. "I like your hair."

"Thanks. I like yours." Brygida was feeling a bit overwhelmed. "Can I get you anything?"

"I'm good. Is this your place?" Xia walked over and patted the trees.

"Yes. I'm leasing it while I work here in Cincinnati."

"I like the trees. The higher air pressure and humidity were a bit of a shock, though."

"You're living in Albuquerque?" Brygida was vaguely aware of where that was: middle of New Mexico, somewhere in the Southwest.

"Just north of there in Santa Fe," said Xia. "I go to school in Albuquerque. Physics and engineering. Father said you have a couple of degrees in those."

"Doctorates in physics and genetics," Brygida replied. "Master's degrees in engineering and genetics. I'm here working as a contractor for an aerospace company. I'm also teaching part-time."

"Gerhardt Industries?" Xia said. "I'd heard they had some crazy starship project underway."

"They have it mostly built in orbit. I'm helping with the fusion engines and coldsleep chambers."

"That must be exciting."

Brygida nodded.

"Father said you were from the North."

Brygida tensed. She didn't sense any animosity from her sister, though. "I grew up in the Golden Kingdom. My mother is still there."

"Have you been to the Ruined Courts?"

"No, I haven't. I want to go."

"I've never been to the Golden Kingdom," Xia said. "Maybe next summer we can go on a road trip together and show each other around."

"Yeah, maybe. That would be pretty cool." Suddenly Brygida felt tears running down her cheeks. She turned away, embarrassed.

She felt Xia's hand on her back. "Are you okay?"

"Sorry. I've had a few rough years where everything looked really bleak. I've spent a lot of time alone. I... I was imprisoned. No one cared. Now I suddenly have a father and a sister. I'm just a bit overwhelmed."

Xia hugged her from behind and rocked her gently.

"My mother died when I was very young," said Xia. "She was killed by... you know what our father does?"

"The Ancient Enemy, yes."

"Okay, yeah. After that, I lived with Father in the House of Drake in the Courts. I grew up with many cousins around. I served in the House army for fifty years, and then I decided I wanted to see these worlds he'd talk about."

"Is that where you got your eyes?" Brygida asked. "I think they're cool."

"I worked as a mercenary in a strange Realm where Earth was the center of an empire with space travel. I was blinded in one of the battles. Burned out with a laser. I had these implanted so I didn't have to wait for them to grow back. I sort of got used to them after that."

Brygida turned around. "They're very pretty. Is that why you go by Lucy, like the Beatles song?"

Xia laughed. "No, that was just a strange coincidence, actually. My mother used to call me *Lu Xi* when I was small. It means *red flower*, because of my hair."

"So Lu Xi became Lucy, when you needed a use name here?"

"Exactly."

"Why change it at all? Why not just go by Xia?"

"Well, it turns out that the sun symbol on the flag of New Mexico is the Zia, with a *z*. People kept misspelling my name."

"People keep calling me Bridget," said Brygida. "It's not a

bad name. I've thought about just going with it."

"Do you use Drake as your surname?"

Brygida shook her head. "No. I knew who my father is, but I hadn't met him. It didn't seem right to use his name, under the circumstances. I didn't meet him until just a few weeks ago, actually. I go by Hakubi."

"Is that your mother's surname?"

"No. I lived in Japan for a couple of decades while going to school there. I needed a name, so I made one up."

"Well, it's yours now, although I'm sure Father wouldn't mind if you used Drake."

Brygida felt tears on her cheeks again. "My mother never married our father."

"So what?"

"So I'm illegitimate."

"I've seen no indication that Father has rejected you."

Brygida snuffled back her tears and wiped her face.

"No, he hasn't. Nor have you. For which I thank you," Brygida said.

"Did you expect rejection?"

"I don't know. Maybe."

"You're not a shapeshifter, are you?"

Brygida shook her head. She didn't know what that had to do with anything.

"You look like you try real hard to not express yourself sexually."

Brygida blushed. "I've never been interested in that sort of thing."

"I meant your biological sexual phenotype. You don't embrace it."

"Oh. Well, I've never thought I looked like much of a woman. Besides, if people are uncertain, they tend to leave me alone. Being flat-chested is an advantage there."

"Tits don't make a woman," said Xia. "I was just wondering

if you'd be more comfortable as a man."

"What? No," Brygida said. "I'm not confused about my sex. I feel that I'm a woman. I don't feel confused about it or anything. I just don't feel that it has to be the thing everyone sees first about me. Why is it so damn important to everyone?"

This was not what she'd imagined having a conversation with her sister about. On the other hand, this was exactly the sort of thing siblings should talk about. Brygida wondered if Xia being so willing to talk about it meant she accepted Brygida for who she was.

"I wasn't being judgmental," Xia said. "If you were a shapeshifter, you could be whatever you wanted to be. Our father has been a woman. I think he even had a daughter once, as a woman. I don't think sex is very important. I just thought that maybe you did."

Brygida shook her head. "Biologically, I'm a woman. Mentally, I'm just a person. I don't know what makes a woman's mind different from a man's, if anything. I'm happy with who I am. I don't need or want that other stuff."

"Look, I just wanted to make sure I didn't offend you by calling you my little *sister*, if you wanted to identify as something else. You look like a woman to me, by the way. What are looks? Hell, sometimes I look like a lizard."

Brygida started laughing then. Xia joined her. It was too funny. *Her sister, the lizard.*

Xia grinned and gave her another hug. "Come on, sis, let's go harass Dad and make him buy us dinner."

"Yeah, that sounds good. Thank you. Let's give him hell."

CHAPTER FIFTEEN

Geoffrey felt uncomfortable riding the bus with his jock cup on.

He'd had to go out the night before and buy a new one. He'd forgotten when talking to Jen that most of his stuff had been stolen or tossed out. His weeks traveling with Drake had started to blur away in his memories. It was like something that had happened to someone else.

From the entrance to Eden Park, where he got off the bus, it took him a while to walk to the old reservoir. He'd left early, though, too nervous to sit at home. He checked his phone; he still had a few minutes before he was late.

Most of the old reservoir was gone from the park. There was a mirror pool and beyond that, the remains of the old retaining wall. Geoffrey saw a few people in renfaire costume over there doing something, so he walked that way.

Jen waved to him when she saw him.

She was dressed in baggy pants and a shirt, with a thick-looking jacket worn open over it. Her hair was pulled back, and she was wearing one of those caps he'd seen on Amish women. He had to admit, she looked kind of sexy in the outfit.

"Geoffrey! You made it!"

"I'm early, aren't I?"

"Really early, for this crowd. I wasn't sure if you'd come, though."

"I said I would."

"You wear your protection?" she asked, eyes dancing.

Geoffrey knocked on his groin with his knuckles. "Yep."

"Okay, let me introduce you to everyone. Hey, guys, this is my friend from school, Geoffrey. He's going to check things out. Maybe try it out, if you don't scare him away." Then she introduced the others to him. "This is Michael, Johnathon, Cindy, Lady Isabella, Lord Constantine, and the Honorable Lord Xavier. Xavier is our field marshal today. All the people with titles are from the other group – our college group is just getting started."

Geoffrey really hoped she didn't expect him to remember all those names.

"You'll probably hear people call me Genevieve. We all take a name in the society that would have been used in the Middle Ages or Renaissance."

"Okay, well, Geoffrey was," he said.

"Yep, like Chaucer."

"So no *lord* or *lady*?" Geoffrey asked.

"No, it's a title you have to earn."

Geoffrey sighed. "Okay."

"Here, check this out!" Jen presented him with a sword.

It was fancy-looking, with hilts that covered the hand. He raised the blade. It was lighter than he'd expected, and very long, almost four feet. It looked a little like Drake's sword, although thinner. It also had a rubber tip held on with gold duct tape.

"Nice," he said.

Xavier walked over with a book and a clipboard. "These are the rules of the list and the rapier handbook. You'll need to read over and sign the waiver before you fight. You're wearing a cup?"

"Yes, sir."

"I'm not a knight," Xavier said sourly. He handed the book and clipboard to Geoffrey and walked away.

"The SCA reserves the title of *Sir* for a heavy weapons knight," said Jen. "Fencers can't get it, and they get a little grumpy about that."

"I was just taught to address all authority figures as *sir*; I didn't mean anything else by it." At least he didn't think he meant anything by it. The *sir* had just slipped out. He hadn't done that since being sarcastic to teachers in high school.

"Don't worry about it. He's always grumpy. Just sign the form, and we'll get you into gear."

"Shouldn't I read the rules?"

"We'll go over them with you. It's easy."

Geoffrey sighed again and looked over the waiver. It basically just said that he was going to participate in something potentially dangerous and was aware of that. He figured it was mostly so people didn't sue if they got a hangnail or something.

"Does anyone ever get hurt doing this?" he asked.

"It's a sport. Injuries can happen."

"Okay." He signed the form and took it over to Xavier. He really felt as if he should read the rules, but if Jen said he'd be fine, he'd roll with it.

Xavier glanced at the form. "Okay, you're good to go. Work with Genevieve first, and then I'll show you a few things."

"Thank you," said Geoffrey.

Xavier nodded and went back to unpacking his gear.

"All good?" Jen asked.

"He said I should train with you first, and then he'd work with me."

"Awesome. I grabbed a bag of loaner gear I thought would fit you. You'll want to get your own stuff if you like doing it."

"Okay, what first?"

"Your pants are twill, so they're fine. You're wearing a cup. You'll need the jacket out of there. Just put it on and button it up."

The fencing coat was a little tight, and it smelled musty, but it fit well enough.

"Now a mask," said Jen. "I picked a big one, since you have a big head."

"Was that commentary on my ego?"

Jen laughed. "No actually."

The fencing mask was metal mesh with padding inside. It had a hard leather cupped part that fit over the back of the head. Jen pulled a hood over all of it.

She held up a leather dog collar with bits hanging off it. "Sorry, should have done this first. Let me slip this in underneath."

It wasn't remotely comfortable.

"Now gloves." She held up grey welding gloves. She helped Geoffrey put them on, since he could see very well.

"Now a sword?" he guessed.

She handed him a rapier. It wasn't nearly as nice as hers, but he figured it was owned by the group, to loan to people. He gave it an experimental swish.

"Okay, we don't flail with these," Jen said. "For today, we'll start with just thrusts – wipe the grin off your face!"

"You can't see my face," said Geoffrey.

"No, but I know you." She punched his arm. "Come over here to the wall." She held her sword and demonstrated a thrust.

She wasn't touching the wall very hard.

"So it's just touch?"

She stabbed him in the stomach. He felt it, but it didn't hurt.

"Practice thrusting gently against the wall," Jen said with a wink. "I'm going to go put my gear on."

Geoffrey practiced touching the wall the way she'd shown him. It was harder than it looked to just touch. He wanted to stab with the blade. He understood why they had to be careful, though.

"In real life, it's pretty easy to slip a blade through someone," Jen said from behind him. Her voice was slightly muffled by the mask. "Even a gentle stab will run someone through."

"Scary thought," Geoffrey replied.

"Okay, you ready?"

"Let's do it."

"Stand like me," Jen said.

She had her feet spaced apart so she was balanced, with her right foot forward. Her left hand was up by her chest, held strangely. She was holding the sword out, with her arm bent.

"You can slap the blade away but not grab it," Jen said. "Thrust *slowly* at my chest. Oh, and if someone calls *hold*, stop whatever you're doing."

He stabbed her slowly, and she used her left hand to slap the blade away.

"Okay, now you do it." She thrust slowly at his chest.

He felt weird slapping the blade away, but it worked.

"Good. Now stab at me again, and I'll show you how to block with the hilts."

He did, and she slid his point off to the side.

"You want to keep your point aimed at me, and I want to get your point aiming somewhere else. Move your hilt as little as possible to deflect the blade. Now you do it."

He deflected a few slow thrusts.

"Excellent. You catch on quick. Ready to just fight a little?"

"Yeah. Am I supposed to aim for anything other than the chest?"

"Basically anywhere is a legal target, including the groin. That's why you needed to wear a cup."

"Is that safe for you?"

"I'm wearing a jill. It's the female equivalent. Ready?"

Geoffrey saluted with his sword.

Jen laughed and saluted back, then attacked.

She was really fast. Geoffrey had to push himself to block her attacks. After a couple of minutes, he was comfortable enough defending and began to attack back. He even scored a couple of hits.

It was fun, although it didn't seem much like actual combat. He wondered what Drake would have thought about it. Geoffrey was almost afraid even to think about that.

"Hold!"

Geoffrey stopped and lowered his sword. He looked around. The others had been watching Jen and him fight. Xavier was walking toward them. He had a blunted dagger in his left hand, which looked fun.

"You've done this before?"

"No, this is my first time." Geoffrey wondered what he'd done wrong. "I've played a lot of video games."

Someone laughed.

"You're just really fast for a beginner," said Xavier. "Fight me."

"You've got this," Jen said, stepping back.

Geoffrey wondered if she was talking to him.

Xavier saluted, and Geoffrey did the same. Then Xavier attacked.

The man was fast. He tagged Geoffrey a couple of time before Geoffrey found a reserve of speed he hadn't known he had and matched him. Geoffrey started parrying everything and finally managed to slip the blade through Xavier's defenses and stab him in the face.

Xavier held up his hand and stepped back.

Geoffrey lowered his weapon and took a step back, as well. He wasn't sure what was going on.

"Well, Jen, you certainly covered the basics with him. I

think you may have found us an actual fencer."

"Did I do okay?" asked Geoffrey.

Xavier laughed. "Yeah, you did good."

Geoffrey pulled off his helmet. He was suddenly aware that he was drenched in sweat. The other fencers congratulated him on his fighting and went back to fence each other.

"Need a break?" Jen asked.

"Yeah, I'm wishing I'd brought some water."

"I brought extra."

"Thank you!" Geoffrey drank about half of the bottle she handed him. "You do this all summer long?"

"All year long," Jen said. "We practice indoors in the winter. You ready to go again?"

Geoffrey finished his bottle of water and nodded. He was feeling the burn from the exercise, but it was a good feeling. *I really do need a car,* he thought. Riding back home sweaty, on the bus, was going to be miserable.

CHAPTER SIXTEEN

Very rarely throughout Drake's life had two of his children been alive at the same time. Being able to spend time with both his daughters was precious to him. It also reinforced his determination to discover who was behind the attempt on Xia's life. Drake didn't believe for a moment that it had been his brother.

His brother had fallen and joined with the Ancient Enemy. The Ancient Enemy didn't hire assassins.

It worried him that Xia said the assassin was a shapeshifter but not from the Ruined Courts. It wasn't that such powers were limited to the Courts, but they weren't exactly common, either. Drake knew of only a few places someone like that could be from.

Xia had gone back to Santa Fe on Saturday night. Drake let her and Brygida know that he'd be leaving soon to head back to Nandegurth and could be gone for some time. He wanted to tell Jason and Geoffrey that in person, too. He hadn't intended to spend the weekend exclusively with his daughters, but he was glad he did.

Jason didn't answer his door when Drake knocked, so he

walked around to the back yard. From the workshop he heard music and the sound of a chisel on wood. Drake knocked on that door and waited.

"It's me, Jason," Drake called.

The music cut off, and the door opened. "I thought you'd left again," Jason said.

"I told you I'd stop by first," said Drake. "My daughter Xia came in from out of town, so I spent the weekend with my daughters."

Jason stepped out of the workshop and locked the door. "Can I get you a drink or anything?"

"I'm good. I assume Geoffrey has left for school."

"Yes, he left about an hour ago."

"When will he be back?"

"Not until this evening. Monday, Wednesday, and Friday are his long days. He has lot of classes, and then there's his new girlfriend."

Drake nodded. "He sounds busy. I'm afraid I can't wait around until he gets home before I leave."

"He's going to be disappointed," said Jason.

"Unfortunately, it can't be helped. Someone tried to assassinate Xia, and I worry that someone may try with Brygida, too."

"We talking ninjas like last time?"

"No. These are shapeshifters of unknown origin and purpose."

"There's no getting any rest with you people, is there?"

"Apparently not."

Jason nodded. "Brygida knows to be careful, right?"

"She is aware of the problem," Drake answered. "I cannot predict exactly how she is going to react, but she isn't a fool."

"I didn't ask, but I assume your other daughter is okay," Jason said.

"Xia detected and killed the assassin sent after her. The

paranoid portion of my mind wonders if maybe she was supposed to. She didn't say in so many words, but the assassin sent after her was wearing my form."

"Oh, shit," said Jason. "If someone did that to one of the people from up North…"

"It would start a war, yes. I'm very much aware."

"Okay, I'll let Geoffrey know what's going on and why you had to rush off. I appreciate you taking the time to let us know."

"I consider you my friends, Jason. I don't have many of those."

Jason nodded, obviously embarrassed. "You're sure I can't get you something?"

"I really must be going," said Drake. "I will return as soon as I can."

"Be careful, Drake."

"To that end, I should collect my armor."

"It's right where you left it," Jason said. "It's too heavy to move."

Drake stripped and put on his armor. He folded the clothes and put them away in a pocket space. His coat, he wore over the armor, as usual.

"Jason, you should seriously consider telling Geoffrey about yourself. It will save you heartache in the long run."

"Maybe," Jason answered. "I'll think about it, at least."

Drake nodded and apported to the Waypoint node in Winton Woods, northeast of his friend's house. That node was connected into a network spanning the globe, but the Waypoint itself was located in the Northeast. He slipped into the node and exited from the node in Andover, nine hundred miles away.

From the town, it was just a short walk to the ancient cave holding the actual Waypoint that powered the entire system on this world. Drake passed the painting of the phoenix on the cave wall. He'd never known before why it was there.

Drake had often visited this Waypoint. It was a mystery. He could sense it, even see it and the controls when he brought up the Instrumentality, but he'd never been able to activate it. It had been locked down, seemingly from the other side.

After talking with Jason, Drake now knew that the Waypoint opened every so often. It appeared to be tied to some celestial alignment. Drake pushed tendrils of Instrumentality against the Waypoint. He could sense the Realm to which it connected. The Realm felt so close that he could almost touch it.

However, that Realm had been closed off, too.

It took a tremendous amount of energy to lock down an entire universe.

From the cave, Drake used the Instrumentality to apport through hyperspace back to the Waypoint on Nandegurth. He was pleased to see that the guards did not relax until his identity had been proven with an Orb of Recognition. Drake saluted the guards and walked to the Citadel.

It was good to be back home.

⊙

Jason was still somewhat discomfited by Drake's arrival earlier that morning.

The man could always manage to make a person feel strange, but Drake had been in rare form. Drake's candor about his daughters, as well as him saying that he thought of Jason as a friend, had left Jason feeling awkward. Drake's last comment about telling Geoffrey haunted him all day long.

Jason distracted himself as best he could. He cleaned the house. He did laundry. He drank a little bit too much. Geoffrey was late getting home that evening. By the time he did get home, Jason was quite drunk.

"Hey, Jason, I'm home!" Geoffrey called. He stopped in the archway to the living room. "Are you okay?"

"I'm… I don't know, actually. I feel pretty good."

"Yeah, you do *now*. How much have you had to drink?"

"Just a couple of beers?" He glanced at the bottles, but there seemed to be more than he'd thought. "And some whiskey."

"All of the whiskey, from the looks of it," said Geoffrey. "What's wrong, man? I don't think I've seen you like this."

"Drake stopped by," Jason said. He wanted to tell Geoffrey the truth. He just wasn't sure how to do it.

"Missed him again, huh?" Geoffrey sat his books down and went into the kitchen. He came back a minute later with a soda and a trash bag. "Here, drink this."

Jason sipped on the soda while Geoffrey cleaned up the bottles.

"Sorry," Jason said.

"Don't worry about it. We all have off days. You feel like telling me what set you off?"

"Drake is worried someone might try to kill Brygida. That was what he had to talk to her about the other night. He's off trying to discover who's behind it. He said they're shapeshifters. One of them posed as him but was killed trying to get to someone else."

"Holy crap," said Geoffrey. "Are we in danger?"

"I didn't get that impression," Jason said. "Sorry I got a little sloshed."

"Was that all that was bothering you?"

Jason nodded. He just wasn't ready to tell Geoffrey. Not yet.

"Well, considering what happened the last time assassins showed up around here, I'd say you getting drunk was a normal reaction. I'm thinking about it, myself."

"How was school?" Jason asked.

Geoffrey laughed. "Fine. All my classes went by quick, as usual. Brygida was as energetic as always. She didn't indicate she was worried."

"Maybe we should imitate her, then," said Jason. "Not be worried, I mean."

"Yeah, easy to say with a fifth of whiskey in you."

Jason frowned. "Did I really drink all of it? I don't remember doing that."

"Yeah, no wonder." Geoffrey laughed again. "Are you really that worried about Brygida? She can take care of herself."

"Maybe it's just the whole situation. I mean, it hasn't been that long since people showed up on our doorstep and tried to kill us. Or tried to kill us in Nandegurth. Or on Masir. Or—"

"Okay, yeah! I get the point!"

"Sorry. I know you don't like to think about what happened."

Geoffrey rubbed his chest. "Well, it turned out okay in the end. Have you had anything to eat today? Or just alcohol?"

"I *think* I had breakfast."

"Then let's tempt fate and order pizza."

"With you it's any excuse for pizza."

"Well, you need to eat something. I haven't eaten since lunch. So, yeah, pizza."

"I'll buy if you order it," said Jason.

"Can't argue with that."

"You have to answer the door, though."

Geoffrey sighed. "Well, *you're* certainly not in any shape to."

Jason really had intended to tell Geoffrey about who he really was. He'd gotten drunk to try to lower his inhibitions enough to say it. That hadn't worked. Now he just felt terrible and still wasn't able to tell the young man.

Well, it had really just been a suggestion from Drake. Jason knew Geoffrey better than Drake did. Jason would tell Geoffrey when the time was right. What the hell business was it of Drake's, anyway?

CHAPTER SEVENTEEN

"I'm going back home to Rhyddid," said Jon.

Lolani smacked him upside his head, which hurt every bit as much as he'd expected. It wasn't as if he hadn't known how she'd react. Lolani was rather predictable.

"Seriously, what the hell are you thinking?" she asked.

Jon rubbed the side of his head. "I'm thinking that Rhyddid just had another revolution, and that the cycle can't continue. Twenty percent of the population has died in the last decade. When is it ever going to stop?"

"And you think you're going to stop it?"

"I think I'm the only one who has a chance."

Lolani sighed. "Aradhana will you talk some sense into him?"

"I happen to agree with him," Aradhana said.

"Oh, for fuck's sake."

"Aradhana is coming with me," Jon said. "I'm not heading into this alone. We'll be safe enough – I don't look like I used to."

"They know the *Chwyldro*, and they'll shoot you down."

"We're going in a commercial transport," said Aradhana.

"We'll be posing as immigrants."

"That's going to go over great," Lolani said. "And no way to escape if things go to hell, which they will."

"I've been practicing apporting Aradhana along with me," Jon said. "I think I can get us both out of trouble if something happens. If I have to, I can apport us to an outbound ship."

"And get spaced as stowaways," said Lolani. She sighed gustily. "You're both crazy."

"If Drake stops back by, will you let him know where we've gone, and why?" Jon asked.

"Of course. I'll recommend he beats some sense into you also."

"Don't do that. He might take you seriously."

"I hope he does. I'd do it myself if it wasn't for Aradhana. When do you guys leave?"

"Tonight," said Jon. "There's a merchant doing the run through Masir to Rhyddid who's willing to take us."

"Willing to take your money, anyway," Lolani muttered.

Jon ignored her. "We don't know how long this is going to take. Would you take care of the *Chwyldro* for me?" He held out the credit stick Drake had gotten for him.

Lolani slapped his hand away. "I don't need your money. Yes, I'll take care of your damn ship."

"We aren't going to be taking foolish risks," said Aradhana. "We'll be okay."

"This whole damn thing is a foolish risk."

"Please, Lolani, this will be a lot easier if we part on good terms," Jon said.

"Idiot," Lolani said. "I'm not angry, I'm worried. If I don't hear back from you soon, I'm calling to Drake again. He *will* kick your ass if you get yourself killed."

"That, he would," Jon said with a grin. "He'd probably bring me back, kill me, and then bring me back again."

"I wouldn't put it past him," Lolani said. "Okay, give me a

hug, you two idiots. Seriously, be careful. I don't want to have
to tell Drake you're dead. He might get weird."

"He isn't weird?" said Aradhana.

"Okay, weird*er*."

"I promise we'll be careful," Jon said. "We don't want to
face your wrath, much less Drake's."

☉

Fridays were supposed to be *easier* than other days.

Brygida had never found that to be true, though. Students
who might be bright and interested at the beginning of the week
were often worn down and tired by Friday. It was an effort to
keep their attention, since they all seemed to have plans for the
weekend.

Her plans for the weekend were to curl up on the couch with
Tadeo and watch classic science fiction. She might even order
out, if it wasn't too much bother. Otherwise, she would just eat
tuna salad on toast, and popcorn. Tadeo would certainly
approve of that.

She was an introvert, and not at all ashamed of that. She
liked people, some anyway. Being around people *drained* her.
She just needed her time to recharge afterwards.

Because she was so tired, her mental shielding wasn't where
it should be. She normally kept her shields tight when in the
city. There was too much mental noise. However, that evening
in the parking garage, it might have saved her life.

Just a few more steps and I can finish this nice and easy.

The thought blasted into her head and she froze. Whoever
had thought it, had been very near to her. The words had been
accompanied by an image of a long knife.

What did she forget her keys or something, come on!

Brygida wished that she'd had a chance to learn some of the

more esoteric uses of the Cynosure. An offensive spell would have come in handy, just then. She could conjure a weapon, but that might not be much use against a skilled assassin. She'd been trained by one of the best martial artists in any world, but she didn't know who she was facing.

She nodded and pulled her keys out. The assassin was going to get suspicious if she didn't keep walking to her car. At least they weren't using a gun. The best she could do against a handgun was to try to hex it and make it blow up.

Brygida unlocked the jeep remotely as she walked up. The assassin leapt up from behind a nearby car and charged, knife raised. The knife was held point down, edge out, along the forearm. It was an efficient fighting method.

She did the one thing she figured the assassin wouldn't think she'd do. She pushed away from the jeep hard and hurled herself onto the killer. The knife flashed down and Brygida grabbed the man's wrist and threw the assassin over her shoulder into the concrete pillar she'd parked next to.

As she did, she felt a line of fire across her face. He'd come very close to sinking the blade into her at the neck, as he'd intended. The blood wasn't in her eyes, so she didn't care about it.

The man hit the concrete hard enough to shatter it. He cried out as ribs cracked and splintered. He dropped the knife as he fell and Brygida followed up on the throw with a smashing knee to his chest that crushed his ribcage.

He collapsed to the floor of the parking structure, coughing up blood as he died. Brygida could hear sirens in the distance, closing in on her position. She started to run, and then decided to stand her ground. She was in the right of it, even if it meant a long session with the police.

The man's dying thoughts were confusing. *Filthy mixed blood abomination. Monika should be slain for mixing with the impure one from the South.*

She knew without looking that the man wouldn't have anything that could be used to identify him, so she didn't bother looking through his pockets. It would have looked bad on the camera anyway. She did wonder how the police had been notified. Had someone seen the incident and called them?

Whoever the assassin had been, he wasn't some local looking for a good time or a bit of cash. The man had been an actual assassin. He'd known about Monika, and that her father was from the South. That meant that whoever was behind this knew an awful lot that other people didn't. It wasn't common knowledge who her father was.

At least, it hadn't been.

She supposed that after their latest visit to the Eternal City, people might have started to gossip about seeing her and Drake together. That could explain how someone might know, but it didn't explain why they might care. It wasn't as if the children of the Royal family could marry each other.

Two police cars squealed to a stop in front of her. The police officers that piled out of the vehicles looked confused. One ducked back into the car to call an ambulance. The other officers drew their guns and approached the dead man carefully.

"We had a report of a woman being attacked by a man with a knife," one of the officers said.

"Yeah, that would be me," Brygida said. "I'm Dr. Hakubi, a professor here. The man's knife is under the edge of the car next to him, where it fell."

"You're bleeding."

"That happens when a man with a knife attacks you."

One of the officers knelt next to the man and felt for a pulse. "He's dead!"

"I was motivated to fight back after he knifed me," Brygida said.

"You should know that anything you say to us could be used against you in a court of law," a woman officer said to her.

The woman was thinking very clearly that Brygida needed to speak up to defend herself.

"I was afraid for my life when he attacked me," Brygida said. "He cut me before I was even able to fight back."

"Do you have any identification?" an officer asked. He sounded angry, or maybe scared. She couldn't tell.

"I have my university ID here around my neck," Brygida said. "My driver's license is in my briefcase."

The officer dug Brygida's wallet out of her briefcase and looked at her license. "You know kung-fu or something?"

"I can assure you that I do not," Brygida said.

"So you killed this guy with your bare hands and you claim not to know kung-fu?"

"Not everyone Asian knows a martial art. As for me killing him, I was *very* motivated, after he sliced my face," Brygida replied.

"Did you know the attacker?"

"I've never seen him before."

"Do you have any idea why he might have attacked you?"

"Because I am a small woman walking alone at night? How would I know? I think I would like to see a doctor, by the way."

The woman officer helped her sit down. "An ambulance is on the way."

The cut on her face burned. I felt as if someone had run a hot iron down her face. She'd caught a glimpse of her face in the window as she sat. She'd looked terrible. The blood on her face made her look even paler. The injury looked far worse than it most likely was. Although the blood was still dripping from her chin.

The woman officer retrieved her license and wallet, and brought them along with her bag over to Brygida. "If there is anyone you'd like to call, now would be a good time. By the way, I'm Officer Holloway."

"Nice to meet you. Where will you be taking me?"

"University Hospital first, and then to our station. We'll try to get the paperwork done as fast as we can and then you'll need to stand before a judge and say what happened. With something like this it shouldn't take long, then you'll be free to go."

"I would think that the security cameras would have seen something," Brygida said.

"We'll pull the tapes, but I doubt we'll need them."

Brygida pulled her phone out of her briefcase. She hesitated for a moment and then called Geoffrey. He answered on the third ring.

"Hey, Brygida, what's up?"

"I may need some help," Brygida said. "I'm getting ready to be taken to the hospital. Could you and Jason come meet me there?"

"Which hospital?"

"University. I'll be in the emergency room."

"We'll get there as fast as we can."

"Thank you."

"Family?" Holloway asked.

Brygida shook her head. "I don't have any family here. There are old friends."

"I'll let the front desk know when we get there, so they can send them back."

"Thank you."

CHAPTER EIGHTEEN

Maelindefel, one of his captains, greeted Drake as he approached the citadel.

"Is it time to move out, general?" she asked.

"Not quite yet, captain. How long would it take to mobilize the forces here?"

Drake followed her as she walked the road around the citadel to the encampment.

"The troops are outfitted and ready, general. We've been on alert since you left. We could mobilize in no more than a day, if you wish to take the camp with them. If it is to be a march directly to battle, I could have them ready in a few hours."

"Very good, captain," Drake said. "Are the other captains as ready?"

"Of course. We stand ready to serve."

Maelindefel was Drake's first division commander, a coveted position she had earned with her ruthlessness and fearlessness in battle. She was also a tactical genius, rivaling even Drake's skill at reacting to the changing tides of war.

His other captains were waiting in the command tent for him. News of his arrival had traveled fast. Some of the horses outside the tent looked hard ridden. Drake smiled as he saw his officers. He trusted them all with his life and more.

"Will we be joining the assault against the Eye, general?" asked Aubriella Scylla. She was a fairly new commander in his army, but she had moved through the ranks quickly. She was as skilled with a spell as she was with a sword. She was the only Omphalos sorcerer on his staff, and she was very good.

"Eventually, captain. First we'll be taking care of something more local. There has been an assassination attempt against my daughter Xia. I suspect there have attempts against others, as well. At least one of the assassins was a shapeshifter who wore my form."

Scylla hissed. "If this person was from one the rival Houses, that means war in the Courts."

"I'm well aware," said Drake. He accepted a glass of purple wine from one of his other officers, a beastman. "However, the shapeshifter wasn't from the Courts."

"That's rare," she said. "Still, I don't like the idea of an imposter wearing your form."

Drake smiled. "I don't, either, but that's the reason we have strict scanning protocols when someone enters this Realm."

"Are you worried one of these assassins will attempt to start a war with the North?" Maelindefel asked perceptively.

"I certainly am. It may be the biggest risk. My daughter, of course, dispatched her attacker with her usual alacrity and skill. She tore an image from her attacker's mind of a tower shrouded in darkness, and someone who bore a close semblance to my brother. I've had other indications that my brother is actively plotting and moving against us."

Drake had no secrets from his officers. They all knew that his brother had entered the Eye and been subverted by the Ancient Enemy. They were rightfully concerned about the strength of such a person moving against them, but it was something Drake had often discussed with them.

"Do you know the location of this tower?" asked Scylla.

"If I did, you'd have already gotten your mobilization orders," Drake said wryly.

"Of course."

"I am actively acquiring information," said Drake. "If I ever get my hands on one of these assassins, then we'll have our answers. Until then, remain ready. We may not have much time. I'd like to pin down the enemy forces and take that tower."

His officers all nodded.

A clatter of hooves and a shout outside the tent caught their attention. A moment later, there was a challenge and response from the guards. A guard ducked into the tent with a salute.

"A messenger has come through the Waypoint from the Courts, general."

"Allow the messenger to enter," Drake said.

He didn't recognize the messenger, but she was wearing the livery of the House of Torenvey. She was breathing hard; she'd obviously traveled quickly. She saluted Drake when she met his eyes.

Drake smiled reassuringly at her.

"Prince Drake, Your Highness, I'm glad you're here. Duchess Eliza of Torenvey sends greetings. She wants you to know that there have been attacks in the Courts. Several sons and daughters of the royal and noble families have been slain. Many of the assassins were slain; none have been captured. Duchess Eliza wishes to extend an invitation to you to join her at your earliest convenience to discuss these matters and others."

The young woman was still breathing hard and had recited her message in a rush.

"Was there anything else?" asked Drake.

"No, Your Highness," the woman answered. "Do you wish me to take her an answer?"

"No need. I'll travel there immediately and speak to her.

What's your name?"

"Petra, Your Highness."

"I shall give a good report of you, Petra. For now, though, rest in the encampment and regain your strength for the return trip. I dare say you can travel with less haste on your return. Guards, find our messenger some food and lodging for the night. Tend to her horse."

"Right away, general!"

Maelindefel waited for the woman to leave with the guard. "It seems your concerns were well founded, general."

"Indeed, although it does little to change our current plans. Keep the troops ready to move out for battle. We'll assault this tower as soon as I learn where it is."

"And the war in the Eye?" Scylla asked.

"Still in the cards, I'm afraid," Drake said. "I would prefer to wait until the situation with the tower and my brother is resolved. I don't want to be surprised by a force entering the Eye behind us."

Maelindefel shuddered. "An assault from the rear, cutting off our only line of retreat? No, thank you. Do you have any idea about the kinds of forces that may be arrayed against us?"

"None whatsoever at the moment," said Drake. "However, I would expect an army of mostly mortal beings, unlike what faces us in the Eye. I doubt there would be many of the Ancient Enemy present."

"Well, that is something, at least," Maelindefel said.

"Any sorcerers?" asked Scylla.

Drake shrugged. "It's possible. My brother is an unknown factor here. Many of the Ancient Enemy seem to have access to something that gives them abilities similar to that of the Omphalos. However, I don't think it *is* the Omphalos. With my brother, rule nothing out. If you find yourself facing him on the battlefield, back off and wait for me to assist. Don't try to fight him on your own. He is at least as deadly as I am. The only good news is that he won't have a sword like Maegril."

His officers nodded. A few looked relieved. They all knew the capabilities of that ancient relic blade.

"Will you be staying the night, general?" asked Maelindefel. "I believe it would boost morale for the troops to see you."

"I will walk around and talk with them," Drake said, "but I should leave before nightfall, for I should make haste to House Torenvey and learn what Eliza has to say."

"May I offer a toast before you leave?" Aubriella Scylla asked.

Drake nodded and glasses of wine were passed around.

Aubriella Scylla raised her glass. "To victory. To death. To the destruction of our enemies, those ancient horrors. To the salvation of our people. To the emperor!"

"Long live the emperor!" everyone answered.

Drake drank the rest of his wine and left the tent.

The troops were in good spirits, well fed and well trained. Drake walked among them, easy in their presence. They were good troops. The men and woman of his Special Forces were quite simply the best of the Courts. No general could ask for better.

As Drake walked, he stopped by their campfires and joked with them. Tried the food they were having. Shared drinks with them. There were too many for Drake to visit with all of them personally, but word traveled around the camp that the general was spending time with them. They were pleased; for some reason unknown to Drake, the troops trusted him. They knew as well as he did that at least one in five of them would die in the coming battles. Most of them were veterans of his other wars. These troops had fought against invading armies and also against the horrors of the Ancient Enemy.

Drake was proud to be their commander.

Away from the encampment, under the citadel, the mines, foundries, and smithies were still hard at work. The mines produced a rare ore resistant to the effect of the Ancient Enemy's dark fire. The foundries turned that ore into a light, strong alloy. The smithies turned that alloy into armor and weapons for his troops.

Drake toured the smithies, stopping to check the quality of the arms. He knew all would be exemplary, as his captains all personally checked the quality daily. The artisans were pleased to see him, though, and eager to demonstrate their skill.

Drake took his leave and walked slowly to the Waypoint.

He had much to think about. He was concerned for Eliza, and for the news she evidently felt was urgent enough to send a messenger. He knew his granddaughter; she wasn't one to fall prey to panic. He also had a foreboding that she wanted to speak to him about more than just these assassinations.

Drake shook his head. There was only one way to find out. The guards at the Waypoint saluted. Drake greeted them. He took one last look around. He didn't want to leave. Nandegurth was his home, his safe haven. However, he was not one to shirk his duty.

CHAPTER NINETEEN

Jason went outside and started his truck while Geoffrey changed clothes.

He backed the truck out of the garage and used the remote to close the door. Jason wished he knew that Brygida was okay. All he'd gotten was that Brygida was headed for the hospital and had called and asked if they could come meet her there.

Geoffrey came running out of the house.

"Did you lock the door?" Jason called.

Geoffrey cursed, ran back, and did that.

"Which hospital is she at?" asked Jason.

"University. The emergency room," Geoffrey said, fumbling with his seat belt.

"At least we're close. Any idea what happened? Was she in a car wreck?"

"I don't think it was anything so mundane."

"You're worried someone tried to kill her?"

"Aren't you?"

Jason sighed and drove as quickly as he dared. It wasn't far from College Hill to the hospital, but it was a Friday night in Cincinnati. The traffic was bumper-to-bumper on Clifton

Avenue. The side streets weren't much better.

It took almost half an hour to drive the six miles. Geoffrey was clenching and unclenching his fists the whole way. Jason wasn't doing much better, his knuckles white on the steering wheel as he pulled into the parking structure. They had to drive to the top to find a place to park.

Geoffrey took the stairs instead of waiting for the elevator, and Jason reluctantly followed him. There was a lot of bare steel in that stairwell, from the angles on each step to the bare metal handrail. Jason would be in bad shape if he fell in a place like this.

They took the sky bridge across the road to the medical center. The emergency room was on the floor below: more stairs. The receptionist wasn't very helpful or knowledgeable. Geoffrey tried several times to get her to understand and finally had to spell Brygida's full name before the woman helped them.

"Oh, the woman with the police. Yeah, hold on."

The receptionist called someone, and Geoffrey and Jason waited against the wall – the seats were all full. A few minutes later, a nurse in scrubs came out and looked around. She spoke to the receptionist and then walked over to them.

"You're with Hakubi?" She looked over them curiously.

"We're friends of hers," said Geoffrey. "She called us and asked us to come. Is she okay?"

"The police cleared you," the nurse said. "Come with me."

She led them through the crowd to a door with a keypad entry. The interior of the emergency room was bedlam. Doctors and nurses rushed back and forth. People screamed and sobbed behind thin cloth curtains. Drops and streaks of blood dried on the floor and ceiling. Some of the lights were old and flickered.

Overall, the emergency room looked and felt like something from a horror movie.

The special exam rooms were in the back, and the nurse led Jason and Geoffrey there. She knocked and then opened the door without waiting. A curtain surrounded the bed. A woman police officer stepped out and greeted them.

"I'm Officer Holloway," the officer said. She had her hand on her pistol. "Who are you?"

"Geoffrey Meeks."

"Jason Grey.

"Sounds like them," Brygida said from behind the curtain.

Officer Holloway nodded. "Okay, go on in. Dr. Hakubi, I'll be right outside the door. Call if you need me."

"I'll be safe with them. Thank you."

Jason glanced at Geoffrey and then stepped past the curtain.

Brygida was sitting up in the bed. Her skin was pale, and her eyes looked bruised, but what caught his attention were the large slash on her face and the blood. There was *a lot* of blood on her face and clothes.

"Oh, my god, Brygida, what happened?" Geoffrey asked.

"Someone jumped me in the parking lot after school. We can talk about the details later."

"Looks like a clean cut," said Jason. "It should heal without much of a scar."

"Thanks, although I wasn't really worried about that. You know I'm not particularly vain."

A different nurse came in pushing a cart. "We need to get that cleaned up," she said. "Also, I'll need to you guys to leave. I need to check for other injuries."

"It's just the cut," said Brygida.

"In assault cases like this, we have to be certain," the nurse said. "Women often don't want to talk about it, but we can help."

"Oh, for—" Brygida muttered something in Thari. "Jason, Geoffrey, do you mind stepping out for a couple of minutes? Just outside the curtain is fine."

They did. The police officer was there, too. She nodded to them. Jason could hear Brygida undressing behind the curtain.

After a few minutes, she called that they could come back in.

Brygida was sitting in the bed with one of those hospital gowns over her. The nurse was washing out her wound with an iodine solution while Brygida sat stoically. The cut oozed a bit but wasn't bleeding badly anymore.

"The doctor will be here in a few minutes to examine you. She may order x-rays, too. The weapon may have hit the bone."

"It did," Brygida said. "The knife cut two millimeters deep through the zygomatic process and deeper, almost four millimeters, through the mental foramen of my mandible. However, the knife was very sharp and didn't chip anything. I believe it missed the nerve."

The nurse gave her an odd look. "I'll let the doctor know."

"Do, please," said Brygida. "I'd like to get out of this place as soon as may be."

Jason thought Brygida looked very small and young sitting in the large examination bed. She was obviously tired and in pain. There were bags of intravenous fluid hanging nearby, unused.

"I'm surprised they didn't hook you up," Jason said, gesturing.

"I refused. I didn't lose *that* much blood."

"Your attacker didn't..." Geoffrey stopped.

"No, I wasn't raped," said Brygida. "I don't think he had that in mind, although we didn't have a conversation."

"Did he get away?" Jason asked.

"He did not, hence the police escort. I'll still have to make a statement and go before a judge tonight."

"You got attacked, and they're treating you like the bad guy? That isn't right!" Geoffrey exclaimed.

The police officer stepped though the curtain. "You don't see any handcuffs, do you?" she asked. "We're treating Dr. Hakubi as if she killed someone, which she did. The judge will make a determination of whether it was self-defense or not. I'm here to provide protection."

"And to make sure I don't run away to Mexico," said Brygida.

"That, too." Officer Holloway smiled. "The nurse said there was no sign of additional assault."

"The encounter didn't last very long," said Brygida.

"What can we do for you, Brygida?" Jason asked.

"Moral support. Officer Holloway here is friendly enough, but I wanted someone around I know. I hope we can get all of this cleared up quickly, but if we cannot, then I'll need you guys to go over to my house and feed my cat. Tadeo always waits for me by the window; she'll be worried."

There was a perfunctory rap on the door, and a sturdy, dark-skinned woman came in and yanked back the curtain. A few tiny drops of blood were spattered on her white lab coat, and she carried a clipboard in her hand.

"I'm Dr. Collins," she said. She shook Brygida's hand and then pulled on rubber gloves. "You've got quite the fan club in here. Let me take a look at that cut."

Jason looked away.

"Looks pretty deep, but the wound is holding closed nicely," the doctor said. "I think we can just butterfly it. No stitches means it will heal with less of a scar. You'll have to be careful with it. No taking a shower or making weird faces."

"My students will be sad to hear that," said Brygida.

"You're a teacher?"

"Professor," Brygida corrected. "I teach physics here at the University of Cincinnati."

"Well, professor, I think you're going to be okay. Even if the knife did nick the bones, I don't feel any chips. You might have an indentation there, though, after it heals."

"I can live with that."

"The nurse said you didn't have any other trauma."

"That's right."

"Well, we're going to give you some literature anyway. It includes a hotline. Any kind of assault can be traumatizing. Don't be afraid to ask for help, okay?"

"I think I'll be fine, really."

The doctor glanced at the police officer. "Did you get the scumbag that did this?"

"She did, actually."

The doctor glanced back at Brygida as she opened a package of Steri-Strips. "Good for you."

"Thanks," Brygida said. "I wish that none of this hadn't happened, of course, but at least it shouldn't happen again."

The doctor applied the adhesive strips liberally along the line of the cut. "Do you need anything for the pain?"

"No, thank you. I still need to face a judge. I'd like to be clear headed."

"Hasn't she been through enough?" Dr. Collins demanded of the officer.

"I don't make the laws," said Holloway.

Dr. Collins sighed and shook her head. "I'm going to write you a prescription for antibiotics and a few days' worth of pain meds. If you have any trouble with the wound, infection, redness or swelling, you come back in here. Ask for me. We'll get you taken of."

"I appreciate that, doctor."

"The nurse will be by in a few minutes with your discharge paperwork." Dr. Collins left the room.

"We'll head from here over to the police station," Holloway said. "You guys can meet us there if you want, but you'll have to wait in the lobby."

"Brygida, what would you like us to do?"

"I'd like for you two to be with me when I go to court. I've never done that before."

"We'll be waiting at the station, then," Jason said.

⊙

Sitting in a police station in Cincinnati was not how Geoffrey had wanted to spend his Friday night. He'd been planning on going out with Jen, but Brygida's call changed that. He'd called Jen as he was changing clothes. She understood and asked him to keep her in the loop.

He texted Jen from the police station to let her know Brygida was going to be okay.

The District 5 Police Station was loud and filled with angry people. The police all seemed angry to be here, and the assorted drug users, drunk and belligerent college students, prostitutes, and petty criminals certainly weren't happy to be here, either. Geoffrey just sat with Jason and tried not to be noticed.

After about three hours, Officer Holloway came out and looked around. She waved to them, and then led them back into the inner offices of the station. To Geoffrey, it seemed as if everyone here was glaring at them.

Brygida, dressed in her bloody suit, sat next to a desk. She gave Geoffrey and Jason a small smile and stood up when she saw them. She looked tired and worn down.

"They're letting me go for tonight," she said. "I have to go before a judge on Monday morning. I could use a ride back over to my Jeep."

"You got it," said Jason.

"Officer Holloway? Thank you for your kindness," Brygida said.

"You've got my card. Call me if you need anything. I'll see you Monday morning."

"Thank you."

Geoffrey took Brygida's briefcase, and Holloway escorted them out of the building. She waved to Brygida as they left. Geoffrey had never met a nice police officer before. He'd assumed they had to exist, but his experiences with the police had been less cordial.

"We're parked around the side," said Jason.

They piled into Jason's truck. It was big enough, and Brygida small enough, that they weren't crowded. As Jason drove to the university parking garage, Geoffrey couldn't help but glance at the cut on Brygida's face. It looked like it hurt. Brygida kept her eyes closed.

There was blood on the ground outside her Jeep. Her blood, Geoffrey realized. Faces bled a lot. There was no other sign that anything had happened, unless the crumbling concrete pillar was related. There was some blood there, too. Geoffrey could imagine Brygida throwing someone against it.

Brygida fumbled with her keys when she got out.

"Why don't you let me drive?" Geoffrey asked.

"That would be great, thanks."

"I'll follow you guys over," said Jason.

"Would you like me to stop at the all-night pharmacy?" said Geoffrey. "We can get your prescription for the pain."

"That would be lovely."

"I'll grab us some food," Jason said. "Meet you guys at the house."

He pulled away, and Geoffrey helped Brygida into the Jeep. He'd never thought she seemed frail, but she did now. She was normally so energetic; now she seemed half-asleep.

"We'll get you taken care of," said Geoffrey.

"Thank you. It means a lot to me that you guys came."

"You're our friend, Brygida. We'd do anything for you."

Geoffrey glanced over when she didn't reply. She was sleeping, her head lolling. She looked very young and vulnerable, and Geoffrey could suddenly see what Jason did. She really was quite pretty.

He carefully backed out of the parking spot and drove to the pharmacy. The sooner Brygida got something for the pain, the better. Geoffrey was glad to be able to help.

CHAPTER TWENTY

The merchant ship stopped briefly at Masir and then continued on to Rhyddid.

There were other passengers aboard besides Jon and Aradhana. Hauling passengers was a common way for a merchant pilot to make some credits on the side. Jon had often ferried people to earn a few extra credits.

Jon flinched and gripped the sides of his seat when the ship entered the atmosphere. The pilot hadn't made an optimal approach for the landing. Jon wasn't the one flying, so he had to just put up with it. He didn't have to like it, though.

Customs was easy, since they had very little baggage.

Immigration was another matter.

"Mr. and Mrs. Owens, please come in and have a seat." The immigrations officer was a tall man, although shorter than either Jon or Aradhana. "I'm Mr. Jones. I'll be working with you as you immigrate."

"Thank you, Mr. Jones." Jon sat in the offered chair. "I trust our paperwork was all in order."

"For the most part," Jones said. He went around the desk and sat. "Your paperwork said you're of Welsh ancestry." He glanced dubiously at Aradhana.

"I am," said Jon. It was true, after all. "Is there a problem with that?"

"Not at all, Mr. Owens. We're open to all immigrants. I'm uncertain what you plan to do for a living here. Your listed profession is ex-pilot. Your wife's is ex-military. Were you planning on working?"

"Not really. My uncle left me a considerable sum of money as an inheritance. I'd heard of Rhyddid as a haven for the Welsh. I've always wanted to retire here."

He noticed that Mr. Jones showed considerable interest when Jon mentioned the inheritance. He'd thought the man might. One common problem with any bureaucracy was corruption. In a bureaucracy in a government in flux, that could always be counted on, either as a problem or as an opportunity.

"While our government welcomes all immigrants, there has been trouble in the past with processing paperwork for non-Welsh wishing to immigrate." Jones made it sound as if, had it been up to him, the world wouldn't work that way, but it was out of his hands.

"I'm sure it's just a matter of paying the right processing fees," said Jon, following his intuition. "To the right person, of course."

"I'm afraid that even the standard processing fee of five hundred credits wouldn't really speed things up that much," Jones said.

"Surely there's an expedited processing available," Jon said. "Perhaps twice the standard fee?" He'd intended to offer much more than that, but his precognitive sense suggested that would send up red flags.

"We'd be able to process your papers today," Mr. Jones said.

Jon shook the man's hand and transferred the credits.

"Welcome to Rhyddid."

Jones was true to his word: Jon and Aradhana had their

papers within the hour.

Most of the fighting in the revolutions had been outside New Cardiff, but Jon could see signs of battle in the city. Many shops were boarded up, and there were burned out buildings on most blocks. Walls had energy weapon pockmarks that had never been repaired.

It was a bit disheartening.

The city had been a jewel before the revolutions. The old palace was still standing on the hill overlooking the harbor; it was the seat of the new government now. Jon wondered idly if anyone had ever found his boyhood stash of art nudes behind the vent in his room.

He'd forgotten it himself when he became old enough to discover the joys of women. Being a prince had some benefits. A part of him missed his old life, and a part of him was happy it was all over. He'd been the only royal family member to survive the purges.

"The city is much larger than I'd imagined," said Aradhana.

"Rhyddid was prosperous, once."

She squeezed his arm. "Come on, let's find lunch and then a place to live. We'll need a base of operations."

Jon nodded. Aradhana was more practical than he was.

They settled on a restaurant overlooking the bay. Jon remembered the place from when he was younger. It had been a favorite with the university crowd.

Jon knew what he wanted, but Aradhana seemed to enjoy looking through the menu.

"I wish I knew what this stuff is. The definitions under each item don't really say much. I mean, what are rarebit or faggots and peas? All it says is *meatballs* on the second one. Is it any good?"

Jon shrugged. "Sort of a working-class meal: meatballs, peas, and chips."

"Chips are sliced potatoes?"

"Sliced and fried, yes."

"I think I might try it."

"The meatballs are usually made from pig's heart, liver, and bacon."

"Ugh! Maybe you should order for both of us. Just don't tell me what it is."

Jon smiled.

The server came over with cups of tea. Jon recognized her. He'd gone to school with her years before. He hoped she didn't recognize him. Maybe coming to this place hadn't been a good idea.

"What can I get you?" she asked.

"*Prynhawn da*," Jon said. *Good afternoon.* "We'd like an order of rarebit, *selsig morgannwg*, and two orders of scouse."

"*Prynhawn da*," the woman replied. "You local? I don't think I've seen you around before."

"My wife and I just immigrated from New Wales on Earth."

"Oh, okay. Didn't recognize your accent, thought I might be losing my mind. Earth, huh? Wow. To come here?"

"Had an uncle from here. Dylan Owen. He'd been dead a long time before the news got to me. Still, he'd told me stories about this world."

"Well, welcome to Rhyddid. Sorry about your uncle. I'll get your order to the cook."

"Thanks."

Aradhana waited for the woman to leave. "Everything okay?"

"Hope so," Jon said. "I went to school with her."

"Shit!"

"Well, I looked different then. Here's hoping."

"Yeah. Okay, so what did you order?"

"I thought you didn't want to know."

"Not knowing is worse."

"Rarebit is grilled toast with cheese sauce. *Selsig morgannwg* is a kind of vegetarian sausage made from bread, onions, and cheese. Scouse is stewed beef with peas and carrots."

"Wow, that sounds like actual food."

"I hope you like it."

Jon was still a worried. He'd noticed the server talking to a man in one of the booths. They'd glanced over in his direction. Maybe it was nothing. Maybe.

Their food arrived about ten minutes later. Jon just took a moment to breathe in the glorious smell of it all. It had been too long since he'd had good Welsh food.

"Wow! This is really good," said Aradhana after trying the rarebit. "What's in the cheese?"

Jon took the other slice and bit into it. "Heaven, that's what."

"I'm serious."

"So was I," Jon said with a laugh. "The cheese traditionally contains ale and fermented tamarind sauce."

"Your people used tamarind?"

"Back on old Earth, the English conquered many nations, including Wales and India," Jon said. "Legend has it that a Welshman tasted tamarind sauce when in India and loved it so much, he tried to take it back home to Wales. The sauce fermented on the way. He ate it anyway and liked the flavor."

Aradhana laughed. "Why is it called rarebit?"

"Sometimes called *Welsh rabbit*, because we were too poor as a country for meat."

"Well, I like it."

Jon noticed the man their server had been talking to exit the restaurant as Aradhana finished eating. The man tried to be discreet, but he watched them as he left. Jon had a bad feeling about that.

"You think we might have a problem?" asked Aradhana.

"Maybe. I think if I'd actually been recognized, the police or military would have swept in already. Maybe they just think we're an easy mark. That we have money."

"We do have money, but I don't want to lose it on our first day."

"We won't. Fight, but don't kill unless you absolutely have to. If things get dicey, I'll apport us to safety."

Jon settled up the bill and left the sever a modest tip – she hadn't exactly been attentive. She made no sign of having recognized him, so he hoped he was just being paranoid. The last thing they needed was to be on the run from day one.

The sun was setting on the west side of the bay, tinting the water like blood. Jon sincerely hoped it wasn't some kind of omen. His homeworld had known too much bloodshed in the last decade. It needed peace, and time to recover.

"We've got a tail," Aradhana said quietly.

Jon cursed. "Just the one guy?" he asked.

"So far. Not the guy from the restaurant, either."

"Okay, then we watch out for him, too."

Jon headed down to the wharfs, sticking to main streets. Their tail stayed with them.

"He doesn't seem concerned about being noticed, the arrogant git," said Aradhana.

"We're probably going right where he wants us to."

"He can't be military or government."

"No. If he was, we'd have been arrested already. Why wait?"

It wasn't long before the man following them was joined by another, and then they saw two more closing in from the front. Jon couldn't quite read their intentions. There was danger, but they weren't triggering his precognitive sense.

"Maybe we should make a stand here," said Aradhana.

"Okay."

The two men behind them continued to close and then walked on past them.

"Pier five, if you want to talk," one of them said as he passed.

"What? I'm confused," said Aradhana.

"Let's walk down to pier five and get some answers," Jon said.

Three men and two women were waiting for them at the end of the pier. One of the men was the guy from the restaurant. Jon didn't recognize any of the others.

"You seem as if you really want to talk," Jon said. "Who's going first?"

"We want you to know that we support you. Your disguise is good. If Lily hadn't known you from school, I don't think she would have recognized you."

"Support me?"

"We're still loyal to Crown," the man said. "You're the last living heir to the throne. We want what you want."

I doubt that, Jon thought. "I just want to see an end to the bloodshed."

The man nodded. "We do, too! Restoring the monarchy would do that."

"I'm not so sure." Jon held up his hand to forestall the protests. "How about we work together and see what we can come up with. We all want peace, right?"

"Right," the man said cautiously.

"Okay, take me to your leader."

"You've wanted to say that to someone for a long time, haven't you?" Aradhana whispered.

"*Shh*. You'll ruin the moment."

CHAPTER TWENTY-ONE

With a focus of will, Drake stepped though the Waypoint on Nandegurth and stepped out on T'era-grata, the legendary ancestral home of the Drake Family. The planet called the Fire Gate was shattered worse than most of the worlds of the Ruined Courts; many ancient wars had been fought here.

This time of year, the Great Eye dominated half the sky. The Walls of Matter shone faintly, a ribbon of light against that terrible darkness. Hundreds of thousands of broken worlds stood between T'era-grata and the Eye, including the one Drake was headed toward.

The ancient ring of metal that marked the Waypoint shimmered as he laid his will upon it and shifted the destination. He stepped though, and out again upon a world trillions of kilometers from where he'd been moments before. The Waypoint system was what had started Drake thinking about the ancient science the Ruined Courts had lost. He'd spent thousands of years researching the forgotten history of his people. There was little left of that history.

The House of Torenvey was smaller than the House of Drake, ruling over maybe a dozen shattered worlds and only a few hundred million people. Of all of the Noble Houses of the Ruined Courts, Torenvey was the one most closely allied to the House of Drake. His granddaughter had ruled this House for a thousand years.

"Prince Drake!" The guards bowed as he stepped though the Waypoint. Drake was mildly surprised that the guard recognized him. His daemonform was better known in the Courts than his trueform.

"I am here to see Duchess Eliza. Please inform her of my arrival."

"At once!" The guard bowed again and called over another guard to send the message.

Suddenly, Eliza was there, in the doorway to the château.

His granddaughter was not a large woman, physically, but she tended to dominate a space with her presence. Eliza was powerful player in the Machiavellian politics of the Ruined Courts, amassing much power through her spy networks. She was ruthless and cruel in the pursuit of that power, and Drake loved her very much. They often played a game when they exchanged information – not that she'd have withheld vital information from him.

"Grandfather!"

They embraced.

"How is my favorite granddaughter?" asked Drake.

Eliza laughed. "You must want something. Come inside and have some tea."

Drake sat in the seat he favored near the fire, and Eliza handed him a perfectly sweetened cup of black tea flavored with bergamot. She poured a cup for herself and curled up in the chair across from him. He was glad she felt comfortable enough to relax around him; she was often very conscious of manners and grace.

"I received your message," Drake said. "Your messenger, Petra, was very diligent. You had an urgent matter to discuss?"

Eliza sipped her tea before replying. "It is a matter which I suspect you are already deeply involved in an investigation of. There have been assassinations and attempts all across the Great Houses of the Courts."

Drake nodded. "As your messenger said. Also, an attempt was made against Xia recently."

Eliza hissed. "I assume her attacker came to rue that choice?"

"Indeed. Xia was unharmed and her attacker slain by her own hand. There was a problem, however."

"The attacker wore your form," said Eliza.

"And was not from the Courts. I see the pattern plays out even here."

"The emperor was forced to form an inquest into the matter, after an attempt on his own life. I would not show myself in the Imperial Court, were I you."

"Emrys can't believe I would do such a thing, could he?"

"Of course not. He knows that had it been you, the assassination would have succeeded. In addition, several of the assassins have been killed. None were taken alive."

"Have you had trouble, yourself?"

"How delicately you ask! Yes, an attempt was made against me. I blasted the fool into oblivion."

"Can you tell me anything of the attempts the successes?"

"None from Cyryth have been attacked. A few from their allied Noble Houses. The assassins seem to target the children of mixed parentage most often, so Cyryth wouldn't have any anyway. You know how prejudiced they are."

"Why am I reminded of the guild meeting?" asked Drake.

"Loranth, the son of the Duke of Cyryth who called out my granddaughter? He said she was of impure blood, did he not?"

"An interesting bit of data," Drake said. "Xia managed to extract a bit from the mind of her attacker. She saw a man she thought might be my brother."

Eliza made the sign of the Eye, to ward off evil. "I thought he was dead. Do you think he could be behind this?"

"No, I think that was another level of deceit. However, I do think it might be linked to the attempt to kill Jon."

"Jon was the Northerner with you before? The one who bore a striking resemblance to Prince Dominic?"

"Yes. I thought then that someone was trying to start another war."

"Whom would war serve?"

"I'm still not sure. Xia saw a tower, shrouded in darkness. The shapeshifters are not from the Courts. I suspect they may be from a Black Realm, though. I was thinking of asking in the Court of the Broken Prince."

"There are no shapeshifters there."

"No, but the Count has an impressive spy ring, and sources within the Families."

"If anyone would know of shapeshifters outside the Courts, it's them," Eliza agreed.

Drake sighed and finished his tea. "As pleasant as it is to spend time with you, I have many pressing matters. I need to get to the bottom of these attempts and determine why they are using my form."

"Before you go, I have a favor to ask of you," said Eliza.

"And I have one for you," Drake said. "What can I do for you?"

"My granddaughter Gillian was going to school in one of the central Realms. She didn't check in, and I fear the worst. Would you be willing to investigate? I can give the Realm coordinates."

"Of course," Drake said. "Gillian was your blonde granddaughter at the guild meeting?"

"One and the same."

"I will leave at once," Drake said, standing.

Eliza stood, too, but didn't move to hug him. "You said you had a favor to ask, as well."

"It isn't as urgent."

"Still, I would know it, if you would tell me."

"I have another living daughter, with Princess Monika of the Golden Kingdom."

Eliza rocked back on her heels. "That is...*interesting.*"

Drake laughed. "My daughter Brygida is an initiate of the Cynosure, but she wishes to learn the ways of the Omphalos. We have become close in recent weeks. She is intelligent and kind."

"When she is free to do so, send her here to me. She will be my guest, and I will see that she learns all that she wishes."

"Thank you, Eliza."

Eliza projected an image of a place for him. "This is the Realm where Gillian was."

"I will go there immediately."

"Thank you, Grandfather."

Drake gave her a hug. "I'll return as soon as I learn anything."

Eliza nodded and then walked him out to the Waypoint.

Drake had the Waypoint take him to T'era-grata first. From there, he took the long step out to Pilgrim's Rest, in the Dancing Mountains. He half expected to find Erin waiting for him there, but the refuge was empty. He felt slightly sad at that. He'd been traveling with others for a long time now; it felt odd to be alone.

Drake rested for a while, to gather his thoughts.

Whoever was behind the attacks, there was an uncomfortable sense of religious fanaticism. The idea that someone's blood could be impure had its roots in an odd sect of the religion of the Omphalos. Drake had thought the sect had been hunted down and destroyed millennia ago.

He'd been one of the principle hunters.

Could that be why the assassins were wearing his form?

It still didn't explain *how* they were able to. Shapeshifters from outside the Courts would have needed to know what he looked like. How could they? *Why* would they?

The obvious reason was that they wanted to start a war between the North and the South. Who would benefit from that? Drake could think of no one.

Well, excepting the Ancient Enemy, of course. The enemy would benefit greatly. Billions of people would die in such a war. The problem was that the enemy was generally unable to organize that way. Was that a blind spot on his part? *Could* the Ancient Enemy have been organizing? It fit the facts well enough.

Drake stood and stretched until his joints cracked.

He began walking North, shifting the worlds around him as he did.

Gillian had been in a state known as Georgia, on one of the central Realms, attending university there. Drake hadn't spent a lot of time in the southern United States, in any Realm that had such a place; nothing there had ever appealed to him.

He kept the Instrumentality in his mind as he walked the road through the Realms. He took larger steps than Jon had, since he was more accustomed to the confusion that moving quickly could cause. As he walked, he sensed turbulent energies moving just off the road.

Gillian had been going to university in Athens, Georgia, east of Atlanta. Drake left the road and stepped through the Realms to cut across the United States. As the last shift faded into rainbows, Drake phased into devastation.

All the way to the horizon, the land was churned up. There were no standing structures or even trees intact. The wind howled mournfully through the ruins. There was no sign of life.

As Drake climbed over the rubble, he could smell the dead, buried under the detritus. He heard a dog barking in the distance. Farther away were helicopters, but he couldn't see them. He made his way to the dog.

The dog was a German shepherd with a dirty cut on its side and its paws bloody from digging at the rubble. He whined and barked when he saw Drake. He didn't seem feral.

"What's wrong, boy?" Drake called to him.

The dog whined and went back to digging.

Drake didn't think he was after food – there were plenty of bodies exposed nearby. He listened carefully and heard someone sobbing. Someone close by.

"Easy, boy, I'm here. Let me take a look."

Drake caught the dog's collar and pulled him back. He petted the dog until he calmed down and then went to where he'd been digging. The sound of sobbing was louder here. It looked as if a house or two had fallen.

"If you can hear me, hold on!" Drake called.

He carefully began lifting and tossing aside the large slabs of concrete. He was strong, and his armor made him even stronger. Shifting rubble exposed a crack, and bloody fingers pushed up to him imploringly.

"Please, help me," a man begged.

"I am," said Drake. "I have some more rubble to move, but you're almost free. You need to be strong and hold on."

"I heard a dog."

"That's what attracted my attention," Drake said. "Did you have a dog?"

"No," the man said. "I always wanted one."

Drake got his hands into the crack and lifted the slab from over the man. "Can you crawl out?" That slab was heavy, even for him.

"I can try."

The man was about halfway out when the dog grabbed his shirt collar and began pulling. Drake got a knee under the slab, reached down, and pulled the man the rest of the way free. The smell of decay came from the hole, but Drake didn't hear anyone else.

"Anyone else in there?" he asked, just to be sure.

"No one alive," the man said.

The dog started licking the man's face.

"Is this your dog?" the man asked.

"I think he's yours now," Drake replied. "You owe your life to him."

The man laughed. It had a hysterical edge to it. "I always wanted a dog."

"There's some kind of aid station to the north," said Drake. "We should get you there."

"I don't think I can walk," the man said. "I think my leg is broken."

"Then I'll carry you." Drake scooped the man up in a fireman's carry, over his shoulders. He figured that would be easier on the man's broken leg.

The dog barked and wagged his tail.

"Come along, dog," said Drake.

"How far is it?" the man asked.

"About four kilometers." Drake was trying to be careful not to jar the man's leg as he walked across the uneven terrain.

"That's a really long way. Are you sure you can carry me?"

"I think I'll manage."

"My name's Jamil, by the way. Figure I ought introduce myself."

Drake laughed. "I'm Drake," he said. "I can see the aid station. We'll get you fixed up soon."

The aid station was run by the military, and the soldiers seemed surprised to see Drake carrying a man in. Two of them ran over and carefully took Jamil from him. Another man started looking over the dog's injuries.

"Where did you find him?" a woman asked Drake.

Drake turned to look at her, and she handed him a very welcome bottle of water. She had captain's insignia on her uniform, and a Red Cross armband. He guessed she was a doctor or a medic.

"About five kilometers to the south," Drake said. "I heard the dog barking. The dog was trying to dig the man out from under the rubble."

"So you dug him out yourself, and then carried him here?"

Drake nodded. "I'm looking for a friend who was attending university. What happened here?"

"You didn't see it on the news?" She shook her head. "Worse hurricane ever recorded, is what. They're saying it's climate change, but I don't know. I never imagined anything like this."

"It looks like the place was bombed," said Drake. "How far does it extend?"

"The whole southern half of the eastern seaboard is just...*gone*, all the way to the Smokey Mountains. Where have you been?"

"I took a hit on the head. Everything is a bit fuzzy. I need to keep going," Drake said. "Thank you for the water. Do you know where the university was from here?"

"Southeast, about three kilometers. Hey, if you find anyone else alive..."

"I'll get them here."

"Thanks. I don't know who you are or where you came from, but thanks. We'll take any help we can get."

Drake nodded and headed back out into the devastation. He'd keep looking until he found Gillian, dead or alive. If he couldn't find her, he'd check the nearby Realms; she might have used the Instrumentality to walk out of the storm.

CHAPTER TWENTY-TWO

There was a collective gasp from the students as Brygida walked into class Friday afternoon. Brygida was well liked by her students; of course they were concerned for her. Most of them wouldn't have heard what had happened, either.

Geoffrey thought Brygida's cut looked a little better than it had the day before. The area was still bruised, but she was healing quickly. Her eyes weren't sunken pits anymore, and she looked as if she'd finally gotten some sleep.

"Good afternoon," Brygida said. "I trust that, with a few extra days, you all read the chapters on electromagnetism."

A girl in the front row, at the end, raised her hand. "Professor, what happened?"

Brygida sighed. "Would you all not rather discuss electromagnetism?"

"We want to know what happened to you," a guy called from the back of the class.

Brygida sat on the edge of her desk. "I assume you mean the cut on my face."

There were murmurs and nods from the other students.

"I wish I could say it was minor, just a cat scratch. The truth is that I was attacked last Friday night in the parking garage. You should all take heed and travel in small packs for protection. I apologize for having to cancel class on Monday. I was in court. Wednesday, I was in too much pain."

"Someone tried to kill you?" asked Elena.

"I am uncertain as to the motivation of the man in question," Brygida said. "I was attacked. He cut my face as I fought back. I planted my knee in his chest, very hard. He must have had a heart condition, because he was dead by the time the ambulance got there."

Geoffrey knew that she'd actually crushed the man's chest. The district attorney in court Monday had wanted to press charges. He'd said Brygida must have run over the guy with her car, but the nice police officer, Holloway, had shown the parking garage surveillance video.

Brygida had thrown the man over her shoulder and kneed him, once.

It wasn't exactly excessive force.

The judge had ruled it self-defense.

"Wait! You killed a guy by *kneeing* him?" a guy called out.

"I'd rather not continue down this line of conversation," said Brygida. "You all wanted to know what happened. This is what happened. Excuse me."

She walked out of the room.

"Poor Dr. Hakubi," said Elena. "It's hard to take a life. She must be really messed up."

"She's having a hard time of it," Geoffrey agreed. "They played the video in court. I saw what happened. She didn't do anything except try to keep the guy from killing her."

"You were there right afterwards, too, right?"

"My friend Jason and I met her at the hospital, and then went to the police station with her after that. She doesn't have any family here. She was pretty messed up. There was so much blood."

"Maybe I should go check on her." Elena stood up and left.

Geoffrey stood and turned to face the other students. "Hey, everybody. Look, Dr. Hakubi is having a rough time with this, okay? She didn't want to hurt anybody. She's just lived through an assault, where someone cut her. Badly. Can we all just focus on science? I think that would make it a lot easier for her."

Several of the students clapped.

Geoffrey felt embarrassed and sat back down.

"That was well said," Jen said to him.

"Thanks."

Elena came back in with Brygida. Elana sat down, and Brygida took a deep breath and smiled at them. "Sorry about that," she said.

Jen raised her hand.

"Yes, Jen?" Brygida asked. She sounded anxious.

"In the second chapter on electromagnetism, the book talks about flux as a scalar quality. Can you elaborate on what that means?"

Brygida closed her eyes and took a deep breath, obviously relieved. "I'm glad you asked that." Brygida turned and started writing on the blackboard. "Magnetic flux through a plane…"

Geoffrey tuned it out and focused on Jen. He'd read the material. He knew what he needed, and Jen did, too. Jen had asked the question to reinforce what he'd asked their classmates to do; she'd asked the question to help protect Brygida.

After class, as they were walking out, Elena grabbed them and pulled them aside in the hallway.

"Do you think she'd go out with us?" Elena asked.

Geoffrey frowned. "What do you mean?"

"I mean we should take Dr. Hakubi out on the town. Take her dancing. Get her drunk!"

Geoffrey laughed. He couldn't imagine that. "I think she's kind of shy."

"Come on, you know her better than anyone. Didn't she

ever cut loose when you worked together?"

"Not really." Geoffrey suddenly remembered the galley on Hephaestus. "Well, actually there was one time when we spent an evening being silly."

"You're going to make me jealous," said Jen.

"As if," Geoffrey said. "She wouldn't be interested in me if I *did* want anything. She isn't like that."

"Let's ask her!" said Elena. "You can bring your reclusive housemate. We'll all get wild and crazy."

Geoffrey laughed. "You're already crazy if you think Brygida and Jason will go out with us to a club."

"Come on!"

"I guess it can't hurt to ask. She'd probably like the art museum better, to be honest."

"We'll keep that as a backup," said Jen.

"Get in there before she leaves!"

"What? Me?" Geoffrey asked.

"Yes, you!"

Geoffrey glared at them when they didn't follow him into the lecture hall.

Brygida was packing up her briefcase. "Forget something, Geoffrey?"

"No." Geoffrey wasn't sure how to start.

"I wanted to thank you for speaking to the class. It really helped to just get back to teaching," Brygida said. "I really appreciate it."

"No problem. Would you like to hang out with us this weekend?"

"You and Jason?" She glanced toward the door.

"Elena had the idea that you might want to go out, maybe to a club. I thought maybe the art museum or something. We just thought you might like not having to be alone."

Brygida smiled. "That's nice. I'm not sure if it's appropriate, though."

"You hang out with me and Jason."

"So you think adding Jen and Elena to our little circle wouldn't be a bad idea?" Brygida sighed. "Maybe it wouldn't be a bad idea, at that. I've sometimes thought Jason and Elena would make a cute couple."

"You know, I've thought that myself," said Geoffrey. "We're doing this for you, though. Please say yes."

"Elena! Jen! Get in here!" Brygida called out.

There was a startled squeak, and then they came through the doorway. Jen was grinning sheepishly, and Elena looked determined. Geoffrey kept his expression blank.

"Geoffrey here is under the impression that we should all *hang out*," Brygida said sternly.

"Look, professor, we don't mean anything disrespectful by it," said Elena. "We just like you and thought you could use a little cheering up."

"And you agree?" Brygida asked Jen.

Jen nodded.

"Good. I think it would be fun," Brygida said. She laughed at their shocked expressions. "Oh, come on. Geoffrey had already succeeded. I think it was mean to send him alone, though."

"We thought maybe you'd save us the trouble of disposing of his body," Jen said, "if you didn't like the idea."

"Hey!"

The all laughed.

"What would you like to do?" Brygida asked. "Maybe dinner and then go out?"

"That sounds good. What do you like?" Elena asked shyly.

"Just about anything."

"There's that Japanese steakhouse place," Geoffrey suggested.

"It's a bit expensive," said Brygida. "Not everyone has a paid internship with Gerhardt. How about Applebee's?"

"Nice enough, and not too expensive," Elena said. "We can afford that. Crestview Hills?"

"That's the closest one, I think. Geoffrey, you should see if Jason would like to come along," Brygida said. "I don't think he gets out of the house enough."

"He'll come if you ask him," said Geoffrey.

"Then tell him that," Brygida said. "I'll come by and pick you guys up around six thirty. We'll meet at the restaurant at seven. Do you have a car, Elena?"

"I do. Jen can ride with me."

"Excellent. Then I will see all of you in a couple of hours. Now, go."

"You don't want me to stay and walk you to your car?" asked Geoffrey.

"No, thank you. I'll be fine. Gone on now. Go home."

They went.

Geoffrey couldn't believe they'd gotten Brygida to agree to go out. Jen and Elena couldn't, either, and were deep into discussions about what they should do after dinner that evening. Geoffrey gave Jen a hug and a kiss, and left to catch the bus.

All the way home, he thought about what to say to Jason. He decided he wouldn't lie, but he wouldn't tell Jason the whole truth, either. He'd tell him that Brygida wanted to go out to dinner and hang out, to keep her mind off last Friday.

⊙

"She wants to do what?"

Jason been relaxing with a beer and a book in the living room when Geoffrey came home from school. The whole situation with Brygida had left him somewhat shaken. He usually did his best to avoid any attention from the authorities, and he'd actually been sitting in a police station only the week before.

"Go out to *din-ner*," Geoffrey said. "You know, food?"

"I thought Friday was pizza night for you."

"Brygida asked if we would go out with her. How could I say no?"

Jason sighed. Geoffrey had a point. "Okay. I suppose you want me to drive?"

"Brygida said she'd pick us up at six thirty." Geoffrey tossed his bag on the couch. "You might want to get cleaned up. You're all sweaty."

"Can I finish my beer first?"

Geoffrey dropped to the couch with a total disregard for the longevity of the furniture. "Are you naturally a jerk, or did you have to study to be this way?"

"Oh, it's natural," said Jason. He finished his beer and stood up. "Where are we going, anyway?"

"Applebee's."

"Good." He could order a burger there and not have to use the cutlery.

As far as friends went, Brygida didn't ask for much. She was quiet and unassuming, and she'd kept quiet about Jason. That went a long way toward making him willing to help her with just about anything.

Jason took a quick shower and dressed in nicer clothes than he normally wore. He didn't relish going out to a crowded restaurant on a Friday night, but if it helped Brygida to not think about last Friday, he was willing to help. Come to think of it, it would probably keep *his* mind off it, too.

CHAPTER TWENTY-THREE

The guys were waiting outside when Brygida pulled up to the house.

She'd gone home after school and showered, and then played with Tadeo with a laser pointer. She'd wanted to spend some time with the scamp, since the little cat had gotten used to her being home for the last week. Tadeo was growing up quickly.

Brygida had dressed in dark jeans, boots, a white shirt with the sleeves rolled up, and a vest: a pleasantly gender-neutral outfit. She never wore makeup, although she was thinking of getting some concealer to tone down the cut on her face.

Geoffrey and Jason climbed into her Jeep. "Hey, Brygida."

"Hey, guys. I glad you agreed to come, Jason."

"You asked."

"Well, I appreciate it." It had been difficult to walk out to her car alone. She knew nothing was going to happen, but anxiety didn't care about rational arguments. She'd gone alone because she didn't want her friends to see how much it bothered her.

The restaurant was crowded when they arrived. She had

trouble finding a place to park. Geoffrey held the door for them when they entered. Jen and Elena were sitting off to the side; they waved.

"I called ahead and placed a reservation," said Elena. "It shouldn't be long."

"Elena, Jen, this is my housemate, Jason Grey," said Geoffrey.

"Nice to finally meet," Elena said. "Geoffrey has told us all about you."

Brygida had to hold back a laugh at the look on Jason's face. Luckily, the hostess arrived and took them to a booth in the back of the restaurant. Brygida sat on the same side of the table as Jen and Elena, which put Jen across from Geoffrey and Elena across from Jason, in the middle.

A waiter materialized out of the crowd and took drink orders.

"I'm glad you came out with us, Dr. Hakubi," said Elena aid.

"Please, outside of academics you can call me Brygida," she said. "Except for you, Geoffrey."

"What did I do now?"

"He's very sensitive," Jen said.

"Guilty conscience," added Jason.

"So, how did you guys meet?" Elena asked.

"I needed a room to rent when I got accepted to school here," said Geoffrey. "Jason had a house and needed a housemate."

"*Need* is a strong word," Jason said. "Don't think I haven't regretted it at times."

"Jerk."

"Asshole."

"You guys are like brothers," said Elena. "Where are you from, Jason?"

"Here and there. Why?"

Elena smiled and shrugged. Brygida could see that Elena found Jason attractive. For his part, Jason was probably only making her more interested by being mysterious.

"If you don't tell us, we're just going to make something up," said Elena.

"I think he's Columbian," Geoffrey said.

"No, I'm not."

"He's on the run from a drug cartel. Had an affair with drug lord's daughter, or wife, or something," Geoffrey added.

Jason punched him on the arm.

"Okay, the drug lord's son."

Jason punched him harder.

"Ouch!"

"They're always like this," said Brygida.

"Could be love," Jen said.

"Hey!"

They all laughed. Brygida thought Jason's laugh sounded a bit forced. He didn't look happy to be the center of attention. Brygida was happy, though. It kept the attention away from her face and what had happened.

She did hope he wasn't too upset with them. She liked Jason, and knew that he liked her and would have wanted more from her if she'd been interested. She wasn't. It wasn't him; she just didn't desire anything more than friendship.

Jen ordered a club sandwich. Elena, Jen, and Geoffrey ordered burgers. Brygida ordered the blackened salmon and a twelve-ounce steak for herself. She'd been craving more protein recently. She thought it might have something to do with the injury and blood loss. Her face still hurt but was healing far faster than was normal for a human.

Brygida had noticed other changes in her body. It started a few weeks ago while traveling, but the changes seemed to have accelerated after her injury. She was getting curves where she hadn't had any before, and was also getting more muscular. She noticed it in the mirror when she'd showered that morning: her arms and shoulders were looking more toned.

The waiter brought the food, and they all dug in. Jason looked relieved.

The salmon was pure heaven. The steak was nice, although Brygida normally preferred steak that was well done. This one was pink in the middle. She noticed Elena giving her a side eye along with a grin.

"What?"

"We're all trying to figure where someone so tiny puts all that food," said Elena.

"You're, like, a millimeter taller than me."

"That's not the point, is it?"

"*They're* natural," Brygida said. "It's called Stahl's ear. I'm aware it has become a fad in some places to have them pointed with surgery, but I was born with mine. I lucked out, and mine look fairly normal. Some people have other ear shapes that are less esthetically pleasing."

"People give themselves pointed ears with surgery?" Jason asked.

Brygida nodded. "This isn't the Dark Ages any longer. People are having all kinds of body modifications."

"Jason is very conservative," said Geoffrey. "You can tell by how he dresses."

Jason was wearing engineer boots, jeans, button-up shirt, a denim jacket, and his ever-present bandana.

"Asshole."

"Jerk."

The waiter came back and collected the dishes. "Anyone for desert?"

"Why are you all looking at me?" said Brygida. "I'm good."

They laughed.

The waiter dropped off the check and left.

"I've got it," Brygida said.

"Too late," said Geoffrey. "My treat tonight."

Geoffrey settled the bill with the waiter, and then they all went outside.

The evening was still warm and damp. The sky looked as if there might be rain later. The cool breeze was welcome, though.

"So…what would you like to do?" Elena asked Brygida.

"Me?"

"We're here for you," said Geoffrey. "Do you want to go to a club? Dance? Drink? Something else?"

"I've never been that into clubs. Or drinking and dancing. I'm more of a sit at home and watch science fiction kind of woman."

"Geoffrey said you like art. There's an art gallery in Covington having an opening tonight," Jen suggested.

"That would actually be really cool," said Brygida. "I don't want to drag you guys there if you're not interested, though."

"Do you want to go?" Jason asked.

"Yeah, I think that would be great."

"Then that's what we'll do."

"Okay, we'll follow you guys over, then," said Geoffrey. "At least we're already on this side of the river."

☉

Jason wasn't sure exactly what was going on, but something was.

"Okay, Geoffrey, spill it," he as they followed the other car. "What are you up to?"

"Up to? Me?"

"You didn't tell me about your friends. Why?"

"Because we were afraid you wouldn't come out with us if we did," said Brygida. "We didn't want to go out and leave you alone at the house.

"I would have come anyway," Jason said.

"Yeah, but you would have bitched about it more," said Geoffrey.

"I'm not." Jason tried to figure out what to say. "I don't feel comfortable around new people."

"Jen and I are dating," said Geoffrey. "It would be nice if she could come over sometimes."

"I never said she couldn't."

"Not in so many words, but you made it pretty clear when I moved in that I couldn't have anyone over. Why do you think I didn't have anyone over for the two years we've lived together?"

"Did I?" Jason asked. He didn't remember that. "I just thought you didn't have any friends."

Geoffrey sighed. "I've dated three girls while living with you. They all thought it was weird that I wouldn't let them come over. I really like Jen. I don't want to mess it up."

"You could have said something."

"I did," Geoffrey said. "I asked twice. The first time, you pretended not to hear me and just sat there reading. The second time, you told me I could move out if I wasn't happy with the arrangements."

Jason didn't remember that, either. On the other hand, it did sound like something he'd have said. He'd been really unhappy with himself for renting the room to Geoffrey, at first.

"Was that pretty soon after you moved in?"

"Yeah, so I never asked again."

"Look, I'm sorry, okay? I was working through some shit," said Jason. "You want to bring Jen over sometimes, go for it. You don't need to ask. Just let me know, so I can decide if I need to be somewhere else."

"I'm not trying to run you out of your house, man."

"I didn't think you were."

"I'm really glad you guys are working this out," said Brygida.

"Could you do it at home or something? This feels kind of awkward."

"Have we ever determined if Brygida is ticklish?" asked Geoffrey.

"Don't you dare! I'm driving!"

"She's definitely ticklish," Jason said. "I don't advise it, though. She's a lot stronger than you."

"Um, good point." Geoffrey looked out the window. "I've never been to an art gallery opening. What's it like?"

"There's usually wine and cheese," said Jason. "There will be some cool people and a few snobs. It's in Covington, so I can't imagine there will be many uppity types there."

"What do you think of Elena, Jason?" asked Brygida.

"She seemed like a nice enough kid."

"He's hopeless," said Geoffrey.

Brygida nodded.

"What?"

"The young *woman* seemed interested in you," said Brygida.

"What?"

"Hopeless and *clueless*," said Geoffrey.

"You're trying to set us up together?" Jason asked. "I don't even know her."

"Kind of hard to get to know someone if you hide at home all the time," said Geoffrey.

"I don't hide at home all the time."

"Jason, do you trust me?" Brygida asked. She pulled into a parking space next to Elena's car.

Jason nodded. "You know that I do."

"Then trust me on this. Elena is pretty and smart, and she's a great person. Geoffrey is friends with her, and I think I could be, too. Just give it a try, okay?"

Geoffrey got out of the car to talk to Jen.

"You know why I'm hesitant," said Jason.

"I do, but you can't spend your life afraid all the time. That isn't living."

"I don't even know if we're going to hit it off."

"No one does, or so I understand. I'm probably not the best person to give relationship advice, having never dated. You're not like me, though. Just be friends with her. Anything else that happens will just be a bonus."

"You know the other reason why I'm hesitant, right?"

Brygida sighed. "Jason, you know I like you. I'd even go so far as to say I love you, as a friend. I don't feel anything else. Not with you or anyone."

"Well, I just thought it should be said."

"Or not said, in this case. Get out of my car. Talk to the woman who does like you. She's intrigued by you, and she finds you attractive. Go forth, young man."

"You know I'm not either."

"Don't be pedantic. You're not nearly as old as some people we both know, and you're male, even if you aren't human."

Geoffrey knocked on the window. "You guys coming?"

Brygida opened her door. "Go away! Jason's brooding."

Jason laughed. "Fine." He opened his door. "I'm coming. Calm down."

Elena was standing nearby and moved closer to him. She was few inches shorter than him and had lovely grey eyes. She wasn't slender, like Brygida or Jen, but compact like a gymnast.

"I hope you didn't us mind teasing you at dinner," said Elena. "We've gotten used to harassing Geoffrey."

"I'm good," Jason said. "Sorry I'm just a bit shy."

"Me, too," Elena said. "I make up for it by being forthright. They're headed in. Shall we follow?"

"We'll probably get mugged if stay out here."

"There's that upbeat attitude from dinner."

Jason laughed. Elena was okay. He liked Brygida. He probably always would. She'd made him feel something he'd hadn't felt in a long time. He understood that she didn't feel it, though, and that was okay. She didn't owe him anything.

They were friends. That was good enough. Elena seemed nice, if shockingly young to someone his age. On the other hand, the age difference between Drake and Monika was far greater, and they'd made that work, at least for a while.

Elena grabbed Jason's hand and pulled him into the gallery.

CHAPTER TWENTY-FOUR

Drake spent three days in Georgia searching for Gillian.

He rescued many people, but he never found her. He was certain she'd survived. If normal humans could survive that disaster, then the granddaughter of Eliza certainly would.

There was no sign of the Instrumentality having been used in the area. He thought he'd caught a trace of a trail at one point, but then he realized it was his own trail from where he'd entered the Realm. He did find other anomalies, though.

At first, he'd thought it looked as if several houses had fallen on the first man he rescued. He was beginning to think that it wasn't far from the truth. Stepping into the nearby Realms, he found similar devastation. It was as if someone had smashed a dozen worlds together.

In one area, he found the same man dead, three different times.

The only thing he knew that could cause this kind of devastation was a Reality Storm. He'd never seen ones as powerful as this must have been. He remembered that Erin had warned him of storms, there on the road North. He wished he'd thought to ask her more about them, but he hadn't quite trusted her at the time.

Gillian just wasn't to be found.

Drake didn't know where she was or how she'd managed to escape, but she had. Considering the bodies that had been carried by the storm, it was possible she'd been picked up and carried away. If that was the case, she'd show up back in the Courts eventually. She was an initiate of Instrumentality; she could always walk back home.

In any case, assassins weren't going to be able to find her if Drake couldn't.

He began working his way back to the Courts.

He spent the night at Pilgrim's Rest. He hadn't slept in those three days, nor had he eaten much. He still had his old backpack in a pocket space. There wasn't much food left in it, but it was enough to sustain him.

He used the local Waypoint to travel back to the Courts. Eliza was waiting on the steps when he stepped though the Waypoint to Torenvey. She led him inside and ordered a meal for him.

"Gillian isn't dead," Drake said as they waited. He explained what he'd found.

"You're certain? Getting caught in a Reality Storm is no minor matter."

"I'm certain that she wasn't dead in any of the Realms I investigated along the path of the storm. I found humans who'd survived, being relocated. I believe she would have survived, too."

Eliza sighed and settled back into her chair. "Well, then, she'll turn up."

"I'm sure she will."

"There are other matters we should discuss."

A servant laid out a large meal on a folding table and left. Drake waited to see if Eliza wanted to eat; she waved for him to go ahead. Drake ate with great pleasure. Eliza always kept a good chef around.

"You can tell me of these other matters while I eat," said Drake.

"Very well. Assassins have struck in the North. Two younger members of the family were killed: Tomas and Dmitri. An attempt was made against Dasha, but she killed her attacker."

"I am glad Dasha is alive. She and Philomena are friends with my daughter Brygida."

"King Andrzej has demanded your head."

"Of course he has."

"Prince Dominic is in the Imperial Court now."

Drake sighed and finished his meal. "I suppose I should put in an appearance."

"They could have you executed."

"Then I will have had an excellent final meal."

"Don't even joke about it. Losing you would be a disaster."

"I love you, too, Granddaughter."

Eliza shook her head. "You're seriously going to go to Court?"

"I cannot clear my name by hiding," said Drake. "I am now well fed, and rested enough."

He stood and gave Eliza a hug.

"Always the fool," Eliza said. "I wish you luck."

Once outside, Drake willed the Waypoint to take him to the Imperial Plaza.

From the looks people gave him, Drake knew the rumor mill had been working overtime. The guards at the gates of the palace crossed their halberds before him, to block his path. Drake had never been denied entry before.

"What is the meaning of this?" he asked.

"We have orders from His Imperial Majesty himself that you are not to be allowed entry unless in daemonform."

Drake drew upon the Instrumentality and felt the change flow through him. He settled his wings and gestured ahead.

"Good enough?"

"Your Highness!" They bowed out of his way.

Drake shook his head at their stupidity. If the enemy had shapeshifters, surely they could mimic his current form. There were shapeshifters in the Realms, though, who were limited to a humanoid range. If that was the case, it could narrow down who might be behind the assassinations.

He was approached by a tall, blue humanoid with horns, wearing an imperial uniform. The person bowed to Drake. "I am the Majordomo Taliz," the person said. "If Your Highness pleases, I'll escort you directly to the Imperial Audience Chamber."

"Please do." Drake was pleased to see this new majordomo was competent and not obsequious, as the last one had been.

Taliz led Drake to the massive bronze doors. Responding to some cue Drake couldn't perceive, Taliz nodded a count of five, and then opened the doors. A hush fell over the court as Drake entered that chamber.

"Prince Daeren Drake," Taliz announced before closing the doors.

Drake was aware that all eyes were on him as walked to the Fire Throne.

Prince Dominic stood there to one side. Drake was a little surprised to see the Duke of Cyryth had already returned to the court. The emissary from the House of Drake saluted, giving a hand sign that the House forces stood ready to assist. Drake returned the sign to stand down. He had no intentions of starting a civil war.

"Prince Drake! We are pleased you have joined us in these troubling times," said Emrys.

"Your Majesty, I came as soon as I heard there were troubles here. I have been off in the Central Realms, where someone had tried to murder my daughter Xia."

"May we assume Xia was unharmed?"

"She is a Drake, Your Majesty. Disturbed by the encounter, but otherwise unharmed."

Emrys and Drake's daughter Xia had once been a couple. They had parted on good terms and remained friends. Drake had known that the fact of an attempt against Xia would shake Emrys, and it had.

"We have been troubled by reports of someone in your form assassinating young people from the North and the South. What say you?"

"My own daughter almost ran me through when we met," Drake said with a chuckle. "Whoever is behind this certainly wants people to think it's me. Which, no offense, is absurd."

"Why absurd?" asked Dominic.

Drake rapidly shifted into Dominic's form and then into his own trueform. "If I were going to assassinate people, I would succeed, and I wouldn't use my own shape. Not to mention the fact that, were I of the inclination, I'd use it in the settling of a vendetta, not to kill innocent youngsters."

"You make a compelling argument."

"Also, some of the assassins have been slain, have they not? The one who tried to kill Xia was slain. He was wearing my form at the time, too. I can't have been all of them, including the dead ones."

"Are we to believe that your daughter has slain one of these so-called assassins?" the Duke of Cyryth said with a hiss.

"Are we to believe it's a coincidence that Cyryth has lost none of *their* sons and daughters?" Drake replied. "Why is that, I wonder. It certainly isn't due to your fighting prowess."

There were snickers around the chamber at his insult.

The Duke of Cyryth did not respond to the question or to the insult.

"We would prefer to focus on the problems," said Emrys, "not feuds that we can ill afford at the moment."

"Of course, Your Majesty," Drake replied. "Notice that

since the Duke of Cyryth is alive and well, I have not been using this opportunity. Instead, I have been trying to investigate the problem. I have several leads, but I am loath to discuss them openly."

"We understand. Court is dismissed. Prince Drake, Prince Dominic, please stay.

"We came here for answers!" Cyryth grumbled. "This is an outrage!"

"File a complaint and go be outraged someplace else. A proclamation will be issued with what I want you to know."

Emrys waited for the room to clear before he sighed. "I hate all of this pomp and theater."

"We all do," said Dominic. "Drake, I'm sorry to hear about your daughter. I hope she is well."

Drake knew Dominic wanted to ask about Brygida but didn't want to mention her if Emrys didn't know. Drake appreciated that. Of all of their cousins in the North, Drake liked and respected Dominic most. Of course, Drake didn't know many of them all that well.

"Xia is fine. Brygida has not been attacked yet," said Drake. "I hope that she will not be. However, if assassins are now moving in the North, she may not be safe."

"Wait – Brygida is Monika's daughter, isn't she?" said Emrys. "Why would she be attacked?"

"Yes," said Drake. "However, such things usually take two. I am her father."

"Oh, wow. I didn't know that."

"Time to fire your spies," said Dominic.

"Right?"

Drake smiled. "As I mentioned, I have several leads. The shapeshifters may be religious fanatics, and they aren't from the courts. They may only be able to shift to humanoid forms. The mind of one held an image of a tower shrouded in darkness."

"Then Xia was able to get something?" asked Emrys.

"She was. She tore the dying man's mind apart, but she was unable to determine how the assassin had traveled to where she was. The man killed three people trying to get to her."

"Despite what some may think, travel through the Realms is not restricted to our two peoples," Dominic said. "We've had a few problems in the North, with things wandering in recently."

"We always have had such problems, down here," said Drake. "The veils between the worlds are thinner in the South."

"Do you have an idea where to start investigating?" Emrys asked.

"I thought I would begin in the Court of the Broken Prince. I have a few contacts there."

"I'm not familiar with that Realm," said Dominic. "Not by that name, anyway."

"It's one of the Black Realms, on the edge of the plains."

"It isn't the place that rains blood, is it?"

"It is, actually."

Dominic shuddered. "That Realm gave me the creeps, the only time I was there."

"It is not one of the kinder Realms," Drake said. "I find myself curious as to what took you there."

Dominic smiled.

Drake had known he wouldn't answer.

"You didn't recognize the tower?" asked Emrys.

"No. Her image was clear, but there was nothing to identify the Realm."

"You think your contacts in the Court of the Broken Prince will know it?" said Dominic.

"Of that I am unsure," Drake replied. "However, I do think I may gain a lead on the shapeshifters."

"Well, I suppose I had better head back North," Dominic said. "Please keep us apprised of anything you think may help."

"Dominic, did Andrzej really call for my head?" asked

Drake.

"Not exactly. He told me to come down here and discover if you *were* behind the murders. I told him I doubted it. If you were the culprit, then I was to bring him your head. If I were able."

"I am glad you feel my head should stay on my shoulders."

"Likewise, Drake. Likewise. Gentlemen, always a pleasure." Dominic strode out of the room.

"An interesting man, my uncle," said Emrys.

"That, he is," Drake said. "I'm glad we generally see eye to eye, so to speak. I wouldn't want to face him on a battlefield. Emrys, I should take my leave, as well. I want to take a Waypoint out of the influence of the Courts, and then walk back in quietly, to cover my tracks."

"As always, you have my leave. Please give my regards to Xia, if you see her again soon."

"I will, and I will let you know what I discover."

"Thank you, and good luck."

CHAPTER TWENTY-FIVE

Two weeks on Rhyddid hadn't gotten Jon any closer to solving what was wrong here.

It hadn't even gotten him particularly close to figuring out *what* was wrong. The revolutions should have been stable; starting with the one that had killed his family, they'd had always been about stopping excess.

Jon's brother hadn't been a good king, so he understood why people wanted to overthrow the monarchy. The revolution had turned unnecessarily bloody, but they'd been pushed by Alliance operatives.

That government hadn't lasted very long, though.

A protest was met with violence, and suddenly there was a spontaneous uprising. The new leaders executed everyone left alive from the previous government. Then they proceeded to do the same things they'd been protesting about. The same bloody cycle had continued every six months or so, ever since.

It just didn't make sense.

"Not everything people do makes sense," said Aradhana.

"What? Sorry. I didn't realize I was thinking out loud."

"Maybe it would help if you did," she suggested. "Tell me

what bothers you about it."

"Well, it *all* bothers me. All the way back to my family being murdered."

"I meant about the cycles."

"It's improbable," said Jon. "There's no reason there should be a cycle of revolutions every six months. The last government wasn't even that bad – as such things go – and then suddenly there was another revolution. Why?"

"How improbable?"

Jon quickly ran the numbers in his head; compared to jump calculations, social dynamics were rather simple. "Approximately twenty-two million to one, against."

"Then there must be a factor you haven't accounted for in your equations."

"It would have to be something that could alter a trend in probability," Jon frowned as a thought intruded that he couldn't dismiss. "Maybe something that feeds on pain and suffering? Something that doesn't want a stable government here?"

"What are you talking about?"

"Drake spoke of monsters. Aliens that feed on pain and fear. He killed one on Earth."

"I saw the broadcast video clip," said Aradhana. "I've never seen anything else like it."

"Drake also killed the doctor who'd botched the jump pilot program. The doctor was one of those things. Dr. Preta purposely altered the genetic material, and hundreds of us died horribly."

"Dr. Preta *was* human. She was in charge of the program that altered me to be an Alliance special operative."

"She *looked* human," Jon said. "Drake can change his form. The enemy can, too. They're somehow related to the Precursors."

Aradhana shuddered. "That's horrible. How could you fight

that? How could you even know if someone was one of those…
things?"

Jon shrugged. "Drake always knew. Something like that
must leave traces."

"Can you render that abstract enough to add to your
calculations?"

"Maybe."

It didn't quite work that way. Jon's probability calculations
were obscured numbers most of the time. As with flying, he just
knew when he had it right.

How did he reduce to numbers what an Ancient Enemy
could do?

Jon shook his head. "I can't quantify the problem, but I can
see that the probability of revolution increases if there are
unknown factors pushing for chaos. A nation should have a
certain inertia. It should be *difficult* to push people to commit
the kinds of horrors that have happened here."

"So the revolutions are only improbable when looking at
purely human factors?" Aradhana shuddered again. "I honestly
never thought I'd live to see aliens. What about these
monarchists –
are they being driven by this thing, too?"

"I wish I knew the answer to that."

The monarchists were a potential problem.

Jon had met with them twice since the day at the docks.
They seemed peaceful, but he wasn't so sure. They wanted him
as a figurehead, a symbol, a rallying cry. They had a
misbegotten belief that a return the *old days* would magically fix
everything.

People who engaged in such thinking often got angry when
nothing went as they dreamed it would. Jon didn't want to find
himself in the crosshairs when the monarchists realized he had
no intention of taking the crown. Revolutionaries didn't like to
be told no.

It also worried him that they'd figured out his identity.

The very bone structure of his face had been altered during the pilot program. There had been a piloting accident, and they'd had to reconstruct his facial bones. He knew his new face was different enough to fool the recognition programs used by the Alliance. It was virtually impossible that some woman he'd casually known at university had recognized him.

Jon had recognized her because he was good with faces, and she'd looked the same as she had at university. He brought up and compared the memory of her from school and the memory of her serving his and Aradhana's food at the café. It was certainly the same woman. What was bothering him about that?

Her build was the same. The shape of her face, unchanged. Her eyes… Nothing different there, which was odd, since she was fifteen years older than she had been. Her hair was even the same length and cut.

"We need to go out to lunch," Jon said.

Aradhana laughed. "That was sudden. I guess I can't complain. At least you want food."

"Actually, I want to see that woman who served our food the last time."

"I should be jealous, but you have that look. Why do we need to see her?"

The probabilities collapsed. He was certain the woman was the key to his problem. He was usually only this certain when he was about to engage the jump engines on his ship.

"Something about her doesn't add up. She shouldn't have recognized me."

Aradhana nodded and stood up. "What do we do if she isn't working?"

"Wait for her, I guess. Maybe ask around. We'll improvise."

She was working, though. The waitress gestured to a corner booth and came over with menus and cutlery in napkins. Everything about her seemed perfectly normal, but Jon's sense of danger screamed at him to run.

Jon and Aradhana sat in the booth. Jon reached out and gripped Aradhana's hand: physical contact made it easier to bring someone along in an apport. Aradhana met his eyes and nodded. She understood. She'd picked up on his mood.

"What can I get you two?" the waitress asked.

"How about the truth?" said Jon. "You tipped off the monarchists. How did you know to do that?"

"My, aren't we thick," she said. Her voice had grown harsher, her tone mocking. "Took you long enough. This is what, two weeks? How do you ever manage to fly a starship with a mind that slow?"

Jon froze and then smiled. "I didn't expect you to just come out with your true nature."

"Oh, my darling little man. What could you possibly know of my true nature?"

"I know enough."

"I doubt that you do," she said, "or you wouldn't be here taunting me."

"What are you going to do?"

Jon had called up the Cynosure in his mind. He was ready to get Aradhana and himself to safety, but he hated to do it in such a public place. Apporting away would be a clear sign of who he actually was. Then he felt a cloudiness come into his mind. It was hard to think, to remember what he was doing.

"I'm not going to anything," she said, "except sit back and enjoy what's done to you."

The glass along the front of the restaurant exploded, and soldiers in riot gear jumped through the windows. Other patrons screamed. One tried to run and was gunned down. The waitress just stood in the center of the room and laughed. The soldiers never even looked at her.

"Jon!" Aradhana screamed.

That broke through the brain fog, and Jon called upon the

Cynosure and apported Aradhana and himself out of the restaurant. He jumped first to their hotel room, but he knew they wouldn't be safe for long. He could already hear soldiers shouting and stomping up the stairs outside.

"Grab our stuff."

Aradhana tossed him his bag as gunshots rang out in the hall. Jon apported them away, dimly aware of the door bursting open as they left. This time, he'd picked a place from his memory, a place in the forest north of the palace, where he'd hidden as a child. It had always been a place of safety for him.

Jon staggered a bit as they arrived in the woods.

Even using the Cynosure, two rapid apports with an extra person along was exhausting. It took a lot of mental processing to make those jumps, and he hadn't figured out how to use the Cynosure well enough to ease the burden.

Aradhana stepped away and leaned against a tree. "I think I'm going to be sick," she said.

Jon nodded. He felt that way, too, but not from the rapid apports. That *thing* had been in his mind. He'd felt it worming its way in, sapping his will to act. It had almost kept him from apporting away. He could still feel its hunger in his mind, as if it was still hunting for him.

There was a sudden *whoosh* of displaced air, and two people impossibly apported to where Jon and Aradhana had been standing a moment before. Both were tall. The man had a mane of dark green hair, and green eyes that almost glowed. The woman had the same eyes, but her hair was long and white. Both were dressed in normal local fashion.

The woman locked eyes with Jon. "You're not who I expected, but you're in a lot of danger if you stay here."

"What? Who are you? How did you…?"

"Apport? You didn't think you were the only one who could do that, did you?" she asked.

"Lyra, I can't keep us hidden much longer," said green-haired man.

"Whoever you are, you've stirred up the hornet's nest," the woman said. "My name is Lyra Rhys-Griffith; my friend here is Emerald. You need to come with us if you want to live."

☉

Jason was working in his workshop when Geoffrey returned from school and came back to speak with him. That was unusual – Geoffrey usually stayed out of Jason's workshop. Jason preferred it that way, to be honest. He liked having a space that was just his.

"Well, what do you think?" Geoffrey asked as he came in.

"About what?" said Jason. He was working on an intricate caving and really didn't want Geoffrey in here with him, but he also wasn't comfortable asking him to leave.

"Elena."

"What about her?"

"Come on, man. She's my friend, too. It really seemed like you guys hit it off the other night."

Jason shrugged. "She's cute."

"Cute?" Geoffrey sat on the corner of Jason's workbench. "She couldn't stop talking about you today in class."

Jason sighed and put down his fine chisel. "What are you doing?"

"What do you mean?" Geoffrey picked up the piece of wood Jason had been carving.

Jason carefully took the carving away from him and put it in a drawer. "Don't mess with my stuff."

"Don't avoid my question."

"You're avoiding mine!" Jason said, exasperated. "What are you doing?"

"We think you and Elena would make a good couple."

"Who is *we?*" Jason asked.

"Brygida, Jen, and me."

"You got Brygida in on this?"

"She suggested it," said Geoffrey. "You had fun the other night, didn't you?"

"Maybe." Jason shrugged. "Yeah, I guess so. The art opening was… interesting. Not really my kind of art, but okay, whatever."

"You're impossible." Geoffrey left the workshop.

Jason looked down at his workbench and shook his head. He wasn't in the mood to work on the carving anymore. He wasn't sure what he as feeling, exactly.

He liked Elena. She had been fun to be around, and she was obviously very attracted to him. He was attracted to her, for that matter. He wasn't sure what to do, though. There were things about himself that he just wasn't willing to let some random person know. It wasn't as if they could ever get intimate; she'd be certain to notice things about him that were different from humans.

Jason sighed again and closed up his workshop. He needed a beer. He also needed to talk to Geoffrey. Jason knew he should tell his friend about himself, but he couldn't bring himself to do it. The longer he waited, the more impossible it seemed to say anything.

Maybe if Geoffrey knew, he'd understand and back off.

Probably not, though. If Geoffrey knew, he wouldn't understand why it was such a big deal to Jason. He might even tell Elena. Jason couldn't risk that.

Geoffrey was already playing a game in the living room when Jason went in. Jason sat in the chair next to the bookshelf and sipped his beer. Maybe it wasn't normal for him not to want to date.

Would dating Elena be more normal? Would it help him blend in and hide better? Probably.

Geoffrey took off his headset and sat down his controller. "What?"

"Tell me about Elena," said Jason.

"Yeah! All right! What do you want to know?"

"She was really talking about me?"

"She was. Wouldn't shut up, actually. Kept asking me about you. She really likes you, man. I think you could really have a shot with her."

As they talked about Elena, Jason thought it wouldn't hurt to go on a few dates with her. It probably looked strange for a man of his presumed age not to date. Elena would be a perfect cover for him.

CHAPTER TWENTY-SIX

A simple ward was sufficient to keep the blood rain from soaking him.

Most of the beasts that lurked in the red-leaved forest stayed away. Drake incinerated the only creature that got close, and the others backed off. For most people, the Court of the Broken Prince was not a place to travel alone at night.

The air smelled of copper, iron, rotting meat, and the normal scent of blood as it soaked into the ground. The shattered world was still dying, bleeding out into the void. Thick clouds overhead continued to rain its blood upon the world.

Drake trekked along the slick cobblestone road until he reached the high basaltic walls. The heavy timber doors of the fortified gates were closed, as he'd expected. Torchlight flickered from within the deep-set windows.

"Guards!" Drake called. "Open the gate!"

A minute or so later, a sputtering torch appeared atop the wall. "We don't open the gates after dark," a guard called down.

"I am Prince Daerandir Drake of the Ruined Courts," he shouted back.

"I'm sorry, lord, but my orders stand."

"Very well."

Drake shifted into his dragon form and leapt to the top of the wall.

The startled beastman dropped his torch to the wet stone and drew his sword.

"I don't think you want to do that," Drake said, shifting back into his trueform.

"Your Highness, please forgive me. I could not see you clearly, and you startled me."

The guard put away his sword and knelt.

"You were faithfully discharging your duty. There is nothing to forgive. Please tell the duty officer that I have entered the town and will be staying with Count Sima. I can be reached there if the officer has any questions."

"Right away, Your Highness."

Drake took the stairs down the back side of the wall. He could have jumped, but his ward wouldn't have stopped the splash from a puddle, and he didn't want to arrive at the count's home covered in blood. It would have been bad manners.

The town was dark. There were no streetlamps, since only a fool would go after dark in a place that rained blood every night. It didn't take Drake long to find the count's home, a fortified manor with a low wall around it.

Surly-looking guards stood under the slight shelter afforded by the overhang at the gate. The guards looked surprised to see him but opened the gate hastily nonetheless. A servant met him at the door to the house itself. Drake dropped his ward as he stepped inside.

"The count has just finished his evening meal, You Highness," the servant said. "I'll escort you to him presently. Will you be wanting a meal, lord?"

"No, thank you."

"Prince Drake," the servant announced as they entered the

room.

The count was a small man with strong cheekbones, a sallow complexion, and a long mustache. He was sitting in a leather chair near a fire, a glass of merlot on the table nearby. He stood and bowed to Drake.

"You honor us, Prince."

"Count Sima, it is good to see you again," Drake replied.

"If you've come seeking your daughter, I'm sorry to say that she isn't here."

"I am aware. I came to speak with you, actually."

"Please sit." Sima gestured to the chair across from his. "Wine?"

"Thank you. I think that would brush off the chill of the road."

Sima poured him a glass. "What brings you to be traveling so late?"

Drake took the wine and sipped it. "Necessity, as you can imagine. I have just come from the Imperial Court."

"The emperor is in good health?" Sima asked as he sat back down.

"Emrys is fine, although not for lack of trying from assassins, it would seem."

"I had heard there were assassinations. I hadn't realized anyone had moved against the emperor."

"The assassins are shapeshifters."

"I assume they were not from the Courts. I also assume you don't think I'm behind it, since I am still breathing."

Drake smiled. "Your loyalty is beyond question. The assassins were not from the Courts. They have struck in the North and the South, and they can move through the Realms by an unknown method."

"That certainly narrows down the options."

"The one who attempted to kill Xia had in his mind an image of a tower clad in darkness," Drake said.

Sima stiffened. "Xia was unharmed?"

"She was unharmed."

"The imagery of the tower in darkness is interesting. I assume you think the tower is in the Southern Realms."

"I know of few shapeshifters in the North, and none from the Earth Realms," said Drake. "These shapeshifters appear to be restricted to humanoid forms. Several have worn mine."

"Unwise of them," said Sima. "Is there anything else you can tell me about them?"

"We don't know much. They may be religious fanatics."

"Those are common enough in any Realm."

"True, but few of them know of the North and the South, and have the ability to travel between them. I was hoping you would either know or be willing to ask the Families."

Sima frowned. "They don't like to get involved in these things."

"I'm aware, but an Institute run by the Families was attacked in the Realm where Xia is going to school. Several people were killed."

"Members of the Family?"

"No, local security."

"Thank the gods, I am sorry the locals died but glad it wasn't a Family member. Those are good people in that Realm.

"So I assumed, since Xia has been staying with them. Will you ask for me?"

Sima nodded and tossed back the remainder of his wine. "If you'll excuse me for a few minutes, I shall go and make some inquiries. I would ask you along, but the Families can be quite secretive."

"I understand completely," said Drake. "I've been walking quite a bit recently. I will sit here and enjoy your wine and fire."

Sima bowed and left the room.

Drake sighed and settled back into the chair. Sima was a good man. He'd essentially raised Xia after her mother had been slain, before Xia had joined Drake in the Courts.

Xia's mother had been slain by the Ancient Enemy during the upheavals at the end of the last century. At least, Drake thought that had been last century – it was all so difficult for him to remember when events happened sometimes.

He'd been alive long enough to see patterns in the cycles of death. The Ancient Enemy never completely relented, but there were times when they were more quiescent. This latest cycle had been very active. Drake could only assume his brother having fallen had something to do with it.

Drake heard Sima talking in the hall and stood as he entered the room. There was an unfamiliar dark-skinned woman with him. Her hair was turning to silver, but there was nothing frail about her body or features.

"Prince Drake, may I introduce you to Lady Thandiwe?"

Drake took her offered hand and gave it a quick kiss. He'd head of the lady; she was the head of one of the prominent Families. Xia's mother had been her granddaughter.

"You are just as handsome and charming as I've been told," said Thandiwe. "However, I came here to tell you personally that we cannot help you."

Drake frowned. "I would think that you could have sent a message if you didn't know, but then you didn't say that, did you? You said you *cannot* help me. Is this because of our history? I must remind you that there are lives at risk."

"It is not because of any history you think we share. It may come as a surprise to you, Prince, but we do not harbor you any ill will for something you had no hand in. We are, and have been, aware of the Ancient Enemy. They have dogged us for our entire history. I blame *them* for the death of my granddaughter."

"But you still will not tell me what you know." Drake paced over to the fire. "Is one of the Families involved?"

Thandiwe looked unhappy. "A transportation contract was

signed, along with an agreement of non-disclosure."

"That's rather unusual, isn't it?" Drake asked. "Doesn't that conflict with the Families non-interference directives?"

"The party in question demonstrated an ability to travel the worlds. They also agreed not to involve the Families in their business."

"Assassination," Drake said. "That is their business."

"No member of the Family has been harmed."

"An attempt was made against your great-granddaughter," said Drake. "She very easily could have been killed, if not for my combat training."

"An attempt was made against Xia?" asked Thandiwe.

"You haven't heard about the Santa Fe attack?"

Thandiwe sighed. "I have not."

"The assassin killed three local staff, trying to get to her."

"The attack happened on the Institute's soil?"

"That was my understanding, yes."

"I will look into this. If what you say is as you say it, then I may be able to help you."

"I will be leaving for that Realm tonight. If you could leave the information with Xia, I would appreciate it," Drake said. "I have another daughter there who may be in danger."

"I will look into it. I will send word to Xia, either way."

"Thank you, Lady Thandiwe."

Sima and Thandiwe left, and Sima returned after a few minutes. Drake finished his wine while he waited.

"You aren't really planning to leave tonight, are you?" asked Sima.

"I'm afraid I must, old friend," Drake said. "As I said, I have another daughter who might be in danger."

"Then I'll see you out." Sima walked with Drake to the front door. "Please give my regards to Xia if you see her again soon. Remind her that she will always have a place here."

Drake gripped Sima's arm. "She knows that. Take care of

yourself. There are dark forces moving."

"I'm aware, Prince. I dare say you're more in danger than I am. Please come back anytime."

"Thank you."

Drake activated his ward and set off to the Waypoint. He still had far to go, to get back to Brygida. He was sure she was in danger, although he couldn't have said from what.

CHAPTER TWENTY-SEVEN

Lyra apported with Jon and Aradhana.

It felt quite different from anything he'd experienced before. Whatever Lyra's power was, it left a buzzing in the back of his head that was almost an itch. That power was not what he used to apport, nor whatever Drake used.

After several quick jumps, the four of them arrived in a modest hotel room. Jon knew somehow that the man with the green hair had used his own abilities to apport. That meant that both Lyra and Emerald could do so. Jon found that very interesting.

"We should be safe here," said Lyra. "I apported us as quietly as I could."

"Quietly?"

"Any apportation creates ripples in reality," said Emerald. "With skill and practice, you can minimize the effect. Whatever you were using made big waves."

"How *were* you able to do that?" Lyra asked Jon.

He shrugged. He didn't know these people, and he wasn't about to discuss everything about his life and capabilities with them.

"I'm a jump-ship pilot."

"I don't see a ship," Lyra said dryly.

"I've learned how to jump short distances without it. What did you mean, I'm not who you expected?"

Lyra smiled. "Interesting that you should ask that and not why I thought you were in danger."

"I knew I was in danger. That's why I was running."

Emerald turned his head, and Jon got the impression that something passed between Emerald and Lyra. What, he couldn't have said. He wished he could read minds the way Brygida did, because he suspected that silent communication had been important.

"What did you think you were in danger from?" asked Lyra.

Jon didn't sense any danger from these two, at least. Whoever they were, wherever they were from, his precognitive abilities suggested they were here to help. He knew that somehow his future and theirs would be entwined for years to come. He felt – for better or worse – that he could trust them.

"From something called the Ancient Enemy."

Lyra's eyes flashed greener for a moment. "You're not local, are you?"

"Actually, I was born here, on this world, in this city. I don't think *you're* local, though, despite your clothes and your Welsh name."

She laughed. "No, obviously not. I suppose we should start with names. I didn't catch yours."

"I hadn't given it." He shook his head. "I'm Jon. This is Aradhana. Are you with Drake?"

"Who?"

"The Precursor," said Aradhana. "Been on the news a lot."

"Precursor? No, we haven't been here very long. I think we must have missed the news on that one. Why would you think that?"

"He's not from around here, either," said Jon. "Why did

you have such a strong reaction when I mentioned the Ancient Enemy?"

"Not many people call them that. Not many people even know about them."

"You guys really haven't been paying attention, have you?" said Aradhana. "There was a vid broadcast of the Precursor killing one on Earth."

Lyra and Emerald glanced at each other for a moment.

"Someone filmed one of the Ancient Enemy being destroyed?" Lyra asked. "And *broadcast* it?"

"It wasn't Deegan. Or Erin, although she was near here," said Emerald. "No others of ours would be so indiscrete."

"I didn't think it was either of them," Lyra said.

"Not that I don't appreciate your assistance," Jon interrupted, "but why did you help us, anyway?"

"There's something wrong on this planet," said Emerald. "We came here to hunt the Ancient Enemy, as you call them."

"You don't seem to be very well equipped for that. Don't you need guns or something?"

"We have other weapons," said Lyra. She held up her hand, and green flames formed in her palm.

Jon had seen flames like those before, although Drake's had been pure white. Those flames had eaten into the body of the monster Drake fought. Jon didn't know what the difference in color meant, if anything at all. Maybe it was just a personal preference.

"You don't seem surprised."

"I've seen a lot of weird shit," said Jon said, "especially in the last few months."

"You said you were running from the enemy," Emerald said. "Did you actually see it?"

"There was a woman at a restaurant. We ran into her on our first day here. She said her name was Lily. She pointed me out to some revolutionaries. Later, I went back to find her because something didn't add up. She's the Ancient Enemy, it turned out. We ran because she'd set up an ambush with the government."

"Pointed you out?" asked Lyra.

Jon sighed. "I'm the last living member of the royal family who used to rule here before the revolutions."

"Seems like it would be quite the risk to come back."

"Some things are worth fighting for. I came back to try to help my people. I didn't realize there was an Ancient Enemy here until I started analyzing the data. The cycles of revolutions are highly improbable."

"We've seen this sort of thing before," said Emerald. "The enemy feed on pain and misery. A cycle of constant revolutions is perfect for them."

"That's sort of what I figured."

"So what are you hoping for here?" Lyra asked. "Do you dream of retaking the throne?"

"Gods, no!" said Jon. "I just want to stop the slaughter of my people."

"Good answer," Emerald said. "Give us a minute, okay? I have an idea."

"Why do I think I'm not going to like this?" asked Lyra.

That sat in silence, one or the other shaking their head occasionally. It looked to Jon as if they were having a conversation. It *had* to be telepathy.

Aradhana pulled him to the other side of the room. "Are you sure we can trust these people?"

"I think so. They risked their lives to help us. Believe me, we weren't safe a few minutes ago, and we are now. You know I can sense danger. I don't feel anything bad from them."

"I really hope you're right."

"Me, too."

"Jon?" Lyra called. "I think we have something. You're probably not going to like it."

Jon and Aradhana walked back over to Lyra and Emerald. "You want to use me as bait?" asked Jon.

Lyra looked startled. "How did you…?"

"It's the most logical thing to do. Honestly, I'm getting used to it. It's what Drake would have done. What did you have in mind, specifically?"

"Do you think that thing posing as a woman would come after you if you made a public appearance somewhere?" asked Emerald.

"She wouldn't have any reason to think I could fight her," Jon said. "But she might suspect something if I'm too open about it. Maybe if I contacted the monarchists. She put them onto me, and it would be natural for me to go to them for help. They're the only people who could."

Lyra nodded. "That sounds as if it could work. She puts in an appearance, you run, she follows you, and we pounce."

"You make it sound easy," said Aradhana, "but Jon is the one who could get killed."

"I don't think it's going to be easy," Lyra said. "I do think we can take this thing and end the problems here. Killing the monster won't fix this society overnight, but the planet will return to normal eventually if we do."

⊙

Geoffrey was pleased that Jason had finally seen reason about Elena, although he was a little suspicious of his friend. Jason had given in a little too quickly. Either Jason had been thinking a lot about Elena, or he was just trying to shut Geoffrey up.

"You should get a cell phone," Geoffrey said.

"You've suggested that before," said Jason. "Shouldn't you be studying or something?"

"I did my reading yesterday."

"When? You were out with Jen all day."

"When I got back."

"Did you sleep?"

"Yes, Dad, I slept." Jason could be annoying sometimes.

Geoffrey was relieved when Jason and Elena hit it off. He'd been starting to wonder about Jason. He hadn't dated anyone, nor talked about having dated anyone. Geoffrey was vaguely aware that some people were just were interested in such things, but it still seemed strange to him.

Geoffrey couldn't remember a time when he *wasn't* interested in girls. Even in grade school, he'd looked at the girls, especially the ones older than him who looked feminine. He'd started dating at thirteen. Of course, back home in the hills of Kentucky, people often married young.

His family had treated him like a freak when he didn't marry before heading off to university. Some of his cousins still made snide comments about him living with a guy, as if renting a room from Jason somehow implied a sexual relationship.

Geoffrey changed clothes and went back down the stairs.

"Where you off to?" Jason asked.

"Work. I do still work, you know."

"I'd begun to wonder."

"I've been working," said Geoffrey. "You just haven't been paying attention."

The bus ride downtown was uneventful.

Geoffrey wished he could afford a car. He probably had enough for a down payment. What he didn't have was a great credit rating. His credit wasn't bad; he just didn't have very much of it. That missing year on his record didn't help.

He greeted the lobby guard at Gerhardt Industries and went up to the tenth floor. Geoffrey spent most of his work time there. His internship hadn't been what he expected. He'd thought he would be building rockets or writing equations on chalkboards. What he did most of the time was clean up after the scientists. He was normally just a glorified janitor – not that he'd tell his friends that.

"At least they pay me well," Geoffrey muttered.

A light was on in one of the labs at the other end of the hall. Geoffrey poked his head in to see if anyone was still working and was surprised to see Brygida, adjusting a weird device sitting on the workbench. The machine was covered in wires and cables.

"Come on in, Geoffrey," Brygida said without looking up.

"Sorry, didn't mean to intrude."

"Not at all. Come on in." Brygida stretched.

"Have you been here since just after class?"

"Yeah. I wanted to get this prototype working. I'm not sure why. Gerhardt axed the project as too costly."

"What is it?"

"It's a quantum-entangled communications rig."

"A what?"

"Come now, Geoffrey, you remember quantum entanglement from class."

"Sure, between two particles, but the quantum state collapses if you try to measure it, right?"

"Very good, but how is that information transmitted between the particles?"

"That's one of the mysteries of science, isn't it?" said Geoffrey.

"It's unknown *here*," Brygida agreed. "Some Realms have more advanced science."

Geoffrey thought about the implications. "So with this thing, you could have faster-than-light communications?"

"No. Nothing can go faster than light. You know that."

"Then what's the point?"

"This rig gives instant communication across any distance."

"How is that not faster than light?"

"Do you remember Cherenkov radiation?"

"Uh, weird blue glow in a nuclear reactor?"

"What causes it?"

"Radiation?"

Brygida sighed. "Cherenkov radiation is electromagnetic energy released when light violates the phase velocity of the medium it's passing through. Remember the maximum speed of light is normally given as through a vacuum. Nothing can exceed that speed. If light moves faster than normal through something like water, it's still under the max speed of light but higher than it should be for the given medium."

"Okay. What does that have to do with entanglement?":

"Nothing, but it illustrates that things *can* go faster than you think they should without violating physics."

"You just said it was a phase violation!"

"Yes, but it's covered by the rules. Let's assume for moment that the information is transmitted between entangled particles through something else, say a microscopic wormhole. The information propagates at the speed of light."

"Right, but it still has to travel through the wormhole. That will take time. If you drag the two particles light years apart, then the wormhole is light years long."

"Is it?" asked Brygida. "What if the wormhole was exactly the same size?"

"How can that be?"

"It isn't cutting through normal space, now, is it?"

"Subatomic space?" Geoffrey guessed.

Brygida nodded. "That's our best guess."

"Wow. Why would they terminate a project like this?"

"It isn't cost effective," said Brygida. "This rig cost tens of millions of dollars to build and can only transmit a binary signal. To make a full-bandwidth video transmission you'd need a much wider bandwidth. It would cost billions."

"Yeah, but you could talk to automated probes, astronauts,

and colonists in real time! It would be cool!"

"That, it would be," Brygida said.

They spent the rest of the evening playing with the communications equipment. They tried it from different places around the building and even the roof and basement. It was painfully slow and not very flashy, but it worked.

Geoffrey had a lot of fun. It reminded him of that time he and Brygida had hung out in the galley aboard Hephaestus. Brygida seemed happier now, more carefree. He liked this side of her.

She gave him a lift home after work that evening.

"Do you want to come in?" asked Geoffrey. "Jason is probably still awake."

Brygida shook her head. "No, I need to be back at work in the morning. Tell him I said hello. Maybe we can all go out again soon. I really had fun last weekend."

"I did, too. We should. It would be fun."

CHAPTER TWENTY-EIGHT

Dark clouds hung low over Cincinnati as Drake made his way into the Realm.

The dense clouds made determining the time difficult, but Drake thought it was probably close to noon. He hadn't been entirely certain where Brygida would be in the middle of the day. He wasn't even sure what day this was.

He stopped by Gerhardt Industries, but the woman at the desk said Brygida wasn't working. That meant she was either home or at work at the university. It was only a few kilometers from downtown to Clifton, where Brygida lived. Drake risked a short apport to her street. He liked the place where Brygida had found a home. Old oak trees lined the street, and blocked most of the rain.

Brygida's cat, Tadeo, was sitting in the window of the darkened house when Drake walked up the drive. Like all cats, she was slightly disdainful as she watched him. Cats were like that, though. Drake appreciated the attitude. He thought it unlikely that the cat would be in the window if Brygida was home, but he rang the doorbell anyway.

When there was no response, he turned and walked west to

Clifton Avenue. The steady drizzle turned into a downpour. Passing cars splashed the deepening water with no regard for the people on the sidewalks. Drake considered activating a ward against the rain but decided not to; he didn't wish to call attention to himself.

The University of Cincinnati was south of Clifton. The sprawling campus was the usual mix of old and new buildings, many of them over a hundred years old. The campus had a pleasing amount of green space, though. The trees and expansive lawns were a welcome sight. The grey stormy sky had been affecting his mood.

A bus stop displayed maps of the university: the Geology and Physics building was on the northwestern corner of the campus, near Clifton Avenue. Drake had never been to the university before, although he'd always intended to investigate it. When Geoffrey applied for school here, Drake had been pleased. The university had a good reputation as a center of learning.

Drake entered the building off Clifton Court. A small, almost undetectable application of power shed the water from his hair and clothes as he stepped through the doors. Students stood by the windows, looking forlornly out at the rain. A few who were more practical braved the weather anyway, running out into the downpour, books held under shirts to block the falling water.

The directory on the wall by the elevators indicated that Dr. Hakubi's office was located on the fourth floor. Drake took the stairs; he generally preferred not to get into small metal boxes with limited maneuvering room. He'd ride in an elevator if he had to, but the stairs were better when it was just a few floors.

A student was in the office with Brygida when he reached the fourth floor, so Drake waited nearby for the young woman to finish and leave. Brygida looked up as he knocked on the door, and Drake knew from the long, healing cut on her face that he's arrived too late.

"Father, what are you doing here?"

"Hello, Brygida. I wanted to see you as soon as I arrived. I'm sorry I didn't get back here in time to stop that."

Brygida shrugged. "It is just a small cut. I'll heal. It's not as if I lost an eye. Or my life."

"Still, I'm sorry." Brygida was such a gentle soul. It pained him to see that she'd been hurt. "If I had known you were in immediate danger, I would have come back faster. Will you tell me about what happened?"

"Please shut the door," said Brygida, and then waited as he did. "I was attacked a little over a week ago. I was slashed, but I bested him. There isn't much else to say."

"Did he say anything?"

"The assassin's dying thoughts were of my mother. He seemed to think I'm an abomination because of my mixed heritage."

Drake nodded. "That fits with what I've been able to discover. There have been attacks in both the North and the South. I suspect whoever is behind this to be some sort of religious zealot. I have not had much luck in tracking them down."

"I didn't sense an entry into this Realm, but then, I didn't detect your return, either."

"I was trying to be as quiet as possible when I returned," said Drake. "I didn't wish to call attention to this place. Again, I am sorry you were harmed."

"I'd have made a better showing of myself if I'd been armed. Of course, then the police would have harassed me more. Unfortunately, I cannot carry a weapon on campus."

"Harassed? Local troubles?"

"Nothing I couldn't handle."

"I was concerned because there have been many deaths in the Ruined Courts. In the North, assassins killed Tomas and

Dmitry. Dasha killed an assassin who tried to murder her."

"Dmitry, I couldn't care less about, but Tomas will be missed. He wasn't bad, for one of my older cousins. I am pleased that the attempt against Dasha failed. Was she wounded?"

"I wasn't told and didn't think to ask. I got the impression that she was fine."

Dasha was Philomena's daughter. Philomena had been friendly to Brygida, he recalled. Drake was glad then that Dasha had fought well. He didn't know anything about Tomas. As for Dmitry, he was only sorry that someone else had killed the man. Drake had wanted to do that himself at some point.

"Who told you, if I may ask?" said Brygida.

"Your uncle Dominic. He was visiting with Emrys, since King Andrzej had asked for my head."

Brygida rolled her eyes. "Andrzej didn't seriously think you were behind it, did he? Did he want you to kill Uncle Dominic?"

"I think the question had to be asked." Drake studied his daughter's face. "I did not take offense at Dominic or Andrzej. Does it hurt – your wound?"

She touched the scar lightly with her right hand. "I'm not sure I'd call it pain, at this point. It did hurt, but not so much that I couldn't defend myself."

"The scar should fade soon," said Drake. "Or if you wish, I can take you to the medical facilities aboard Hephaestus."

"It's fine. I think the scar makes me a bit intimidating."

"I'm sure your student admirers think so."

"Don't take this as me complaining, but I don't think I have any student admirers," said Brygida. "I honestly hope not, anyway. Do you have any leads on the assassins?"

"I've made some inquiries. Did Xia mention the Families to you?"

"I don't believe so. What families?"

"There are people in the Central Realms who developed technology to travel the worlds. Some of them grouped together to form a sprawling trade empire, a thousand years or so ago. They are referred to as the Families."

"You think these people might be behind the attacks?"

"No, but I think they have unintentionally aided those who *are* behind them. I know so, in fact. I spoke to one of the Family Matriarchs, and she told me a transport contract had been signed. She's working to have it overturned, since whoever is behind this attacked Xia on Family property."

"The more I learn of the universes," said Brygida, "the less I actually know."

"I enjoy not knowing everything."

"I never thought I could know *everything*, but I do wish I knew more." Brygida sighed and shook her head. "Have you seen Geoffrey and Jason yet?"

"Not yet," Drake replied. "I wanted to make sure you were all right. They weren't injured, too, were they?"

"No, I was alone when I was attacked."

"I stopped by your house earlier and saw Tadeo in the window. The assassin didn't attack you at home?"

"I was leaving here, actually," said Brygida. "I was attacked in the parking structure across the street."

Drake nodded. "I wonder how they knew to find you there."

"I've wondered that myself. I can only assume that I was followed from home, and then the assassin waited for me to return to my car."

"That seems an odd choice. Your home would provide more operation security for an assassination. It's isolated."

"Maybe whoever is behind this wanted it to look like an accident or a mugging gone wrong."

"Why would they care?" asked Drake. "The assassins have been open and aggressive in other instances. They've even used shapeshifters who wore my form. Why try to hide at this point?"

Brygida shrugged. "Maybe they feared retribution."

"You mentioned that the assassin knew of your mother, and thought of you as an abomination due to mixed heritage," said Drake.

"That's right."

"How did he know?"

Brygida frowned. "I… I didn't think to wonder about that."

"Almost no one knows of your mixed heritage."

"There was no thought of you in his mind," said Brygida. "To most people back home in the Golden Kingdom, my father was just someone from the Southern Realms. I remember, back when I was just a child, encountering a man in the Eternal City. I was with my mother. We were walking back to the palace after having lunch near the docks, and this man started screaming at us both. I still remember him shouting as the guards took him away that my blood was impure."

"He couldn't have known about me," said Drake. "That suggests he thought you were impure because one parent was from the Realms. Do you know if the others who were attacked had a parent not from either the Golden kingdom or the Ruined Courts?"

"Xia?"

"Her mother was from the Court of the Broken Prince, one of the Black Realms."

"Dasha's father was from a central Earth Realm, not unlike this one," said Brygida. "I don't know about the others."

"I think it would be safe to say that for each, one of their parents was not from the North or South."

"It does seem likely." Brygida stretched and stood. "Let me check if there are any students waiting. My office hours ended a few minutes after you arrived, but I'd hate to exclude someone who needs to talk to me."

"Of course." Drake stood and opened the office door. "No

one there."

"Good, then we can get out of here. Are you going to stay in town for a while? You can have the spare room again."

"Thank you. I don't have any plans at the moment. It would be nice to stay with you a while and catch up. If the Families learn anything, they'll relay the information through Xia."

"Would you like to go out for dinner, or grab food on the way home?"

"I'll leave that to you."

"Let's wait a bit and then order delivery," said Brygida. "I usually spend some time with Tadeo when I get home. She helps me relax."

"She's very cute," Drake said. "I'm looking forward to spending some time with her again. When last I stayed with you, I awoke some mornings with her sitting on my chest and staring at me."

"She wanted food."

"So I gathered. I told Tadeo that *you* are her mother, and she needed to tell you about it."

"Oh, she does," said Brygida. "Loudly."

CHAPTER TWENTY-NINE

Jon was nervous as he walked through the darkening streets.

There was an expectant emotional pressure in the city. The military had been ruthlessly cracking down on dissidents and rebels. The checkpoints throughout the city were guarded by cold-eyed men and women with body armor and rifles. It was not a night to be out walking.

Jon had to apport a few times to keep from being discovered by the roving patrols. It bothered him to see the troops in the city. It reminded him of the day of the first revolution. His memories of that day were of fear, blood, fire, and death. The feelings of grief, loss, and hopelessness had come later.

The silence had awakened him that day. Jon woke up in the late morning, as usual, after being out late with his friends the night before. Then, the city had held expectant emotional pressure, much like today. In his youthful arrogance, Jon thought he could redirect the burgeoning revolution. He'd thought it would be peaceful.

Jon's brother, the late king, had been an incompetent fool with a little too much fondness for decadence, but he hadn't been the monster the revolutionaries made him out to be. There had been no trial for his brother or the rest of his family. Someone had killed them all as they gathered around the breakfast table.

Jon had never understood before how his people had turned so violently against the royal family. Now he knew it was because of the influence of the Ancient Enemy. Hell, maybe it had actually *been* the Ancient Enemy that killed them.

He didn't know, and he hadn't waited around to find out. He ran, out of the palace and through the burning city, to the spaceport, where his signet ring bought him passage offworld. He hadn't even looked back.

Had it been Jon who'd drawn the Ancient Enemy here? Was it because of Brygida and her damn jump ship pilot program? Dr. Preta had been one of those monsters. Had she been working with the one behind Rhyddid's revolutions? There were too many variables to come to any meaningful conclusions, and thinking about it triggered Jon's feelings of guilt. He didn't need that right now, not on top of all his other problems.

Osian, Jon's point of contact with the monarchists, was standing at the end of the pier, right where he should be. Jon couldn't be sure Osian wasn't one of the Ancient Enemy, but Lyra had assured him that the enemy *rarely* worked with others of their own kind. She said the Ancient Enemy had *sometimes* been encountered in groups before, but they were *usually* fighting each other.

There were too many qualifiers in Lyra's statements for Jon to feel reassured by what she'd said. Lyra and Emerald were unknowns. They weren't from Rhyddid, that was certain. Jon didn't think they were even from this universe.

My life has gotten really weird, he thought.

Osian didn't turn as Jon walked up to him. "You're late," the man said.

"I couldn't exactly walk straight here."

"It seems that you're the main topic of conversation around town," Osian said. "We thought you were going to keep a low profile."

"I had intended to."

"So what happened?"

Jon sighed. "I didn't expect Lily to betray us."

"What's this, then?"

"Lily asked me to meet her at the restaurant. Moments after I got there, the military stormed the place. I barely escaped."

"Yes, how *did* you escape?"

"We had help, of course," said Jon. "You can't expect me to divulge names, can you?"

"No, of course not. Keep that information to yourself." Osian shook his head. "We had a lot of hopes placed on you, lad. I suppose all that's for naught now. What do you need from us?"

"I need a way off planet for my wife and myself."

"Thought she'd be with you."

"I left her someplace safe."

"What you're asking isn't going to be easy," Osian said. "We're taking a big risk even talking to you."

"And I appreciate it," Jon replied. "If I can get off planet, I can reach out to some friends who've offered assistance. Maybe I can even come back and take the throne."

Jon hated lying, but he needed help from these people, although not to take the throne or even to get him off world. He needed them to believe they were helping him, so he could lure Lily out of hiding. He was the bait for the trap, but the trap couldn't be set without the Monarchists.

Osian shifted his weight uneasily. "I'm not sure how we'd feel about outsiders coming in."

"You misunderstand," Jon said, thinking quickly. "Many of our people left after the purges started. Some were already offworld. I've been in contact with them. They wouldn't come and fight, but they could supply resources."

"Weapons?" Osian asked eagerly. "We've had a hell of a time getting ahold of enough weapons."

"Weapons and money, which can be just as useful," Jon lied.

Osian nodded. "Okay, yeah, I can see that. We know a captain. Owes us some, you know. We can probably get you two on his ship. It isn't the fastest, but it'll get the job done. Then, once you're safe, we'll have a long talk with Lily. If she betrayed you, or us, we'll make her into an example of why that's a bad idea."

"I have a few things I'd like to say to her myself."

Jon felt sick at the glee in the man's voice. Osian *wanted* to hurt Lily. Of course, considering what Lily actually was, Osian wouldn't have enjoyed interrogating Lily as much as he thought he would.

"We can have some of the boys pick her up tonight," said Osian.

"I think it would be for the best. That way, we know about her, one way or the other."

"Follow me, and keep quiet," Osian said. "I'll get you to a safehouse and have her brought there. Maybe we'll have some fun."

"I think you and I have very different definitions of fun," said Jon.

Jon realized then that Osian was under the influence of the Ancient Enemy, whether he knew it or not. Jon doubted that the man would have ever even thought of the things he was hoping for, if he hadn't been pushed toward... *evil* by the enemy. Jon didn't know if he really believed in pure evil, but the Ancient Enemy certainly qualified, if anything did.

☉

Traffic was light for a Thursday.

Brygida drove home in just over half an hour, which was something of a miracle for Cincinnati traffic. The rain stopped as she pulled into her driveway. She saw Tadeo jump down from the window, no doubt to wait by the door.

Tadeo pounced on Brygida when she came in, meowing loudly to tell her all about that time she was a cat. Brygida scooped her up and hugged her, eliciting a vibrant purr. Behind her, Drake came in and took off his coat.

"Hello, little cat," he said.

Tadeo purred louder and slow-blinked at him.

"She likes you," said Brygida.

"She has good taste."

Brygida laughed and hung up her coat while juggling the cat, who wouldn't get down from her shoulder. "Can I get you anything?"

"I'm good, thank you. I think I'll go change." Drake went into the spare room.

Brygida changed out of her work clothes. The scar on her face stood out as a pale line when she glanced in the mirror. She'd thought about using makeup to hide it, but in the end, she just couldn't be bothered. It would fade in time.

Her father was sitting on the couch, dressed in jeans and a green tee-shirt, when she went back into the living room.

"Still interested in dinner?" Brygida asked. "There's a good Korean place near here that delivers."

"I am rather partial to bulgogi," said Drake.

"I'll order us some kimchi and bulgogi. Can I get you a beer?"

"Sit down and relax. I'll get it. Order the food and then spend some time with Tadeo."

Drake left the room and rattled around in the kitchen while she placed the order.

Brygida was relieved to settle into her favorite spot on the couch and pet her cat. Tadeo wanted to play fetch and was running around with a toy mouse when Drake came back from the kitchen. He had several bottles of Jeju Wit Ale, which Brygida knew she hadn't had in her fridge.

Brygida raised an eyebrow at the beer.

"Figured we'd get in the spirit better with a Korean beer." Drake sat down on the couch across from her. "How have things been?"

"Fine, other than the assassination attempt."

Drake grimaced. "I am sorry I didn't get back sooner."

Brygida brushed her fingers over her scar. "Me, too, if I'm being honest, but it might not have changed anything. What's done is done. The wound has healed. The scar will fade. Geoffrey and Jason will be glad to see you. They were very supportive after the attack."

"They're both good people," said Drake. "How have they been?"

"Well. They've both been dating, which seems to occupy much of their free time."

"Jealous?" Drake teased.

"Not in the least. I've never been interested in such, as you know."

"I meant jealous because of them spending less time with you, not jealous of the romance. I respect your choice."

"Oh, well, maybe a little jealous." Brygida shrugged. "I miss traveling with all of you. We had some good times together."

"I'm sure we will again in the future."

"I certainly hope so."

The doorbell rang, and Brygida got up and took the food from the delivery driver, giving her a generous tip for being prompt. The food smelled good. Brygida got plates and flatware from the kitchen. Drake was holding Tadeo when she returned.

"The scamp tried to get into the bag," said Drake.

"She's still a little feral," Brygida replied.

"Aren't we all?"

The servings were generous, and the kimchi was very spicy. They spent some time just enjoying the food. Drake cleaned up the dishes afterward. Tadeo raced around the room, leaping from the furniture and making strange noises with her mouse toy in her mouth.

"So, Jason and Geoffrey have girlfriends? Do we approve?" Drake asked as he came back in.

Brygida laughed a little. "Not sure it would matter if we didn't, but yeah, Jen and Elena are good people, too. Not sure how serous Geoffrey and Jen are, but Jason and Elena have really hit it off. Geoffrey and Jen spend a lot of time together, but Geoffrey is very young."

"Has Jason gotten less inhibited?"

"Not in the least. I don't think he's told her about his true identity."

"How about Geoffrey?"

"What about him?"

"Has Jason told him?"

"I doubt it," said Brygida. "Jason isn't exactly forthcoming with the information."

"I may have to intervene," Drake said.

"Go easy on him. If you scare Jason too much, he might drop everything and run. He has a good life here now."

"I don't plan on scaring him at all," Drake said. "He isn't afraid of me, is he?"

"I think anyone with sense is afraid of you."

"Even you?"

Brygida scooped Tadeo up and flipped her over in her lap. She rubbed the kitten's belly as she tried to decide how to answer. Her father seemed mellow, but she'd personally witnessed him commit extremely violent acts.

"Let us say that I respect you," she said. "I don't think you'd ever harm me. I have no intention of ever giving you a reason to."

"I would never harm you," Drake said softly.

"What if I fell?"

"You wouldn't."

"But what if I did?"

Drake sighed. "I'd try to get you back. If I could not, then I'd put whatever you had become out of your misery as humanely as possible. I have never liked such hypotheticals. If you fell, you would no longer be yourself, and therefore a promise never to harm you would not apply."

"Some people might see that as splitting hairs."

"I would be causing more harm to you by not killing you."

"Touché." Brygida smiled. "I've never liked such hypotheticals, either."

"On that note, I think perhaps I should go to bed," said Drake.

"I probably should, as well," Brygida said. "Tomorrow is Friday. Jason will be at home, and Geoffrey will be home from class around three. If you're going to talk to them both, that would be a good time."

CHAPTER THIRTY

Jon sat in the darkened warehouse and tried not to think of all the things that could go wrong in the next few minutes, not the least of which was him dying. Lily was one of the Ancient Enemy, beings that might even match Drake in capabilities. Jon wished he knew more about them, but he was also kind of glad he didn't.

Osian was pacing and muttering to himself.

The revolutionary had sent out a team to collect Lily half an hour ago. They still weren't back. That didn't necessarily mean anything bad; the streets were full of bands of troops they had to avoid.

Jon was probably more worried than Osian, but then, Jon knew Lily wasn't human.

Twenty minutes later, the men returned, bringing a woman with a bag over her head. Osian signaled to move her in front of the floor lamp and remove the bag, and Lily stood blinking in the pool of light. She didn't seem concerned about the men standing behind her. She smiled as her eyes met Jon's and blew him a kiss.

"Osian? Is that you, dear friend? Why have I been brought

here like this? Have I not been a good friend of the revolution?"

"That remains to be seen," Osian said. "Jon thinks you tipped off the soldiers about him."

"Hmm. Anything else?"

"You admit to it?" Osian asked.

"Did Jon really tell you nothing else about me?" said Lily. "He didn't even warn you?"

"Warn us? About you?"

Lily sighed. "I suppose it's possible you simply don't know enough to be afraid. I thought you said you knew all about me, Jon. If you really had known anything, you'd have been too terrified to come back and confront me like this. Oh, well. Maybe I'll save you until last. Then you'll understand better what's coming."

"Shut the fuck up, bitch!" said Osian.

He raised his hand to slap her. He never got the chance. His hand began to swell, and then his arm. He screamed once, and his face and throat swelled up. Jon had one last look at the terror on the man's face before Osian popped like a balloon.

The others turned and ran for the exits.

Lily stood laughing as she killed them one by one. She appeared to take her time, but Jon's sense of time told him only moments passed. She seemed surprised when she turned back to him.

"You're still here? I hoped you'd try to run again. Maybe lead me to that woman you were with. She looked like fun."

"You won't touch her."

"My dear boy, there is nothing you can do to stop me."

"I don't intend to try, but they might."

Lily cocked her head and turned around suddenly.

Lyra and Emerald appeared, walking forward as they apported in, both bathed in green flames.

Darkness seemed to gather around Lily then. "I don't know you, human," she said. "However, you and your Mo'Ceri friend are outmatched. You should flee."

"Your kind don't talk unless you're scared," said Lyra.

"What? No call for me to surrender? How sad. I thought you were the heroes of this little farce."

"No, we're the pest control," said Emerald.

Jon shouted a warning as the dark energies around Lily slashed out at Lyra and Emerald. He needn't have bothered; they weren't there. Searing lightning clawed at Lily. Jon could see Emerald directing the energy at her. Lyra had gone high into the catwalks of the warehouse, where she rained green fire down onto Lily.

At least down onto what had been Lily.

Lily's form twisted and changed into something Jon's mind didn't want to comprehend. It was much more horrible than the thing Drake fought back on Earth. Jon had to apport away as the thing began lashing out in every direction with its dark fire.

Where that fire struck wooden crates, they dissolved into putrefying puddles. The very walls of the warehouse began to crumble. Still the darkness, the green flames, and the lightning lashed back and forth. Something caught fire, and the warehouse filled with smoke, lit from within by the terrific energies of the battle raging.

Jon had no idea how the battle was going.

He hadn't expected this... sorcery.

Drake could do amazing things, but what Drake did always seemed to be rooted in technology. Jon couldn't determine how the energies being unleashed in the warehouse could possibly be technological in nature. Even with something like the Cynosure, there had to be a structure and a purpose to the release of energy. This chaotic battle was... *elemental.*

A resounding concussion blew the windows out of the warehouse. Most of the smoke and flames were blasted away, as well, revealing the thing that had been Lily collapsed in the center of the open space, bathed in green fire. The fire crawled over its body, eating into the gnarled, twisted flesh as it screamed.

Emerald and Lyra were standing close to the body. Lyra had her hands stretched out toward the dying thing, and flames flowed from her to it in a continuous stream. Emerald was clutching his left arm, which looked badly burned to just above the elbow.

Jon wasn't sure what he was supposed to do.

He felt sick to his stomach. He hadn't known what was going to happen. If he'd known, he would have apported away. He didn't have any doubts about Lily, or whatever it was, needing to die. He just wished he hadn't been here to witness it.

The thing stopped screaming and began to dissolve into the concrete of the floor. Lyra stopped directing fire at it. Jon could only assume the thing was actually dead.

"Yes, it's dead," said Emerald. "They don't die easily, but they do die."

"Am I getting older, or are these things getting tougher?" Lyra asked.

"I think I'll decline to comment," Emerald said, holding his arm.

"Emerald? Why didn't you dodge that?" said Lyra.

"Ah, yes, how could I have forgotten such a thing?"

Lyra shook her head. "Go have Leander take a look at it."

Emerald glanced at Jon.

"I'll be fine here," said Lyra. "I won't be long. Go on home."

"You're sure?" he asked.

"I'm sure. I want to talk to Jon before I return."

Emerald apported away.

"Is it always like that?" Jon asked. "Honestly, I thought you'd use weapons or something."

"You're an initiate of the Cynosure," said Lyra. "Are you

aware of its true nature?"

"You mean that it's a machine?" Jon asked. "Yeah, I'm aware."

"What I'm using is similar. You said you'd seen someone claiming to be a Precursor kill one of the Ancient Enemy."

"Well, I saw part of it," Jon said. "He used a sword."

"A sword?"

Jon shrugged.

"I'm surprised a conventional weapon could hurt an Ancient Enemy."

"I think it was a *very good* sword. Also, he was bathed in flames, like yours and Emerald's, only white."

"White flames?" Lyra asked. "What did he look like?"

"Big guy, red hair."

"Hmm. I think someone I know may have been up to some extracurricular activity." Lyra shook her head. "Jon, thank you for your assistance."

"I didn't do much. You and Emerald did all the fighting."

"You stood your ground and lured the thing in. That helped more than you can know. It isn't easy to stand in the face of those things. You did well. If you ever need help, don't hesitate to ask us."

"I won't, or wouldn't if I knew who you actually are."

"I'm a member of the Circle of Aurora. We try to hunt down things like the Ancient Enemy, to make the universes safer for normal people."

Jon felt her mind brush against his and received an impression of a beautiful world of green fields and forests, with four suns in the sky. With the impression came a sense of where that universe was. How he knew, he couldn't exactly say, but he knew he'd be able to go there if had to.

"Aurora, I presume?" he asked.

Lyra nodded. "I wish I had the time to stay and talk. You remind me of someone I know, and I'd really like to know if you know him, as well."

"I doubt we know any of the same people," said Jon. "As I told you, I was born here."

"Hmm. Well, don't be a stranger." Lyra apported away, leaving a rainbow afterimage.

Jon could hear sirens in the distance. He took one last look around the warehouse, but all of the monarchists were dead. Maybe it was for the best. They'd wanted him back on the throne, and that wasn't something he would ever seriously entertain.

He apported away before the soldiers arrived. He and Aradhana still needed to find a way off the planet. That wasn't going to be easy. At least with the Ancient Enemy gone, his people would have a chance, a real chance to recover from the endless cycle of bloodshed that had plagued them for so many years.

CHAPTER THIRTY-ONE

The next morning, Brygida offered to come home for lunch and drive Drake over to Jason's house, but Drake didn't see the point, since Jason lived nearby. The rain stopped sometime after noon, and Drake walked the couple of blocks from Brygida's house. The sky was overcast, and a cold, heavy fog had settled over the city, making the trees seem like giants as they loomed out of the mist.

The garage door was open, and Drake could see Jason bent over, working on the engine of his antique truck. Jason glanced up as Drake came up the driveway. He had dark grease smeared on his face, and he wore his usual bandanna holding back his hair and covering his ears.

"Drake! You're back," Jason called. "Have you talked to Brygida yet?"

"I had dinner with her last night. She told me about the attack."

Jason nodded, wiping his hands on a rag. "Kind of hard for her not to tell you, with that scar and all."

"It seems there have been a series of attacks," said Drake. "An attempt was also made on my daughter Xia. There were other attacks in the Courts and the Eternal City. I regret I was gone as long as I was, but I was implicated and had to clear my name."

"Damn. Is your daughter okay?"

"She was unscathed, thank you."

"I'm glad to hear that." Jason closed the hood of the truck, using the rag in his hand, and gave the hood a wipe to remove any oil stains. "Geoffrey isn't home yet. Would you like to come in and have a beer?"

"That would be good," said Drake. "I want to talk to you before Geoffrey arrives anyway."

Jason shot him an unreadable look and then went into the house.

Drake followed him inside. Jason was washing his hands in the sink with soap that smelled of oranges. It seemed effective for removing the grease.

"You have a little on your face, as well," Drake said.

"Thanks." Jason finished washing and then pulled a couple bottles of beer from the refrigerator. He opened them by popping the lids off against the counter and handed one to Drake. "What's up?"

"I think it's time we clear a few things up between us, such as how you came to be on this world."

Jason choked on his beer and glared at Drake.

"I've known since we first met that you are not of this Realm," said Drake. "However, with all that has come up, we never had a chance to really talk about it."

"And you decided that today was the right time?"

"It seems as good a day as any, and maybe better than most. With all that is going on, I may not be around much."

"Gee, that would be terrible."

"I'm not in the mood for your defensive sarcasm, Jason. I know you aren't from this world, but you've been here for some time. I also suspect that you came here through a Waypoint. I would very much like to know where that Waypoint is and how you activated it."

Jason tossed back the rest of his beer. "I didn't even know what it was until I met you," he said. "As for how it was activated, if I knew that, I'd have returned home a long time ago."

"Is it close to here?"

Jason shook his head. "No, it's up north, just inland from the east coast."

"The locked Waypoint in Maine?"

"Fuck, I'm going to need another beer."

Drake waited while Jason got another beer and took a few sips while leaning against the kitchen counter. "Well?"

"It was a long time ago, Drake. At least it feels like a long time to me. I was young and stupid, and my friends and I had the idea to explore some caves. I suppose you could say it was something of a *wanderjahr* for us. One last romp before we settled down and got serious about life. We found a portal to another world. It was open when we got there."

"So you went through the portal."

"Yeah. There were people on the other side, here in North America. The native people were friendly, and we stayed with them for a while. This world was so different. After a time, we got homesick, decided to go back, but the portal was gone, closed, whatever."

"So you came through with others. Are they still here?" asked Drake.

"They all died a long time ago," Jason said, looking away. "This world isn't kind to people who look different."

Drake nodded. "Humans can be cruel. I can understand why you keep yourself hidden."

"Can you?" Jason said. "You don't bother to, because you don't have to. You can fight, and just leave if things go to hell. Not everyone has the option."

"I never thought otherwise. And I haven't always had the skill and power that I do now. Believe me, I understand the despair that can come from feeling helpless and hunted. I've been in that position, too. I am curious about the Waypoint, though. It you didn't open it, then it must be one that opens on its own periodically. Has the portal never reopened?"

"I haven't always been able to go check," Jason said, and finished his second beer before continuing. "I know of at least one time, but… I don't know. I couldn't get through. I've just about given up, to be honest. So much time has passed, I don't even know if there's a reason to return."

"We could go and take a look at the Waypoint," said Drake. "It's possible that I could open it."

"Don't do that, Drake."

"Don't do what?"

"Don't give me a false hope."

"I only say it's possible. That's all. I need to examine it to be certain. Will you take me to it?"

"It would take a couple days to drive there."

"Have you forgotten how I can travel?"

"No, but I don't know how to tell you how to get there if you've never been there."

"Let's assume I might have been there before," said Drake, setting down his empty beer bottle. "However, I still want you to tell me where it is. It's possible there is more than the one Waypoint."

"It's north of Andover, Maine. You were right with your first guess."

"You might want to grab a coat."

"You can't be serious."

"I think you'll find that I often am." Drake shook his head and smiled. "I promised you before that I'd try to get you home if I could."

"Don't take this the wrong way, but I didn't believe you."

"I know you didn't. I'm not offended. At the time, I had given you little reason to truly trust me. I hope the situation between us is somewhat better. Let me try now."

Jason sighed and left the room.

Drake didn't want to take Jason through the normal node jumps to reach the Waypoint. Nor did he wish to jump directly there. One could never be certain who might be watching. So he pulled up the area in his mind and found a node near the Waypoint. There was a stream with a beautiful little waterfall called Devil's Den. Drake remembered making love to a native woman there, long ago. She'd had the most incredible cheekbones.

"I'm ready when you are, Drake," said Jason.

"Sorry, I was thinking about Andover. Jason, I want you to talk to Geoffrey when we get back."

"I talk to Geoffrey every day."

"I am going into darkness and danger. I don't when or if I'll be able to come back. You're my friend. You need a support network. You need people who know who you really are."

"Damn it, Drake, it isn't that easy. I've spent my whole life hiding. Any time I've told people about who I am, things have gone badly for me."

"And you think Geoffrey will care that you aren't human?"

Jason snorted. "Geoffrey wouldn't care if I had two heads."

"Then tell him."

Jason sighed. "Can I think about it?"

"You're hoping I'll open the portal, and you can return home without saying anything."

"Stop trying to guess what I'm thinking. Let's go, before I run away and hide."

"Yes, let us go."

Drake caught Jason and himself up in the apport. Jason's house blurred away to reveal trees, rocks, and a little stream. A signboard displayed a map of local trails. A park ranger picking up trash did a double take and then wandered off, shaking his head.

"One of these days, Drake, someone is actually going to see you," said Jason. "Where are we?"

"North side of Andover, in a little park on the Appalachian Trail called Devil's Den."

Jason nodded. "Appropriate enough. You must have been here before."

"I have," Drake replied dryly, "but it already had the name before I arrived."

"We still have a ways north to go. It's sort of that way," Jason said, point northwest.

Drake concentrated and sensed the pulse of power in that direction. "Yes, I can feel it," he said. "Are you ready? I'll take us right there."

"You might want to come in fifty feet to the south. The portal is in a cave."

Drake nodded and caught them up in another apport.

This time, they arrived in a forest, on the slope of a rocky hill. The air was rich with the smells of tannins from the fallen leaves and the only slightly disagreeable, musty smells of leaf mold and wood rot. A light dusting of snow was mixed in with the leaves.

Up the hill, fallen stones shielded the dark maw of a cave. Drake touched the tumbled, moss-covered stones. The stone of the hillside was old, weathered granite. There was almost no trash, just a ragged old plastic bag caught in a bush, probably blown there.

"This is the cave," said Jason.

Drake nodded; it was much as he remembered it. He removed one of the remote devices from his pocket. A mental pulse caused it to emit light, and it floated to above his right shoulder. The leaves and twigs crunched under Jason's feet as they walked.

"How do you do that, Drake?" asked Jason.

"Do what?"

"Walk completely silently, even here?"

"In the forests of my youth, it wasn't safe to make even the slightest noise. You learned to be silent, or you died."

"Sounds like a great place."

"It was very beautiful," said Drake. "This place reminds me of it somewhat."

"Threnendar looked much like this, too," Jason said. "The trees were larger, and it was more mountainous, but it this is close enough to hurt."

"I understand," said Drake. "Shall we make our way inside?"

The cave wasn't difficult to enter. An optical illusion from the fallen stones made it look as if the cave stopped a meter or so past the entrance. It didn't. The cave reached far back into the darkness. A phoenix was painted on the wall.

"Your work?" asked Drake.

Jason just nodded.

Drake stopped about ten meters into the cave. He could feel the power of the Waypoint pulsing through the cave. It was one of the old devices, a relic of the expansion of his people after the universes were first formed.

Drake called forth the Instrumentality and sought the mechanism of the Waypoint. He could feel the controls tucked away into a pocket space. Something was blocking him. He shook his head.

"I'm sorry, Jason. I've tried to open this one before. This Waypoint has a specific set of controls, but I can't determine what they are. I think it might be tied to planetary alignments."

"What?"

"I can feel the mechanism, but I can't access it."

"What does that mean?"

"It means this will be harder than I thought."

Drake drew on the power of the Instrumentality and drove

tendrils through the interstices of reality. He could feel the universe on the other side. A pulse of power shot back down the tendrils, and Drake rocked back on his heels from the force of it. Someone or something on the other aside didn't want him to open a path to that world.

Too bad, Drake thought.

He drew more power, spreading his hands to pull open the interface. Drake was shaking from the effort, and rainbows lit up the cavern as reality tore open under the awful force of the Instrumentality. For just a moment, Drake saw a cave not unlike the one he stood in. A woman was there, shining too brightly for his eyes to focus on her.

Not yet, came a thought into his mind. *Come back in fifty years. That world isn't ready to join with this one. Go away, child of Chaos.*

I'm not waiting fifty years, Drake thought.

You don't have a choice.

The brightness of the woman burst upon him, and Drake cried out as the interface snapped shut. He could feel that the universe on the other side had been sealed with a power greater than he was able to bring forth, even with the Instrumentality. Something tickled his face, and Drake wiped blood away from his nose.

"*Marrah,*" Jason whispered.

"I'm sorry, Jason. I can't open the Waypoint, nor get through to the other side, at this time. The woman you saw said to come back in fifty years. I don't know who she is, or what power she has, but I believe her when she says it won't open until then."

Jason nodded. "What's another fifty years at this point?"

"Come on," said Drake. "Let's get you home. I could use another beer, too."

"Yeah, that sounds like a good idea."

CHAPTER THIRTY-TWO

Geoffrey was surprised that Jason wasn't home.

His truck was in the garage, and there were empty beer bottles on the counter in the kitchen. It wasn't like Jason to leave bottles out instead of chucking them into the recycling bin. His friend wasn't out in his workshop, either.

Geoffrey called Brygida. "Hey, it's Geoffrey. Have you seen Jason?"

"Can't say I have," said Brygida. "He might be out with Drake."

"Drake's back?"

"He was planning on dropping in on you guys. Don't let him drag you off on some adventure. Midterms are next week."

Geoffrey groaned. He'd been trying not to think about that.

"Calm down, Geoffrey. You'll do fine. Just actually study a little when you get together with Jen, okay?"

"Yes, ma'am."

Brygida laughed. "I'm sure I'll see you guys over the weekend. Say hi to everyone. I have to go. I have a student waiting to talk – it's my office hours."

"Okay, thanks, 'bye."

Geoffrey had just sat down on the couch with a beer when Jason and Drake appeared. Jason was wearing a coat and didn't look happy. Drake had a little bit of dried blood visible near one nostril. It looked for all the world as if Jason had struck Drake, but Geoffrey knew that couldn't be it: Jason didn't have a mark on him.

Jason took his coat off and went out into the hall.

"If you're going to make coffee, grab me a beer," Drake called.

"Yes, I'm making coffee. Get your own damn beer."

"He's in a great mood," said Geoffrey. "Where did you guys go?"

"Just a little road trip," Drake said, sitting down on a chair.

Jason came back into the room and gave Drake a beer along with a glare.

"Jason has something he wants to talk to you about," said Drake.

"Doesn't look like it," Geoffrey replied.

Jason had left the room again in a hurry. Geoffrey could hear him banging cabinet doors in the kitchen. Jason preferred real coffee to instant. Geoffrey couldn't really blame him, but Jason was almost a snob when it came to coffee.

"I think the ritual of making it soothes him as much as the coffee itself," said Drake.

"Are you okay?" Geoffrey asked. "Your nose…"

"Ah, yes. My nose. I encountered someone who forced me to make more of an effort than I have in some time. My nose bled a little. It isn't anything to worry about."

"If you say so."

"I do."

Jason came back in with his coffee mug and sat on the couch next to Geoffrey. He didn't look at Drake. Jason's mug rattled as he set it down; his hands were shaking slightly. If he hadn't known better, Geoffrey would have said Jason was scared.

"What's going on?" Geoffrey asked.

"As I said, Jason has something he wants to tell you."

"And as I said, it doesn't look like it," Geoffrey replied. "Jason, I don't know what's going on, but don't worry about it, buddy. Just relax and drink your coffee. Drake is just being an ass. If you don't want to talk about anything, don't."

"No, he's actually right, for once," said Jason.

Drake snorted and sat back, drinking his beer. His odd green eyes were focused on Jason, though. Geoffrey couldn't imagine what was going on, but it was clear Drake was pushing Jason to do something he didn't want to do.

Jason sighed and pulled off his bandanna.

Geoffrey glanced at him and then at Drake. "What? You finally convinced Jason that his bandanna is a fashion disaster? Is a haircut in his future?"

Drake laughed. "Sorry, I forgot I clouded your perceptions." He waved his hand.

Geoffrey shook his head as a sharp, fleeting pain went off behind his eyes. He blinked a couple of times. He didn't know what Drake was talking about. He glanced at Jason, to see if his friend knew anything about it.

That was when he noticed Jason had pointed ears.

Geoffrey groaned. "Please tell me you're not related to Drake!"

"Oh, hell, no," said Jason.

"Thanks," Drake said wryly. "Would being related to me be so bad?"

"No offense, but yeah, kind of," said Geoffrey.

"Hmm." Drake looked as if he wanted to say something else, but instead he just shook his head and drank his beer.

"Okay, you've got pointed ears. So what? Am I missing something?"

"You really don't care?" Jason asked.

"Well, I have a million questions, but otherwise no, not

really. I mean, have you met our friends?"

"Good point."

"I think I should get another beer," said Drake. "Geoffrey, do you wish another?"

"That was the last beer, Drake," said Jason. "Sorry. We didn't know you were coming, or we'd have stocked up."

"No worries."

Drake waved his hand, and two glistening six-packs of bottles appeared on the coffee table. The bottles were labeled *Magennis* but otherwise were black and gold with the familiar harp symbol. Geoffrey wondered who was going to be missing them, in a universe next door.

"You could have just summoned beer at any time?" said Jason. "You realize we're on a bit of a fixed income, right?"

"Make and sell more furniture, then," Drake replied. "Geoffrey, how is your internship going with Gerhardt? Is he paying you well?"

"It's going fine," said Geoffrey. "He's paying me well enough. Um, shouldn't we all talk about this?"

"About what?" Drake asked.

Geoffrey gestured at Jason. "About Jason? I mean, how long have you known?"

"All my life," Jason quipped.

"Since I first met him," said Drake. "It was somewhat obvious. I mean, covering his ears? His problems with iron?"

"Can we not talk about me like I'm not here?"

"Was I?" said Drake.

"Kind of."

"Does Brygida know?" Geoffrey asked. "Jon?"

"Yes, Brygida does," said Jason. "She figured it out, back when she was helping Lolani with her illness. I don't know if Jon knows."

"He figured it out," Drake said, "before that."

"Unbelievable. You are such an asshole, Jason. I moved in

with you! After all we've been through, and you didn't tell me until now!"

"Yeah, like I was going to tell somebody I'd just met. 'Hi, are you interested in being my housemate? By the way, I'm not human.'"

"It's not as if you were a secret cigar smoker – ugh. Anyway, you should have told me when we got back."

Jason shrugged. "Well, I didn't. Get over it."

"He may be more dwarf than elf," said Drake. "At least, he's as surly as one."

"Do I need to say it?" Jason asked with narrowed eyes.

"It would probably be best if you didn't," Drake replied. "For you."

"How long?" Geoffrey demanded.

"As I said, my whole life."

"I mean, how long have you been on Earth?"

"A while."

"Like, since before I moved in with you?"

"Obviously it had to be a bit before that." Jason finished his coffee and left to make more.

"Am I just slow, or what?" Geoffrey asked Drake.

"Should I answer?" Jason said from the other room.

"I clouded your mind so you wouldn't notice." Drake shook his head. "Maybe it was a mistake, but at the time, Jason was worried about anyone finding out. I think he's had a very rough life. As for how long he's been here, I don't know. A few centuries, I would say."

"Wow. I always thought we were almost the same age," said Geoffrey. "Now, I feel like an ass."

"You are an ass," Jason said as he came back in and sat down. "But so am I. I should have told you, after everything we'd gone through. It's just easier to pretend to be normal, you know?"

"What about Elena?" asked Geoffrey.

"What about her?"

"Are you going to tell her?"

Jason sipped his coffee. "I hadn't planned on it, no."

"It doesn't bother you? Lying about being so much older than her?"

"*That's* the part that bothers you?" Jason said. "My age?"

"That's the only part that really matters," said Geoffrey. "Isn't it? I mean, you seem human."

"That's debatable."

"You're from the same root stock," said Drake. "I would guess your ancestors were colonists from the Courts. Elena, I assume, is a native of this world. Her genetics are likely incompatible with yours."

"Why?" Geoffrey asked. "You seem to be, uh, *compatible* with lots of different people."

"My people are shapeshifters," said Drake.

"That's genetics?" Geoffrey asked. "Not magic or something?"

"Yes."

"I think you would have made my old biology teacher cry."

"Without a doubt."

"So you don't think I'd be able to ever have children?" Jason said. "With a human, I mean."

"I can't imagine you've been chaste your entire time on this world," said Drake. "Have you ever had any children?"

"No," Jason replied flatly.

"This is so weird," said Geoffrey. "Man, if I had pointed ears, I'd have been flaunting them."

"You'd probably be dead, then," Jason said. "You don't think the government takes an interest in such things?"

"Jason, there are people who have surgery to point their ears."

"There are?" said Drake. "I didn't think the idea of elves was common in your culture."

Geoffrey shrugged. "Movies, games, books: yeah, elves are a

thing. Some people want to be like them."

"Not just space elves?" Jason asked wryly.

"Hey, I like *Star Trek*," Geoffrey replied indignantly. "People don't care as much about pointed ears and stuff nowadays. Brygida doesn't hide hers."

Jason sighed. "Look, I know I have hang-ups. Let me deal with them in my own way, okay?"

"Yeah, okay." Geoffrey opened one of the beers. It tasted like Guinness. "How long are sticking around for, Drake?"

"At least the weekend," Drake said. "I won't run off again without saying goodbye, if at all possible."

"I talked to Brygida. "She mentioned maybe getting together for dinner one day this weekend."

"That sounds good."

Geoffrey wondered what Drake wasn't telling them. Someone had tried to kill Brygida, and Geoffrey didn't think Drake was going to let that stand. He'd traveled with Drake to the ends of the universes to discover why someone was trying to kill Jon. Drake wouldn't do any less than that for his friend Brygida.

CHAPTER THIRTY-THREE

Drake awoke to the smell of bacon the next morning.

The rich odor drove him to dress hurriedly. Tadeo was in the dining room window, chittering at the birds gathered on a feeder. Brygida was in the kitchen, frying the bacon.

"Bacon and biscuits," Brygida said. "I'm terrible at cooking eggs – sorry."

"Do you have eggs?"

Brygida nodded. "I bought some last night. I didn't think about how badly I cook them until this morning."

"I could assist in the cooking," Drake suggested. "I'm rather fond of eggs."

"If you don't mind. You'll find the eggs on the fridge door."

Brygida set out a pan while Drake was retrieving the eggs, cheese, and butter. "How do you like your eggs?"

"Not raw or burned," Brygida said. She finished crisping the last piece of bacon. "Do you want the bacon grease?"

"No, thank you. Butter will suffice."

Drake deftly whisked the dozen eggs in a bowl with a fork while the butter was melting in the skillet. He poured in the eggs and waited until they began to bubble before adding the cheese. He kept stirring and agitating the eggs as they cooked. When they were light and fluffy, he divided the eggs onto the two plates Brygida had set out.

They spoke little while eating.

"How did it go with Jason?" Brygida asked.

"Well, I think. Geoffrey was somewhat surprised but not bothered about it."

"I didn't think he would be," Brygida said. "Did you talk to them about who Geoffrey really is?"

"It didn't seem an opportune time."

"That could come back to haunt you."

"It already has." Drake shook his head. He'd wanted to tell Geoffrey about his father, but it just wasn't the time. Geoffrey was safer not knowing. "No, I think it best for now that he remains ignorant."

Brygida nodded. "As you wish."

"Thank you. I appreciate your discretion."

"Geoffrey has taken up fencing – did he tell you?"

Drake smiled. "No, he did not. Competitive?"

"No, historical rapier."

"Well, it isn't the best for actual combat, but it should help him defend himself, if need be."

"I have tried to subtly influence him on this," said Brygida, "although it's his girlfriend who actually got him interested."

Drake sighed. "I suppose it was too much to hope for, to think that he simply had a drive to learn for himself."

"Not everyone is like you," said Brygida, smiling to take the sting out of her words.

"I never thought everyone was, my dear daughter. I do remember you handling yourself quite well in combat, though."

"I learned to fight because it was what was done. I remember being quite cross at my mother and Uncle Dominic for making me learn, although I did enjoy the thrill of combat once I began. I suppose it wasn't much different from my other classes in that regard."

"Have you thought of giving Geoffrey fencing lessons?"

"He hasn't asked."

"Maybe I should do so," said Drake. "I haven't the time to properly train him, but I can certainly instill the basics. He'd be better than most opponents he'd face, at that point."

"I'm sure he'd be thrilled," Brygida said. "Once he gets over his terror."

"You don't think he'd be afraid of training with me, do you?"

Brygida shrugged. "Let us just say that he has a great respect for your combat prowess."

"He's seen me fight," Drake mused. "However, fencing is certainly a different art."

"I think he would benefit from the training, not to mention the bragging rights."

Drake laughed. "I'm essentially unknown here."

"If you were to train him, he'd become a better fighter and be able to impress his girlfriend."

"You mentioned her before."

"Jen is good for him, I think," said Brygida. "He met her in my physics class. They're a good match."

"He is rather young to thinking of settling down."

"I don't think it's like that." Brygida stood up and started collecting the dishes.

Drake stood and began to help her.

"I've got this," she said. "Why don't you head over and see if you can catch Geoffrey. He has practice on Sundays, so a few lessons today could go a long way."

"I don't mind helping with the dishes."

"There aren't many," Brygida said. "Go on."

Drake nodded and left the house. The morning air was brisk as Drake stepped outside. It felt strange to be walking around outside without his armor. He was accustomed to being protected at all times.

Not that I can't defend myself, Drake thought. He just preferred not have to think about it all the time. He preferred to think about his family and friends. Drake didn't often allow himself to relax.

His daughter Brygida wasn't much like him – not that it bothered him. Drake had grown to love the strange young woman. She was very intelligent and talented. She just didn't have the same drives and desires as most people.

In some ways, it would have made his own life easier if he'd been more like her. Drake had suffered much loss because of his drive to be with someone. He'd had many lovers over the years, and he'd loved them all. Of course, a few stood out.

Princess Monika, of the Golden Kingdom, had been one who stood out. He'd loved her very much. Perhaps too much. He didn't even remember why they had gone their separate ways, but he regretted it. She's been with child when she left him, but she hadn't told him about Brygida.

Drake would have liked to be a part of Brygida's life when she was growing up.

Not that Drake had any complaints about who his daughter had become. As they traveled together, Drake had come to know Brygida quite well. He loved his daughter for who she was. Perhaps that is what made having not known her sooner so difficult.

Of course, he still desired her mother, Monika.

Monika was an exceptional woman.

Traffic was light in the city this morning. Drake could hear cars and trucks a few kilometers away on the expressway, but there were few to none on the back streets he was walking. It was curiously peaceful, walking along these tree-lined roads.

Drake missed the forests of his youth. It felt like so many lifetimes ago, although it had been over forty-five thousand years since he left, by his reckoning. He was uncertain how much time had passed in that Realm. He hadn't known how to determine such things, back then. He could only assume that everyone he'd known there was dust now.

He left a lover and a child when he'd gone into the darkness of the East to seek revenge for the death of his mother and father. He never returned to that world. At first, it had been because he been afraid to lead the Ancient Enemy there. Later, it had been because he couldn't bear to learn what had happened to his wife and daughter.

Maybe he'd return one day.

Drake shook his head to clear his thoughts. He didn't want to think about that. He was too much a realist to believe he was going to survive the coming war. He could smile and pretend for others, but he felt in his heart that he was going to die.

He was content with his fate.

Drake had put off the war, dealing with the problems of his friends, but he couldn't put it off much longer. The assassinations of children from both the Courts and the Golden Kingdom was proof that he needed to get back to what he'd been doing before Jon entered his life.

Someone, possibly Drake's fallen brother, was sending people out to hunt down and kill the non-pureblood children of two Realms. Drake wasn't entirely certain why, nor did he understand why the assassins sometimes wore his form. It may have been an attempt to corrode support for Drake and his army.

Drake needed to find that tower shrouded in darkness and end this. If what he suspected about why Jon had been created was true, then Drake needed to do something about the Stasis Tombs in the Eye, as well. That was a far more terrifying proposition.

CHAPTER THIRTY-FOUR

Jon and Aradhana set off the next morning to try to escape from the planet.

Jon had not had a good night, his dreams haunted by the specter of what he'd seen in that warehouse. He'd been unprepared to see it, and only his shock had insulated him and allowed him to function as well as he had. Having traveled with Drake probably helped a little, as well.

While it was true that Jon had encountered the Ancient Enemy before, it hadn't prepared him for what Lily had done to Osian and the others. No amount of knowledge about the Ancient Enemy would have been enough to prepare him for that horror.

In some ways, maybe it was good that the slaughter bothered him. At least he knew he was still capable of being moved by such horror. He was just glad Aradhana hadn't been there, glad she hadn't had to see that.

"Do you really think the spaceport is going to be open?" Aradhana asked.

"Commerce is the lifeblood of any planet. I used to make my living moving goods to and from planets like this."

"You mean smuggling."

Jon shrugged.

Other people were out on the streets; the city wasn't locked down. Jon had been worried that after the fire at the warehouse, the city might be put under stricter martial law. Instead, this seemed to be a day much like any other. There were no more troops on the streets than normal.

It saddened him that seeing troops on the street was normal to him now.

There was a military checkpoint at the entrance to the starport. Jon presented his and Aradhana's papers and waited as the soldier looked over them, frowning. An officer approached, and they stood talking quietly behind a privacy barrier.

The officer stepped forward. "Mr. and Mrs. Owens?"

"That's us," Jon replied unenthusiastically.

"These are immigration papers."

"That's right. We're moving here from New Wales."

"Congratulations," the officer said. "You're here. Why are you at the starport?"

"We're immigrating, but we haven't moved our assets. We needed to return home and pack, have things shipped here."

"You should have thought of that before. These papers are for immigrating. Now that you're here, you must obey our laws. You say you want to return home? Then turn around and start walking. This is your home."

"Perhaps I misspoke," said Jon. "I meant to say we needed to return to our *former* home, to pack our things for moving here. We didn't pack before, since we didn't know the condition of the housing market here in New Cardiff."

"I suggest you contact a moving company," the officer said. "All off-planet visas have been canceled. Not that you bothered to acquire one."

"We have immigration papers, but we aren't citizens here yet," said Aradhana. "We're still citizens of Earth."

The officer spat to the side. "Well, then, you're even more fucked. If you aren't citizens, you can't buy property. Now *cer i grafu*. I'm busy."

Jon caught Aradhana's arm and pulled her away from the checkpoint.

"What did he say?" Aradhana asked. "That bit at the end in Welsh?"

"Go and scratch," Jon replied. "Basically, *fuck off*. I'm just relieved he didn't decide to detain us."

"So now what the hell do we do?"

"Anything in the luggage you're really attached to?"

Aradhana shook her head. "Nothing I can't live without. What are you thinking?"

"We apport onto the field and try to bribe our way onto a ship."

"Fuck."

"I know it isn't the greatest idea."

"Yeah, no shit." Aradhana sighed. "Let's just do it."

Jon took her hand and concentrated on the other side of the fence. Suddenly they were there, between two buildings, with the landing field only fifty meters away. Three ships waited on the field. Two had Alliance markings; the other ship was marked as coming from Masir. Jon would have preferred the Masir ship, but the closest Alliance merchant looked ready to take off.

"That one," Jon said, nodding toward the merchant ship. "Walk casual. They're still loading cargo, but I can see the crew disconnecting the fuel lines. They'll be taking off soon. You still have your Earth papers?"

"Yeah. Not sure how much good it will do."

"I plan to offer a sizable bribe."

"What's to keep them from taking the bribe and then handing us over to the port authorities?"

"Do you have a better idea?"

Aradhana sighed. "No, let's go."

No one stopped them as they walked across the field, but Jon felt his skin crawling between his shoulders. He kept expecting to be shot. The feeling wasn't prescience, though. He was just afraid.

The woman supervising the loading carried a slim digital tablet and showed lieutenant's bars on the shoulders of her uniform. She gave Jon and Aradhana a curious glance as they walked up but finished checking off the items being loaded before she turned to them.

"Can I help you?"

"We were hoping to purchase passage on your ship," said Jon.

"This is a merchant vessel, not a pleasure yacht."

"We're Alliance citizens, and the locals wouldn't even consider letting us leave the planet, lieutenant," Aradhana said. "We just want to go home. We're from Earth."

The woman frowned. "What do you mean, they wouldn't let you leave?"

"We had to sneak onto the field."

Jon kept quiet. The lieutenant looked as if she would respond better to Aradhana.

"Bide a moment." The woman raised a com unit. "Captain? We have a couple here that are looking to book passage back to Earth. Yes, sir, that's what I told them, but they're persistent. Roger, I'll let them know." The woman lowered her com and looked at them. "The captain will see you in his office. I'll lead you there. Don't think that because we're letting you on the ship, you can stay. If the captain says you go, you go."

"We understand, lieutenant," said Aradhana.

Jon nodded.

"All right, follow me." The lieutenant led them into the ship. The merchant vessel wasn't much bigger than Jon's ship, the *Chwyldro*. It was taller, though, and a maze inside. They passed through the lower decks and then climbed a ladder to the upper. They passed the bridge before coming to a door marked *Captain's Office*.

To Jon, that seemed a bit pretentious for such a small ship.

The lieutenant buzzed the intercom and announced them. The door slid open to reveal a very small office just big enough for the small desk. Before the desk stood two chairs, and behind it a heavyset man with bulging eyes and a beard.

"Please sit," said the captain. "I'm Captain Laurent, master of the *Avignon*. You are?"

"Mr. and Mrs. Owens," said Jon, sitting in the offered chair. "Thank you for seeing us, captain."

Aradhana sat in the other chair.

The lieutenant leaned against the doorframe behind them.

"So, what seems to be the problem?" Laurent asked.

"My wife and I had thought about immigrating to this world," said Jon, "but the government is a tad too authoritarian for us."

Laurent guffawed. "I imagine so, if you're from Earth. Not much law there at all, is there?"

"It certainly isn't as suffocating as this world. We'd like to book passage to wherever you're going, as long as it's away from here. We have money. We're not looking for a free passage."

"I'm not in the habit of taking on passengers."

Jon was sure that was true, but he was also sure Laurent wouldn't have wasted his time if he wasn't interested. "What would it cost us?" Jon asked.

"Fifteen hundred credits," said Laurent. "Each. In advance."

Jon sighed and nodded. It was nothing short of highway robbery, but the captain was a shrewd businessman and could probably smell their desperation. "Very well."

"Make it two thousand each."

"What?"

"You agreed too easily."

Jon shook his head. "Seventeen hundred each. We aren't rich."

"Sure, you're not." Laurent glanced past them at the lieutenant. "Please escort these people off my ship."

"Fine," said Jon. "Eighteen fifty, but that's the best we can do, really."

The captain sighed and shook his head. "All right, you got passage. Don't expect any meals. You'll sleep in the cargo hold. Don't mess with anything, or I'll have you spaced. Do we understand each other?"

"Absolutely, captain," said Jon. "We don't have any luggage. I assume you'll want payment in advance?"

"Of course." The captain held out a credit stick.

Jon entered the insignificant amount and touched sticks with the captain.

"Thank you for your business. Lieutenant Murphy, show our new guests their quarters. We're ten days to Proxima. You can find passage to Earth from there."

"Captain, not to take their side, but they won't make it ten days without food or water," the lieutenant said. "I'm not comfortable taking them in and then having to space the bodies later."

The captain sighed and shook his head again. "Fine. One meal a day, no more."

"Thank you, captain," said Jon. "That will be sufficient."

"Go on now. I don't want to see you again."

CHAPTER THIRTY-FIVE

Drake didn't have to wait long for someone to answer the door.

Jason opened the door with a sigh and a gesture to enter. The house smelled of coffee, and Jason didn't look as if he'd gotten much sleep the night before. He was wearing his signature bandanna again. Drake hadn't intended to cause his friend distress.

"You're not a coffee drinker, are you, Drake?"

"No, thank you."

"Can I get you anything else?"

"I'm good. I actually just wanted to stop by and see how you're doing. Also, Brygida mentioned that Geoffrey is learning to fence. I thought I would offer to practice with him."

Jason sighed. "I'm fine, Drake. No thanks to you."

"You have a doubt about having told Geoffrey?"

"No, not really. I just have problems with telling *anyone*. Damn it, this isn't easy to deal with. I've been *hunted*, Drake. Do you know what that's like?"

"You know that I do, and I do sympathize. It's one of the reasons I thought you should tell Geoffrey, so you'd have someone else to help you if you needed it. I will always gladly assist, but I can be difficult to contact."

"Yeah, you do tend to disappear."

"I assure you it's because I must deal with other important matters. Some of those matters are making themselves felt most harshly at the moment."

"Like the assassin who tried to kill Brygida?"

"Exactly that, and other things." Drake shook his head. "I have duties as the General of the Rim that I have not been taking care of properly. There is still a war raging; this is just a lull."

Geoffrey came down the stairs, rubbing sleep from his eyes. "Oh, hey, Drake."

"I heard you have taken up fencing," Drake said.

Geoffrey looked startled. "Yeah. I joined a historical group. My girlfriend is a member, so it seemed like the thing to do, you know?"

"I'm sure it will come as no surprise, but I am something of a fencer, as well," said Drake. "I would very much like to practice with you."

"I appreciate the offer, but this group uses special rules and stuff. I don't think you'd like the restrictions. I mean, we use blunted swords with rubber tips."

Drake nodded. "Practice weapons, yes. I am familiar with the concept. I trained the Emperor himself in fencing. You don't think I risked stabbing him, do you?"

"How can I say no?" Geoffrey made it seem more a question directed at Jason.

"I'm not sure he wants to spar with you, Drake," said Jason. "I think he's a bit intimidated."

"When beginning to fence, you can only be as good as your master," Drake said. "I'm sure the person teaching you is skilled, to a degree, but they won't have the skill that I can impart."

Geoffrey sighed. "Can I have breakfast first?"

"Of course. Do you have a copy of those rules you mentioned? I can read them while you eat."

"Give me a minute." Geoffrey trudged back up the stairs and came down a minute later with a ring binder holding a thin sheaf of papers inside. "Our rules."

"I shall acquaint myself."

"Fantastic."

Drake sat at the breakfast table and read over the rules. They were rather straightforward, as far as combat was concerned. He was happy to see draw and push cuts were included in the rules, although the injunction to thrust as lightly as possible seemed pointless. Drake was of the opinion that pain was a good training aid and motivator. However, he'd follow the rules as written, for Geoffrey's sake.

Geoffrey sat at the table with a bowl of hot oatmeal. He ate it rather lumpy, and washed it down with a glass of something like milk. Drake couldn't be certain, but from the smell, he suspected the milky substance was also oats, which seemed odd to him.

The fencing manual had a lot of information about the types of materials allowed for the gear, but not much information about how to fence. When Drake mentioned this to Geoffrey, he was informed that the historical group preferred to have such knowledge imparted in person. It was also, apparently, very informal.

"Do you have gear I could use," Drake asked, "or do I need to acquire some?"

"I have an extra sword, but I don't think my coat would fit you."

Drake nodded. "Let me see your gear, and I'll acquire my own."

Geoffrey stood up and washed his bowl and glass in the sink. "My stuff is in the garage. Do you really want to do this,

Drake?"

"Why wouldn't I?"

Geoffrey sighed and went into the garage.

Drake followed him. Geoffrey was laying his gear on the workbench. The fencing coat was of an unfamiliar style, more historical than Drake had expected. The rapiers were simple affairs with dished cups over the hand, and long flexible blades. The mask looked sturdy enough.

"The mask is strong, for epee and saber work – not that we do that," said Geoffrey. "The hood is made much like the coat."

"Where did you buy the swords?"

"From an online place. I know they aren't the best, but they're all I could afford."

"Could you show me some of these online swords?"

"Sure." Geoffrey got out his phone and then showed Drake some pictures.

Some of the swords were quite beautiful. Drake assumed they were also expensive, given the long numbers assigned to each of them. He found one he liked.

"Do you fancy any of these?" Drake asked.

"I'd love to have this one," said Geoffrey, showing him a sword with an elaborate swept hilt. "I can't afford it, though."

Drake smiled as he called upon the Instrumentality. It took only a moment to find the weapons and pull them to him. He also pulled scabbards and a sturdy black mask.

Geoffrey gasped as the swords appeared on the workbench.

"Go ahead, see if you like the balance," said Drake.

With the Instrumentality still in his mind, Drake shifted his clothes to that of an Eastern European fencing jacket from the fifteen hundreds that he'd once seen in the fencing manual of Joachim Meyers. The clothes were of the fashion of that time, although Drake had them in all black. He made sure the coat was of sufficient density to suit the rules. He also made a black hood for his fencing mask, and black leather gloves.

"Drake, I don't know what to say. This sword is amazing!"

"I'm glad you like it."

Drake drew his own blade from the workbench and flourished it. The practice sword wasn't as perfectly balanced as Maegril, but it was nice enough, of a similar quality to the practice swords in the Courts. It would suffice.

"Where do you normally practice?" asked Drake.

"Huh?" Geoffrey was still looking in awe at his sword. "Oh, uh, over in Eden Park, near the old reservoir wall."

"Is it far from here?"

"Maybe a mile."

"Not too far to walk, then.”

"We could ask Jason for a lift," Geoffrey suggested. "I don't want to walk through Cincinnati with a sword."

"I do it all the time."

Geoffrey looked uncomfortable.

"Fine, let us ask," said Drake.

Jason was amused. "Sure, why not? Geoffrey's been trying to get me to go to his practice for a while. I can watch you kick his butt, or laugh if he kicks yours."

It took as long to drive to the park as it would have taken to walk there. Drake didn't understand Geoffrey's reluctance, although he did notice that many people stared at him as he followed Geoffrey over to the old stone wall. Well, he did make a rather striking figure in the black velvet.

"Okay, so you can deflect a blade with your hand," said Geoffrey, "and you have to be careful not to hit too hard. They're really particular about that."

"I did read the rules, Geoffrey," said Drake. He pulled on his mask and hood. The sword felt good enough in his gloved hand. "Shall we?"

Geoffrey sighed and pulled on his own mask and hood. He held his sword looser than Drake did, and kept his left hand near his chest. "Ready?" His blade was somewhat in *quinte*, but flatter.

Drake saluted with his sword. "*En garde.*" He held his blade in *octave* with his left hand off to the side of his head.

Geoffrey advanced and lunged. Drake parried to sinister and countered with a moulinct draw cut across the right side of Geoffrey's helm. Geoffrey stepped back.

"Good cut," he said. "Damn, you're fast. I didn't even see that."

Drake smiled. "I was moving at less than half my normal speed. I shall slow down a little more."

"Yeah, he's just human, Drake, take it easy on him," Jason called.

"Of course."

Drake once again settled his blade in *octave*. Geoffrey was more cautious. He thrust, and Drake parried, countering with a low thrust which Geoffrey deflected. They went back and forth for a few minutes this way. Someone had done a respectable job of teaching Geoffrey the basics of fencing. Drake could see a mix of styles from at least two of the great Italian masters.

Geoffrey lunged after a parry, and Drake parried to dexter, then switched hands and thrust from sinister to center mass. Geoffrey cried out and stumbled back, dropping his sword. He shook his head and rubbed his chest.

"Damn it, Drake! That was too hard."

"I apologize. I thought I *was* striking lightly. That thrust would have barely entered you, had it been a real sword."

"Well, it needs to be lighter." Geoffrey picked up his sword. "May I?"

"Please do." Drake spread his arms.

Geoffrey tapped him on the chest.

"I barely felt that."

"That's how hard it's supposed to be," said Geoffrey. "You're supposed to release excess force by relaxing the wrist and elbow, allowing them to bend out of line of the strike."

"Are you ready to try again?" Drake asked. He switched the sword back to his right hand.

"Yeah. Just don't actually kill or maim me, okay?"

"No promises," Drake replied. "*En garde.*"

CHAPTER THIRTY-SIX

After practice, Geoffrey took a shower and tried not to think about how sore he was.

Drake had left, and Jason was reading in the living room. Geoffrey wasn't sure why Drake decided to train him or to give him a better sword, but he wasn't going to complain about it. The sword was amazing; it had really improved his fencing. Jen told him that spending a little more on a sword would be worth it. She was right. Only it hadn't cost him anything. Well, not money, anyway.

Geoffrey groaned as he sat down on the couch.

"I'm not driving you to the university," Jason said without looking up.

"I wasn't going to ask you to."

Jason glanced at him. "Are you really that sore?"

"Yeah. I thought I was in good shape. I was wrong."

"Drake really put you through your paces. I thought you did well."

"Thanks." Geoffrey stretched. "Have you ever fenced?"

"You may have noticed that I'm not overly fond of iron," said Jason. "Swords are made of iron. At least the ones here are."

"You had swords made from something else, where you're from?"

Jason sighed and put down his book. "I don't want to talk about that. I'm… I'm not comfortable with… I don't ever talk about that stuff."

"We're cool, Jason. I don't even really think about it. We were just talking. You mentioned it first. I won't push."

"Okay. Thanks for understanding."

"No problem."

Jason picked up his book. "I'm still not driving you to the university."

Geoffrey sighed. "Well, at least it isn't far."

"Have fun."

The weather hadn't warmed up. The sky was still overcast, but at least it wasn't raining. Geoffrey buttoned his coat and set off for Jefferson Avenue. It was only a few blocks away, not even a mile. He knew he should get out and walk more, but cars were just so damned convenient. He wished he could apport, like Drake or Jon.

Jen was meeting him at The 86, a coffee bar they both liked. A friend of hers had some art on display there, with the opening tonight. Geoffrey didn't care much for modern art, but he cared a lot about Jen, and this was important to her.

There wasn't much Geoffrey wouldn't have done for Jen. She was an amazing woman. He was sometimes still in shock that she seemed to feel the same way about him. He'd thought that after Kalea, on Kai, he wouldn't love another woman. This was different. What he felt for Jen contained just as much lust as he'd had for Kalea, but it also held more… respect. He liked Jen for who she was, not just what she looked like. Not to mention that she was brilliant and talented.

Traffic was light on Taft road – for a Saturday, anyway. Geoffrey darted across and walked past the giant Kroger supermarket, which was always busy. He and Jason did most of their shopping there, as did everyone else in the area.

Jason isn't human, he thought.

It was a weird thing to think. A year ago, he'd have been freaked out by it, probably hiding and gibbering somewhere. After months of traveling with Drake, though, Geoffrey couldn't really feel much of anything about it.

What did it mean to be human?

Jason was a different species but looked mostly human. Hell, he *did* look human. So what about the pointed ears? Geoffrey had seen people with pointed ears before, in real life. Other than Brygida and Drake. Unless those people hadn't been human, either.

Geoffrey wasn't sure what to think about that.

The 86 was on the far corner of Jefferson Avenue. Jen was standing outside, talking to a couple of people he didn't know. He checked his phone, but he wasn't late. Jen looked around and waved when she saw him. She said goodbye to the people she'd been talking to and walked over to greet him.

Geoffrey hugged her tightly. The thing with Jason had shaken him more than he wanted to admit. It didn't change how he felt about his friend, but it seemed as if it had changed how he felt about himself. It didn't make much sense, but there it was.

"You doing okay?" Jen asked.

"Yeah, I think so." He laughed a little. "What am I talking about? I'm doing great. I'm here with you!"

"You looked like you were moving a bit stiff."

"I'm just a little sore. My uncle is in town. He found out I'm learning fencing and decided to give a few pointers. Now, I'm sore as hell."

"Well, that's disappointing," Jen said, pretending to pout.

"Not *that* sore," Geoffrey assured her.

She laughed. "Come on inside and warm up."

Jen pulled him indoors. There were more people than

normal in the bar. Paintings covered one wall. Jen ordered a weird coffee, and Geoffrey tried a local craft beer brewed with holiday spices. The beer was okay, although it was a bit sweeter than he preferred.

"So your mysterious uncle fences?" said Jen.

"Yeah. He's really good." Geoffrey felt that he'd just made the understatement of the century, but what the hell was he supposed to say?

"Sport fencing or historical?"

Geoffrey shrugged. How did the term *historical* even apply to someone like Drake, who'd been around since before the dawn of human history? "He mentioned a lot of fencing terms, but also mentioned German *Fechtbuchs*. I don't know. Maybe both? I don't think there's much about any kind of fighting that Drake doesn't know. He fights in an odd style I haven't seen anyone here use."

"You think he'd come out to a practice?"

"God, I can't imagine that. I'm not sure I'd want him to. He's really eccentric."

Jen nodded, sipping her coffee. "You did mention he was a mercenary or something."

"Yeah, emphasis on the *or something*," Geoffrey muttered.

Fortunately, Jen was distracted then. "Oh, there's my friend! Come on, let's go say hi. I'll introduce you."

Jen dragged Geoffrey over to the wall of paintings. A young woman in a Goth uniform was talking to a woman with a buzz cut, dressed in coveralls. The woman with the short hair had a lot of piercings on her face and ears. Geoffrey wasn't sure which woman was Jen's friend.

"Carmila!"

"Jen!" Buzz Cut hugged Jen. "This must be Geoffrey."

"As far as I know," Geoffrey said cautiously.

Carmila laughed.

"Carmila is the artist who did all of these," said Jen. "Aren't they amazing?"

"Well, only this section are my work," Carmila replied modestly.

Geoffrey glanced at the paintings. They were in a surreal style, very freaky subject matter but very well executed. Nude women and strange monstrous creatures sipped wine, ate food, and had sex under bizarre trees and flowers with startlingly animalistic internal structures.

"Nice," Geoffrey said. "They remind me a bit of Hieronymus Bosch."

"Oh, he's a keeper, Jen."

Jen snuggled up against him, which he didn't mind at all. "I know," she said.

The rest of the evening passed in something of a pleasant blur. Geoffrey was introduced to a lot of people he promptly forgot. He was sore and stiff from his fencing workout, but the steady supply of beers really helped with that.

Off and on, he thought about Jason and who he really was, but he couldn't really think about that with all these people around. Besides, Jen was hugging and leaning on him a lot, which usually meant that she was horny. In the scheme of things, he'd much rather think about that than about Jason.

CHAPTER THIRTY-SEVEN

The ship is slowing down, Jon thought.

His perception of space was dampened, sitting in the cargo hold of a ship that wasn't his, but he could still feel something. They had come out of the jump an hour before. If they were in the correct system, then they still had over an hour until they reached the spaceport. If the ship was slowing down now, it could only be bad news.

An alarm sounded, and they could hear people yelling and running throughout the ship. The crew spoke a sub-variant of French. He didn't know what they were saying, but they sounded agitated. Aradhana shook her head, she couldn't make it out either.

"What's going on?" Aradhana asked.

"I don't know. Stay here. I'll go see what I can find out."

Jon left the cargo hold and climbed the ladder to the upper deck.

The captain glanced at Jon as he leaned into the Bridge. "What's going on?" Jon asked.

"We're fucked, that's what," muttered the captain. "I knew you and that woman were bad luck. Now we're being boarded by an Alliance destroyer. Just who the hell are you?"

"Why do you think it has anything to do with me?" Jon asked.

"Play the message," the captain ordered.

"*Avignon,* this is the Alliance Destroyer *Valley Forge.* We have reason to believe that you are carrying two fugitives, wanted by the Alliance. Stand to and prepare to be boarded." The message looped again until the captain growled at the coms officer to turn it off.

"You think that means my wife and me?" Jon asked.

"I bloody well don't think it's anyone from my crew," the captain replied. "You're the only new thing on this ship. I knew you were trouble. I should have listened to my first officer and spaced you both."

"Thanks for the passage. Sorry for the inconvenience," Jon said as he backed out of the bridge and ran to the ladder.

He slid down the ladder as fast as he could and arrived in the cargo hold just as a shudder ran through the ship, accompanied by a loud clang. Jon was almost knocked from his feet as the ship suddenly slowed even more. Aradhana was standing in the center of the hold, looking worried.

"Are we being boarded?" she asked.

"Alliance destroyer," Jon answered.

"So we're screwed."

Jon was trying to concentrate and call forth the Cynosure in his mind. "Do you trust me?" he asked.

"You know I do, what are you thinking?"

"I'm thinking about trying to apport to Kai," Jon said. "I don't know if I can, and it could kill the both of us."

Aradhana shrugged. "We're dead if they get ahold of us. You know that. They probably won't be quick about it either. I believe in you Jon. You can do this. If you fail, fuck it, at least I'll die in your arms."

Jon shook his head. Aradhana was a hell of a woman. He'd

always have feelings for Lolani, but he loved Aradhana. He didn't know what the future held for them, he'd always had a blind spot in his precognition about himself, and those he loved.

The boarding alarm sounded.

"It's now or never," Aradhana said. She stepped close and held him tight. "Do it."

Jon ran all of his jump calculations through the Cynosure. He was always amazed at having a connection to such a powerful machine. He didn't have precise information about where they were in space. He had a good idea, but a good guess really wasn't enough. He didn't have any choice. The cold numbers filled him with dread as he funneled energy into the jump and the cargo hold of the ship dissolved into rainbows.

Intense light and pain shocked him. Jon gasped, but couldn't find anything to pull into his lungs. He felt a burning pain, such as he'd never felt before. He tried to scream, but didn't have any air to scream with. He could feel blood vessels bursting in his lungs, skin, and eyes.

His bleeding eyes wildly sought anything to identify as he and Aradhana tumbled. There! A flash of light over water. A reflection of sunlight through clouds. A familiar chain of islands.

Jon had jumped to Kai, all right. He'd just jumped into orbit, as if he'd been piloting his ship. Only seconds had passed, Jon knew they'd okay if he could just refocus. The pain slowed him down. He should have hyperventilated and exhaled before he'd jumped, but how could he have known he'd jump into empty space?

It felt like an eternity, but he could feel the coordinates for the beach solidifying in his mind. Getting his sluggish exhausted brain to use the Cynosure was another matter. Jon felt intense spasms wrack his whole body, and ice forming across his bloody eyes. He had to jump and hope for the best.

A flash of rainbows and Jon and Aradhana were on the beach. Aradhana let go of him and fell over into the sand. She was trying to scream but could only gasp as she convulsed on the beach. Jon reached for her, but couldn't see and fell over himself. His whole body felt on fire, and his muscles wouldn't stop spasming. Someone must have seen them appear because it wasn't long before he heard Lolani calling their names.

"Jon, Aradhana! What happened? Oh my god, you look terrible!"

"Vacuum exposure," Jon gasped. His eyes were too bloody to see. "Bends."

"Shit! Get them up and to my ship, fast."

Jon felt hard hands grasp him under his arms. His feet dragged along in the sand. His heels caught on the steps, but he was past caring about incidental pain. He felt pressure and a prickling sensation, and the darkness swallowed him.

Some indeterminable time later, Jon came to.

It was a nice to just lay in on an acceleration couch and not be in pain. From the fading echoes of nightmares, Jon knew Lolani must have used one of her precious nanotech medical packages on him. Nothing else could have repaired the damage to his body so quickly either.

His eyes hurt when he opened them and tried to look around.

So, mostly repaired.

Lolani was sitting nearby watching over Aradhana.

"How is she?" Jon asked. He didn't recognize his own voice. It sounded harsh.

"A little better off than you," Lolani said. "She kept her eyes closed."

"I didn't have much choice. I had to see where we were so I could jump."

"I figured." Lolani shook her head. "Bruh, you ain't a cat with nine lives. You need to be more careful. What'd you say to piss off a captain so much she space you, huh?"

Jon started to smile and then decided against it. He hurt when tried. "Wasn't like that. I miscalculated a jump."

Lolani shook her head. "You?"

"I guess it was pretty good, all things considered."

"Where you jump from?"

"Proxima Centauri, I think. About an hour past the jump point into the system."

"Next time, try using a ship."

"Ouch, don't make me laugh, please. I hurt too much. How long have we been back?"

"Only a few hours. Meds still working on you."

"I'm sorry you had to use them on us."

"Idiot," Lolani said. "You could have died, you know?"

"Believe me, I know. We didn't have much choice. An Alliance ship was boarding the merchant ship we were on, looking for us."

"They not gonna give up, are they? What does Drake have to do? Nuke a few planets?"

"I hope not," Jon said. "Certainly not for my sake."

Lolani sighed. "At least they only came after you in Alliance space. What were you thinking going there, bruh?"

"I was thinking we needed to get off of Rhyddid, fast."

"So your quixotic mission failed?" Lolani asked.

"No, I think I was actually successful," Jon said. "I met some people there that helped settle things on Rhyddid, once and for all."

"That sounds pretty final. Who'd you have to kill?"

"We found the… *thing* responsible for the cycle of violence there. Now that it's dead, the revolutions will stop and the people will have a chance."

"Well, well, look at you. Just out of curiosity, when you say *thing*…"

"Like Drake fought on Earth, or Dr. Preta, yeah."

Lolani shuddered. "Damn, bruh. I guess I shouldn't give you so much shit."

Jon smiled. "I rather you didn't stop."

"Jon…" Lolani glanced at Aradhana.

"I'm with her now, and happy," Jon said. "You'll always be my best friend though. You're like a sister to me."

"All right, as long as we good."

"Yeah, we're good."

CHAPTER THIRTY-EIGHT

Drake was in and out of Cincinnati repeatedly over the next few weeks. Geoffrey wasn't sure, but from little things Drake let drop, Geoffrey suspected he was trying to track down the origin of the assassin who'd tried to kill Brygida. Every Saturday, Drake insisted on training Geoffrey in fencing. Geoffrey didn't mind, although his SCA instructor didn't seem too happy about it. Geoffrey was getting used to fighting Drake, who was inhumanly fast even when trying to slow down for training's sake. After that, fighting a normal human seemed pretty easy.

Geoffrey was surprised when final grades were put up; he'd aced every one of his classes, even Brygida's. He hadn't been confident about his answers on the physics final. It didn't feel as if anything came easily to him, except maybe fencing. Unfortunately, he didn't have a class for that. He went up talk to Brygida after his final class with her.

"You're unhappy with your grade?" asked Brygida.

The scar on her face had faded to a faint, pale line. He knew Brygida knew that he was looking at her scar, but she ignored him as she packed her books and papers into her satchel.

Geoffrey didn't mean to stare, but he often did anyway.

"No, not as such," Geoffrey said. "I just want to be sure I actually earned it."

Brygida put down her satchel.

"Geoffrey, I would think that you know me well enough by now to know that if you hadn't done the best you possibly could, I would not have given you an A."

"The best I possibly could? So you *did* give me the grade?"

Brygida sighed. "Is your self-confidence really so low? You earned the grade. Would you like me to give you the answer key and your test, and let you grade it yourself? I've had students think they should have gotten a higher grade but never one complain about an A."

"I just didn't think I did very well on the test," Geoffrey said stubbornly.

"You missed eleven questions," said Brygida. "There were one hundred questions, each worth one point. I included three bonus questions, each worth five points. Those weren't easy questions to answer. You missed one of them – wildly off mark, I might add. However, you answered the other two bonus questions perfectly. Do the math."

Geoffrey nodded slowly. "I'm sorry, I just… Jen and Elena are both brilliant… I didn't want to take away from what they did. I mean, they just got A's, too."

Brygida smiled. "You scored a ninety-nine on the test, an A. Elena and Jen didn't miss any questions, including the bonus questions, and scored one hundred fifteen each. Does that satisfy your need to humble yourself?"

Geoffrey blushed and nodded.

Jen grabbed him from behind and laughed when he jumped.

"What are you guys being so serious up here for?" said Elena. "The semester is over. It's time to celebrate!"

"We're going for a bite. Care to join us, Dr. Hakubi?" Jen asked.

"The semester is over. Call me, Brygida." She smiled. "I think going out and celebrating would be a lot of fun. Is Jason coming?"

"He will if he knows what's good for him," said Elena.

They all laughed at that.

"Where do you want to eat?" asked Brygida.

"Jen and I were thinking of The Melting Pot," Elena said.

"Mmm, fondue," said Brygida.

"Isn't that kind of expensive?" Geoffrey asked.

"I thought you were Mr. I-have-an-internship-and-can-afford-to-spend-money," said Elena.

Geoffrey laughed, holding up his hands. "I surrender!"

"Hey, back off. He's mine!" Jen said with a mock growl.

Brygida laughed. "Okay, go away! Call me when you're ready to head over there."

Geoffrey, Jen, and Elena walked to the edge of campus together. The weather was cold, with a few inches of snow on the ground. Real snow wouldn't come for a couple of weeks, but Cincinnati was on the edge of the snowbelt and got about thirty inches of snow every winter. Not all at once, fortunately. Not *usually* all at once, anyway.

"Remember to tell Jason about dinner tonight," said Elena, "so he doesn't spoil his appetite."

"I'll remember to ask him," Geoffrey said.

"Don't ask him shit," said Jen. "Just *tell* him dinner is a seven, and we're all going out. You give him a choice, and he'll stay home."

Elena laughed. "Yeah, do that."

"I will," Geoffrey said. He gave Jen a hug and a kiss. "See you guys at seven."

"Be safe walking home," said Jen.

"I will."

It wasn't that cold outside, and Geoffrey's military surplus parka was nice and warm. The biggest hazard while walking home was the slush from speeding cars and trucks. There was a light fog, and the snow and ice picked up the city lights, sparkling.

Of course, the city lights were mostly orange sodium lights that gave a ruddy glow to the sky and made it feel as if he was walking on an alien world. Geoffrey hadn't visited any alien worlds that looked like this, however. All the ones he'd actually been to had been much like Earth, except for maybe the Courts.

Geoffrey stopped for a moment and took a deep breath.

He'd been to alien worlds.

It was difficult to wrap his brain around that.

Jason was in the kitchen making coffee when Geoffrey got home. Geoffrey took off his soggy boots and hung up his coat. He hoped Jason wouldn't try to get out of going to eat. Geoffrey didn't want to have to call Brygida and get a lift.

"How'd you do in your classes?" Jason asked.

"Straight A's, even in Brygida's class."

"Congratulations," Jason seemed in a good mood.

"Thanks. Some of us are going out later to celebrate," said Geoffrey. "We're having dinner at the fondue place."

"Sounds good. Have fun."

Geoffrey sighed. "Elena is going to be there. I think she's getting tired of you giving her the cold shoulder."

"I haven't been!"

"Yeah, you kind of have," said Geoffrey. "When was the last time you guys went out?"

"She had papers and finals and stuff. I didn't want to be a distraction."

"Well, the semester is over. You don't have an excuse to hide anymore."

Jason set down his coffee mug. "First of all, I'm not hiding. Second, I don't need any excuses. Third, mind your own damn business."

"You and Elena are both my friends, so it is my business."

Jason rubbed his face. "You have to know that my relationship with Elena can't go anywhere. I can't afford to let her too close to me. She could discover what I am. That isn't safe. For her or me."

"If you just tell her who you are, then she doesn't have to discover anything."

"You know why I can't do that."

"Actually, I don't," said Geoffrey. "I really don't see what the problem is."

"Damn it, you are so fucking naive sometimes."

"Fuck you, man. I'm not the one who's been stringing some girl along for months. Did you know Jen says that Elena cries over you? She doesn't understand why you're so standoffish, and you won't tell her anything!"

"I never intended to hurt her," Jason said quietly.

"What *did* you intend?" said Geoffrey. "Why did you start dating her? So you could feel normal? Do you even care about her at all?"

"I care about her a great deal. Geoffrey, please understand how difficult this for me. Maybe I did start dating her to feel normal, but… Yes, I do have feelings for her. Can't you understand how dangerous it could be for her?"

"Frankly? No. I've known for months, and nothing's happened. Brygida goes around as alien as can be, and no one's bothered her. I get that you've had a hard life, man, but you need to understand that it doesn't have to be like that anymore."

"What could I possibly offer her, Geoffrey? We could never have a family together."

"This may come as a shock to you, but most women don't want kids," said Geoffrey. "Especially smart ones like Elena. What could you offer her? How about a guy to date, who doesn't judge her because she has brains. Maybe even likes that about her."

"I do."

"No one can know if these things are going to work. But if it doesn't, and it doesn't end because you do something stupid, then you'll have a friend for life. That woman would do anything for you, man. She loves you."

"When did you get so wise?" Jason asked.

"It just slips out sometimes," said Geoffrey.

"Sounds like a personal problem."

Geoffrey smiled. "The Melting Pot, seven this evening. Jen is making reservations."

"How can I say no to melted cheese and bread?"

"Well, technically only the cheese is actually melted."

"Asshole."

"Jerk."

"So it's settled. We're all having dinner to celebrate the end of the semester."

"Okay."

"What about Elena?" asked Geoffrey.

"What about her?"

"You need to figure out what you're doing before you really hurt her. And don't even think about breaking up with her right before Christmas."

"You're not giving me many options here."

"I'm not saying you have to tell her – that's your secret. I do think that to be fair to her, you should at some point. Let her decide if she cares about you being older."

"You still think my age is the sticking point here?"

"Yeah, actually."

Jason sat down at the table and sipped his coffee.

Geoffrey sat down across from his friend.

"I know you dealt with the truth about me really well," said Jason, "but – forgive me for saying so – I think you're somewhat exceptional."

"You think, because I didn't make a big deal about it, that

it didn't freak me out?"

Jason looked surprised.

"I *was* a little freaked out," Geoffrey said. "I kept it to myself because I didn't want to worry you. Oh, I don't care that you aren't human, whatever that means, exactly. I was mostly just shocked that I hadn't noticed."

"Drake *did* whammy your brain."

"Yeah. I tend not to pay attention to stuff like that anyway. I remember being out with Jen one day, and these assholes said something derogatory to her. I made them apologize, but I didn't really understand why they'd said what they did. Then Jen said it was just part of being a mixed-race woman in modern America."

"Assholes are everywhere." Jason said. "You leave them alive?"

"I'm not Drake, so yeah. I don't understand why it bothers people. I'd like her any color."

"Even green?"

"You know, I always thought Orion women were hot in *Star Trek*, especially the one in the new movie."

"Gaila was one of the few good things about that movie."

"Rachel Nichols, yeah," Geoffrey said with a sigh. "Anyway…"

"Jen is about the same height as her, isn't she?"

"*Anyway*," Geoffrey said. "We were talking about you and Elena."

"I thought I was doing a good job of changing the subject."

"Come on, Jason."

"Will it suit your sensibilities if I just keep dating her as normal but don't let it get too serious?"

"I'm fine with whatever, man. I'm not sure how she'll feel about it. She *is* human, and she isn't asexual, either."

"That's a thing?" Jason asked. "Hmm, maybe I should try that."

Geoffrey sighed. "Just don't hurt her, okay? She's my friend, too."

"I have no intention of hurting her."

"I didn't think you would, or I wouldn't have introduced you."

"I thought that was more Brygida's doing than yours," said Jason.

"You're my housemate, so I'm taking the credit. It's just after six. We need to get ready and get going, if we're going to be there at seven."

"Where are we going for dinner?" Jason asked as he stood and rinsed his coffee cup.

"I told you, the Melting Pot."

"Oh, yeah. Semi-fancy. Okay, I'll dress up nice."

"Your bandanna is really going to stick out."

"Can't be helped," Jason said. "It's part of my culture."

"Asshole."

"Jerk."

CHAPTER THIRTY-NINE

The semester was over.

Final grades hand been reported, panicked students consoled, and other students advised for the upcoming semester. Brygida took one last look around her office and decided she'd be happy not to see it for a few weeks. Teaching while working on the side for Gerhardt had been exhausting.

Brygida sighed as someone knocked on her door. "Enter!"

"Hello, daughter."

Brygida looked up quickly.

"Father, I didn't realize you had returned."

"I only just arrived," Drake said. "If I recall correctly, the semester is over and you will be free for a few weeks."

"That's right," Brygida said. "I've been looking forward to relaxing and catching up on some reading."

"You're taking off time from Gerhardt's project?"

"I solved the problems he was having, and a couple he didn't know he had. Yeah, I decided I am done for a while with that. I'll pick it back up next year."

"I thought perhaps I could fulfil a promise I made to you."

Brygida frowned. She didn't remember any promises her

might have made her. "What promise?"

"To see the Ruined Courts and have the opportunity to acquire access to the Instrumentality."

"I thought the problem before was time," Brygida said. "It seems as if training in the use of the Instrumentality would take months or even years. With the time differential that could be as much as a decade here. I really don't want to lose that time."

"I understand that," Drake said. "But I think you are in an interesting position compared to others. You already have Cynosure, therefore you are already trained in the use of something very similar to Instrumentality. I remember the Emperor saying that Cynosure came easy to him, as he had already mastered the Instrumentality. Surely it would go the other way, also."

"One might think," Brygida said.

"There is also the fact that you know the two powers are actually machines. I doubt you'd use the Instrumentality in the same way as another initiate. Your scientific background alone would change how you approached it. There seems to be little reason for you spend years learning spells, when you know for a fact that it is the application of willpower and focused desire that achieves results."

"You make a compelling argument," Brygida said. "But will it sway the minds of the people in the Courts who act as the gatekeepers of knowledge? Will I be allowed to gain the Instrumentality?"

"I'd like to see someone attempt to deny me," Drake said.

Brygida nodded. "I'll need to stop by and see if Jason minds taking care of Tadeo while I'm gone."

"Of course, although I think you'd only be gone for a day or so."

"I'd rather not risk it," Brygida said. "Besides, I would think that there would be a small chance that the attempt might kill me."

"No Drake has ever failed the attempt."

"I'm only half Drake."

"As are all in the House. *We* don't intermarry."

"My car is in the parking structure," Brygida said, ignoring the implied insult to her mother's side of the family. Some of her extended family there had gotten a bit too close to each other. "Would you care to ride over with me to see Jason?"

"Certainly," Drake replied.

Brygida slung her satchel over her shoulder and then locked her office door. Drake walked silently beside her, out to her Jeep. It was cold, for early December. Brygida put on her gloves before starting the engine. Drake might not be affected by the cold, but she was.

She called Jason as she was driving over to his house.

"Hello?"

"Hey, Jason, this Brygida."

"Is everything okay?"

"Everything is fine. Drake is wanting me to go to the Courts with him, and we were going to stop by. I just wanted to give you a call, instead of dropping in unexpected."

"I appreciate that," Jason said. "You can come by anytime. Geoffrey isn't here. He's out with Jen, Christmas shopping, or something."

"Thank you. We'll be there in a few minutes."

Jason opened the door as they approached. He had cleared the sidewalk of snow, and laid down some salt. The snow-covered trees around Jason's house were lovely. There were no Christmas decorations, not that Brygida expected any.

"Come on in out of the cold," Jason said. "You can hang your coat up if you wish. Can I get either of you anything?"

"I'm good, thank you."

Drake nodded that he was good.

"I actually want to ask a big favor of you, Jason," Brygida said.

"What can I do?"

"Time gets a little wonky in the Courts, so I can't know how long I'll actually be gone for, I was wondering if you mind taking care of Tadeo?"

"Sure," Jason said. "Did you want me to just check up on her, or bring her here?"

"Either," Brygida replied. "I may only be gone a day or two, in which case just making sure her food and water is topped off will be fine. However, it could be longer, in which case I'd be grateful if you'd bring her here and give her some company."

"No problem," Jason said. "She's a sweet little cat."

"Thank you, Jason."

"So what has you rushing off to the Courts," Jason asked. "Does this have something to do with the assassinations?"

Brygida felt her scar twitch. "No, this is just a good time to go."

"She has never been to the Courts," Drake added. "The holiday break seemed a good time."

"Look on the bright side," Jason said. "You'll get to miss all the nauseating holiday music."

"I would if they hadn't been playing it for the last month," Brygida said. She fished her spare key out of her satchel. "Tadeo will be fine tonight."

"I'll check on her in the morning," Jason said, taking the key. "And again in the evening."

"Thanks, say hi to Geoffrey for us."

"Will do."

Back home, Brygida refilled Tadeo's food and water bowls. She checked the thermostat to make sure the temperature would be good. She hugged and kissed on Tadeo until the little cat squeaked and wriggled free. Tadeo raced across the room and climbed into Drake's lap, where he was sitting on the couch.

"The little traitor," Brygida said.

"All cats are fickle," Drake replied. "That is part of what makes them so intriguing. Are you ready to go?"

Brygida sighed. "I think so, yes. Do I need special clothes?"

"I think what you're wearing will suffice. We will be visiting with my granddaughter, Eliza."

"Then I am ready."

Drake stood and placed Tadeo into the warmed spot on the couch where he'd been sitting. The little cat curled up immediately and laid there watching them both. The tip of her tail was twitching.

Drake nodded, and the living room dissolved away in rainbows. For just a moment, Brygida had an impression of a snowy forest, and then the world became a swirling tunnel of grey. Brygida knew that her father was taking her through a hyperspatial tunnel, across all of the universes to the Ruined Courts. The sensations were not pleasant. Just as she thought the mind-numbing grey swirl would drive her mad, the tunnel dissolved into rainbows.

They had appeared on a raised dais of some sort. An ancient weathered ring of metal stood in front of them. Strange runes flickered on the metal, and the interior was like a shimmering pool of water.

"T'era-grata," Drake said. "The ancestral homeworld of the Drake Family."

"This worldlet, is very small," Brygida said, staring at the very close horizon. "How does it have gravity and an atmosphere?"

"Ancient engines provide the gravity and stability. They also keep the shattered worlds from colliding."

Brygida swallowed hard. "I hadn't thought about that."

"Look to your left."

Half of the sky was a black so deep it hurt to look at. Brygida could see faint glimmers, which must have been other planets. A shining ribbon bisected the darkness, and Brygida realized she was looking at the Eye, the supermassive black hole that dominated the first universe. The rest of the sky was a deep baleful red.

"Wow."

Drake laughed. "I perceive that you are somewhat overwhelmed."

"How big is that black hole?"

"As large as the Milky Way Galaxy is across."

"And we're in orbit around it?"

"Indeed," Drake replied. "All the shattered worlds of the Ruined Courts are."

"Are there any stars?"

"Not anymore," Drake said. "The stars and uninhabited planets were dismantled to build the Walls of Matter, the ribbon across the Eye."

"What is the function of the Walls of Matter?"

"Threefold," Drake said. "First, the walls hold back most of the gravitational effects of the black hole. Secondly, the walls convert the gravitational forces into energy."

"And thirdly?"

"The Walls of Matter hold the mechanism of the Instrumentality."

Brygida rubbed a hand across her face. It was a lot to take in. That ring had a diameter measured in hundreds of thousands of light years. It was boggling. The mathematician part of her brain was gibbering in a corner. The physicist part of her wanted a closer look.

Drake waved his hand and the portal in the ring flickered. "I'd give you a tour of the House of Drake, but I know you're pressed for time. This portal will lead to the House of Torenvey."

"And your granddaughter?" Brygida asked.

"Countess Eliza married into the House almost two thousand years ago. Her husband died in one of our countless wars, and she became the head of the House. She has led them for a thousand years. She is ruthless and powerful. She also has little love for the North, having lost children and relatives in the war with the Golden Kingdom."

"Do you trust her?" Brygida asked.

"Implicitly. She is my granddaughter, after all."

"Do you think she'll hate me because of my dual-heritage?"

"Not at all. She knows you're my daughter. Be careful what you tell her though. She is something of an information broker."

"Ah, like Aunt Philomena."

Drake looked surprised. "I didn't realize she fulfilled the role of spymaster."

"She's full of surprises," Brygida said. "She's a good one though."

"And you trust her?"

She gave him a sharp look. "As much as I trust any of my family from the Golden Kingdom."

Drake nodded. "Ah. Shall we?"

"We shall," Brygida said. "We'd better, or I'm going to run home."

Drake stepped through the simmering portal, and Brygida followed him.

CHAPTER FORTY

Drake greeted the guards as he and Brygida stepped through the Waypoint at the House of Torenvey. They knew him, of course. Drake wished that Torenvey used the genetic scanner, the way the House of Drake did. However there weren't many of the ancient devices still in use. The Imperial Court didn't even have any.

"Countess Eliza is expecting you, Prince Drake," the guard said. She glanced curiously at Brygida. "She is awaiting you both in the sitting room."

A doorman open the door for them as they approached. "Do you need a guide to the sitting room, Your Highness?" he asked.

"I know the way, thank you."

Brygida was quiet as she followed Drake. She was looking at all of the ornate carvings. She seemed particularly taken by a golden statue of a dragon.

"It is sculpted from time-locked flame," Drake said.

"Time-locked flame?" Brygida asked, touching the smooth statue. "How do you do that, and how do you carve it if it's time-locked? It can't be stasis, the statue is warm."

"Perhaps time-slowed would be a better description," Drake

said. "If it was true stasis, the statue would be silver. In answer to your question, we don't know how to do it any longer. It is an ancient statue, perhaps predating the Ancient War."

Brygida shook her head. "It is an amazing display of just how powerful our ancestors were."

"They did build the Instrumentality."

"Good point."

Drake led Brygida to the sitting room where Eliza was waiting. His granddaughter was dressed in a rusty velvet doublet and pants that matched her hair in color. She stood when they entered the room.

"My dear Drake, did you get lost coming from the front door?" Eliza asked.

She usually called him grandfather, but she didn't know Brygida.

"Not at all," Drake said. "We stopped to admire your displayed artwork, which is why it is there, after all. Countess Eliza, this is my daughter Brygida, also the daughter of Princess Monika, of the Golden Kingdom."

"I'm pleased to meet you, Your Highness."

"The north does things differently," Brygida said. "I'm no princess. If you must insist on titles, I am technically a duchess. However, if you must, then please call me doctor. I earned that one, and it means much more to me."

"I like her," Eliza said. "Please have a seat, Brygida, grandfather. I made your favorite tea."

Drake smiled. Brygida might seem quiet and reserved, but she was no pushover. He sat down after the ladies and accepted the cup of tea. Brygida shot him a questioning glance as Eliza handed her a cup. Drake nodded. The tea was safe.

"I am pleased to finally meet you," Eliza said. "I was curious as to what you'd look like, but I see you take after Drake. Might I enquire as to your scar? It looks recent."

"Eliza," Drake said quietly.

"It's okay," Brygida said. "I'm not vain about it. An assassin almost succeeded in ending me. If the blade had been poisoned he might have."

"You're not a shapeshifter?" Eliza asked.

"Not that I know of."

"Hmm."

"Eliza, I assume that our conversation is a confidential as always?" Drake asked. "I didn't bring Brygida to meet to so that you could acquire tidbits of information to sell."

"My dear grandfather, I am surprised that you would think such a thing of me. I am merely exercising curiosity about my aunt."

"Sure."

"I am also curious about her life in the Golden Kingdom."

"I'm sure that you are," Drake said. "However, that information isn't on the menu for today. I brought Brygida here so that she could attempt to gain the Omphalos."

Eliza laughed. "It takes years to prepare for that, as you know."

"Brygida is already an initiate of the Cynosure, surely that would have prepared her."

"I suppose that would be possible," Eliza said. "Have you spoken with Emrys?"

"I have," Drake replied. "The Emperor, of course, did it the other way around. He was an initiate of the Omphalos before he traveled north and acquired Cynosure. However, he thought it worked much the same way. Brygida isn't seeking to learn spells or incantations."

"What are you seeking then, if I may ask?" Eliza said.

"To be honest, I'm not sure," Brygida replied. "I think I wish access to the… *Omphalos* in order to be closer to this side of my heritage. I think I might feel more… *complete*."

"I wish I knew more of the Cynosure. Emrys said the use of it is much the same. I believe that the mental focus would be much the same. I cannot say how the Omphalos will react to the presence of the Cynosure imprinted upon you. You need to be prepared to face the horrors that it may generate. People have died making the attempt."

Brygida nodded and glanced at Drake. "They sometimes die with the Cynosure as well. I know myself well, I think. I do not fear making the attempt."

Eliza smiled. "You are a true Drake."

"Thank you."

"How long would it take to get ready?" Drake asked.

"We'll need to convene a guild meeting first…"

"There will be no guild meeting," Drake said. "Any grandmaster of the guild may sponsor an initiate."

"Sponsor, yes. This is completely different and you know it. Not to mention that she'd have to be inducted into the guild."

"Have you forgotten what almost happened to your granddaughter?" Drake asked. "Brygida killed the attacker that came at her before. Now you wish to paint a target on her, by alerting the guild? No. We take her to the initiation chamber and wait until she has finished."

Eliza sighed. "This is against all established procedure."

"I've never been one for rules," Drake said.

"Only when they suit you."

"I don't wish to be a problem," Brygida said.

"Oh, you're not, my dear," Eliza said. "Drake just doesn't like to let anyone know what he has planned. Don't take our banter as anything negative. We're both on your side."

"I'll try to keep that in mind."

"You said you'd earned the title of doctor," Eliza said. "I take it you left the Golden Kingdom and sought an education one of the Earth Realms?"

"I did, yes."

"You remind me a bit of my granddaughter."

"Have you heard from Gillian?" Drake asked. "With all that

has been going on, I haven't had a chance to look more for her."

Eliza shook her head. "I think she is just enjoying herself, traveling the Realms. She'll turn up eventually. If you can't find her, then the assassins won't be able to either."

"I did discover how the assassins were traveling the Realms," Drake said. "That has now stopped."

"That will certainly help. Have you had any luck discovering where they were coming from?"

"A little," Drake said. "I'm still looking into it. I need one of the assassins, alive."

"You may be in luck," Eliza said.

"What do you mean?"

"Let's not get sidetracked, grandfather. We should move quickly with Brygida, while no one is watching. As soon as word gets out that you're back in the Courts, all hell will break loose. And I do mean that quite literally."

Drake sighed. "Very well. I shall restrain my curiosity for now."

"If you have a chance to discover more information, then you should do so. I don't have to do this right now," Brygida said.

"No, I promised you," Drake said. "The other can wait. You have time constraints, the other problem does not. I assume one of the assassins has been taken prisoner?"

"Let the prisoner rot in the dungeon," Eliza said. "For now."

"You have a dungeon?" Brygida asked.

"No, but the Emperor does."

"Ah."

"I assume the prisoner has already been put to the question?" Drake asked.

"Such polite euphemisms," Eliza said. "As I understand it, no one was able to break through the mental wards."

"Indeed."

"Well, they weren't you," Eliza said with a smile.

"No, they were not." Drake shook his head. "Brygida, daughter of mine, do you need time to prepare yourself, or rest?"

"No, I wouldn't get any rest," Brygida replied. "I'd rather get this done."

Eliza stood up and Drake and Brygida followed suit. "Follow me, then."

Eliza led them out to the Waypoint, she nodded to Drake and gestured at the Waypoint, it flickered into life. They stepped through into a vast basalt chamber. Hundreds of inactive Waypoints were set into the outer wall of the chamber. There was no one else in the vast space.

It was also very dark. Only a single feeble globe of ball lightning flickered on the ceiling. Eliza gestured again and called forth a smaller globe of light to float over them. The globe of light moved with them as they walked down the long stairs to the platform in the center.

"This place is huge," Brygida said softly.

"We hold guild meetings here," Drake said. It seats a hundred thousand people, give or take."

"Are there that many people who can use the Instru— I mean the Omphalos?"

"You're teaching her bad habits, grandfather," Eliza said. "That machine heresy that you ascribe to will be your downfall. No, there aren't that many initiates, not anymore."

"May I ask why?" Brygida said.

Eliza sighed. "I don't really have an answer for you."

"It is cyclical," Drake said. "The number of people who use the Omphalos waxes and wanes over the millennia. I've seen it come close to dying out a few times. Usually the numbers are much as they are now, with a few dozens in each of the houses initiated."

They reached the center.

"There are stairs up on the other side," Eliza said.

"I admit to having mixed feelings about being here again," Drake said.

"You did forge an indelible memory in the minds of the guild members the last time you were here," Eliza said.

"What happened?" Brygida asked.

"I fought a duel," Drake said.

"He defended the honor of our house, and saved my granddaughter," Eliza said. "He flayed the fool alive and then dissolved him into his component atoms."

"Oh."

Drake sighed. "It was unfortunate, but had to be done."

"The fool challenged you to a duel to the death, what did he expect?"

"I think he was too young to really know who I was."

"Half the houses of the Courts tell bedtime stories of your exploits," Eliza said.

"And the other half use me as a boogieman. It doesn't matter. Are you okay, Brygida?"

"I can feel a lot of old psychic traces here. Many duels have been fought on this platform. Many have died upon it."

Drake nodded. "That is the way of things in the Courts."

"Are you ready, Drake?" Eliza asked.

"I am ready." Drake called forth the Instrumentality and projected his image of it onto the platform. He was aware that Eliza was doing the same. The images rotated and synced. Suddenly the three of them sank through the floor into the chamber below.

"What just happened?" Brygida asked.

"It takes two grandmasters to access this chamber," Eliza said. "This leads to the chamber of the Omphalos. From here, you must go alone. Walk down the corridor. You'll know when to stop. I wish you luck, young lady."

"Thank you." Brygida looked around at Drake.

He nodded to her. "Go on. This next part is up to you. We'll be here waiting for you."

Brygida took a couple of deep breaths and then walked into the corridor.

"I think she'll do well, grandfather," Eliza said. "She'll be okay."

"Of course she will," Drake said. "I just worry for her. She is a sensitive soul, and the imprinting process isn't easy on anyone. It was hard on me the first time."

"The first time? Out of curiosity, how many times have you done it?"

Drake just smiled.

To tell the truth, he didn't know.

CHAPTER FORTY-ONE

Living on Kai wasn't quite paradise, but it was as close to that as Jon had ever gotten.

The extreme weather and lack of technological infrastructure were the biggest drawbacks. On the other hand the landscape of the island was breathtaking. It was nice to have an ocean to swim in every day, and the temperature was always perfect.

Of course, it was also where Aradhana lived, so there were other benefits.

Jon had never had much luck dating on Rhyddid. Being the brother of an unliked king was bad enough. Being well above two meters was its own problem. Women might like tall men, but they didn't like giant freaks.

At least, that was how he'd always thought of himself.

Aradhana was close to two meters tall herself, and had experienced similar problems with dating. Lolani had been right, they were perfect for each other. Dating Aradhana made Jon feel almost normal. It was much the same for her.

It wasn't just the compatible height.

They loved each other, and were friends. They had agreed

to forge new lives for themselves, which had nothing to do with where they had come from. For Jon, that was difficult, as he didn't know what the genetic modifications would do to him in the long run. Would he stay young practically forever, like Drake? Did it matter? If he worried about that, he'd never be with anyone, and that would be a very lonely existence.

Aradhana like to joke that she'd hit the jackpot. He'd always look young as she got older.

Jon looked younger than his years, but not by that much.

Neither of them were really worried too much about it.

Lolani was fighting in the interisland championship that night. Not because she had to, Drake had left them an obscene amount of credits. Lolani just liked to fight. Now that Brygida had healed Lolani of her metabolic issues, the woman was unstoppable.

After Lolani's victory, they all went to celebrate at their favorite local bar. Jon ate a little, and drank a little more than he should have, but it was a celebration. Alcohol didn't do much to his nervous system anyway.

He left Lolani and Aradhana partying. They'd be up all night long, and Jon wasn't up to that. The night was nice, it wasn't raining for a change, so Jon walked back to his and Aradhana's apartment, taking a detour to walk down by the beach.

He loved the beach.

Jon wanted to head back to the apartment he shared with Aradhana, but he was feeling restless. Something wasn't right. A merchant ship had landed earlier, and Jon found himself drawn to it. Whatever was wrong, was tied to that ship in some way.

Starships didn't land on Kai all that often. The planet was self-supporting, and didn't really import or export all that much. Jon and Lolani both made runs to other planets for goods when someone needed something, but it wasn't common. On the other hand, it wasn't uncommon enough to really draw suspicion.

The ship had Masir markings, and crews were currently unloading floating pallets of boxes. The boxes had various logos, but were mostly small-scale consumer electronics. Refrigerated cargo containers of fish sat nearby, so the ship must have been expected. Masir did buy fresh fish from Kai. Everything seemed normal, except for the bad feeling Jon had.

Jon followed his instincts and walked across the landing field to his and Lolani's ships. He checked the exteriors for anything that shouldn't be there. The ships were clean. The feeling wouldn't go away though.

"Hey! What are you doing over there?" a voice called.

Jon straitened up and turned to face the speaker. It was one of the officers from the merchant ship. The man looked like a Masir native, but Jon couldn't be sure. People of the same ethnicity were not uncommon on other planets.

"Just inspecting my ship," Jon replied. "What's it to you?"

"Oh, sorry, you must be Captain Livingston. You match the description anyway."

"Description?"

"Yeah, we had a couple of passengers this last trip, you know how it is. Sometimes you have to pick up a few extra credits however you can."

"I know what that's like," Jon replied. "What about them?"

"As soon as we landed they started asking questions. Pestered the captain until he looked up the registry on those two ships. Which are real beauties, by the way. Jump ships?"

"Yeah."

The man whistled. "Never thought I'd see one of those. Anyway, these two guys had descriptions of you. Said they wanted to hire you. I didn't believe them. They didn't look like they could afford a jump ship charter. I was happy to have them off the ship, to be honest. They kind of gave me the creeps."

"Thanks for the heads up," Jon said. "I take it these two disembarked?"

"Yep, they made a beeline for the bar. Heh. Can't say as I blame them. I'd be there myself if we weren't on a tight schedule."

"I'll go check it out."

Jon had been feeling more and more uncomfortable as they talked. It wasn't that he didn't believe the man. On the contrary, he did, and he was worried about what the man had said. The two men could be Alliance assassins, or worse. It was just barely possible that someone from the Golden Kingdom or even the Ruined Courts would send assassins after him. Just because Drake was okay with the fact that Jon might be capable of unleashing literal hell, that didn't mean everyone was okay with it.

There was definitely something wrong.

Light and noise poured out of the bar, and a light rain began to fall. Jon circled the bar, but other than a vague feeling of wrongness, he didn't get any definite visions or precognitions. That was strange in and of itself. His prescient was usually much clearer.

A figure stepped out of an alley nearby and Jon tensed, but then he recognized the leather trench coat and long red hair in a braid. The figure raised his hand as if in greeting. Jon's hair stood on end, something was wrong.

"Drake?" he said softly.

A line of fire brushed against his head from his temple back. Jon had instinctively dodged, but whatever had been fired at him had been fast. The pain fogged his mind. The injury hurt out of proportion to what Jon thought the weapon could have done to him.

Jon apported again as a beam passed through where he'd been. He got a better look at the person he'd thought was Drake. It looked much like him, almost exact in fact, but the person didn't move like Drake. It wasn't him, and that gave Jon hope. Drake was fast and somewhat prescient himself. Jon had always suspected that a fight with Drake wouldn't last very long, and not in Jon's favor either.

"Come on, Jon. Stand still. Make this easier for yourself."

The voice sounded like Drake's but it wasn't. It lacked the subtle intonations and inflections that Drake's voice held. Drake voice was rich. This voice was flat, devoid of all emotion.

"Why should I make it easier, imposter?" Jon asked.

Jon apported to a nearby rooftop. He was acutely aware that the merchant he'd spoken with had said there were two people asking about him. Jon needed to find the man's accomplice before the man found Jon.

Fake Drake was looking around for Jon. Jon knew that the real Drake would have known exactly where Jon was. Jon wasn't sure if Drake used psionic abilities, or just could hear very well, or both. Either way, Jon was sure now the man wasn't Drake.

Jon ran along the rooftop and apported into the air behind the imposter, hitting him in the upper back with both knees. They both went down and Jon smashed his elbow into the man's temple. The man had dropped his small pistol, Jon stomped it, feeling it crush under his boot. The man drew a wicked looking knife. Jon apported away. His knees and elbow hurt.

He still didn't know where the other man was, but he'd worry about that later. Jon apported behind the man and punched him in the back of the head. Jon apported away before the man could react. He kept doing that until the man was staggering under the blows. The man's features flowed and shifted into someone else.

At some point the man dropped to his knees, the knife slipping from numb hands. Jon snatched it up and apported behind him, holding the knife to the man's throat. Jon didn't know if he'd really be able to cut the man's throat, but the man couldn't know that either.

"That's enough!" a voice called out.

A pale man stepped out of a nearby doorway. He carried something in his hand, held high. Jon's feeling of something bad about to happen started trying to knock a hole in his skull.

"We're at an impasse," Jon said. "I don't know either of you, although I can guess where you're from. If you attack me, this guy dies. Put down whatever that is, and let's talk."

"Kill him if you want, it makes no difference to me," the man said. "However, if you do, I'll release this trigger, and then the bomb I left in the bar will detonate. Kill me, and I'll drop it, and the bomb will detonate. So, you see, it is you who will surrender. Don't worry, we'll be quick and merciful. We just want you dead."

"What a coincidence, that's just how I feel about you," Jon said.

Jon apported close to the other assassin and gripped the hand with the dead man switch. As he arrived Jon threw the knife hard behind him, hitting the other man in the eye. The knife sunk in to the hilt, and the man dropped like a puppet with cut cords.

The man with detonator tried to get free. Jon slammed a forearm into his throat, and the man retaliated with a knee to Jon's groin. They staggered back and forth trying to wrest control of the detonator. Jon apported them both out to the beach, where they fell into the surf.

"It's no good," the man growled. "The detonator doesn't have a range."

The man suddenly reach up and grabbed Jon's head, gouging with his thumb across where Jon had been shot earlier. The pain was overwhelming, and Jon instinctively brought both knees up into the man's stomach. They fell over rolling through the wet sand. Jon tried to push the man's head into the water, but the assassin was just as strong as Jon and shoved back.

Jon could feel himself weakening. His head injury must have been worse than he'd first thought. People were yelling in the distance. The sound of the tides pounding the barrier reef were overwhelmingly loud, and Jon knew what he had to do.

Jon apported them both ten thousand feet above the sharp rocks of the reef. The assassin had probably never been in freefall before, but Jon had. The man cried out as they fell, and Jon twisted, never letting go of the man's hand, and the detonator. Jon spun himself around, using the weight of his falling body to spiral fracture the man's arm.

He felt the spasms in the assassins arm cause the man to loosen his grip and Jon ripped the detonator from him. They were barely a hundred feet above the sharp rocks when Jon shoved himself away from the assassin. Jon knew the look of terror on the man's face would haunt him, but Jon apported away, back to the beach, alone.

Jon hit the sand hard, but didn't let go of the switch.

"Jon! What's happened?" Aradhana cried out.

The wind had been knocked out of him when he'd hit the beach. Jon struggled to sit up. Aradhana was there, and Lolani. There were other people there also, all shouting. Jon shook his head, which hurt really bad.

"Bomb!" Jon managed. "In the bar. I killed the assassins. The detonator has a dead man switch." He raised his hand with the detonator.

People cried out and stumbled back.

Lolani was trying to do something to his head that felt as if she was pulling his scalp off.

"Jon, calm down," Aradhana said. "We found a body in the ally, and a smashed pistol. What happened? Did the man try to mug you? What is this about a bomb?"

Jon groaned. His head hurt so back he couldn't think straight. How could he explain to any of them about who the assassins had been, where they had been from, and why they had wanted him dead? He couldn't explain any of it, he realized. There was something they would understand though.

"Alliance," Jon said. "They sent two operatives, on the merchant ship. They planted a bomb, wanted to use the bomb to force me to surrender, so they could take me back with them."

"There were two strangers on our ship," a familiar voice said. "They were asking about Captain Livingston here. I warned him about them."

"Where is the other operative, Jon?"

"One dead in alley," Jon managed.

"We found that one. What about the other one?"

"On the rocks. I dropped him there. He's dead."

Suddenly everyone was talking at once. Jon just wanted them all to shut up. He just wanted to sleep, but the pain in his head wouldn't let him. Lolani jabbed him with something and suddenly the pain was gone. It was so abrupt, that Jon felt like he was floating.

"Jon, let me have the detonator," Aradhana said.

"What?"

"We found the bomb. It's a nasty little satchel nuke. It would have destroyed the whole town. Lolani is going to throw it into the sun. We have to take the detonator with it, in case there is a distance trigger."

Jon let her take the dead man switch from him.

"You're safe here in your ship," Aradhana said. "We'll be back just as soon as we can. You're going to be okay. Just sleep. You can sleep now."

"Sleep…" Jon muttered.

That sounded too good to be true.

CHAPTER FORTY-TWO

As Brygida walked down the long corridor seemingly carved from solid basalt, she was aware that something was happening around her. A rainbow nimbus clung to everything, even her. She looked behind her, but the room she'd walked out of was gone. Her perceptions, from walking the Realms, told her that she was shifting through realities, but it wasn't quite the same as walking through the Realms. This was something else.

Brygida closed her eyes, but the there was still a parade of sensations.

Her memories were playing out. They were being pulled from her mind, like taffy. She had no choice but to observe her life. It wasn't something she'd have chosen to do on her own.

Sensations she'd forgotten, warmth, a feeling of being loved. Faint voices echoing, dampened by a barrier of flesh and embryonic fluid around her. The sound of her mother's heart was very loud. Her mother's mind was even louder.

Pain and fear, the shock of cold air on her skin. Birth. Warmth, food, a feeling of being held and loved. The realization that even as a newborn, she could hear the thoughts of people around her. It forced her to grow up much faster than she was ready to. That was a good synopsis of her life.

She'd grown up before she was ready.

Other memories flowed past her. Learning to ride. Grooming the horses in the stables. She'd loved those horses. She'd always loved animals. Pain, fear, and loss when a rabbit she'd raised had died. The knowledge that things wouldn't live forever was unbearable. Why did things have to die? Why did her rabbit die?

Being a child in the Golden Kingdom hadn't been easy. She was the daughter of a princess, but she was different. Her ears didn't look like everyone else's and she was teased for it. Some of her aunts and uncles hated her for it. Her cousins said they'd cut her ears off. In a fit of rage and self-loathing, she'd taken a knife to her ears herself, to round them. There had been a lot of blood, and her mother had been even angrier with her.

She'd tried her wrists next, but that hadn't worked any better.

She didn't like those memories, but they were a part of who she was. She wasn't ashamed, she was angry. People who claimed to love her, had driven her half mad. They had made her hate herself. At least for a while. She understood them, that didn't mean she had to forgive them.

Brygida had thought that leaving the Golden Kingdom would solve all her problems. The Cynosure had given her the ability to walk away from her mother and the others. She'd thought that being out from under her mother's shadow would make her feel better. She hadn't been able to walk away from the feelings inside of her though.

The University of Tokyo had just been a new set of problems to deal with. Brygida wanted to think that all people were equal. The students and professors at her new school tried their best to disabuse her of the notion.

Brygida had picked the school in Tokyo, because she thought the people there looked somewhat like she did, like she imagined her father must have looked. She'd never known her father. It was her uncle Dominic that had told Brygida about the man. He was a prince from the Ruined Courts, in the hated South. Dominic had urged her to seek him out. Brygida didn't understand why her mother had picked such a man, but it did help Brygida understand the prejudice she'd faced as a child.

What she didn't understand was the prejudice she faced at the university.

She didn't look like the locals. Okay, she could deal with that. She was used to that. The sexism was a shock. People thought that she couldn't be smart because she was a woman, so what? It had an effect, though. That was when she started dressing more androgynous. Not that it had helped. She had a very feminine voice.

Brygida resolved not to care.

She focused on her studies and earned degrees that the bigots said she couldn't. She forced her peers to accept her, at least grudgingly. Then she set out to make her mark on the Realms. She wanted to use her skills in genetics. Not on animals –she couldn't hurt animals– on people.

The jump ship program had seemed like the perfect place to experiment with the genetics of her family. If Brygida was being honest –which she didn't seem to have any choice about in that place, there inside the Instrumentality– then Brygida had to admit that she'd started the program to see if she could change herself into someone her mother would accept.

Along the way she'd realized that no matter how much she changed, her mother wouldn't accept her. Her family in the North would always be prejudiced against her. She thought about seeking out her father. She figured it couldn't be any worse with him.

Rhyddid needed those pilots. The independent worlds needed them. Then her kids, the people in the experiments, had started dying. It had been the same heartbreak as her rabbit all over again. Then the revolution on Rhyddid, the Alliance had stepped in and Brygida had found herself in prison on a space station.

It was an effective way to imprison her. She was in solitary. There was no place she could walk to in the Realms. If she tried, she'd die in the vacuum of space or be shot as an intruder on another version of the station. She thought about dying that way. She's have done it to avoid working on a genetics project for the Alliance.

Then, against all probability, her father had rescued her.

What could she say about it? She'd been in shock, but she recognized him. He even had pointed ears, like she did. Her ear tips had grown back after a few years, before she'd even left home. Her father had the same hair and eyes too.

The most shocking had been that he'd instantly accepted her for who she was.

It had been a revelation. This was the man her mother seemed to hate. The man loathed by most of her family to the point that they hated, ostracized, and blamed her as a child. He was a good man. Oh, he certainly had his quirks, but he seemed to genuinely care about people.

She realized that she had a new family.

She had friends that cared about her. Her father loved her. It was good enough.

It took her a while, but she gradually was able to come to terms with everything that had happened. She was even able to come to terms with herself. She felt at peace.

She understood what was happening, perhaps better than most. A copy of her mind was being uploaded to the Instrumentality. At the same time, there had been another sensation. The Instrumentality was imprinting itself onto her.

Her life finished playing out and Brygida opened her eyes.

She was aware of the cold scrutiny of the Instrumentality.

"Well? Do I pass?"

It isn't about passing, although failing has deadly consequences. The power of the thought was mind-numbing.

"I'm not dead, so I assume you approve?"

You'll do well with my assistance. I sense the taint of the lesser one on you. You'll have no need for it. Shall I remove it?

"I think I'll keep it," Brygida said. "My father said it had once been a part of you. Perhaps this way I'll have full access to what I need."

Drake has ever meddled in things he should stay out of, came the powerful thought.

Brygida realized she was walking back down the basalt corridor. She could see her father and her... *niece* waiting for her in the chamber under the platform. Drake was smiling.

"Are you feeling okay, my dear?" Eliza asked. "You seem remarkably calm."

"I saw nothing I hadn't already dealt with," Brygida said.

She walked past Eliza and hugged her father. She was aware that he was startled, but he hugged her back. She just rested in his arms.

"Thank you."

"You're quite welcome," Drake said. "Was this for anything specific?"

"No."

"Forgive me for interrupting," Eliza said. "It is customary for the new initiate to spar, to demonstrate that the imprint was successful."

"I have nothing to prove to you," Brygida said.

"For yourself, then," Eliza replied.

Brygida called forth the image of the Instrumentality she'd just realized was within her. It was a simple matter to refract it and double it. The two images filled the small chamber. An application of will rotated the images until they synced.

She and the others floated up through the ceiling to the platform.

Brygida aligned the errant photons in the chamber, and the whole cavern began to glow.

"Is that sufficient?" she asked.

Eliza nodded, a shocked expression on her face.

"Do you still contain the imprint of the Cynosure?" Drake asked.

Brygida looked within and realized she'd been using both of the powers at the same time. Her image of the Instrumentality contained the Cynosure. It was like a separate layer in a drawing. She could lift it away, and use one or the other, but she liked how it looked best, with both.

"Yes, the Instrumentality offered to remove it, but I declined."

"The child is delirious, grandfather," Eliza said.

Drake studied Brygida's face. "I don't think so. It has spoken to me. If my daughter says the Instrumentality spoke to her, then the Instrumentality spoke to her. "

"Thank you, father."

Eliza shook her head. "I can see her ideogram of the Omphalos, it looks wrong."

"Actually yours does," Brygida said. "No offense intended. Yours is imperfect. I have an image of what it once was, as does the Emperor, I suspect."

"His looks much like yours," Drake replied. "Would you like to meet him while you're here?"

"I think so, yes."

"I thought you were trying to keep her a secret," Eliza said. "Aren't worried about some fool challenging her?"

"I think any idiot that challenges a Drake will find themselves wishing they hadn't," Drake said.

"Perhaps I should just go home for now," Brygida said. "I miss Tadeo. I can always meet my cousin later."

Drake smiled and gestured to the correct Waypoint. Brygida wondered how he knew which one it was out of the hundreds.

She wondered if it really mattered.

CHAPTER FORTY-THREE

Drake returned to Cincinnati with Brygida.

He had been intending to spend the rest of the holiday break with her, but Hephaestus contacted him shortly after he arrived. Drake was a little concerned about leaving Brygida alone. The imprint process wasn't easy to endure. It was difficult to face your life, with all of its highs and lows. Brygida was doing very well, under the circumstances.

Prince Drake, there has been an incident on Kai.

Drake cursed. *What happened?*

Assassins tried to kill Jon. The word is it was the Alliance, but I don't think it was.

Is Jon…

He is alive, but injured.

I'll go. Drake shook his head. "Brygida, I'm sorry. Something has happened. I have to go."

"Is Jon okay?" Brygida asked.

"Hephaestus says he is wounded, but alive. I won't know more until I go there."

Brygida gave him a hug. "Go, but come back and hang out when you can."

Drake smiled. "I will."

Drake apported from her living room to the closest Waypoint node in Winton Woods. From there he jumped across space and through the Realms to outside the bar on Kai. It was becoming a familiar jump point for him.

He startled a couple of locals when he arrived.

"Do you know Jon?" he asked in the local language. "Lolani?"

The couple both pointed to the landing field.

Drake apported onto Lolani's ship, as she had the better medical facilities. Every alarm in the ship went off when he arrived. Lolani and Aradhana came charging into the room with rifles, but stopped suddenly when they saw him.

"Is that really you, Drake?" Lolani asked.

"It's me, I came as soon as I heard about the attack."

"Prove you're you, bruh. Tell me something an assassin wouldn't know."

"I kissed you under the wing of this ship."

Lolani blushed and lowered her rifle. "Jon's in medical."

"How is he? What happened?" Drake asked. "Also, it is good to see you both. I was worried that you may have been hurt."

"I'll let you talk to him and he can tell you what happened," Aradhana said. "Maybe you can make more sense of it."

Jon was sitting up in an acceleration couch in the closet that passed for a medical room on the *Ahi'iwa*. He looked bruised and battered. He'd obviously been through a hell of a fight. His head was shaved, and he had a long line on his head that glistened under the medical cement. Drake could see that the skin had been badly burned, then debrided and sealed. Lolani had probably done the impromptu surgery.

"You've looked better," Drake said. "You might want to try dodging next time."

Jon laughed. "I would have if I hadn't thought it was you."

"Well, that answers my next question," Drake said. "I didn't know if it was Alliance or…"

"I've been letting people think it was Alliance," Jon said. "Kind of hard to explain the other."

Drake moved closer. "May I take a look?"

"Go ahead, although Lolani has already worked me over."

Drake carefully felt the wound. "This was done with a thermal weapon. A very hot one."

"It was a pistol of some kind. I stomped it in the fight, so there isn't much left."

"I don't suppose the assassin is around to question?"

"There were two assassins, actually," Jon said. "But no, neither is alive. I did what I had to do. They had a nuke…"

"I understand," Drake said. "You know I'd be the last person to judge your actions in any case."

"So it was an assassin from the Courts?" Jon asked.

"I don't think so," Drake said. "They are shapeshifters that are not from the Courts. They are limited to humanoid forms. It isn't that common of an ability. I'm still trying to track them down."

"This one knew me pretty well. He really looked like you, at first anyway."

"How did you tell the difference?"

"You mean other than him shooting me? His voice wasn't right. It didn't have the same tonal quality that your voice has. His eyes seemed dead. His movements weren't smooth and graceful."

Drake nodded. "So he wasn't used to moving in my form. That implies he'd only recently adopted my form. Interesting."

"Drake, what the hell is going on?"

"I don't know, Jon. Given the time it would take for them to travel from Earth, the timing is probably okay. I made arrangements to stop any more travelers like them from entering this Realm. I hope the other party abides by the agreement. This shouldn't happen again."

"Not your fault, Drake."

"Maybe not," Drake said. "But I intend to end this. I'm tired of hearing of friends and family being attacked."

"Is everyone ok?" Jon asked.

"Of those you know, Brygida was attacked. She is okay. She was injured, but not severely. The single attacker only used a knife there. I find it interesting they sent two after you."

"I'm glad she is okay. What are you going to do?"

"What I do best." Drake shook his head. "Don't worry about it. Get to feeling better, Jon. I'm glad you have good people here to take care of you."

"I'll be okay. I'm healing. Thanks for coming so quickly."

"If you need me, Hephaestus is always listening."

Jon nodded.

Drake called upon the Instrumentality to apport to T'era grata, and from there to the Waypoint in the Imperial Plaza. Drake shifted his armor to a heavier set, using the Instrumentality. The guards at the palace bowed out of his way without a word.

The majordomo sped up to him. "Prince Drake, I wasn't informed you were visiting the court today. If you'll give me a moment, I'll prepare a time for an audience and announce your—"

Drake walked past the little person without a glance.

The guards took one look into his eyes and opened the huge bronze doors to the audience chamber. The Emperor was seated on the Fire Throne. There was a crowd of people inside the room, as usual. Drake walked past them all, and they moved out of his way. One stood their ground for a moment, but Drake didn't slow, and they too moved from his path.

"Prince Drake, welcome to our court."

Drake stopped three paces from the throne, and bowed deeply. "I have an urgent need for an audience, Your Imperial Majesty."

Emrys stood. "This audience is adjourned! Please, follow me, Drake."

"Thank you, Emrys," Drake said quietly.

They entered the room behind the throne and closed the door.

Emrys shrugged out his heavy robes. "Help me with these."

Drake took the heavy garments and helped Emrys step out of them, then hung them on the peg next to the door. Emrys was wearing jeans and a tee-shirt under his formal clothes. Drake smiled. The court would have been scandalized.

"I can only think of one thing that would have you march in here like this," Emrys said.

"You really captured one alive?" Drake asked.

"We haven't been able to make him talk. Trust me we've tried everything from truth agents to thumb screws. Nothing works. We've tried three different methods of mental infiltration. Someone locked this guy up tight. I'm not even certain he knows anything at all."

Drake sighed. "I'll take anything I can get. I haven't been able to capture one of the assassins alive, and all the corpses were either too old or too mangled to be of use to me."

"You're welcome to try Drake. I can't imagine you'll do any worse. Hell, even if the guy dies."

"I appreciate it. I want to end this threat as soon as possible."

"So do I, come on, I'll walk you down."

Drake followed Emrys out of the private chamber into the main audience hall. From there they took an unobtrusive door on the right down a long flight of stairs. Several guards were playing cards. They stood and saluted as Emrys approached.

"At ease. Prince Drake need to see the prisoner. He has my full approval to do whatever is necessary."

"Right away!"

"You just have one prisoner down here?" Drake asked as they followed the guard.

"I issued a general amnesty when I took the throne. You wouldn't believe how long some of these poor sons of bitches had been down here."

"Oh, I don't know," Drake said. "I vaguely remember spending a year or five in a cell down here during Emperor Cedric's reign."

"That was ten thousand years ago, Drake."

"Time flies when you're having fun."

Emrys snorted back a laugh.

"Here we are, Your Majesty, Prince Drake." The guard unlocked the cell door.

"I can't decide if I should stay with you or not," Emrys said.

"Do you want to have nightmares tonight?" Drake asked.

"Yeah... no, come see me in my private audience room after you've finished."

Drake nodded and entered the cell.

The prisoner was a young man. He'd been ill used, from the condition of his face and hands. Drake had expected nothing less. The man glared at Drake balefully as he entered.

"Do you know who I am?" Drake asked.

The prisoner just glared at him.

"Some of your people have tried to kill my family and friends," Drake said. "I take that personally. I'm not going to lie to you. You won't leave this cell alive. However, if you tell me what I want to know, I can make your passing easier."

"I don't know anything." The man's words were slurred. He was missing most of his teeth.

Drake shook his head at such primitive torments.

"I think you do know something, or you wouldn't be in this cell," Drake said.

"You'll get nothing from me, lesser one. So don't bother to ask."

"I'm not planning to ask you anything," Drake said. "Nevertheless, you'll tell me everything you know, and even things you didn't realize you knew. You see, I think you know who exactly is behind this, which is why for the first time you're actually scared. I can hear your heart beating faster. You're sweating, even though this room is cold."

Drake knelt down close to the man.

"Don't think death is an escape either."

The guards outside the cell grimaced at the horrific screams. They didn't know what the infamous Prince Drake was doing to the prisoner. They didn't want to know.

CHAPTER FORTY-FOUR

Geoffrey straightened the wreath on the door one more time and looked out through the glass storm door to the sidewalk and driveway. Both were still clear of snow. The glass in the storm door had ice around the edges, but he didn't care about that.

He shut the front door and looked back down the hallway. It was painfully barren. Jason had refused to allow Geoffrey to put up any Christmas decorations. Even the pine wreath on the door had been fought over. Geoffrey knew Jason wasn't religious, but he thought Jason was being a bit unfair. It wasn't as if Geoffrey was particularly religious, either.

Christmas wasn't really a religious holiday in the United States – not for most people anyway.

Not like it had been when Geoffrey was younger. Or maybe it was just where he was from. His family in Kentucky had been more religious than most people. Maybe that was it.

Geoffrey lit some scented candles in the living room.

The house was about as ready as he could make it. Jason was in the kitchen, making hot chocolate on the stove. The rich smell drifted through the house, and smelled like heaven to

Geoffrey, although Jason has been scandalized at the suggestion that they should get some marshmallows for the hot chocolate.

There was a knock on the door: Brygida with some bags and her cat carrier. Geoffrey helped her inside and gave her a hug. She seemed different since she'd gone off with Drake. It seemed to him that some of her sadness was gone. She also seemed happier, although she was as quiet as ever. Tadeo raced out of the carrier when Brygida opened it, and they both laughed as Jason yelled for the cat to get off his leg.

"How are you doing, Brygida?" asked Geoffrey.

"I'm well. You?"

"Doing well. Is it strange that I'm looking forward to getting back to school?"

"That's because you don't have to teach," Brygida said, taking off her coat and setting it on her carrier. She wandered off into the kitchen to save Jason, who was swearing at the cat again.

Geoffrey answered the door again, and was engulfed in an embrace and cold, wet kiss. Jen then pushed past him, dropped her bags, and kissed him again. Geoffrey certainly didn't mind.

"Who's here already?" Jen asked when she came up for air.

"Brygida and Tadeo."

"She brought Tadeo? Oh, I see the cat carrier. I'm going to go say hi."

Jen handed him her coat and went into the other room.

Geoffrey grinned as he hung Jen's and Brygida's coats up. He avoided the temptation to peek into the bags. Brygida would know if he did.

Elena showed up a few minutes later. She put her bags down and hung up her coat before hugging Geoffrey. He thought she seemed sad.

"Where is everybody else?" she asked.

"They're in the kitchen."

Elena sighed and nodded. "Can we talk?"

"Of course. Are you okay?"

"Yeah, I just... I don't want to put you in a difficult place, but..."

"Is this about Jason?"

"Hard to guess, huh?"

Geoffrey had been expecting her to want to talk to him. Jason had been a little better with her recently, but he'd still been a bit standoffish. Geoffrey knew why, but it wasn't something he could tell Elena. That made it a awkward.

"I just don't know what we're doing," said Elena. "We've been dating for months, but it just feels... stagnant. I mean, usually a girl has to slap away a guy's hands after the first week, if she doesn't want to move too fast. Five months, Geoffrey! What the hell am I doing wrong?"

"You know it isn't you," Geoffrey said. "Jason is just going slowly because he's been hurt before."

"Cry me a fucking river, Geoffrey. Everybody who dates has been hurt. Even those who don't, like Brygida. Is Jason planning on breaking up with me?"

Geoffrey shook his head. "No, he isn't. I won't lie: he thought about it. Not because he doesn't care about you. Just the opposite, in fact. He cares deeply about you, but he's really inhibited. He's embarrassed about his... He doesn't feel like he can be intimate."

"You know women don't really give a damn about the size of a guy's dick, right?"

Geoffrey blushed. "I don't think it has anything to do with that. Not that I would know."

"I thought you guy's all checked each other out in the bathroom or something."

"Eww, gross. *No.* God, no."

Elena laughed. "Okay, calm down."

"Jason really does care about you, Elena."

"I wish he'd show it."

"There are other ways than physical, you know."

"Uh-huh. Like you and Jen can keep your paws each other. You know people can hear you two when you sneak off, right?"

Geoffrey blushed again. "If you want that with Jason, you're going to have to make the first move."

"You think I should just jump his bones?"

"Yeah, actually."

"You're as much a perv as Jen. You guys are perfect for each other."

"I didn't mean tonight," said Geoffrey. "You're coming to the New Year's Eve party at my cousin's place, aren't you?"

"I don't know. It feels a little weird."

"Jason is going as my housemate. Jen is going with me as my date. Come with her. Hell, get Jason drunk and find a coat room. It wouldn't be weird – he wants you. He just needs a push."

Elena laughed. "You make it sound more like a college frat party."

"Well, Alan is a bit boisterous."

"Do you really think Jason wants…?"

"Yes," Geoffrey said. Elena was really pretty, and Geoffrey knew Jason wasn't gay or ace. "Yes, he wants you that way. I don't know how long it's been for him, since he was with a woman. A long time, I think."

"Hey! What are you guys whispering about in there?' Jen called. "You'd better get in here and get some hot chocolate. Jason got the rum out, but it won't last!"

"Not the way you drink!" Elena shouted back. She gripped Geoffrey's arm. "Thanks."

☉

Jason had made four quarts of hot chocolate from scratch,

so there was plenty. He turned the heat off once everyone had a mug of it. Jen found the RumChata in the pantry and was splashing the spiced rum cream liberally into each mug.

Geoffrey had found himself a wild one.

Jason wished he was as uninhibited.

Elena moved close and stood next to him, drinking her hot chocolate while watching the others. Jason felt his pulse quicken as he looked at her. She was a lovely young woman. Jason wanted more than anything to kiss her, but he worried it would send the wrong signals. She obviously wanted more from the relationship than he could afford to give her.

It wasn't just his... otherness. Jason did feel the gulf of their age difference. He was a lot older than Geoffrey had guessed. Not anything like Drake, of course, but Jason was a more than a hundred times older than Elena. How did anyone get past that? If he told her how old he was, and gave her reason to believe it, the smile would drop from her face, and she'd move away in horror. He'd be lucky if all she did was leave him.

Did he have the right not to tell her, though?

He sighed.

Elena glanced at him. "Are you okay?"

He bumped his shoulder against hers. "I'm good. Just a little tired."

Brygida left the room with her cat perched on her shoulder and came back a minute later with a large crock pot. "I made a pot roast," she said.

"I can smell the rosemary and onion," said Jason. "Smells good."

Brygida left the kitchen again.

"You like her, don't you?" Elena asked.

"I'm sorry? What? Who?"

"Brygida," Elena said. "You like her."

"We're just friends," said Jason. "There's no need to be jealous."

"I'm not," Elena replied. "I know Brygida isn't interested in that. I just think you wish it was different."

Jason shook his head. "Where is this coming from? We're just friends."

"How is that, by the way?" Elena asked. "I mean, Geoffrey worked with her, before school. You don't work, though."

"I work," Jason said. "I make custom furniture. It's a dying art. My business has been thriving. That's part of why I'm tired. I have a lot orders to fill, this time of year."

"Don't change the subject," said Elena. "How do you know her?"

"I met her while traveling with Drake," Jason said without thinking.

"Ah, the enigmatic Drake... Funny how we've never met the man. Geoffrey said he's a mercenary, or something. Why would *you* have been traveling with him?"

Jason's heart was beating a lot faster now, and not in a good way. "I don't really want to talk about it."

Elena slammed her mug down on the counter hard enough to break the handle off it. "That's the problem, Jason. You never want to talk about anything. Not even a simple question like that."

"There is nothing simple about that question," said Jason. "I met Gerhardt and Drake at the same time. After that, I traveled with Drake for a while. I really can't talk about it."

"You are so full of shit! What, the mercenary needed you to make some furniture for him? What do you really do back there in that workshop? Cook meth or something?"

"What?"

"Why have you never taken me back there?"

"The key is on the hook by the door," said Jason. "Be my guest, if you don't believe me."

"You're fucking hopeless."

She stomped out of the kitchen. Jason heard her raised voice from the other room, and Jen and Brygida trying to calm her down. He was embarrassed, and he didn't know what to do.

"What the hell did you say to her?" Geoffrey demanded as he came into the kitchen.

Jason didn't think he'd ever heard that edge to Geoffrey's voice before.

"Taking her side already?"

Geoffrey sighed. "This isn't about sides, Jason. I'm your friend, and hers, too. She's in the other room crying. You're not. So what the hell did you say to her?"

"She questioned me about Brygida and how we'd met. Through Drake, I told her. Then she demanded to know how I knew *him*. Through Gerhardt, I said, and she didn't believe me."

"You need to learn how to lie better, buddy."

"I was trying to be honest."

"The *trying* part is where you usually fuck up," said Geoffrey. "She thinks you don't care about her, because you haven't put the moves on her. Give her *something*, man."

"I've been trying not to lead her on."

"I think you're a few months past that, Jason. Just snuggle with her, kiss her or something. Damn, man, you're older than me – surely you know what the hell to do."

"I can't let it go too far," said Jason. "You know why."

"Let it go a little further," Geoffrey said. "For all our sakes. Now get in there and apologize."

"I didn't do anything wrong."

"Do you really think that matters?"

CHAPTER FORTY-FIVE

Everyone was looking at Jason, and he hated it.

This was exactly why he'd avoided having a lover or even friends most of the time. Why were people always so obsessed with sex? It was dangerous to him to let someone get close – didn't his friends understand that? Of course, Brygida wasn't human, and she was glaring at him, too. Jason sighed and knelt next to Elena, who was sitting on the floor with her back to him.

"Elena, I'm sorry," he said. "I'm... I have problems letting anyone in. That's my fault. I acknowledge it, but I don't want it to get between us."

Elena sniffled and wiped her eyes. "I just don't want to feel as if I'm dating a stranger."

"I get that," said Jason. "It's mostly just bad timing. I lost someone important to me, in the winter, a long time ago. I've never gotten over it. So I just... close myself up, to keep from feeling the pain of it again, but that isn't fair to you."

"Oh, Jason, I'm sorry. I didn't know." Elena suddenly turned and hugged him tightly.

He was acutely aware of her thin blouse and firm breasts

pressed against him. He felt himself blush, because he wanted her badly just now. Everything always happened at the wrong time. Jason hadn't let himself get too close to her, but he could see now that it was just as dangerous to keep her away as it was to bring her in closer.

Nor hell a fury, to quote William Congreve, he thought. *What a depressing fucking play.* Jason had seen it in 1697, in England. *Why did I think of that?* Maybe because Elena looked a little like a woman he'd known then. Maybe because Elena scared him a bit.

"Jason?"

"I'm sorry. Hey, Elena, why don't you grab your coat?" Jason asked.

"What?"

"You were right. I should have shown you my workshop before now. I love woodworking, and I… I… I think I should share that with you. May be you'll understand me more if you see my work."

Elena jumped up and ran to the closet.

Jen was smiling, and Geoffrey gave him a thumbs up. Brygida was looking down and petting Tadeo, but she had a faint smile on her face. Jason sighed and met Elena by the back door. His coat was still hanging up there. He shrugged into his coat as she waited.

Elena's eyes were puffy from crying, and Jason's heart felt as if it would burst. He'd never meant to hurt her. He could see how his behavior had, though. No wonder she'd thought he was pining away for Brygida. Jason figured he was lucky she hadn't thought he was after Jen.

"You ready? It's cold out there."

"I'm good."

Jason took the key from the peg and led Elena across the yard to his workshop. He hadn't thought to clear the snow, and it crunched under his boots and her shoes as they walked. Jason tried not to think about how much he hated the cold and the snow. It wasn't her fault, after all.

He left a radiant heater on in the workshop over the winter, so it wasn't too cold in here. He shut the door behind Elena, turned on the light, and then turned on the other two heaters: large, electric ceramic ones that put out a lot of heat fast.

Elena was gently touching the carving on a chest he'd been working on. "It's beautiful," she said. "I'm sorry about what I said earlier."

"Don't be," said Jason. "You were right. I keep too much to myself. I should have told you, when the first snow fell, about why I was having problems. I shouldn't have retreated into my head and expected you to just be okay with it."

"You could tell me now."

My friend died in the snow after being attacked by dogs, Jason thought. "I lost a close friend in the winter."

"I'm so sorry. It must have been recent, for you to be so upset about it still. I won't ask about it again."

It was in the fourteen hundreds. Why haven't I been able to move on? Or forgotten about it, for that matter. I shouldn't be able to remember it.

"What are these tools made of? I've never seen anything like them."

"It's a special kind of bronze. Expensive, but harder than steel. They don't wear out as often, so it's worth it in the long run."

Elena jumped up his workbench in front of him and sat. "Very sturdy," she said.

Jason swallowed hard. "Yes, it has to be."

Elena pulled him over and kissed him. He caught her hands before she could push his bandana off, and pressed her hands against his chest. She had other ideas and dropped one hand lower. Jason moaned involuntarily as her hand cupped his groin.

"You know, Geoffrey tried to tell me you were worried about this, but I don't think you have anything to be ashamed of."

"He what? Oh, never mind." He kissed her back. Her lips and tongue were sweet and hot. She tasted of chocolate and rum.

Elena straightened and unbuttoned her jacket and then her blouse.

"What are you doing?"

"Shush."

She undid her bra and pulled his face into her breasts.

It had been a long time since Jason had been with a woman. She was firm and hot, and he wanted to kiss every part of her and more. He wanted her so badly, he thought he'd burst.

He tried to pull back, but she pulled him against her. "No," she said.

"I can't, Elena. I don't..."

"I don't have any, either. We'll worry about that next time."

"Next..."

Elena pushed him back, jumped down and then pushed him against the workbench. She started working his belt buckle, and then unzipped his pants. Jason thought he should stop her, but really didn't want to.

She kept her eyes locked with his as she knelt down and went down on him. All Jason could do was hold on to the workbench, to keep from falling. This was certainly going to change his feelings toward his workshop.

☉

Geoffrey felt really awkward sitting here in the living room. Everything happened so quickly with Jason and Elena that Geoffrey hadn't known what to say or do. He was just glad they'd made up, although they were taking their time coming back in.

Jen began to giggle, and then Brygida couldn't keep it together and started laughing.

"What?" asked Geoffrey.

That just made them laugh harder.

"Did I miss something?" Geoffrey asked. "I'm still freaked out about them getting into a fight, and you're laughing."

"Make-up sex is always the best," said Jen.

"You don't think…?" Geoffrey blushed.

"I think that maybe it's time for dinner," said Brygida, her cheeks rosy. "They'll find their way back in eventually. The workshop is heated, right? We don't have to worry about them freezing?"

"I'm not going out there to check on them," Jen said. "Send Geoffrey."

"Yeah, no," said Geoffrey, "I'm not going out there. He keeps a heater on all winter and has extra heaters, too. They'll be fine."

Brygida nodded. "Better for the wood that way."

Jen started laughing again, covering her face.

"You don't think…?"

"What are you worried about, Geoffrey?" Jen asked. "I'm sure they've got it well in hand, or whatever."

"I don't think he has any…"

"Condoms?" Brygida said. "You don't have to be worried about my sensitivities. I may not wish for such things myself, but I am aware of how it's done."

"Sorry," said Geoffrey. "Yeah, that."

"I would think that you two would be aware that there are other options," Brygida said. "Do I need to find you a book?"

"We're good," Jen said, blushing.

"You mentioned dinner?" Geoffrey said, hurriedly changing the subject.

"I made pot roast. Come on, let's go have some."

"Shouldn't we wait for them," asked Geoffrey.

"I think they have other things on their mind."

Brygida filled up large bowls with the roast while Geoffrey got bread out of the cupboard. Jen had brought a merlot, and she filled three glasses with the deep purple-red wine. Geoffrey couldn't help but think of the purple wine Drake had served them on Nandegurth, after they had first met. It had tasted of cloves, as did the roast.

"Why did you get bread out, Geoffrey?" asked Jen. "There's plenty of potatoes and carrots."

Geoffrey shrugged. "My family always had bread with roast."

"This is really good, Brygida," said Jen. "Thank you."

"Yes, thank you."

"You're quite welcome. Eat up – there's plenty." Brygida caught Tadeo as the cat made a leap for the table. "Not you. You can't have any. It has onions. Excuse me."

Brygida got up, and Geoffrey heard her opening a can in the other room.

"I brought canned cat food in anticipation of her antics," said Brygida. "That should occupy her for a few minutes, at least."

Jason and Elena came back in just then, looking a bit disheveled.

"You guys hammer out all the kinks in your relationship?" Jen asked, winking at Geoffrey.

Elena blushed.

"Did you guys leave any roast for us?" said Jason.

"Worked up an appetite, did you?" Jen said.

Jason smiled. "Yes, actually. The roast?"

"There's plenty," said Brygida. "Not sure about wine, though. I think we finished this bottle off."

"I brought three," Jen said. "I thought I was going to have

to get Jason drunk for Elena."

"What good would he be drunk?" asked Geoffrey.

"This is really good, Brygida," Jason said. "Thank you. All Geoffrey wants to eat is junk food."

"Pizza is not junk food."

"It isn't this, either," Jason said. "I'll have to make guys my fish chowder some time."

"That would be great," Brygida said. "When you guys are done eating, we should exchange gifts. I'm impatient."

"Oh yeah, we've got one of those meat and cheese trays in the fridge," Geoffrey said.

"Charcuterie," said Jen.

"Whatever."

"See? Junk food," said Jason.

"Um, gonna have to disagree with you on this one, Jason," Elena said. "Meat, cheese, and crackers is food."

"She's not wrong," said Jen.

Jason sighed.

"Does anyone want anything else to drink?" Geoffrey asked.

"Wine is perfect for charcuterie," said Brygida.

Geoffrey took the tray into the living room. He left the lid on, thinking of the cat rampaging across the meats and cheeses. Jen brought small plates for everyone.

"Who wants to go first?" asked Jen.

"Oldest first?" Elena suggested.

"Sneaky," said Brygida.

"I am older than I look," Jason said.

"Well, flip a coin or something," said Geoffrey.

Brygida smiled. "Jason, do you wish to do the honors?"

"You have to put this on first." Geoffrey handed him a Santa hat. "Don't worry, I got one for everyone."

"Sure."

Jason handed out small bags to everyone.

Geoffrey opened his. It was a set of nice pair of Sony

headphones. "Oh, man, thank you. These are awesome."

"I figured they'd be better for your games."

"They're great. Thanks!"

Jen got a knitted scarf, hat, and gloves. "You didn't knit these yourself, did you?"

Jason grinned. "I have many talents, but knitting is not among them."

Elena's gift was a leather winter coat with a thermal lining.

"Your coat didn't look warm enough," said Jason. "I hope it fits."

Elena tried it on. "I love it. Thanks."

"This bag is suspiciously heavy," said Brygida. "It is a bomb?"

"You won't know until you open it."

Brygida starting laughing.

"What is it?"

From the bad, she pulled out a plasma ball thing like those sold at Spencer's Gifts. Jason had made a wooden plaque to go with it that read *Mad Scientist Starter Kit.*

"Thank you. It's perfect."

They finished exchanging gifts, and then had a great time playing with the cat and eating crackers and meat and cheese. Jason and Elena stayed very close, with Jason frequently hugging her. Geoffrey was glad they'd figured things out. It would have been really awkward if they broke up.

Brygida still seemed a bit off, from how she'd been before.

Geoffrey wasn't sure what to make of it, but he wasn't too worried, either. He was a little unhappy that Brygida wasn't interested in dating. It seemed sad to be alone at Christmas, but she seemed happy enough hanging out with them and Tadeo.

Maybe she just wished Drake and Jon could have been here with them. They'd spent so much time traveling together. Geoffrey hoped that wherever he was, Drake was having a good time, too.

CHAPTER FORTY-SIX

Drake stepped away from the unconscious prisoner in the chair and looked at the projection on the wall of the cell. Drake had used the Instrumentality to construct and project a real time magnetic resonance image of the man's brain. The prisoner wasn't lying, he really didn't have any idea where the tower was in the Black Realms. That part of the man's brain had been burned out by someone. Drake was pretty sure he knew who.

That wasn't to say that Drake had gotten nothing so far from the interrogation. The tower was definitely in the Black Realms near the Courts. Drake had gotten enough to know that it was a Realm with perpetually black skies. Drake only knew of a few of those, and they were clustered together. The would-be assassin had used a Waypoint to reach the Realm, so Drake couldn't be sure it was actually an Earth, and not some other world. On the other hand, very few of the Black Realms were full universes.

Drake remotely stimulated the man's hypothalamus, rousing the prisoner. The man screamed and thrashed under the stimulation of the nanotechnology Drake had placed in his brain. Drake eased back and observed the man. For all of the torment that had been inflicted upon him, he remained steadfast. The prisoner was a fanatic, Drake decided.

"Calm down," Drake said. "I believe you when you say you don't know where the tower is. The information isn't there, or I'd have had it by now."

"Just kill me."

"Not yet," Drake said. "I think you know more. Tell me about the organization of your assassins. What is your purpose?"

The man spit blood. "We are a brotherhood devoted wiping out things like you!"

"Obviously you've never met my brother."

"I have not met the Great One," the man said. "But he will triumph."

"You poor deluded fool. Don't you realize he has joined the Ancient Enemy?"

"Lies!" the man shrieked.

"I wish that it were so," Drake said. "Tell me of what your groups plans."

The man was silent.

Drake sighed and stimulated the prisoner's dorsal posterior insula, driving his perception of pain beyond bearable levels. Given the damage to the man's body, it wasn't difficult. Drake stimulated the man's hypothalamus to keep him from passing out from the pain. A tweak to the hippocampus made the minutes feel like hours for the man. Drake eased off as the man spasmed, giving him a minute to gasp in a few breaths.

"I really don't enjoy this sort of thing," Drake said. "If it was just me you were going after, I'd ignore your brotherhood and just kill your people as they came at me. However, you are going after others, including those I care about, so I must do what I have to do to stop you."

Drake glanced at the MRI on the wall. The man's hippocampus and prefrontal cortex had lit up as Drake mentioned people he cared about. The man was remembering something.

"Tell me, and I'll end this."

"I don't know anything," the man sobbed.

"You just remembered something, tell me what it was."

Drake forced his awareness through the fog of pain in the man's mind. It was no good, the man had already hidden everything away again. Drake shook his head. The man was stubborn.

"Do you need more incentive?" Drake asked.

"Please just kill me."

"I promise I will," Drake said. "As painlessly as possible. You just have to tell me what I need to know first."

The man sobbed.

Drake could see the memory regions of his mind lighting up again.

Suddenly the man began shrieking and convulsing. Drake was confused, as he hadn't done anything to the man. The MRI of his brain lit up with a steady pulsing. The screams became inhuman.

Starting at his feet and fingertips, the man was dissolving. Drake recognized the effect, he'd used it on his enemies himself. This time, someone else had done it.

"No!" Drake cried. He threw his image of the Instrumentality against the man to stop the process. There was a thunderclap and Drake was driven backwards. Something else was at work. He could see the faint image of whatever it was. The ideogram was dark and pulsed with menace. Drake has never seen anything like it. Whatever it was, it had overpowered Drake's use of the Instrumentality, which shouldn't have been possible.

Drake reached into the man's mind. The pain had destroyed

the blocks. There was the knowledge Drake was seeking. Two assassins were already on the Earth Realm where Brygida was. They were going after Brygida and Xia again. Drake had the impression of a vision of a party, and a clock counting down. That was when they were to strike, when the two women were together at the party. The assassins had orders to run if they saw Drake. They were not to be captured.

Drake drew his sword and drove it through the man's skull, ending his suffering. It also had the benefit of preventing the enemy from knowing that Drake had managed to retrieve information from the man.

The image of the MRI on the cell wall flickered out.

The body finished dissolving. Drake hadn't been sure the effect would end there, but it did. Someone out there was very powerful, and several steps ahead of Drake. He suspected it was his brother, Galuchin. His brother had been more talented in his clairvoyance than Drake had been. There was no reason to believe he wasn't still.

The dark power he'd used bothered Drake.

Nothing should be able to block the Instrumentality.

The Instrumentality was the most powerful weapon in any universe, wasn't it? He wasn't so sure now. A little nagging memory in the back of his mind suggested there was another more powerful power. It wasn't dark though. However, if there was a higher power, then there could also be an antithesis to it. Obviously, there was. Something had blocked him after all.

Drake left the cell.

The guards stared at him nervously, so Drake smiled reassuringly at them. They did not seem reassured. Drake walked past them and apported to the top of the stairs to avoid having to walk all the way back up to the audience chamber. He was very tired from what he'd had to do.

"Enter," Emrys called out when Drake knocked.

Drake sat down in the offered chair and accepted the mug

of warm mulled cider thankfully.

His mind hurt from what he'd been forced to do. Drake was also trying to calculate exactly how much time remained before New Year's Eve back where Brygida and the others were. He didn't have much time.

"Did you learn anything from the prisoner?" Emrys asked.

Drake sipped his cider. "I learned enough, I think. By the way, you no longer have a prisoner, and it wasn't my doing. Someone found him and destroyed him, with a power I've never seen before. I was unable to stop it."

"Well, that's disconcerting." Emrys glanced at Drake's sword. "Could it have been what made those?"

Drake shook his head. "The mythical Plaza of the Worlds? No, I don't really believe it exists, not anymore anyway. I once found some old records that suggested it had been destroyed in the Ancient Great War."

"The Plaza blades all still have power, though," Emrys said. "I've seen my father's blade, hell, I've used it. I'm not sure if the Instrumentality could make such a weapon."

"They are all different, also," Drake said. "This was something else, though. It was… dark, and malevolent. I don't think if the Plaza of the Worlds is real, it would feel like that. That kind of evil would have tainted the blades."

Emrys nodded. "So what did you learn?"

"The tower I seek is in the Black Realms," Drake said. "The prisoner really didn't know where it was any longer. That part of his brain had been burned away. The neurons had actually been destroyed."

"That takes some exceptional skill," Emrys said.

"I haven't said anything before, but I believe my brother, Galuchin, is behind this."

Emrys choked on his cider. "I thought he was dead?"

"I thought that he was also," Drake said. "Twice over. I had thought he'd died when he was lost in the Eye. Then, I found him again years later, Fallen."

Emrys nodded. "I remember you telling me about it."

"I thought I'd killed him then, also. Being stabbed with my sword, Maegril, is usually pretty final. However, he had escaped, wounded. I'd thought he'd died, but obviously not. What I saw today in that cell…I was unable to stop it with the Instrumentality, Emrys."

"That's all we need. Did you discover anything else? There are a lot of Black Realms."

"The tower is in one with perpetually black skies. There aren't many of those."

"Do you want me to send out scouts?"

"No, I'll find it. I have another plan."

"You have that look, Drake."

"What look?"

"The look that says I'm not going to like what you're going to say."

"I have a look for that?"

"Oh, yes. I've seen it often."

Drake smiled. "As the prisoner was dying, I was able to pull just a little more information from his brain. In fact, I think he'd been about to tell me about it, which is what actually got him killed. Xia is still on that Earth Realm, the same one my daughter Brygida is on."

Emrys inhaled sharply.

"They know each other, and somehow the enemy has learned that they plan to get together at a New Year's Eve party. The assassins intend to strike at midnight."

"I assume you're going there now to stop it?"

"Indeed, although they have orders to run if I appear."

"So what are you going to do?' Emrys asked.

"I am a shapeshifter," Drake said. "I will be there and stop them. I will not reveal myself until I want them to run."

"You plan to let them escape?"

"I do. One of them anyway. I intend to track that one back to the tower, and my brother."

"You don't really think they'll lead you back there, do you?"

Drake smiled. "Don't worry, my faculties weren't damaged. They will run back if I make it look good, but don't actually chase them."

"If you don't chase them then how can you..." Emrys looked surprised. "You know a way to track them across the Realms, don't you?"

"I'll know where they end up," Drake said.

"Can I ask how?"

"I'll use a passive quantum entangled device that emits no radiation."

"You always manage to surprise me, Drake. I'm dying to learn how you know about such things, but I know you're in a hurry to get to your Earth Realm. Honestly, I'm eager for you to go as well, I worry about Xia. I still care for her, you know."

"My daughters are both quite capable, but the enemy knows this as well. I suspect they will try something subtle like poison or a nuke."

"Only you would think a nuke was subtle."

"I meant as opposed to actually attacking them openly with swords or knives. Recently, a team of assassins tried to kill Jon. They used a nuke and an ancient pistol."

"An ancient pistol?" Emrys asked. "Why do I not think you mean a flintlock?"

"This one would have been used in the Ancient Great War," Drake said. "It was destroyed before I had a chance to examine it, but from the damage to Jon's head, the pistol seemed to generate a beam around five thousand degree Celsius."

"That is as hot as the surface of a star," Emrys said.

"A yellow dwarf star, yes. I have ancient rifles that are hot enough to ignite the atmosphere of a planet."

"I think I'm developing a new ulcer."

Drake finished his cider and stood. "You should have thought of that before you took the throne."

Emrys snorted. "As if I had a choice."

"I'll let you know what I discover, when I can."

"Drake?" Emrys stood and shook his hand. "Good luck."

Drake nodded and left.

CHAPTER FORTY-SEVEN

Geoffrey felt an odd tension as Jason pulled his truck up to Alan Patterson's house outside Berea, Kentucky. Maybe it was just because it had been a while since he'd seen his cousin. Maybe it was just because he didn't like parties.

It had taken them almost two hours to get here from Cincinnati. Jen and Elena pulled in next to them in Jen's car. Brygida's Jeep was already here. They all stepped out into the cold night. Music pulsed from the sprawling, ranch-style house. There was a barn off in the distance.

Geoffrey was surprised to see that Brygida wasn't alone. There was a woman he didn't recognize with her, tall and Asian, with short, red-and-black streaked hair. She was dressed in black and had on a lot of jewelry and make-up.

Jen hugged him. "Who's that with Brygida?" she asked.

Geoffrey shrugged. "I don't know. She didn't say anything about bringing anyone."

There were a lot of cars parked at his cousin's house. Geoffrey hoped all those people were just friends of Alan's and not any of his family. Geoffrey really didn't want to have to deal with any of them.

Brygida joined them. "This is my sister, Lucy."

Geoffrey glanced in surprise from one to the other. They didn't look anything alike, except both looking Asian. The tall woman moved with a feline grace.

"Nice to meet you," Geoffrey said. "I didn't realize Brygida had a sister."

"I go to school out West," said Lucy.

Jen elbowed him and nodded her head toward the door of the house. It was cold out here, and she wanted to go in. Geoffrey grabbed the gift basket from the truck and led the way to the door.

His cousin opened the door when he knocked. Alan was a little shorter than Geoffrey, with brown hair that was already starting to thin. He grinned widely when he saw Geoffrey and engulfed him in a hug. Alan had always been good to Geoffrey, even when the rest of the family would have ostracized him for it.

They all came in out of the cold and Geoffrey introduced everyone. He felt a little bad about bringing so many people, but Alan said to bring all his friends, so Geoffrey had. Alan shook everyone's hand and pointed to the room to the side.

"You can just toss your coats in there," said Alan. "Food is laid out in the dining room. Drinks are in the kitchen or the bar between the kitchen and dining room. There's a keg in the living room. Some idjits are out back playing cornhole in this weather."

"Hey, I hate to ask, but…?" Geoffrey wasn't sure what to say.

"You don't have to," said Alan. "This party is friends only. You're my only family here."

"That's a relief."

Alan laughed.

"Oh, we brought you this," Geoffrey said, handing the basket to Alan.

The basket held a bottle of decent wine and a loaf of French bread. It had been Jen's idea, as a housewarming gift. Which reminded Geoffrey that he hadn't really introduced Jen.

"Oh, and this my—"

"Your girlfriend, Jen," Alan finished. "I've heard a lot about you, Jen. I thought Geoffrey was fibbing when he talked about how awesome you are, but I think he was understating. What are you doing with this guy, anyway?" Alan winked to let them know he was joking.

"I just keep him around to make me seem smarter," said Jen. "And because he's pretty."

"Hey!"

The all laughed.

"Seriously, congratulations on your new job and your house," said Jen.

"Thank you. Go on and enjoy yourself. Get some food. Most of the people here are either work friends or people I knew from college. I gotta get – more people at the door!"

"I like him," Jen said.

"Yeah. Me, too. He was the only member of my family who was good to me, growing up."

Geoffrey looked around. All the others had dropped off their coats and were mingling. He took off his coat and carried Jen's into the other room. Coats were all over the place on the spare bed and other furniture.

"So who did Brygida say her friend is?" Jen asked. "She's pretty."

"She *said* she's her sister," said Geoffrey. "I didn't know she had a sister."

Jen rolled her eyes at him. "Oh, come on, Geoffrey. We're in Eastern Kentucky."

"What does that have to do with anything?"

"When two women who don't look alike introduce themselves as sisters, they're usually together."

Geoffrey shook his head. He wasn't getting whatever she was trying to say. He looked over at Brygida and Lucy. They were hanging pretty close together. That did seem odd for Brygida.

"You're hopeless, but I love you, anyway," said Jen.

Geoffrey blushed as he figured out what she'd meant. Brygida identified as ace, but he supposed maybe she could have met the right woman. Ace people might not feel sexual attraction, but they still needed emotional support and love. He shrugged. It really wasn't any of his business, as long as she was happy.

Jen tucked her arm in his, and they moved into the dining room. The table was laid out with a lot of different kinds of food and Arcade Fire's *The Suburbs* was blasting over the sound system. Geoffrey felt a little envious. Alan had made a good life for himself. He was an accountant or something in Richmond. Geoffrey hoped that when he got out of school, he'd do as well for himself.

He glanced over at Jen, who was loading a paper plate with food and chatting with a woman dressed in business casual. Geoffrey hoped everything would work out long-term with Jen. They weren't ready to tie the knot or anything – not yet. They'd talked about it, though. Jen wanted to wait until after college, maybe graduate school.

Geoffrey had never thought he'd be so lucky. Jen was really smart and beautiful. If everything worked out, and they got good jobs in aerospace after getting out of school, they'd be set. He'd worried about her family, but they seemed to love him when he went home with her over Thanksgiving break.

That odd tension crept back to Geoffrey more, the longer he was at the party. Something felt off, and he couldn't figure out what it might be. Just about everyone here was friendly. A couple of people stood out to him as acting strange, but hell, most people probably thought *he* was weird, too.

Jen was talking to a tall, blond, carnivorous-looking woman in a slinky red dress. Geoffrey couldn't tell what Jen was talking about, but she kept laughing. Alan came in and met his eye, and then he gestured for Geoffrey to move over to him.

"What's up?" Geoffrey asked.

"You got a minute?" Alan seemed distracted.

"Sure."

Alan pulled him into a quiet nook by the kitchen. "Who's Drake?"

"What?"

"Don't play coy. That blonde woman your girlfriend is talking to said she's a friend of your Uncle Drake. I don't think she realized I'm your cousin and know that you don't *have* an Uncle Drake. I wouldn't have thought much of it – people crash parties like these all the time – but I asked your friends Elena and Jason, and they confirmed it, although they didn't know who the woman is, either."

"I can explain, but I'm not sure you'd understand," said Geoffrey.

"Hey, man, I'm not judgmental, you know that. So what, you got a sugar daddy or something?"

"What? Oh, hell, no! I'm not—"

"Keep your voice down, Geoffrey. What was I supposed to think?"

"Not that!"

Alan laughed. "Okay, so explain it to me."

Geoffrey didn't know how he could. The things that had happened to him in the last year and a half just weren't things that happened. To anyone. Geoffrey didn't have any proof, either.

"You know I have an internship with Gerhardt Industries?"

"You've mentioned it."

"Drake sometimes works for Gerhardt. He's a mercenary. He really is my uncle." It was the only thing Geoffrey could think of. He hated to lie to Alan, but Geoffrey didn't want him thinking what he was thinking, either.

"Geoffrey, we have the same family. Cousins, remember?"

"Not entirely," said Geoffrey. "You're related on my mother's side."

"Wait, this guy is claiming to be your deadbeat dad's brother?"

"He said he felt bad for how his brother had acted. He got me that job with Gerhardt. It's how I met Brygida. Hell, he got me a full scholarship."

"What's he want in return?" asked Alan. "I don't trust shit like that, and I can't believe you did, either."

"He seems to be exactly what he says," Geoffrey said. "If it's some kind of mistaken identity, so what? I've got an internship, a scholarship, and a foot in the door with a defense contractor."

Alan put his hand on Geoffrey's forehead, and Geoffrey slapped his hand away.

"What the hell, man?"

"Just checking that you aren't feverish and hallucinating. Anybody else ever meet this guy?"

"Jason and Brygida have both met him," said Geoffrey. "I don't understand why you're so sure this can't be true."

"Because it *sounds* like *bullshit*, Geoffrey. Your dad was just some scumbag your mom banged when she was drunk at a party. She doesn't even remember him, just the car wreck afterward that put her in the hospital. Don't forget, he walked away from her there."

Geoffrey clenched his fists and took a deep breath. "You know what? It doesn't matter. Maybe he was a scumbag, and maybe this Drake guy is just some stranger helping me out for no reason. What difference does it make? He isn't asking for anything from me."

Alan raised his hands. "Okay, I'll back off. Just be careful. You're the only decent family I've got."

"I'm good, man. Really. Drake has acted like an uncle to me, and not a weird one like Uncle Tracy, either. He really did help me. He's helped Brygida and Jason, too. He seems like a nice guy who's trying to make up for something his brother did."

"Except the fact that he's supposed to be a mercenary or something. Guys like that usually don't have much of a conscience."

"Maybe he's trying to make up for that, too. I don't know. I do know that if he ever asked for anything inappropriate, I'd run the other way, fast. Don't worry about me, okay?"

"I'll try."

"What are you guys being so serious about?" asked Jen as she came up and hugged Geoffrey.

"We were discussing Uncle Drake."

"One of these days, you're going to have to introduce me," Jen said. "I was just talking to Sonja there about you. Oh, she's gone. Weird."

"Was that the blonde?" Geoffrey asked.

"Yes. She said she's a friend of your uncle. No offense, but she looks expensive, if you get what I mean."

Alan laughed. "I thought that, too. That dress is a bit skimpy for a party like this."

Geoffrey frowned. "Did she ask you any questions? I don't know her."

"She asked if we were staying until midnight. She seemed to think it wasn't worth it, but who leaves a New Year's Eve party before midnight?"

"Something weird is going on. Drake never mentioned anyone like her."

"Well, I guess I don't have to worry about Uncle Drake if a woman like that is stalking him."

"We're good, thanks, Alan."

"Okay, I won't worry so much about Drake. Besides, I think

Jen would kick his ass if he tried anything. Have fun. Say 'bye before you go, okay?"

"Will do." Geoffrey waited for Alan to walk away. "I need to talk to Jason. Have you seen him?"

Jen frowned. "I haven't. What's up? What did your cousin mean about 'if Drake tried anything'?"

"Alan doesn't know Drake."

"How is that possible?"

"Drake is my uncle on my dad's side."

"Oh."

"Did that woman say anything else?" Geoffrey asked.

"She seemed to know you pretty well. Maybe she was expecting your uncle to be here."

"That's what I'm worried about. I think she might be here to kill him."

Jen starting laughing, but she stopped at the look on his face. "You're serious."

"It's probably nothing, but I'd like to find Jason and Elena. I should tell Brygida, too. She'll know what to do."

It didn't take them long to find Brygida; she was looking for them. Geoffrey told her about the woman and what he suspected. She nodded along with his suppositions and then smiled.

"It's okay, Geoffrey. Don't worry about her."

"You know her?"

Brygida looked aside. Her friend Lucy asked Jen about drinks, and they left together for the kitchen.

"I do, Geoffrey, and so do you. Do you remember Masir?"

Geoffrey rubbed his chest. "I remember more than I want to about it. Why?"

"We had dinner at Malouf's? A woman had dinner with us?"

He suddenly remembered. "Oh shit! You mean that's D—?"

Brygida covered his mouth. "Hush. There's a plot afoot.

You don't need to know the details, but you don't have to worry, either."

"Every time someone tells me not to worry, I worry more," said Geoffrey.

Out of the corner of his eye, he saw two muscular-looking men stand up and walk together into the kitchen. It only struck him as odd because they were both wearing their coats, and he hadn't seen them earlier. A woman with sharp features was staring at him. She waited for Brygida to turn away and then left through the front door. Maybe Geoffrey was just being paranoid, but those people seemed odd to him.

"Don't worry about them, either," Brygida said with a smile. "Really, we've got it covered."

"Tell me about it later?"

"I promise."

"Brygida," Geoffrey said as she turned away, "the woman you're with. Is she really your sister?"

"You can't tell whether she is or not?"

"No."

"Good."

CHAPTER FORTY-EIGHT

The music pounded into Jason's head.

It was good. He liked music, even the stuff modern humans came up with. Music had changed a lot over the centuries, and yet he could sometimes hear traces of those older songs in the modern ones.

Jason usually didn't allow himself to even think about not being human; he usually didn't feel safe enough to do that. Not for a long time, anyway. Maybe Drake was right. Maybe telling Geoffrey, and being accepted, had been what he'd needed.

He still wasn't happy about not having a choice, though.

There were a lot more people at the party than Jason had expected. Jason had met Alan once or twice before – he couldn't remember when or where. Right now, Jason just wanted to run away from these people he didn't know. He'd only agreed to come with Geoffrey because it seemed important to him.

"Great party!" said Elena. She handed him a beer.

Jason smiled. "It's great to be here with *you*."

Elena took his arm and steered him into the dining room. "Let's get some food before it's all gone."

Jason looked at the obscene amount of food laid out on the

table. "You're right, that certainly seems like the food could run out at any time."

Elena punched him lightly on the arm and handed him a paper plate.

Jason was relieved to see the paper plate and plastic utensils. He'd decided he would just say he wasn't hungry if plastic hadn't been an option. Bringing his own cutlery would have been noticed; people would have thought it was weird.

He heaped two fried chicken breasts, baked beans, coleslaw, and mashed potatoes on his plate. Elena took much the same. She perched a biscuit on top of his chicken, and they found a quiet place out of the way to eat.

Jason was surprised to find he felt very comfortable with her.

He'd been worried that after their impromptu make-out session in his workshop, things would be weird between them. Instead, Elena was more relaxed and open. The semi-sex had acted like a confirmation that he liked her, although Jason still couldn't figure out why she'd thought otherwise. They had been together every day since then, but nothing else sexual happened between them.

Jason felt both relieved and frustrated.

He was relieved that they hadn't gone further. That she didn't have to wonder about why he kept his bandana on during sex. In this modern age, couples – and more people – got completely naked around each other. It was just expected.

Jason hadn't been *completely* celibate in the thousand-plus years he'd been on this Earth. He'd managed to hold out for almost a century, the first time, and he usually managed to hold out a few decades each time since then. He'd been quite happy during the Victorian Era, when couples were never expected to see one another completely naked.

He wasn't ashamed of his body. He'd been fairly fit even before spending months walking the worlds with Drake, and now he was in great shape, probably the best he'd ever been. He just didn't feel comfortable letting someone know that he wasn't human. He really envied Drake and Brygida, walking around and showing off their pointed ears without a care in the world.

Jason sighed.

"You okay?" asked Elena. "I'm not really into parties, either."

"I thought you liked it," Jason said. "Are you not having fun?"

Elena snuggled up close. "I just keep thinking maybe we should have stayed at your house. Geoffrey wouldn't have been there. We would have had the whole place to ourselves."

That was the other reason Jason had agreed to come to the party.

Elena suddenly stood up. "Come on."

"What? Where are we going?"

Elena shrugged. "Don't know. I just don't want to just sit. Let's go for a walk."

"Outside?"

"Well, we can't walk that far in here."

"It's cold outside."

"I think you'll survive."

Outside was clear and very cold.

At least there wasn't much snow. They were far enough south to be out of the Snowbelt, which mostly stopped at the Ohio River. Kentucky generally got freezing rain in the winter. Jason was glad he didn't live in Kentucky.

There wasn't much wind, so the cold wasn't intolerable. Jason could see the stars from the back yard, which was nice – he couldn't see them in Cincinnati. The Milky Way was bright, and the constellation of Orion stood out from the other stars. Jason tried not to take it as an omen. The hunter could stay in the sky where he belonged.

Elena walked next to him but somehow still set the pace.

They walked along the fence, looking out at the frozen fields of bluegrass. A few low mountains blotted out the horizon to the east.

"Do you think he has horses?" Elena asked.

"Because this is Kentucky?"

"Because it's a farm, and that's a horse barn."

"I don't know," Jason said, reluctant.

She took his hand. "Come on, let's find out."

"I don't know if we should go poking around," said Jason.

"Do you really think Geoffrey's cousin would care?"

"Probably not."

"Then come on."

It was a little bit warmer in the barn, and very dark. There weren't any horses. Maybe Alan just hadn't had time to buy any; he'd only recently bought the property. Jason didn't even know if Alan intended to buy horses. Lots of people bought farms just to have some space out in the country.

Jason kept thinking of doing that, himself.

"I'd like to have a place like this one day," he said.

"I was just thinking the same thing," Elena said. "Farms are a lot of work, though."

The barn smelled of hay, sweet feed, and old manure: an odd but pleasant mix of scents. Once his eyes adjusted, the barn didn't seem so dark. There was translucent plastic over the barn windows.

"Jason?"

"Hmm?"

"Kiss me."

Jason moved close to Elena and embraced her. He shivered a little as her hands slid under his shirt. Her hands were cold. Her mouth was very warm, though. His need for her grew into a fire, and he pushed her against the side of a stall and started kissing her more urgently.

She pushed him away but held onto his jacket.

"What are we doing, Jason?"

"I hadn't really taken the time to think about it," Jason replied. "Making out?"

"No. We aren't doing that," said Elena, letting go of his coat.

"Okay." Jason was confused – hurt, even.

Elena unbuttoned her coat and then her shirt.

"What are *you* doing?"

"Hush."

She took off her shirt and coat and then deftly shrugged out of her bra. Her breasts were small and firm, her nipples hard in the cold air. She unzipped her pants, kicked off her shoes, and stood naked before him.

"Elena, what are you doing?" he asked, his voice cracking.

"Hush."

"No, don't shush me. Somebody could come out here, and it's cold!"

"No one is going to come out here," said Elena. "If you're worried about me getting cold, come warm me up."

"Elena—" She silenced his protest with her lips.

She felt like fire where she pressed against him. Her hands unbuttoned his shirt and then his pants. She pulled him back and down onto her and her discarded clothes.

"Elena, we can't. I–"

She held up a condom.

"It isn't just that. I'm–"

"Older than you look. I know, and I don't care. I want you." She tore open the condom package and deftly rolled it onto him before he could protest.

Jason wanted to stop her. No, he didn't want to stop her. He just felt that he should.

He knew he should get up and run from the barn. He couldn't do what they both wanted. He just couldn't. She would discover who he was. What he was.

He'd lowered his guard before, in the past. The woman he'd been with hadn't taken the discovery of his true self very well. Jason was forced to run, again, leaving his entire life behind.

He'd had to run away too many times.

When Elena's hands grabbed his head to pull his face against her breasts, he didn't resist. He wanted her. He was too occupied kissing her as he thrust into her to worry any more. He needed her. Evidently, she needed him just as badly.

It wasn't just lust; that, he could keep in check. He… *loved* Elena. He wanted to be with her, and not just for sex or a clever disguise for his identity. He wanted to be with her as long as they could be. As long as she… He couldn't think about that.

She pulled his face up to hers, and they kissed hard.

Her hands felt so good on his head, his face, his ears.

He froze.

"We'll talk later," Elena said, staring into his eyes. "Don't you dare stop now."

He didn't stop. They needed each other too much. He needed her too much.

Afterward, they lay in silence, just holding each other. His sweat cooled almost painfully, but he didn't care. She had felt so good under him So right.

"We should get dressed before we freeze like this," said Elena. "That would be embarrassing."

"At least we'd die happy."

Jason cleaned himself with his handkerchief and then got dressed. He was embarrassed but still feeling the strong afterglow from the sex, so he didn't worry too much about Elena discovering what was under his bandana. They both got dressed. Mostly, anyway.

Elena was playing with his bandana.

"I thought it was weird," she said, "how you wear this thing everywhere."

"I have several, actually. I do wash them."

"Hmm."

"Elena, I wanted to tell you…"

"Tell me what?" she asked. "Are you related to Brygida? You don't look much like her."

"No, I'm not remotely related to her."

"Okay, you have pointed ears like hers, but you aren't related. The odds seem a little extreme, but whatever. I don't get why you hide them. Were you bullied in school or something?"

"It's a lot more complicated than that."

"Well, uncomplicated it. You're acting as if I just discovered some deep, dark secret." She tossed him his bandana. "What is the big deal? Your ears look nice."

Jason carefully covered his ears with the bandana and then sat down next to her. He had dreaded ever having to reveal himself to someone, but at least with Elena, it didn't feel wrong. He did have strong feelings for her. Feelings that made his chest tight. That had just made love, and he already was craving her touch again.

"I wanted to tell you for a long time," he said. "It's just… difficult for me."

Elena frowned. "Why do I think you're not just talking about your ears?"

Jason rubbed his face. A cold horse barn was not where he wanted to have this conversation. Not that he *wanted* to have it anywhere, but Elena deserved to know.

"Look, can we talk about it later? I promise I'll tell you everything."

Elena stood and paced. "Since I can't even imagine what the problem is, I'll just end up worrying. No, I think whatever it is, you should tell me now."

Jason sighed. "You've seen my ears. What do you want me to say? That I'm not human?"

Elena laughed. "Because your ears are different?"

"Not just that."

"So you're either crazy or just fucking with me."

Jason stood up. "Neither, Elena."

"Oh, come on."

"I *am* serious," he said. He'd never expected she wouldn't believe him, not after seeing his ears. He had dreaded someone finding out. He never expected they just wouldn't care.

"Fuck you." Elena shoved him hard enough that he fell. "So, what? You figure you'll fuck me and then just blow me off with some bullshit story? Get in, get off, and get out, huh?"

Jason felt tears welling up and hated himself for it. "It isn't like that at all."

"Then tell me the truth!" Elena shouted.

"I am," Jason said. "I'm trying to. This isn't easy for me."

"Not easy for *you*? Okay."

"Elena, please."

Elena just stood looking at him. Then she shook her head. "I don't know what the hell to make of you. If you'd just wanted to fuck me, you could have done it months ago. Jason? Are you just delusional? I mean, do you really believe what you're implying? I think I'd rather believe you're crazy, than that you're just an asshole trying to get rid of me."

"I don't know how to convince you, if you won't believe your eyes. Find something iron and touch me with it. Then you'll see that it burns me."

"What is that supposed to prove? Some people have weird allergies." Elena knelt down and touched his face. "Jason, what happened to you, to make you believe something like this? Because I really think you believe it, and that scares me."

"I'm sorry," Jason said.

Elena's phone rang. "Shit. Hold on." She answered the phone. "No. What? Yeah, I think you're right. It is time to go. No, I don't want to talk about it." She hung up and put the phone back in her pocket.

"I don't want to lose you," Jason said.

"I need some time to think about things."

Jason stood up and moved to hug her, but she backed away.

"I need time," she said, "and space."

Jason nodded. "If you want to talk, you know where to find me."

"Yeah." Elena walked out of the barn.

Jason stood in the cold for a long time before he went back out to the house. Most of the guests had left, so it must have been past midnight. He thought about just leaving, just getting into his truck and driving. Somewhere. Anywhere. The only thing that stopped him from panicking was the fact that Elena hadn't believed him.

Somehow, that hurt more.

CHAPTER FORTY-NINE

Drake found the bomb in the kitchen. It was disguised as a beer keg. He glanced at the clock on the wall: a quarter 'til midnight, it said. He didn't have much time. The lid of the keg came off easily. There was a mass of wires and circuitry inside the case. The bomb looked to be of local manufacture.

He supposed that made sense. Why import technology when what was available would suffice? Still, it was a somewhat impressive weapon. The keg was lined in lead. Shaped charges englobed a sphere of what might be beryllium. He could only guess that something radioactive was inside the globe – he suspected uranium or plutonium. An electronic counter counted down to midnight. Drake replaced the lead-lined lid.

"Hey, what're you doing?"

Drake stood and looked at the two men who'd entered the kitchen. There were muscular and had knives and a pistol each under their coats. To his eyes, they looked to be local thugs who'd been hired without being told what they were doing. They'd be disposed with the others when the bomb went off.

The woman he'd seen earlier wasn't local. She hadn't seen through his disguise, but was able to sense the Instrumentality on her. She was from the Courts. Drake had discreetly planted a tracker on her.

"We asked what you're doing," the other man said.

Drake smiled and called upon the Instrumentality to rapidly change his form back to normal, along with his armor and weapons. The men went pale as he started to change. They drew their pistols but hesitated long enough for Drake to step forward and grip the ends of the weapons.

The sound of the guns going off was muffled by his armor.

Drake jerked the pistols from their hands and crushed the metal and plastic together like so much tinfoil. "You might want to run," Drake suggested.

They ran.

"What was that noise?" asked Alan as he walked into the kitchen. He stopped when he saw Drake. "Who the hell are you? How did you get in here?"

Drake glanced at the clock: only five minutes left.

"I don't have time to explain, Alan," said Drake. "Those men you saw running from here brought a bomb. I need to defuse it." He pointed to the bomb.

"That's a keg, man. How much have you had to drink?"

Drake lifted the lid off it.

"Holy shit! Is that what I think it is?"

"If you think it's a makeshift atomic fission weapon, then yes, it is. Time is wasting, and I'm not sure what to do."

Geoffrey came into the kitchen, and Drake could hear him asking questions, but he ignored them both. The bomb held his whole attention. The simplest solution would be apport the weapon into the sun, but he had to assume that whoever built the thing must have thought Drake or Brygida might try to defuse it. He was also leery of using his sword against it. The nanotechnology the blade used to destroy things might set the weapon off.

In some ways, it was the primitive nature of the device that was throwing him off. He couldn't be sure what the massive wires and circuit boards were meant to do. It was possible they were nothing more than circuitry to time the implosive charges together. On the other hand, they could be something else entirely.

The clock on the display ticked past one minute.

From the other room came the sound of a mass of people counting down. The television was tuned to the ball drop in Times Square, the signal in the United States that a new year had begun.

"Can you reach the power source?" Brygida asked from next to him.

"No. It's under the beryllium sphere, and there are mercury switches designed to discourage moving the device. I'm not sure what these sensors are, but I think they're to detonate the weapon if the Instrumentality is employed."

The party guests began to count along at ten seconds.

"Ah, fuck it," Drake said. He reached in quickly and jerked the beryllium sphere free of the casing, snapping the wires. The clock ticked to zero and beeped. People were cheering in the other room.

"That was too close," said Brygida.

Drake nodded.

"Will someone explain what is going on?" said Alan.

Drake apported the beryllium sphere and uranium into oblivion. He then stood up and turned to look at Geoffrey and Alan. Brygida stood up next to him.

"Uh, Alan, this is Drake," said Geoffrey.

"Okay. And that?" Alan pointed to the bomb.

"Someone snuck a bomb in here," said Brygida, "probably to kill me."

Alan shook his head. "You're Geoffrey's friend, right?"

"Dr. Brygida Hakubi," she replied. "I'm a physicist. I'm working with Klaus Gerhardt on his starship engines. I suspect someone really didn't want me continuing doing that. Drake here also works for Gerhardt, in special security. He learned of the bomb plot and came here to foil it."

Alan looked around at them all. "I'm... confused."

Drake picked up the bomb casing and replaced the lid. "Let me get this out of the house, and then we'll talk."

Xia came back in as he entered the living room. "I chased the woman and allowed her to get away, as instructed."

"Good," Drake replied. "And thank you."

"Let me take that," said Xia. She took the bomb and left.

"Okay, now can someone explain?" Alan was looking confused and anxious. "Geoffrey says you're his... *uncle?*"

Drake shot a sharp glance at Brygida.

It's what you told Gerhardt, Brygida thought to him.

Right.

Drake nodded to Alan. "Daeren Drake. I'm sorry about crashing your party."

"You seem to have been right on time," said Alan. "There was a blonde woman here earlier. Is that the woman you're talking about? Did she bring the... the... the thing?"

"No, she was working for me." Drake looked around. "Has anyone seen Jason?"

"He and Elena are in the horse barn," said Brygida.

"You might want to round them up."

"I'll send Jen," said Brygida. "I think we should all think about heading home. See you later?"

"I'll be there," Drake said. "I may be delayed."

"Can I talk to you?" Alan asked. "Alone?"

"Sure."

Alan led Drake back into the kitchen. "What have you gotten Geoffrey into, and who the hell are you, really?"

Drake smiled. "I told you who I am. As for what Geoffrey has gotten into, he's his own man."

"I mean, are you really his uncle?"

Drake hesitated and then nodded. "Yes."

Alan frowned. "And his father?"

"I haven't seen him in some time," said Drake. "He may be dead."

"You don't seem real shook up about that."

"He was not a good man."

"What was his name?"

"George," Drake said without hesitation. "George Drake."

Alan shook his head again. "I suppose he was mixed up in all this, too?"

"Most certainly."

"Are we safe?" Alan asked. "I mean, that *was* really a nuke, right?"

"Welcome to the world of high-stakes corporate espionage."

"Man, shit like this just doesn't happen."

"It does," Drake said. "You just don't hear about it."

"And the other?" Alan asked. "Are we safe?"

"You're safe. So is Geoffrey. I'm surprised that this happened, but I'm close to tracking down who's responsible."

"I'm guessing I don't want to know what you're going to do," said Alan. "I can't imagine it'll be legal. That other woman, Lucy. Was she a guard or something?"

Drake smiled again. On this Earth, his daughter Xia often went by the name Lucy. "Yes, actually. You have a good eye for this sort of thing."

"Oh, man. Okay. I'm going to need another drink. Probably more than one. When this all catches up to me, I'm going to be sick."

Drake gripped his shoulder. "You'll be fine. Don't worry about what happened."

"Yeah, I'll try."

Drake nudged the man's mind slightly. He wouldn't even remember that anything *had* happened, once Drake left. He hated to do it, but it would be the best for Alan and for

Geoffrey.

Drake stepped outside.

Brygida and Xia had already left, as had Elena and Jen. Drake was disappointed; he'd hoped to meet Elena and Jen in his own form. He liked the young women. Geoffrey and Jason had made good choices.

Geoffrey was talking to Jason, who looked a bit disheveled, with hay sticking out from under his bandana. He also didn't look as happy as Drake would have expected him to. Drake had been certain Elena and Jason had gone to the barn to have sex. It had sounded as if they were enjoying themselves. He wondered what happened.

"My friends, I'm sorry to have to depart again so soon," Drake said. "However, I must track down the origin of that bomb."

"Bomb?" said Jason. "What bomb? And when did you get here?"

"I'm sure Geoffrey can fill you in."

"I could if I knew anything about what's happening," said Geoffrey.

"An assassin tried to kill Brygida with a small nuclear device," Drake said. "I disarmed it, but the assassin escaped. I need to leave to track her down."

"Well, I guess that puts things in perspective," said Jason. "Suddenly my problems seem trivial. Will you be back soon?"

"As soon as I can," Drake said. "One never knows where these things will lead. I trust you two will stay safe. Brygida will be around if you need help."

"Thanks," said Jason. "Don't worry about us."

Drake nodded. "I trust you'll be well. Until we meet again."

"Goodbye, Drake," said Jason.

"Come back when you can," Geoffrey added.

Drake called upon the Instrumentality and apported away to Hephaestus. He had much he needed to do. He only hoped the tracker he'd planted on the woman worked.

CHAPTER FIFTY

Jason was quiet for most of the trip back to Cincinnati.

Geoffrey didn't want to bother him, especially since the roads weren't in the best shape. The weather had turned colder, and it had snowed again to the north. Jason's old pickup truck didn't do well on ice. The expressway got better once they passed Crittenden.

"Will you tell me what happened?" Geoffrey asked.

Jason glanced over at him and shook his head.

"Come on, Jason. It isn't a secret that you Elena went to the barn. Jen said Elena was going to try to get you alone."

"And you thought that was a good idea?"

"Well, yeah. You had sex, didn't you?"

Jason sighed. "There is more to a relationship than sex."

"Yeah, no shit."

Jason drove on in silence.

"Well?"

"Yes, okay? You happy?"

"I am," said Geoffrey. "I just don't understand why you aren't."

"My bandana didn't stay on," Jason said. "She asked me

about my… So I told her."

"Okay, that sounds good, I think. She deserved to be told."

"She didn't believe me," said Jason. "I don't know if thinks I'm an asshole liar or just plain crazy."

"She didn't believe you?" Geoffrey said. "After she'd seen your ears?"

"She's seen Brygida's."

"Yeah, but Brygida isn't human, either."

"She doesn't know that."

"Good point."

"Funny."

Geoffrey leaned back his seat. "She was pretty angry?"

"What do you think?"

"I think she's going to talk to Jen about it."

Jason groaned. "Damn it."

"On the upside, they'll probably ask Brygida."

"And what is she going to say?" said Jason.

"I think that depends on what you say to her. I think you need to talk to Brygida, give her a heads up that this could be coming. Let her know what you want her to say."

"That sounds like a fun conversation."

"Got to be better than the one you had earlier."

Jason didn't say anything for a few miles. Then, "Tell me about what happened at the party."

"Oh, man. Okay. Drake must have known something was going to happen. He was there in disguise."

"The blonde in the red dress?" said Jason.

"Yeah. How did you know?"

"I thought I recognized her from a television show you made me watch."

"Really?" Geoffrey thought about it. She *did* seem familiar. "Anyway, the bomb was set to go off at midnight. There was another woman who got away. *She* planted the bomb."

"The *nuclear* bomb."

"Yeah."

"Geoffrey, we have gotten into some weird shit."

"*This* is what it takes to make you think that?" Geoffrey said. "After all we've been through?"

"Okay, go on."

"There isn't much left to tell. About the only other thing that happened was Alan grilling me about Drake. He and Drake talked later, though, so I think we're cool."

"Yeah, sorry. I didn't know what to say when Alan asked me. I mean, Drake has been telling that lie for a while, as a cover. Although he does kind of act like a crazy uncle."

"No, my Uncle Tracy was way crazier."

"Crazier than Drake?"

"Kind of," Geoffrey said. "Yeah."

"Well, maybe it was being called *Tracy* all his life that did it."

"That was his name," said Geoffrey. "It isn't that uncommon in Eastern Kentucky. I have an Uncle Whitney, too."

"Eastern Kentucky. Enough said."

"Hey!"

"Geoffrey, what am I going to do about Elena?"

"You really like her?"

"What do you think?"

"You love her?"

"Yeah, I do."

"Then give her a little time to process it. I mean, my brain melted a little when you told me, and I already knew there were people here who aren't human."

"You think she'll come around?"

"Does she love you?"

"Without a doubt."

"Then she'll come around."

Jason took the bridge across to Cincinnati and then turned

up past Eden Park to go home. There was fresh snow on the streets in town. They went through a sobriety checkpoint and then turned to their neighborhood.

"You think Brygida made it back okay?" Geoffrey asked.

"I'm not worried. Hey, did you ever find out who that woman was with her?"

Geoffrey laughed. "Lucy? No, I didn't. I think she's an associate of Drake's. She took the bomb after he'd defused it."

"Do you think she's really Brygida's sister?"

"No," said Geoffrey. "I asked Brygida, and she didn't answer."

"Oh, well, it isn't any of our business."

Jason pulled into the drive, waited for the garage to open, then pulled in. They got out as the door was closing. The air was cold, and they hurried into the house.

"You don't think those assassins are going to try again, do you?" said Geoffrey.

"I think Drake is going to do everything he can to make sure they don't."

⊙

Drake was aboard Hephaestus, looking at the data he had gathered from the device Drake planted on the assassin. The signal from the quantum entangled device was a little odd. The assassin had used several Waypoints, as well as walked the Realms.

It was evident that the assassin was trying to cover their tracks. Xia had followed the woman just enough to put some fear into her. Drake hoped that the assassin was going to go back to the tower, in the Black Realms.

"My Prince, your new armor is finished," Hephaestus said. "It awaits you in the armory."

"Thank you. I'll go try it on. Keep an eye on this?"

"I have been monitoring the remote since you deployed it."

Drake smiled and walked back through the ship.

He missed having his friends aboard. The ship seemed too empty without Geoffrey, Jason, Jon, and Brygida there. They had really had some good times together.

Drake removed his coat and sword belt when he reached the armory. His new armor gleamed in the center of the room. Hephaestus had made it entirely of illythrum, as the black alloy had some very special and useful properties. It generated a natural quantum field that resisted entropy, not to mention it was a platinum alloy, and naturally durable and resistant.

Drake stepped out of his armor and into the new armor. It fit perfectly, of course. Hephaestus had scanned Drake's body again before construction.

"Does this have the modifications I asked for?" Drake asked.

"It has all of them, yes. I also included the stasis field generator we talked about," Hephaestus replied.

"You figured it out?" Drake was surprised. Hephaestus hadn't thought a generator that small could be incorporated into the armor.

"I discovered an ancient set of diagrams in my databases. They were from before the Great War."

Drake wondered again about Hephaestus. The machine intelligence of his starship was beyond ancient. Drake knew Hephaestus had been constructed before the ancient war that had almost destroyed the Courts. Sometimes Hephaestus spoke of times even older. The Great Expansion, when the first universes were created.

"How is the armor?" Hephaestus asked.

"It looks and feels good," Drake said. "It may be slightly more responsive than my older armor. Just how tough is this stuff?"

"The armor itself can withstand temperatures in excess of

eleven thousand Celsius, and withstand pressures of up to twelve hundred bars. However, with the stasis field generators, there is no theoretical limits to the temperatures and pressures you could withstand. You could fall through the heart of a star."

"What if the stasis field flickers out while in the heart of a star?" Drake asked.

"The stasis field will remain active if external pressures and temperatures exceed the suit limits."

"How can that work?" Drake asked.

"Time does pass within a stasis field, even though the occupant is removed from spacetime, as it were. It passes at the rate of one picosecond per second on the outside. When the stasis field triggers, it only activates for five picoseconds. That gives the circuits more than enough time to scan the external environment with quantum sensors. If conditions are not optimal, it triggers another five picosecond cycle, and so on."

Drake nodded. About one trillionth of a second. "Okay, I'm convinced. How fast does it activate?"

"One femtosecond."

One quadrillionth of a second. If Drake was facing an enemy that could hit faster than that, he was in trouble. The materials of the armor would hold up far longer than one femtosecond. He should be fine.

Drake buckled on his sword belt and shrugged into his coat. The leather coat might seem an odd choice, but Drake had grown fond of wearing it over his armor. It helped in technological Realms, where wearing armor in public wasn't normally done, except by police and military forces.

"Prince Drake, the signal has stopped," Hephaestus said.

"Where is it?" Drake asked.

"The signal faded out in the Court of the Broken Prince."

"That can't be where the tower is."

"It is in close proximity to the Realms of Eternal Darkness."

"You said the signal faded out?"

"The remote could have been noticed, or there may simply be too much quantum interference at this distance. I'm surprised we could detect it from here as it is."

"Hmm. So I may pick up the signal once I'm in the Court of the Broken Prince?"

"If the remote is still active, then yes."

"Then wish me luck," Drake said. "And also, thanks for the new armor."

"Of course, My Prince."

Drake nodded and the armory faded away in rainbows.

CHAPTER FIFTY-ONE

Drake arrived in the Court of the Broken Prince through the Waypoint east of Darkton. It was in the small hours of the morning, and the blood rain was starting to taper off. Drake closed his helmet around his head and walked on toward town.

He followed the town wall around to the south, where the road exited the gate. The guards on the walls shouted at him, but Drake ignored them and turned south. There was another Waypoint far to the south, but Drake intended to be long gone from this Realm before he ever reached it.

It took three shifts to bring him clear of the blood rain. The forest in this Realm was much the same as the last, black gnarled trees that twisted and shifted, without any wind. Snarling things with red glowing eyes followed him. He shifted, and they had green eyes, another shift, yellow, another, and the beasts were gone.

When the vegetation ceased, Drake knew that he had reached the first of the Realms of Eternal Darkness. The sky overhead was filled with turbulent clouds. The rocks began to float alongside the road. Phosphorescent minerals glowed dully in veins in the rocks, providing scant light. The red sky found in the other Black Realms had shifted into the ultraviolet in the Realms of Eternal Darkness. The ultraviolet didn't provide any visible light —unless you could see in that spectra— but it did provide energy to the phosphorescent minerals and lichens.

Drake stopped and consulted the tracker in his helmet. The quantum entangled remote was still broadcasting, his helmet found a faint signal, to the south. It was most likely in another Realm.

He kept following the road, shifting slowly, one veil at a time. The signal grew in strength as he walked the worlds. No creatures followed him on his lonely trek. The demi-Realms in that place had been hard hit during the Ancient War. The Ancient Enemy had sucked almost all traces of life from those worlds.

The signal reached maximum strength, and Drake knew he was in the right Realm. The road wormed its way south through slot canyons and the ruins of ancient cities, now long forgotten. The ruins were so old that Drake had never even seen a suggestion that such places had existed. He wondered what kind of people had lived there. Had they been colonists from the Courts, or indigenous? There was no way to now tell.

Nor did it really matter.

The road clawed its way up a crumbling mountain of slate. Even with his superior vision, Drake had difficulty seeing to the other side of the U-shaped valley that the road plunged into. He could see campfires and torches burning, almost painfully bright in the intense darkness.

There was an entire army down there.

Drake wondered what they were using as fuel. He couldn't make out the manner of beast or man that was encamped. He doubted they bore regular forms anyway. He hoped it wasn't an army of the Ancient Enemy, such as was found in the Eye. It was unlikely though, the Ancient Enemy wouldn't have needed campfires.

Drake crept along the ridge to the south.

He stayed low and moved carefully and silently. He doubted any of the enemy had better senses than he, but it was always better to be safe. He wanted to scout the enemy position, find the accursed tower, and then get back out without being detected.

He didn't want whoever was in command of that army to flee.

Few of the enemy soldiers bore human forms. The rest flopped or crawled upon a wide range of overly complex and impractical body forms. Some of those forms he recognized from his travels, but there were many that surprised him. All of them had one thing in common, they were armed with lethal-looking hooked weapons, horns, claws, spines, or all of the above.

The tower of black basalt sat in the cirque at the head of the valley.

There was a ring of fortifications around the tower. Large ballistae sat at regular intervals, ready to rain massive iron bolts down on attackers. He doubted that the current occupant had built the edifice. It was most likely a relic of a bygone war, perhaps even the Great War.

An aura of dark menace emanated from the tower.

The passive signal of the tracker showed that the assassin was in the tower. Drake had no doubts that other horrors were there as well. He couldn't tell from a passive scan if his brother was in the tower, and he didn't want to do anything to reveal himself.

It took Drake the better part of a day to work his way back out of the defenses. He needed distance from the tower before he used the Instrumentality to leave that Realm. He was certain the enemy would be vigilant for the use of a major power.

Walking away from that world was much the same as going to it. He welcomed the red sky when it finally faded in. He'd missed the light, even if it was dim and ruddy.

He was far south of Darkton, so he took the Waypoint there, instead of the one he normally used. Three jumps later and he emerged from the Waypoint on Nandegurth. He knew his army was standing ready to move. Within a few hours they would be marching to that world shrouded in darkness.

The guards cleared him and Drake walked down the road to his fortress. The symbolism of his brother's tower was not lost on him. Nandegurth had bright white skies. The other was always in darkness. The towers were similar though, they may have even been built during the same era. His brother had been the General of the Rim before Drake had been. Galuchin knew the capabilities of the army that Drake would bring against him.

Drake was hoping that Galuchin wouldn't know much about the Special Forces from Nandegurth, though. The troops on this world had been specially selected and trained by Drake to fight against the forces of the Ancient Enemy. The equipment of his troops was far superior to that of the Army of the Rim.

Drake hoped it would be enough.

About the Author

Paul B. Spence is a practicing archaeologist who hopes to one day get it right. He currently lives in New Mexico, where all the cool kids hang out, with too many cats.

Like most authors, he had an eclectic career path. He's worked as a retail gofer, a food service monkey, brute laborer, a rennie, a writer for the RPG industry, and many other rewarding jobs that didn't pay enough to feed him or his cats.